The Secrets of
Ashmore Castle

The Secrets of
Ashmore Castle

Cynthia Harrod-Eagles

sphere

SPHERE

First published in Great Britain in 2021 by Sphere

3 5 7 9 10 8 6 4 2

Copyright © Cynthia Harrod-Eagles 2021

The moral right of the author has been asserted.

A CIP catalogue record for this book
is available from the British Library.

ISBN 978-07515-8181-2

Typeset in Plantin by Palimpsest Book Production Ltd, Falkirk, Stirlingshire
Printed and bound in Great Britain by Clays Ltd, Elcograf S.p.A.

Papers used by Sphere are from well-managed forests
and other responsible sources.

SPHERE
An imprint of
Little, Brown Book Group
Carmelite House
50 Victoria Embankment
London EC4Y 0DZ

An Hachette UK Company
www.hachette.co.uk

www.littlebrown.co.uk

To Tony, who makes everything possible

DRAMATIS PERSONAE

AT ASHMORE CASTLE

The family
William Tallant, 5th Earl of Stainton
— his eldest daughter, Linda, married to Viscount Cordwell
— his eldest son, Giles, Viscount Ayton
— his second son, Richard
— his daughter Rachel
— his daughter Alice
— his widowed mother, Victoire (Grandmère)
— his half-uncle Sebastian
— his wife, the countess, née Maud Stanley Forrest
  — her brother Fergus, 9th Earl of Leake
  — her sister Caroline, widow of Sir James Manningtree
  — her sister Victoria, Princess of Wittenstein-Glücksberg

The servants
Moss, the butler
Mrs Webster, the housekeeper
Crooks, valet to the earl
Miss Taylor, maid to the countess
Mrs Oxlea, cook
Frewing, hall porter
James, William, Cyril, footmen
Rose, Daisy, Dory, maids

In the stables
Giddins, head man
Archer, groom to the earl
Josh Brandom, groom to the young ladies
John Manley, Joe Green, coachmen

On the estate
Markham, land agent
Adeane, bailiff
Moresby, solicitor
Saddler, gamekeeper
Cutmore, woodsman

In the village
St Peter's Church
— rector, Dr Bannister
— choirmaster, Mr Arden

Tom Holyoak, policeman
Persons, station master
Mrs Albright, post office stores
Eli Rowse, blacksmith
Axe Brandom (brother to Josh), assistant blacksmith

KITTY'S FAMILY

Father - Sir John Bayfield of Bayfield Court, Hampstead
Mother - Catherine Harvey, jam heiress, deceased
Stepmother - Jayne, née D'Arcy

NINA'S FAMILY

Father - Major Anthony Sanderton, deceased
Mother - Antonia Marie Dawnay, deceased
Aunt - Alexandra Schofield, née Sanderton, of Draycott Place

CHAPTER ONE

3rd December 1901

It was a hard walk up the hill, especially carrying a valise. Sometimes she had to pick her way through muddy hollows, where hoofs and wheels had churned the ground. The recent long, cold spell had broken, and it had been mild and wet, though today there was only a fine drizzle. At one point, she had to step aside as two grooms posted past, each riding one dapple grey and leading another. Carriage horses being exercised, she thought wisely, noting that they matched. They pranced and lifted their knees high, trying to toss their heads, and seemed very big, their weight displacing the air. She was prepared to smile and wave to the men, but they did not look at her as they passed. Horsemen were usually friendly, she had found, but an earl's grooms were above ordinary mortals.

The big white house on the hill looked down over the Ash valley and dominated the view from the village of Canons Ashmore. It was called Ashmore Castle – she didn't know why – but was always referred to as just 'the Castle'. There was prestige in getting a place there, and when you left, a reference with that name on it was worth a lot. She followed the minor path round to the back, as instructed, and arrived eventually in a yard behind the kitchens where she discovered two men in footman's livery, smoking. They

1

had chosen a spot where the overhang kept the drizzle off them; they were jacketless, with long green aprons over their striped waistcoats and shirtsleeves.

One was tall and thin, with a hard, noticing face and rather bulging eyes. The other was shorter, plump, and with a face that denoted either good humour or stupidity.

'Hullo, what have we here?' said the thin one. His raking look took in the valise. 'Fresh blood?' He had been lounging with one foot up on the wall behind him. Now he pushed himself off and stood straight, continuing to examine her in a way that made her feel he could see right through her clothes. 'Who are you, then?'

'I'm the new sewing-maid. Dory Spicer.'

She looked at the plump one enquiringly.

'William,' he said, 'William Sweeting.'

'Nice to meet you, William,' she said.

The thin one gave a derisive snort. 'Ho, aren't we polite?' he mocked, in mincing tones. Then he thrust his face closer. 'You listen to me, Dory Spicer – what sort of a name is Dory, anyway?'

She didn't answer. She hated her name, Dorcas, and never let anyone find it out if she could help it.

'Well, I'm James,' the thin one went on, 'and I'm first footman, so I'm an important person to get on the right side of. Be nice to me, and you could go far. I run this house.'

'Isn't there a butler? I heard there was a butler.'

'Oh, Mr Moss,' James said witheringly, and left it at that, as though nothing more needed to be said about him.

She looked at William, who swallowed nervously and said, 'Mr Moss has been here for ever, nearly. Years and years. Him and his lordship go right back.'

'What's his lordship like?' Dory asked, to encourage him.

James intervened. 'You don't need to know that. *You'll* never see him. You'd best go and report to the housekeeper,

Mrs Webster. Watch out for her – she's a Tartar.' He grinned at her, and his face was so thin she could see the muscles move and rearrange. It was unnerving. 'Sewing-maid, eh? Watch you don't go the same way as the last one.'

She knew he wanted her to ask him what that was, but she clung to one last grain of defiance. She wouldn't ask him. Instead she said, as if meekly obedient, 'All right,' and went towards the nearest door.

'Not that one,' James called sharply. 'That's the kitchen. *That* one – rear lobby. Go through it and turn left, house-keeper's room's at the end.'

She changed direction and muttered, 'Thanks,' without looking at him again.

'You don't want to go in the kitchen without being invited,' he called after her. 'Lots of sharp knives in the kitchen.'

He's just trying to scare you, she told herself, as she scurried past. But she didn't like the hints of a divided, fractious household. He might be just a troublemaker, she thought, stepping through the rear lobby, with its smell of wet mackintoshes and boots, but that didn't mean it wasn't so.

It was a good day for hunting: the mild smells of earth rose damp and sweet through the thready mist, and the scent was breast high. Hounds were running well – a pocket handkerchief would cover them, as the saying was – and the clamour of their music echoed eerily on the winter air.

Behind them, the field galloped, strung out as the pace increased. The Earl of Stainton was well up with the leaders. Hunting was his passion. It was not about the kill, it was about the run: the speed, the sound of slamming hoofs and snorting breaths, the thrust of great muscles beneath him, the sting of the wind past his face. Joy filled him, fierce and exhilarating, blotting out any troubled thought. For a little while he could forget himself, his difficulties and responsibilities, and become a creature of pure sensation. He and the horse and the moment were one, a united thing of taut, glorious perfection.

The fox was old and cunning, and had led them a dance, but the earl had hunted this country since he was eight years old, and carried a map in his head of every contour and copse. It was his land, and he knew it as well as the fox did. He felt instinctively that Charlie was heading for the farm at Shelloes, where the large pig yard would foil the scent. Stainton took his own line whenever possible. He turned aside, sending Jupiter thundering diagonally across the slope. Ahead was a big blackthorn hedge, a formidable jump, and the approach was awkward, but it was well within Jupiter's scope. Two paces away, the big bay pecked slightly, but Stainton pulled his head up, gave him a thwack behind the saddle, and shouted, 'Come on!' Jupiter grunted, thrust off, and rose magnificently to the challenge.

They soared. The earl cried out, 'God!' in simple ecstasy.

In the parlour of a small house in Ridgmount Street in Bloomsbury, four hands freed the notes of Schubert's Sonata in C from the keys of the piano in a steady, accomplished rhythm. Dust motes swirled in the stream of pale winter sunshine that filtered through the net curtains, and glinted on the two golden heads, one middle-aged, one young.

Suddenly Mrs Sands threw up her head and cried softly, 'God!'

The music tumbled to a halt.

'Mummy? What's wrong?' Chloë asked.

Molly Sands had put both hands to her head. Now she opened her large, pale blue eyes, and took a shaky breath. 'It's all right. I'm all right,' she reassured automatically.

Chloë continued to look at her anxiously. 'Is it a headache?'

'No – not . . . I just felt . . . I don't know. Strange. As

though . . .' It had been as though she was falling – a black, swooping sensation. But it was momentary, and she did not like to see her daughter alarmed. She grew brisk. 'It's passed now, whatever it was. Begin again, please, from the triplets.'

Chloë didn't immediately obey. She and her mother were very close; and there were just the two of them. They lived in a small but comfortable way on Mrs Sands's earnings as a piano teacher. If anything happened to her mother . . .

'Mummy?'

'It was nothing. A moment's dizziness. I'm quite all right now,' Mrs Sands said firmly. 'Begin, please.'

The music resumed.

The earl's groom, Archer, following his master on the second horse, Tonnant, saw Jupiter's knees strike the dense top of the hedge. Recently cut, it was bristly and unyielding. The enormous impetus of his jump flipped the horse over in a complete somersault. The earl went flying off. Archer jerked Tonnant away and aimed him at a spot further down the hedge, to avoid landing on whatever might be on the other side. The hedge was lower here, and Tonnant cleared it easily. His blood was up and it took half a dozen paces before Archer could check him and turn. By that time, Jupiter had already struggled to his feet, and was standing, trembling, one forefoot held off the ground, the saddle twisted round under his belly.

Beyond him, the earl was lying in a crumpled heap, unmoving. He was an experienced rider, hunted three or four times a week, had taken hundreds of tumbles in his time. He knew how to fall, should have got straight up. *Must have winded himself*, Archer thought, sliding down. And yet he knew. Something about the stillness of the body, the awkward angle of the neck . . . A cold dread settled in his stomach.

Tonnant was excited, threw up his head, snorting, would not be led nearer. But two other riders came over the hedge where Archer had jumped – Mr Whitcroft, a local farmer, and his son Tim.

'What the—?' Whitcroft exclaimed, pulling up so sharply that Tim's horse cannoned into him. Both men quickly dismounted. Whitcroft took Tonnant's reins from Archer and cried, 'Go to him!'

Archer knelt on the bumpy grass, feeling strangely remote, as though the world was at the wrong end of a telescope. The earl must have hit the ground at an awkward angle. His head was twisted to one side, and one blank eye seemed to peer up at the sky. There was nothing to be done. He was gone.

Archer stood up shakily, met Mr Whitcroft's gaze, and shook his head. Tim looked from one to the other and said, 'He's not—?'

'God rest his soul,' Archer replied, and Tim gulped.

Whitcroft turned to his son and said sharply, 'Ride to the Castle, quick as you like, raise the alarm. Bring help.'

Archer roused himself. 'Take Tonnant,' he said. 'He's faster'n your plug.'

The boy looked white and shaken, but he had wits enough to obey, to separate out Tonnant's reins, and cock his knee for Archer to leg him up. He was away while still feeling for his off-stirrup, Tonnant leaping straight into a gallop, still excited, eager to be moving again. Archer hoped the boy could stick on. Maybe he should have gone himself. But he couldn't leave his master.

'Shouldn't we straighten him out?' Whitcroft said, the shock evident in his voice.

Mr Whitcroft was right, Archer thought. You couldn't leave the earl all bunched up like that. 'Twasn't respectful. He straightened him out as best he could, then rose again awkwardly. Whitcroft took off his hat, and Archer followed suit. *Must see to the horse,* his groom's instincts told him, but this moment had to be observed.

'It's the way he would have wanted to go,' Mr Whitcroft offered tentatively.

'Yes, sir,' Archer said again. It was true, he thought. Not old and feeble in his bed, but with a horse under him and the damp winter air on his lip*s*.

Now there was nothing to do but wait.

The head man, Giddins, took charge when the sweating Tonnant skidded into the yard and his rider almost fell off, babbling his news. By the time the butler, Moss, had been summoned, Giddins had sent off four men to bring back the body and two to help with the horses, and was ready to cut through Moss's immediate paralysis with urgent, respectful suggestions.

'Doctor'd better be sent for, Mr Moss.'

'Yes. Of course.'

'And the undertaker.'

The word shocked Moss. 'But we don't know that he's dead yet!'

Giddins gave him a steadying look. Archer was no fool. He'd seen dead men before, and dead horses. He wouldn't make a mistake like that. 'Better Mr Folsham's on hand when he's wanted. Nobody upstairs needs to see him waiting.'

'Yes, you're right,' Moss said.

'And rector,' Giddins went on. 'He'll be wanted. And Mr Markham did oughter be told.' Markham was the agent.

Moss pulled himself together. He had his position to consider. Couldn't have a stableman telling him what to do. 'I will see to everything,' he said. 'I must tell her ladyship at once, before rumour reaches her.' But he paused, all the same, staring at nothing. 'He was such a good rider,' he heard himself say, puzzled.

Already it was the past tense for his lordship, Giddins noted. 'Accidents happen,' he said.

William George Louis Devereux Tallant, fifth Earl of Stainton, came home to Ashmore Castle for the last time on a withy hurdle, with estatemen pulling off their caps as he passed, and women coming to their cottage gates to stare. He was carried into the rear yard, where a number of servants had gathered in worried or excited groups, whispering among themselves. Dory was among them, and found herself quite close as the litter passed, close enough to see the white face. *That James was wrong*, she thought. *I did see him.* Much good would it do her! She wondered if her job was safe, and dismissed the thought. There'd be all those armbands to sew on, and who knew what else in the way of mourning clothes? They'd need a sewing-maid now more than ever.

The earl's lady received him with white, stinging fury, though from long training, nothing showed on the outside. He had made her a widow – a dowager! How *dared* he? It had not at all been in her plans to be widowed at the age of forty-nine. Stainton was only fifty-two, and in stout health. She had expected him to last for many more years, and when the time came, to go in an orderly fashion, with plenty of notice. She had imagined a dignified death-bed scene, the whole family gathered in respectful silence to hear his last words and witness the last breath. Not like this! Not carried in, broken and muddy, by yokels! Nothing was arranged! No plans were in place! How could he do this to her? She had done her duty by him, and now he had reneged on the deal. She was beside herself with rage.

'A telegraph must be sent to his lordship,' she said, managing to keep the tremble out of her voice. Moss, the butler, would have thought it a tremble of grief rather than anger, but she did not show emotions to the servants, not even understandable ones. Her eldest son, Viscount Ayton, was in Thebes, attached to a group conducting excavations on behalf of the Egyptian Department of Antiquities. 'He must come home at once.'

She met the butler's eyes and read the question in them. How long would it take Ayton to get back from Egypt, and could the funeral be held off that long? Thank God it was winter. A cascade of considerations flooded through her mind: the people who would have to be informed, the visits of condolence that would have to be endured, the funeral to arrange, the ramifications of will and finances, succession and titles . . . It went on and on. Damn Stainton for doing this to her!

'I will see to it at once, my lady,' Moss said, with a tremble in *his* voice. He could afford to show emotion – it was laudable in a servant.

The earl's unmarried daughters, Lady Alice, fifteen, and Lady Rachel, sixteen, had been hunting that day, but the point had been so fast that when hounds checked at Shelloes – the earl had been right about Charlie's destination – no-one yet knew about the accident. Josh Brandom, groom to the young ladies, did not wait to see if the scent would be picked up again. Pharaoh and Daystar had had enough, he decreed. It was time to go home. They did not argue with him. He had Archer's authority, and Archer had their father's.

Josh insisted that they trot all the way, through the gathering dusk and the increasing cold. It was agony to trot for long on a sidesaddle, but that was also Archer's orders, as the girls knew: cantering was too tiring for the horses after a day in the field, but they would get cold at the walk. 'Don't want chills in our stables,' Josh said implacably, when Rachel complained and Alice pleaded. 'When you're grown-up, you can do as you please.' He sniffed, the implication being that if they did as they pleased they would be ruining good horses, but it wouldn't be his problem then.

When there was a hunting party at the Castle, there was always tea in the Great Hall – a baronial anachronism added by their grandfather, useful for large gatherings – but there was no company today, so the young ladies would have theirs in the former schoolroom, which they now used as their sitting-room. Josh took pity on them and let them off at a side door, taking their horses round to the stable-yard himself.

Their first few steps were stiff and painful. 'My back's got knives in it,' Rachel complained.

'My sit-upon hurts,' Alice countered.

'Don't be vulgar,' Rachel chided automatically. They started up the stairs. There was no-one about. 'Never mind – hot baths soon. And boiled eggs, and muffins.' Always boiled eggs, always muffins after hunting.

'I hope there's anchovy toast,' Alice said, holding her heavy skirt clear of the stairs. Her riding boots were leaden.

'Won't be,' said Rachel. 'No company. But there might be cake.'

'Not if Mrs Oxlea's drunk again,' Alice giggled.

Rachel shushed her. They weren't supposed to know about the cook's weakness – or, at least, they certainly weren't supposed to speak about it. It wasn't seemly.

The schoolroom was warm, but the fire hadn't been made up recently and was dying down. Alice put coal on – the last in the scuttle. 'Shall I ring for more?'

'Better not,' Rachel said. They weren't supposed to ring without permission, the summoning of servants being a privilege wholly reserved to grown-ups. 'We can ask when they bring tea.'

But time passed and tea didn't come. 'We've been forgotten,' Alice said.

Rachel went to the door, opened it, listened. 'Doesn't it

sound awfully quiet to you?' It was always quiet up here, at the top of the house, but it seemed more so than usual. And they hadn't passed any servants on the way up.

'We should ring,' Alice said. 'I can't last until dinner time. I shall faint away.'

'Something's wrong,' Rachel said. She closed the door and went back to Alice by the fire. Her anxiety communicated itself to her sister, and they held hands, listening, wondering.

The forge in Canons Ashmore was at the end of the village street. The assistant blacksmith, Axe Brandom, came running out as the rector's carriage passed and stopped it. The living was a wealthy one, and the rector kept a smart black brougham drawn by a spirited high-stepping bay. Fortunately, the bay knew Axe from many professional encounters and stopped with no more than a snort and one toss of the head, even though it was heading for its own stable.

The rector let down his window and Axe stepped up to it. 'They're looking for you, sir, up at the Castle. My brother Josh was here a bit since – went to your house for you, asked me to keep a look-out for you.'

'I was at the Grange at Ashmore Carr,' the rector said. 'Old Lady Bexley—'

'Yes, sir – they said at your house she had took queer. I hope she's not—?'

'Just one of her turns. I sat with her a while and she's quite all right now. Is someone unwell at the Castle?'

Axe looked solemn. He was a massive young man, with red-gold hair, and golden hairs like wires on his bare forearms. The smithy grime on his face made his blue eyes look brighter. 'It's his lordship, sir. Had a bad fall out hunting. They do say as he broke his neck.'

'Dead?' The rector was startled.

'That's what Josh heard, sir.'

11

'Good God!' the rector said blankly. Just as it had in Lady Stainton's mind, a flood of consequences and ramifications cascaded through his thoughts. The earl, dead? He pulled himself together. 'I had better go straight there.' He craned out of the window to address his coachman. 'Deering, drive to the Castle.'

Deering, who had heard everything, of course, was ready. He winked at Axe – an inappropriate gesture, the smith thought – and touched the bay with the whip. As it sprang forward, Axe heard the rector mutter, 'What a terrible thing,' as he wrestled the window up.

Terrible, Axe thought, as he turned back to the forge and the waiting carthorse. *And surprising.*

Rachel finally got up the nerve to ring, and they waited in trepidation for it to be answered. No-one had come near them and, going frequently to the door to listen, they had found the house remained ominously quiet. They were sure now something was wrong.

'We should go down and find out,' said Alice, always the bolder of the two.

But Rachel was the obedient one, too sensitive, hating to be in the wrong, hating to be told off. 'Better not. They'd send for us if we were wanted,' she said.

And at last someone came – not Daisy, who had been their nursemaid and was now the housemaid who generally saw to their needs. It was the head housemaid, Rose, tall, thin, hawk-nosed and always rather daunting, who came in bearing the tea-tray. She regarded them with an unsmiling face – that was nothing new – but with a hint of sympathy in her eyes that was unsettling.

'Your tea, young ladies,' she said. 'I'm afraid you got forgotten in all the fuss.'

'Where's Daisy?' Rachel asked.

'Couldn't say, my lady, but she'll be in trouble when she turns up.'

'What fuss?' Alice picked up the word. 'What's happened?' 'I'm afraid I've got some bad news for you,' Rose said. 'His lordship's had an accident, out hunting.'

'Father?' Rachel said. She reached blindly for Alice's hand. 'He had a fall,' Rose went on. 'I'm afraid he's dead.'

She turned her back on them while she set out the tea on the low table by the fire, giving them time to absorb it. Neither of them made a sound. 'Everything's at sixes and sevens downstairs,' Rose said, taking a normal tone, which she thought would help brace them. 'I had to make your tea myself. Mrs Webster'll have something to say about it when things settle down. There's no excuse for not following routine. I did you boiled eggs. There's no muffins – Cook didn't make any – but there's extra toast, and I brought the good strawberry jam. You must be starving.' She turned at last and saw them still stiff and staring, not knowing – she suspected – how they were supposed to react. 'Eat your tea. Going hungry won't help,' she said. 'That's a poor-looking fire. I'll make it up for you.'

'There's no coal,' Alice said, her voice sticking in her dry mouth.

Rose tutted. 'That Daisy! I don't know! Well, come and have your eggs, anyway, before they go cold.'

It was good to have someone tell them what to do. They came and sat, watching blankly as Rose poured the tea.

Alice found her voice, afraid Rose would leave before she had had time to ask anything. 'How did it happen?'

'The horse came down, jumping over a big hedge, was what I heard. Jupiter, is that its name? His lordship took a bad fall and broke his neck.'

Rachel made a little sound, an indrawn gasp. Rose's words

seemed to run round the room in a soundless whisper, a little rustling ghost phrase, like mouse feet or dried leaves: *broke his neck . . . broke his neck.*

Rose gave a little shiver. *Goose walked over my grave,* she thought automatically.

At last Alice asked, in a small voice, 'Do you think . . . Did it hurt?' She looked at Rose, her eyes wide and appealing. 'Does it hurt, dying?'

To anyone else, Rose would have answered, 'How should I know?' But she felt unaccountably sorry for the young ladies – daughters of a great house, yes, but the least considered of anyone in it. Shut away up here and kept quiet until they were old enough to be married off – like goods for the market that had to be kept unmarked so's they'd fetch the best price. So she said, 'I don't suppose he'd have known anything about it, my lady. It's quick, is a broken neck. One second you're alive, the next you're dead. No pain at all.'

Rachel reached the end of a train of thought. 'Mama,' she said. 'Shouldn't we go to Mama? She must be . . .' The word *upset* was the only one she could think of, and it didn't seem appropriate. Not nearly dramatic enough. How *did* you feel if your husband was killed suddenly?

'She'll be far too busy for you,' Rose told her firmly. 'You'd only be in the way. Much better stay here until sent for.' She saw it was an answer that comforted them, and headed for the door, shrugging them off with relief.

But Alice stopped her as she opened it with another question. 'Where is he?'

'In the small dining-room,' she answered reluctantly. She did not want to get involved with the details. Folsham the undertaker had brought a temporary coffin with him, not having anything grand enough for the earl until it was made specially, and it was positioned on the dining-table, a purple cloth under it and another over. Folsham had brought those, too. There it stood while decisions were made.

14

Alice said, 'Can we see him?'

The question surprised a sharp answer out of Rose. 'Of course not. The very idea!' She regarded them, sitting, backs straight and hands in laps as they'd been taught, looking very forlorn. Her lips tightened. They were not her responsibility. She had enough to do without that. 'I'll get one of the girls to bring up some coal,' she said. And went out.

Giles Tallant, Viscount Ayton, had stepped out of the tent for a moment to stretch his neck, and stood under the canopy, surveying the scene. Gold and blue was the palette, the gold of the sand and the blue of the sky. Like an heraldic achievement, he was thinking, azure and or with lesser dabs of white, grey and brown, when the message was brought to him.

It was misspelled as usual, written down by someone whose first language was not English – and who probably rarely wrote things down even in his own language – but the meaning was unequivocal. *Your father is dead. Come home at once.*

Shock rolled through him at the stark words. His mother, of course, would not waste money on a gentler phrasing – and, besides, as she never spared herself, why should she spare anyone else? Shock, followed by . . . He would not allow himself to feel anger, which would be inappropriate, but his anguish at this news was at least in part made up of frustration. He had known all his life, of course, that this day would come, and the awareness had been a brooding shadow in a corner of his mind. But his father had been a fit and healthy man, and Ayton had hoped to have many more years of freedom. It must have been an accident, he supposed: illness would have been longer foretold. *Father, dead!* Inwardly, he damned the Fates that had allowed it to happen. Outwardly, he turned his face up to the sky and closed his eyes, looking like a man struggling with sorrow.

He felt the dry heat of the sun beat on his eyelids, felt the prickle of sand on his skin, heard the background sounds of the workings – the susurrus of shovels in sand, the ring of metal on stone, the grumbling groan of a camel, the creak of wooden poles and canvas as the sunshades worked in the occasional breeze. This was his world, the clean dryness of the desert and the constant undercurrent of excitement about what might be discovered. He did not want to go home. He thought of the grey wetness of England, the sameness of day-to-day, the stultifying rules and immutable traditions, the confinement and responsibility that awaited him. He did not want to be earl. *He did not want to go home!*

He had never got on with his father. They were too different. The earl had quite liked his younger brother Richard, though he cost him money and embarrassment. Had Ayton been sacked from Eton for misconduct, had he spent his time at university drinking and girling, his father would have roared at him, but it would have been a roar that rose from a depth of understanding, even affection. Had Ayton been an idler, an expensive wastrel, running up debts, chased for unpaid bills by tailors and wine merchants, his father would have punished him and loved him.

But he had spent his time at Eton studying, then insisted on going to University College London, to study under Flinders Petrie, rather than to Oxford as a Tallant should. He had won that great Egyptologist's approval for his application and his methodical habits, and had gone on his first expedition at only nineteen, when Petrie had recommended him to Percy Newberry, who took him to the excavation of el-Bersheh. The fever had entered his blood. It was all he wanted to do. He had taken his degree – which was, if not disreputable, at least *odd* – and afterwards hoped to apply his knowledge in the field for as long as his cadethood lasted.

Stainton could not understand it. It was not what his heir should do. It was not right. It was not *done*. He had raged and blustered, tried at first to forbid him, but Ayton was of age and could defy him. He could not even cut him off,

16

because the cadet title came with an independent income – not large, but enough for a young man with modest tastes and no desire to gamble and carouse. Abroad, he spent little. And archaeological expeditions were, in any case, paid for by rich families like the Stanhopes and the Cecils, or by associations like the Egypt Exploration Society. Ayton mixed, both in England and on the Nile, with titled men of good family, which made the earl roar all the more, baffled, because he could not put his finger on why it was wrong. He just knew it *would not do*. So Ayton kept away as much as possible, and when he had to be in England, he stayed with friends, or in the cheap lodgings in London he kept up. He visited Ashmore Castle as little as possible.

I am not ready for this, Ayton thought. The Castle was not home to him: it was a prison. The cage door would clang behind him and he would never get out again, to breathe the air anonymously, to be just himself.

He felt a trickle of sweat run down his back, and realised that standing out in the sun with his face turned up for roasting must look mad.

A voice said, 'Are you all right, Ayton?'

He lowered his head and turned. It was Howard Carter, chief inspector of the Egyptian Antiquities Service, who was supervising the excavation. He was looking at Ayton with mild concern, his big, handsome face bisected by the dark moustache that always somehow looked well groomed, no matter what the conditions.

In his hand he held a small figurine, in the shape of a large-eared, long-backed cat sitting very upright: the goddess Bast. Made of jade, it had been found just an hour ago. Carter had been drawing it for the record. Ayton did not blame him for his desire to keep holding it. It fitted beautifully in the hand, the smooth stone good to the touch.

'Not getting a touch of sunstroke, I hope?' Carter said jokingly.

17

'I've had a telegraph,' Ayton said bluntly. 'My father's dead. I have to go home.'

'My dear fellow, I'm so sorry,' Carter said, surveying his colleague's face. 'My deepest condolences.' He saw the young man's clenched fists, and suspected some other emotion than sorrow. He knew how keen Ayton was on archaeology, and the indications were that they were on the point of some interesting finds. He must be disappointed to be summoned away. 'Of course you must go. But you can come back when everything's settled?' he said, making it a question. 'We've so much more to do out here.'

'I don't think,' Ayton said slowly, 'that it will be in my power to return for a long time. If ever.'

'Well,' said Carter, awkwardly, 'I'm very sorry for it. But if you have to go, you had better leave at once.' He pulled out his watch and squinted at it. The sunlight bounced off the silver case in a glint of pure burning white. 'If you leave now, with a bit of luck you should be able to make Alexandria by Sunday night, and catch the *Imperator* on Monday morning. She's comfortable, and as quick as anything is out here.'

It was a mail service, and took four days from Alexandria to Trieste, where a train would be waiting, a *de luxe* express that took just two days to reach London.

'You'll be home in not much more than a week,' Carter concluded.

'I'd better send a cable,' Ayton said, seeming almost dazed.

Carter had never seen him indecisive. 'You can do that from the hotel. Go now, old chap, don't delay. No time to waste. Family duty must come first.' And as Ayton turned away, he added, 'All this will still be here. Egypt has waited for you for three thousand years – it will wait a bit longer.'

The sun beat down, glinting blindingly off flecks of mica. The sand pulled at Ayton's soft boots as he tried to walk quickly, like clutching hands anxious for him not to go.

CHAPTER TWO

Perhaps the person who most sincerely mourned the earl was his valet, Crooks. 'Twenty years,' the pudgy, watery-eyed manservant had been saying whenever two or three senior servants gathered together. Moss, the butler, only nodded sympathetically, but her ladyship's woman, Miss Taylor – grey of hair and mauve of face – found his moist self-pity irritating. Years of biting her tongue in the presence of Lady Stainton had honed it to sharpness when talking to lesser mortals.

'Twenty years or not, you're superfluous to requirements now,' she told him. 'You're like one of those Indian wives: when their husband dies they're thrown on the funeral pyre.'

'The settee,' Moss murmured. He read encyclopaedias, and liked to appear omniscient.

'*Sut*tee,' Mrs Webster corrected impatiently.

Moss caught up with what had been said. 'But there's no need to be talking so shocking, Miss Taylor,' he said sternly. 'There'll be no emulation here.'

'Immolation,' said Mrs Webster.

'Either way,' said Miss Taylor, 'a valet whose master dies is for the chop. It's not as if there's anything else he can do. And at your age,' she added to Crooks, her voice brimming with malicious pity, 'you'll never get another place.'

Crooks had been saying the same thing himself, but he

19

didn't expect to be agreed with. 'Perhaps his new lordship will need a man,' he said in a wobbly voice.

'Bound to have one already,' said Miss Taylor. 'He's not a child. How old is he?'

'Twenty-six,' Moss provided.

'But he may not have a man suitable for an earl,' Crooks said. 'Someone who knows what's due to his position.'

'Quite, quite,' Moss said soothingly. 'I believe he's been living very modest. And abroad such a lot of the time.'

Mrs Webster asked, 'You've known Lord Ayton longest, Mr Moss. What sort of a man is he?' She had only been at the Castle six years.

Moss pondered. 'He was very good-natured when he was a boy. Unusually so, given he was the heir – no side to him. But who knows how he'll change when he takes on the mantle, if I might speak poetical?'

'There's bound to be changes,' said Mrs Webster. 'He'll have his own ideas. We'll all feel it.'

'I don't know,' said Crooks. 'It's her ladyship runs the house. A gentleman wouldn't trouble himself about domestic details.'

'If she's still here,' said Mrs Webster.

'What can you mean?' said Miss Taylor stiffly. 'Her ladyship is in perfect health.'

'But she'll be moving to the Dower House, won't she?'

Moss and Miss Taylor exchanged an amused glance. 'Have you ever *seen* the Dower House, Mrs Webster?' Moss enquired.

'Of course I have. Pretty little square house at the end of the village.'

'Little's the word,' said Miss Taylor. 'Her ladyship couldn't stick it.'

'And I believe it's in poor repair,' said Moss. 'No-one's lived there in – well, it must be fifty years. His lordship's mother – his *late* lordship's mother, I should say – didn't care for it.' The fourth earl had caused a scandal by bringing

20

home from his travels a lively Frenchwoman, Victoire Ballancourt, for a bride. She had found the English countryside too cold and English country houses too damp, and as soon as she was widowed had decamped to London and a cosy house in Bruton Street.

'Besides,' said Miss Taylor, 'his new lordship's unmarried so she'll have to stay and run things for him.'

'*I* run the house, Miss Taylor,' said Mrs Webster, 'so there's no need for her to stay. Her ladyship can go to the Dower House any time she likes. And you'll go with her, of course. I'm sure you'll love it there – once essential repairs have been carried out.' She had no personal spleen against Miss Taylor, but she liked to keep the balance of power in the house, and Taylor had been bullying poor old Crooks all day.

'We'll see,' said Miss Taylor, her nostrils flaring. 'And if I might venture an opinion, Mrs Webster, *some* changes might be welcome in this house. I think you'd hardly claim that everything is entirely as it should be.'

Mrs Webster reddened, but with vexation rather than embarrassment. 'I do the best I can with what I have. I've asked and asked for more staff—'

'I'm sure I wasn't blaming you,' said Miss Taylor meaning exactly the opposite. 'And we all know that fool in the kitchen isn't up to the job. That pork last night – practically raw! I cannot and will not eat raw meat.'

'Indeed, it's true, pork should always be well cooked,' Moss ruled ponderously. 'And chicken, and game also. It's acceptable for lamb to be pink, however. And roast beef, now that can be rare – gentlemen often prefer it that way. His lordship's father, I believe – his late lordship's father, I should say—' he corrected himself with a quiver, 'liked it bloody.'

'I will not have blood oozing out of my meat,' said Miss Taylor. 'I am not a vampire.'

'Come, come,' Moss said, disturbed. 'There's no need for that sort of talk. You can't be calling his lordship's father—'

'The fact is,' said Miss Taylor, impatiently, 'neither the earl nor her ladyship ever cared a jot about food, or they'd have done something about it and sent that cook packing.'

'Well, perhaps his new lordship will have fresh ideas about food, having lived away for so long,' Mrs Webster said. 'He might have London tastes. He might even want foreign dishes prepared.' Which, she thought, might make Mrs Oxlea uncomfortable enough to leave of her own accord. Modern cooking was beyond her – she was fit only for roasting vast joints, as if they were still living in Tudor times with spits and cauldrons. 'Anyway,' she added, 'when he gets married, there'll be a new mistress. Then there really will be changes.'

Crooks groaned, 'I hate change. I wish we could just go back to the way things were. Twenty years I was with his lordship. Twenty years!'

Miss Taylor ignored him. She was thinking, and the fruit of her thoughts she offered to Mrs Webster, being of the opinion that Crooks and Moss were both fools. 'It occurs to me,' she said slowly, 'that he might not settle here at all.'

'What do you mean?' Webster asked, intrigued.

'He's never shown any liking for the Castle, and he's lived abroad whenever he's had the chance. He might just close the place up.' She smiled maliciously. 'Then you'll all be out of a position.'

'So will you,' Mrs Webster pointed out.

'Her ladyship needs me. Even if it's in that nasty Dower House, I'll keep my job.'

Mrs Webster shrugged. 'Well, I can always get another place. I'm young enough. And most of the servants will be all right. It's Mr Moss and Mr Crooks who are most at risk.'

Moss was looking from her to Miss Taylor and back, trying to follow their argument. 'Surely you don't think—'

'Has to be considered,' Mrs Webster said unkindly.

'Twenty years!' Crooks bleated.

* * *

22

In the formal dining-room at Holme Manor, in Frome Monkton, Dorset, Linda, Lady Cordwell faced her husband down the length of the table. Even with as many leaves as possible taken out, it was still uncomfortably long for dining *à deux*, and the room itself was too big, difficult to heat. But the smaller dining-parlour's ceiling had come down when the roof leaked last winter, and there had been no money yet to repair it, and Lord Cordwell refused to dine in the morning-room, even when it was only the two of them. Which, his lady reflected, was all too often these days – and if you didn't entertain, you tended to not be invited back. We really must do something about having a dinner-party, she thought. Invite twenty or thirty people. It would be a large expense, but it would be good for reciprocal invitations for months. Dining out at other people's houses, while saving the equivalent expenditure at home – and winter was the time to do it, when need was greatest – they might be invited to hunting and shooting parties, Saturday-to-Mondays, the house all but shut up for three whole days! If you caught the right party to start with, the invitation train could carry you right through until the Season started.

She'd have expressed all this to Cordwell, but the effort of speaking down the table was too much for anything but short sentences. She addressed herself instead to the minuscule fillet of fish on her plate, with its dab of sauce. Like her mother Lady Stainton, she was not greatly interested in food, but she was always hungry, these days, and knew from her looking-glass that she was getting gaunt. Really, when they were alone, they should go back to nursery food, cheap and filling – big plates of mutton and potatoes followed by rice pudding – but Cordwell clung to the refinements due to a viscount. She had always thought it admirable that he would not lower his standards, but lately she had come to think it more foolish than noble. She had not known – her parents had not known – when she married him how impoverished his estate was. Times were hard, particularly in the West Country, rents had fallen, and returns were low. Gerald Cordwell had been saddled with his father's debts when he came into his inheritance unexpectedly young. His father had died in a shooting accident – Linda secretly suspected the old viscount might have blown his own brains out in despair at his financial condition, and she wondered sometimes whether Gerald suspected it too. Her dowry had floated the ship off the rocks, but with expenditure stuck at the 'twenty pounds aught and six' mark, they were bound to sink again.

And there were two children now to provide for, Arabella and Arthur. It was annoying, Linda thought, that she had got a girl first time round. If Bella had been a boy, she could have stopped at one and saved half the expense.

Gerald was saying something, and she roused herself from her reverie to ask him to repeat it. 'I said, I wonder if your father will have left you something in his will. Do you know when it will be read?'

'At the funeral,' she said. 'It's traditional. Always straight after the funeral.'

'You haven't had the invitation yet, have you?' he said, and she was annoyed at the anxiety in his voice.

'I don't suppose they can fix it until they know when Giles will be home. They can't have it without him.'

'No, I suppose not.'

He sounded so glum that she said, to cheer him up, 'We can certainly stay at the Castle at least two weeks. I think Mama will expect me to be on hand to support her in her grief. She may even need me for longer – a month, say. And she'll want to see the children. We'll take them with us.'

'A month,' Cordwell said, brightening. Shut the house for a month! Even the nursery! When they *were* invited anywhere for a Saturday-to-Monday they always had to leave the children behind, which meant coals and hot water and meals for them and the nursery staff. But if they took them to the Castle, they'd take the nursery staff too, and they'd all be kept at the Castle's expense. And the other servants could be given a holiday, whether they wanted one or not.

'You haven't seen Giles for a long time,' Cordwell said thoughtfully. 'You always got on well with him, didn't you?'

'Whatever Papa left me in his will won't depend on Giles,' she said impatiently.

'Yes, but there's the question of future invitations . . .'

'Oh, don't worry, I can handle Giles. I'll revive childhood memories with him, and make myself indispensable to Mama, and you – well, you only have to be affable. I'm sure Giles liked you when you last saw him.'

'I can't remember when that was.'

'Never mind, people generally like you. And if he takes to the children, we might even persuade him to have them there permanently. It can't matter to them to have two more. And even when he marries and gets brats of his own, having cousins to play with is always a good thing. I foresee a golden period opening up before us.'

Cordwell could not quite reach her heights of optimism. 'What about the allowance?' he asked quietly – so quietly she almost missed the words. When she caught them, she frowned.

'What do you mean?' she asked.

'I mean, was the allowance in your father's will?'

'You know damn well it was an informal arrangement between us,' she said shortly. 'He might have had it written into his will, but—'

'But he didn't know he was going to die so soon,' Cordwell finished for her. 'What if it isn't?'

'We'll cross that bridge when we come to it,' she said briskly, not willing to show him she was worried. Without that allowance . . . 'Even if it isn't, Giles is bound to honour it. He's a very virtuous person, he'll always do what's right. Anyway, I can talk him round. I could always make him do what I wanted when he was a boy.'

She had offered too many assurances. Cordwell was not comforted. Absently he finished his fish in one mouthful, instead of eking it out, and the footman and butler, who had been standing against the wall (he felt it imperative to keep up the style of a viscount, even if everything was crumbling about his ears) stepped forward to clear the plates and bring on the next course. He looked in dismay at the leg of pheasant on his plate, knowing how little edible material there was among the tendons and sinews of a pheasant's leg. But they'd had the breasts yesterday. At least there'd be pheasant soup tomorrow. He helped himself to potatoes and cabbage. He'd hoped there'd be carrots, but perhaps they were being saved for the soup.

Linda was having a gloomy thought of her own. They could not have a dinner-party, and trigger lots of invitations for the winter, because she'd be in mourning for six months. Damn it! It was more than ever imperative that they got an invitation to stay on at the Castle after the funeral. Once installed, trust her to stretch it out.

The journey had seemed interminable. The *Imperator* was a well-appointed ship, and Giles's stateroom was luxurious – he'd have been happy with more modest accommodation, but by the time he booked his passage the cheaper cabins had all been taken. Still, he'd enjoyed long baths in his own private bathroom, and even submitted, slightly shamefaced, to the ship's barber shaving him. The man had admired his razors – a rare present from his father when he had reached eighteen, a pair of ebony-handled blades from Truefitt and Hill, the very best that money could buy – but had shaken his head at the state of the edge, and had taken them away to sharpen them. Giles could have explained the difficulty

26

of keeping a strop from drying out in a desert climate, but would not demean himself further. He did not have a manservant, which the barber, like the cabin steward, had already kindly overlooked, while making it clear that a gentleman of his eminence needed looking after by professionals. The steward took away all his clothes to brush and clean and launder, which was agreeable, but Giles baulked at having his trousers held while he stepped into them, or his socks put on for him. 'I've been dressing myself since I was four,' he said, with good humour but firmly. The steward gave him the sort of kind smile you accord the mentally incompetent. Giles realised he was being written off as an English Eccentric.

Unused to being confined, he took his exercise by walking round the deck fifty times every morning, and again in the evening. He'd avoided contact with the other passengers – it was one thing for foreigners to be outgoing, but he did not understand why being on a ship should make the normally reticent English so excessively sociable. He had only to pause and lean on the rail for half a moment to find himself being wheedled to make up a table for whist or biritch, play deck quoits, or engage himself to eat dinner with this or that party. News of his bereavement had somehow spread, and he was always receiving warm and sympathetic looks – especially from a Mrs Cadwallader, who was travelling with an unmarried daughter in her twenties. Sometimes he feared actually to be embraced.

Fortunately he had books with him in his luggage, and could retreat to his stateroom and read. For much of the crossing he was happily engrossed in a recently published tome by Professor Montalcini of the venerable University of Siena. Montalcini documented similarities between Etruscan and Minoan wall paintings, quoting the Etruscan expert, Giles's old friend and mentor Flavio Lombardi. He proposed that they stemmed from a common influence, the Egyptian.

Civilisations that have been in contact for centuries may develop a common artistic vocabulary, whose origin is lost in time, he read. The author compared fragments of wall paintings from Knossos with the Etruscan murals of the Tomb of the Roaring Lions. The Egyptians were great painters of murals on lime plaster . . . Asia Minor . . . Lydia . . . Herodotus . . . the Aegean region . . . the island of Thera . . . Thucydides recorded that the Etruscans lived on the island of Lemnos in ancient times . . .

Absorbed in the world in which he felt most at home, he passed the hours happily. When he did emerge from his cocoon, it was to find the weather gradually worsening as the ship ploughed westwards, leaving the eastern Mediterranean climate behind. His walks around the deck were sometimes lively, as he found himself tipped against railings and having to cling to handholds. It was a reminder of what he was going to: the iron grey of English winter skies, the iron weight of responsibility.

He had been Viscount Ayton all his life and was used to being addressed as 'my lord' and 'your lordship', but his new position was driven home to him when one of the passengers – an American, and almost as keen a deck-walker as himself – stopped him on the last morning, touching his hat and saying, 'Morning, Earl! Brisk today, don'tcha think? Fresh, I call it, but my wife won't leave the cabin – thinks there's a storm brewing!'

Giles had given him a startled look, and murmured something vague.

His tormentor gave him a rueful grin. 'Dare say you'll be glad to be getting home to dear old England. I never liked being at sea myself. Not looking forward to crossing the Atlantic again, I can tell you. You'll be home a lot quicker than me, Earl, and that's a fact.'

'Yes,' said Giles. 'I suppose I will.'

★　★　★

The village of Canons Ashmore lay in the valley of the river Ash, built along either side of one long street, which had been a coaching route until the railway came. It was a pretty street – the wealthy second earl had added stone façades to the old Tudor and medieval houses, so now only the wavering roof line and jumble of chimneys suggested what mismatched horrors might lie behind. The same earl had built the dower house for his mother when he succeeded at the age of thirty – his mother and his wife did not get along – but it was his grandson, the fourth earl, who had been railway-minded. He had sold the necessary land and helped push the Bill through Parliament, against the wishes of most of his neighbours. The railway ran along the high ground to the north of the village, while Ashmore Castle was built halfway up the slope on the opposite side of the valley, so it was of little daily inconvenience to him. Indeed, he loved to travel, and as the railway provided him with a quicker escape to the Continent, he could see nothing wrong with it.

Giles was almost asleep at the end of his long journey when he arrived at Canons Ashmore station. He had to scramble to gather his effects together and descend to the platform, looking around rather wildly, afraid the train would move off before he'd got his trunks out of the luggage van. He needn't have worried. The telegram he had sent to tell his mother what train he was taking had not passed unnoticed through the village post office. There was a welcoming committee waiting for him, headed by Persons, the station master, flanked by his two porters, and supported by a number of worthies Giles felt he ought to recognise but didn't. Because of the solemnity of the occasion, his father's death, they were trying to look mournful while attempting to convey how happy they were to see him. Words stuttered out at him. 'Tragic circumstances . . . shocking accident . . . our noble patron . . . her ladyship's fortitude . . . homecoming in happier circumstances . . .'

Giles had the impression that if he weren't in mourning, there might have been bunting and a band.

'My luggage,' he managed to suggest.

'All will be taken care of, I assure your lordship. The Castle brake is here. Please do not concern yourself for an instant. And there's a carriage outside waiting for you, my lord. Hossey, take his lordship's portmanteau! This way, your lordship. Oh, your ticket – no need, I assure you, your lordship, but – oh dear! – thank you.' Persons was caught between shame that the lord of Ashmore Castle should have to show the same permit as ordinary mortals, and the awareness that Head Office would expect his returns to tally.

Outside, a closed carriage awaited Giles, drawn by a pair of his mother's greys. The black leather harness lay in satisfying contrast against the shining dappled curves of flank and neck. They tossed their heads a little in their eagerness to be off; their breath smoked on the chilly air. He had forgotten how beautiful English horses were, sleek and well fed, round bodies and delicate heads – so unlike the poor thin scrubs of hot countries.

There was also quite a crowd of villagers, who parted to make passage for him to the carriage door, but stared in frank curiosity, whispering to each other. Some tried to catch his eye, smiling ingratiatingly. He recognised Millet, the proprietor of the Crown, and Mrs Albright, who ran the post office stores. He gave them a rather dazed nod and hurried into the carriage, disconcerted by the reception. This, he supposed, was what it would be like from now on – constantly in the public eye. He felt a weight of gloom descending.

The greys trotted him briskly down the high street, turned sharply left at the end into Ash Lane, and moments later they had passed over the hump-backed stone bridge, through the gates, and were on Stainton land. He stared through the window at the lush wetness all around him. Even in winter,

England was green, and Buckinghamshire was surely the most verdant county of them all. But the sky was low and grey, seeping moisture, and there was so little natural light it felt as though night was coming already. He had grown used to acid blue skies and a white sun, and to having to seek the shade. So much green was depressing. He felt ever more out of his place.

In all the years of arriving home as Lord Ayton, he had been content to be driven round into the stable-yard and to go in by a side door. But, presumably on orders, the coachman swung the horses left at the top of the slope and then right, up the shallow incline to the paved terrace in front of the main entrance. Someone – either his mother or Moss, he supposed – had evidently decreed that his first entrance as earl should be a grand one. Shallow steps led up to the great door, and the servants were arranged in two rows slantwise down them, creating a sort of deer-trap to funnel him in. *No escape!* One or two he recognised and he tried to remember names, but they had never been important to him – *the* staff, not *his* staff. But they were his now. They bowed and curtsied as he passed, and one or two looked keenly up into his face, as though he had answers for them. *I know nothing! Leave me alone!*

At the head of the lines, nearest the door, were the house-keeper, Webster – he remembered her name, and greeted her by it, and she bobbed a curtsy – and Moss. The butler had been in situ most of his life. He felt it appropriate to shake his hand.

Moss seemed moved. 'Welcome home, my lord,' he said fervently, his eyes moist. 'A sad occasion.'

'Very sad,' Giles responded, though he meant something different from Moss.

'But we are most glad to see you, my lord, even so,' Moss said. 'Ashmore Castle welcomes you home.' He made a little

31

gesture with his hand, as though reminding Giles that *all this* was now his.

But I don't want it! Giles thought. He took one last look round at the grey twilight of deep winter – even the skies seemed to be weeping for him – and went in.

In the great hall, there were good fires in both fireplaces, and lamps were lit. His sister Linda was the first to reach him. Good God, how thin she'd grown! She seized him in an embrace, an unaccustomed exercise in which she had no skill. She grasped him like a sheaf of corn she was about to stook. She felt like a bundle of broomsticks to him. Her hair smelt sour and her cheek was lean and cold.

'My dear, dear Giles! Little brother! How wonderful to see you again! It's been so long – too long. We've missed you so much while you've been away. You must never go away for so long again!'

She had never been a gusher. And 'little brother'? He was only a year younger than her. Giles eased himself out of her grip, frowning. If Linda was being nice to him, she must want something. But what? He had nothing she'd be interested in, he thought – forgetting, with frightening ease, that he now had everything.

'Good to see you, old girl,' he said awkwardly. She was beaming at him – *beaming*! She clicked her fingers behind her and her husband shuffled up shamefacedly to shake his hand.

'Stainton,' he muttered, embarrassed.

'Cordwell,' Giles responded. He heard Linda hiss, and saw a little exchange between them, her scowl at Cordwell's inadequacy and his little *moue* of regret – *I can't help it.*

But there were others to greet, and he was passed from hand to hand. They were all in black, which looked particularly odd to him after Thebes. Grandmère, still elegant, though dressed in the style of twenty years ago – which suited her – had diamonds at her ears. She kissed his cheek

– hers smelt of scented powder – and addressed him in French, *Poor boy, don't let them eat you up!* Then Uncle Sebastian, actually his father's uncle, with a stomach that arrived first, cigar ash on his front, brandy on his breath. Genial, gripping his shoulder with unexpectedly strong fingers. Uncle Sebastian lived mostly at the Castle, though he actually had a small house of his own in Henley. He used it only when something interesting was happening on the river.

Here was Aunt Caroline, his mother's sister, very fashionable, with many jet beads and a smile for him that seemed to offer real sympathy – she had always been kind to him when he was a child. Uncle Stuffy, his mother's younger brother, Lord Leake, so immaculately dressed he looked almost out of place in the shabby surroundings. Two little children, six or seven years old. They were thrust at him by Linda, who seemed to be everywhere. She gave him an ingratiating look, as though being offered her children were a great treat. Some cousins he vaguely remembered. Last and least, his two younger sisters, hanging back, but staring at him with great interest. They smiled uncertainly and shyly but did not speak, looking oddly waif-like in black.

And again he had been funnelled, this time to the place where his mother stood, all in heavy blacks, her back stiff and her face grim, her lips set tight as though she did not mean to speak for several years at least.

'Mama,' he said, and since she did not move a muscle, he leaned forward and dutifully kissed her cheek. He felt he should have some words for her, but he had no idea what they might be. She was surveying him now with a sharp, critical eye.

'Your hair needs cutting,' she said. 'And why are you not in mourning?'

'I've been travelling ever since I received your telegram. I've had no opportunity to—'

She interrupted his excuse. 'You should have been here.'

He was startled. Did she blame him for his father's death? Did she think he could have prevented it? 'I understood it was an accident,' he said.

He was angry that his voice sounded so feeble. She always did that to him, creating guilt by her assumption of it. Why should he have to justify himself? 'I came as soon as I got your – telegraph.' He almost said *summons*.

'You should have been here to deal with things,' she responded.

'But no-one could have foreseen—' he began.

She lifted a hand sharply to cut him off. 'Your excuses do not interest me. Your place was here, at his side, on the estate you were to inherit, learning about your duties, preparing yourself for your future role. Not indulging yourself in that selfish manner.'

'Mother—'

She would not let him speak. 'We have had to delay the funeral while we waited on your pleasure. Everything is in suspension. I would say that you have disappointed me, except that I hardly expected any better from you. You were always selfish, Ayton. Selfish and wilful.'

It was Uncle Sebastian who intervened. 'Now, Maudie,' he said genially, 'let the boy get his breath back. I dare say it was a horrible journey, and he'll want to wash the grime away and change his linen before he can be rational. Why don't you go to your room, Giles, and clean up? Tea can be waited half an hour, can't it, Maud? Poor feller doesn't know if he's coming or going.'

Going, Giles wanted to say. *Definitely going.*

His mother was about to say something, but Aunt Caroline, who had drifted to her other side, now said, 'That's a good idea. We can manage without bombarding you with questions for half an hour. We're longing to hear about your adventures. Go *on*, Giles.'

He escaped gratefully. His mother, he was sure, did not want to hear about his adventures. She had never wanted to *hear* from him, only *tell* him. He wished Richard were here. Richard could always soften her.

At the turn of the staircase, Mrs Webster was waiting to waylay him. He didn't really know her, but he liked what he saw. She looked intelligent, dark as a gypsy, with an all-seeing sort of eye. 'Her ladyship wanted you to be put in the Queen's Bedroom, my lord,' she said without preamble, 'but we have not yet managed to remove all his late lordship's effects, so I've had the Blue Bedroom prepared for you.'

'Thank you,' Giles said, with feeling. The great state bedroom in which several monarchs were said to have slept had always been his father's. He had been thinking of his own simple, modest room – one of the bachelor chambers on the second floor. It hadn't occurred to him that being earl would force him not only into his father's metaphorical shoes but his literal bed. He was about to ask to be moved to his old room, but Mrs Webster forestalled him.

'The Blue Bedroom is a *compromise*, my lord, until your further wishes can be known.'

'Very well,' he said. He understood. The Blue Bedroom was the compromise that it had been possible to sell to her ladyship, while a bachelor room was unthinkable. And, for the moment, her ladyship still ruled.

'I have had hot water sent up,' she went on. 'I understand that you do not have a manservant, my lord. Shall I send one of the footmen? James is accustomed to looking after gentlemen – he attends to Mr Sebastian.'

Giles was prepared to stand firm here. 'No, thank you. I am quite used to dressing myself.' He was in no mood to have a stranger pawing over his things.

Webster bowed her head graciously and stepped aside,

and he took the rest of the flight two at a time, like a man fleeing.

The Blue Bedroom was a handsome one, with a dressing-room attached. It had blue and white Chinese wallpaper and a *bleu-de-roi* carpet. Favoured guests usually had it, by which he gathered that the mattress on the massive four-poster was one of the better ones. He could put up with it, he supposed, for a day or two.

But he still could not be alone, for when he entered the room he found old Crooks, for Heaven's sake, his father's man, waiting for him, looking pink, damp and nervous. Giles stopped short, and snapped, 'What are you doing here?'

'I beg your pardon, my lord, for the presumption, but I understand that you have no manservant, and thought that perhaps I might offer my services for the time being. Having no other duties, as it were . . .' The second sentence seemed added on impulse and trailed away into the sand, but it did explain the first.

Giles had no wish to feel sympathy – he wanted to cling to his irritation – but in an unwelcome flash he saw that the old man was afraid, and realised that his father's death had put Crooks out of a position. At his age, what was he to do? There was also the possibility that Crooks had felt affection for his master, and was mourning him. And while he emphatically did not want the man who had folded his father's under-drawers to unfold his, he had never been the sort of boy who tortured small animals. *Damn it, why can't they leave me alone?* But he saw Crooks's lower lip tremble, and his chalky hands, locked together in front of him, writhe a little.

'I really don't need looking after,' he said, exasperated, but in a kinder tone than he might otherwise have used. 'I am accustomed to dressing myself.'

'Of course, my lord, but now you are the earl, there may be things – expectations – my experience – at your service . . .'

Crooks swallowed, and added, 'I cannot help noticing, my lord, that you have no mourning clothes.'

'There hasn't been time—' Giles began impatiently.

'Of course, my lord. If I might suggest, a mourning band for this evening?' Crooks produced one from his pocket, like a magician. 'And for the funeral tomorrow—'

'Tomorrow?' He'd assumed he would have at least a day's grace. Why so soon?

'Her ladyship did not want to wait any longer than necessary,' Crooks said apologetically. 'But, if you'll forgive me, it would not set quite the right tone if you were not in mourning. I took the liberty of investigating your lordship's old room, and there is a pair of black trousers in the wardrobe that would be suitable. If you will allow me, I can alter his late lordship's mourning frock to fit you, just as a temporary measure – it would only mean taking in the seams at the sides. You are much of a height, though his lordship carried more weight. Then, one of his black cravats. And if your lordship does not have a silk hat—'

'I don't.'

'—I can put a clean band inside one of his late lordship's, and attach the crape. It can all be done by tomorrow morning.'

So the trap, the gentlest yet, closed velvet jaws on him. 'Thank you, Crooks,' he said, and felt obliged to add, 'That's very thoughtful of you.'

A rush of blood to the valet's face was probably as much relief as pleasure. But he beamed. 'I am glad to be of service, my lord. Might I lay out a change for you, my lord, while you wash? I have unpacked your bags in the dressing-room. And would your lordship care for me to shave you?'

'My lordship wouldn't,' Giles growled. 'I can shave my own damned chin, thank you.'

'Indeed, of course, quite so, my lord,' Crooks murmured, and scuttled away into the dressing-room, taking the rest of the permission for granted.

Giles watched him go with despair. Not only having the earldom thrust upon him, but inheriting his father's manservant as well! It was too much! He felt a little like weeping. But Crooks had done him a service over the mourning clothes, saving him from maternal unpleasantness tomorrow. He supposed he could put up with him for a little while. He'd find some way of scraping him off at some point. Wearily he began to shrug off his jacket. He felt a thousand years old.

CHAPTER THREE

It rained on the day of the funeral. Canons Ashmore stood sodden under a sky almost low enough to touch. Trees dripped; roofs and cobbles glistened; gutters and downpipes gurgled steadily. In the row of carriages outside St Peter's that went all the way up Church Lane, the horses stood with heads drooping and ears out sideways, their breath making little clouds about their muzzles, where raindrops caught and trembled on their whiskers.

Inside the church, there was the dank smell of wet wool and the mouldy smell of chrysanthemums; sniffs and the occasional hollow cough were the counterpoint to the familiar words of the funeral service. The neighbourhood had turned out to see off the earl. Giles was aware he was being scrutinised: he felt the eyes on the back of his neck. What sort of a landlord would he prove? Was there anything to be made out of him?

At the graveside, all was black umbrellas, an astonishing number, like a sudden growth of mushrooms brought on by the rain. The inside of the grave was grey and slippery, indecent, like a wound, an exposure of something never meant to be seen. Giles felt faintly nauseous – though perhaps that might have been hunger. He had been unable to eat at breakfast. He'd had little appetite since he'd left Thebes.

The rector nodded to him, and he stepped forward and threw a lump of clay down, hearing it thump hollowly on the coffin, and tried for decency's sake to think about his father and feel grief for him. But nothing came. He couldn't remember a single moment when his father had spoken to him naturally or with unalloyed affection. Perhaps an earl had always to be acting a role. It was a depressing thought. When they had driven through the gates this morning, the gatekeeper had come out carrying his little son, presumably having been engaged in doing something for him when the carriage passed. The child had his arm around the gate-keeper's neck, his cheek resting comfortably against his father's, as though this were an accustomed perch. It was what people did, in the real world. They touched, they smiled, they spoke unguardedly, from the heart. It was impossible for Giles to imagine his own father holding him like that.

He stepped back from the graveside. There was a smear of clay on the fingers of one glove, and he wiped it absently with the other, spoiling both. *I have nothing for you, Father*, he thought. *But then, you never had anything for me.*

His mother's face was carved in stone; but Aunt Caroline was holding her elbow, as though she might need support. Giles noted that his little sisters were crying: Alice with a tremble of the lip and a tear or two, but Rachel was weeping as though broken-hearted. He was surprised, but then remembered that Rachel had always been too tender-hearted. She could not bear a mouse in a trap or a butterfly beating against a window. Even a sad song or story could reduce her to tears: *The Constant Tin Soldier* or *The Fir Tree*. When they were all young together, Richard, he recalled, had enjoyed teasing her by quoting certain lines from *The Little Match Girl*: '. . . frozen to death on the last evening of the old year. Stiff and stark sat the child there with her matches . . .' Sometimes simply drawing a box of matches from his pocket with a significant look would be enough to set her off. Giles did not suppose she had ever had more of a relationship with their father than he'd had, but for Rachel, the mere idea of his being dead had tears beslobbering her face.

Well, he thought, *it's good that someone cries for him.* No-one should go unwept to their grave. The fifth earl of Stainton had Rachel – and the sky. It had to be enough.

When he arrived back at the Castle after the interment, and entered the great hall, the first thing he noticed was that there were two dogs – lurchers, a grey and a brindle – lying by the fire. They got up as people began to come in, and Giles heard his mother make a sound of annoyance. But the dogs skirted round her and came to Giles, heads low, tails swinging uncertainly.

'Moss, what are they doing in here?' Lady Stainton said sharply.

'They must have slipped in, my lady,' Moss said. 'I had no orders about excluding them.'

Alice, coming up behind Giles, said, 'They're Papa's, Giles – Tiger and Isaac. How they must miss him!' She squatted to caress their rough heads. 'You don't understand, do you, poor boys?' Tiger turned his muzzle to her, but Isaac was pressing against Giles's legs, shivering.

And Giles, somewhat to his own surprise, heard himself saying, 'Let them stay.'

Even more surprising was that his voice came out commandingly. He saw his mother's mouth open to contradict him, then close again as a slightly puzzled look came over her face. After a moment, she said, 'As you please,' and turned away. Alice, still crouching, threw him an adoring look, and then they all had to move to admit the rest of the party. The dogs went with him, as though attached by invisible leashes. So he had gained two new friends – or three, counting Alice.

★ ★ ★

41

Dory reached the bottom of the back stairs to find the passage blocked by a knot of whispering maids. 'What's going on?' she asked.

The nearest one, in the pink dress of a kitchen-maid, turned to her, and Dory recognised her. Ida, wasn't that her name? 'It's Mrs Oxlea,' she said. 'She's shut herself in her room and won't come out.'

'Drunk again,' said one of the housemaids.

'She's not drunk,' Ida said angrily. 'Don't you go spreading lies, Doris Clavering. She's very upset. Crying fit to bust.'

'What about?' Dory asked.

'His lordship, of course,' said Ida.

Dory thought it was good that someone was weeping for his lordship. 'Why don't you just leave her alone?' she asked.

'Because *they*'ll be back any minute,' Ida said.

'There's the meal, you see,' Doris elucidated. 'They'll all expect to be eating and drinking and nothing's been done.'

A wave of chattering broke out as everyone gave their own version of the situation, but it ceased abruptly as James appeared, thrusting his way through them imperiously. 'What's all this? You sound like a yard full of hens!' When the situation was explained to him, he took Ida by her shoulder in a grip Dory could see must hurt. Ida was the senior kitchen-maid, and in a few sharp questions he had found out what needed to be done. Dory didn't like him, but could only admire. The food was all ready in the kitchen – a cold buffet, apart from the soup. He despatched Ida and Brigid to heat it up, and sent everyone else to carry things upstairs, delegating William to supervise down here while he took the third footman, Cyril, with him upstairs to see it was all laid out suitably on the buffet. 'And hurry it up!' he goaded them, as effectively as a touch of the whip. Finding Dory just behind him he grabbed her – yes, that grip did hurt! – and said, 'Go and find Mr Moss, tell him he should be here. *They*'ll be here any minute and they'll want something to drink. Come and tell me when you've found him – I'll need you for messages.'

'What about Mrs Oxlea?'

His lip curled. 'We don't need her. Leave her to stew. Look lively, girl!'

She found Mr Moss in the butler's room. He was sitting in a collapsed way in his armchair, with a glass of wine in his hand, which he was holding up in front of a candle flame. He didn't look surprised to see her when she came in. He seemed, she thought, slightly dazed – or slightly foxed. 'It was his favourite claret, the Talbot,' he said lugubriously, swirling the wine in the glass. 'Her ladyship didn't know. Wanted me to serve a Margaux. Said our guests wouldn't know any different. But *he*'d know. He wasn't fond of the Margaux. Said it was too soft. And it's his funeral – it should be his choice. I told her, "it's what he'd want, my lady," I said.'

'I'm sure you're right,' Dory said soothingly, 'and what a good thing he has you to look out for him. But they'll be back any minute, Mr Moss, and won't the bottles have to be opened and ready for them?'

'They're open and breathing,' he said. 'D'you think I don't know what's what?' He looked up at her blearily. 'Who are you?'

'The sewing-maid, Mr Moss. Dory. Only Mrs Oxlea's not well, and nothing was ready, and James said you ought to be out there. He's getting things taken up, but—'

Moss heaved himself to his feet, his face contracting with either alarm or annoyance, possibly both. He swayed, and then was steady. If he was drunk, Dory thought, he could handle it. 'It's not his job to order things, or send me messages. You go and tell him that! *I* shall take control, and *I* shall have everything ready and waiting when they arrive. The very idea! His lordship would turn in his grave if he thought I needed a footman to tell me my duty!'

43

He went on muttering, but he was on the move, and in the right direction, so she ran the other way and up the back stairs to find James. He was directing activities, like a conductor with a large orchestra, and the cold feast was taking shape on the long white-clothed table at the end of the great hall. He received her message impassively, hardly seeming to see her. 'Run down and find William, tell him to help Mr Moss bring up the bottles to the anteroom. And find Mrs Webster and tell her we'll need bowls for the soup, and napkins. She'll know which ones. Run!'

Dory ran, and found Mrs Webster in the china room loading housemaids' trays with bowls. She received James's message with a quick frown, but only said, 'The bowls are coming, as you see. And Rose is getting the napkins. He takes too much on himself,' she added, almost under her breath. She seemed to register Dory for the first time. 'Run to the nap-closet and help Rose.'

Dory obeyed, thinking that if James hadn't taken too much on himself, there might have been an unpleasantness. She didn't like him, but she liked him more when he was too busy to look at her in that undressing way, or make sly remarks.

Funeral baked meats. The words arrived unbidden in Giles's head, and he thought what an odd idea it was. Was it the Irish who laid out a feast on the chest of the corpse and summoned the sin-eater to consume the food and the departed's sins with it? He had eaten nothing all day, but the idea of food sickened him. A buffet had been laid out, of cold meats, rolls and cakes, such fruit as could be mustered in mid-winter, and wine and port to drink. Giles thought, after the cold graveside, many would have preferred hot tea. Then a wheeled trolley made its appearance, with a great tureen of steaming soup on it, and he tipped a mental hat to the cook, or whoever had thought of it.

Moss appeared at his elbow. 'Mr Moresby is here,
lord, in the library.'

'Moresby?'

'Of Moresby, Tuke and Moresby, my lord, solicitors.'

'Oh,' said Giles. 'The reading of the will.'

'Mr Moresby specifically requested to speak to you fi1
my lord, alone. As a matter of urgency.'

'Very well, I'll come.'

Moss made his stately way out (he seemed more state
than ever today, almost as if he wasn't sure of his footing
and Giles followed him, trying to do it unobtrusively. Th
two dogs got up and attached themselves to his shadow
and he heard their nails clicking on the marble floor. It was
a comforting noise, like a clock ticking in the background.

The footmen, James and William, presiding at the buffet
table, followed him with their eyes, and James slewed his
lips sideways at William and muttered, without moving them,
'That's trouble!'

Moresby was a handsome man in his forties, with black hair
going grey all over, like a badger, and a bushy moustache.
His eyes were blue and intelligent and his gaze was direct,
a little assessing. Giles liked the look of him, and offered his
hand, and Moresby shook it with an air of faint surprise, as
though he had not expected to be received so affably.

'Moresby, Tuke and Moresby,' Giles said. 'Which Moresby
are you?'

'The latter one, my lord. My father is nominally his late
lordship's man of business, but he has pretty much retired,
and his health lately is not of the soundest. But I assure
your lordship that I have a complete grasp of all aspects of
the estate and his late lordship's affairs.'

Giles took a seat and waved Moresby to another. 'Well,
you had better say what you came to say. I understood you
had come to read the will.' Moresby opened his mouth to

45

reply, and Giles added, 'I'd be obliged if you would speak to me like a fellow human being, and leave out as many *your lordships* and *his late lordships* as possible. I'm not made of glass and I shan't shatter from the shock of a plain pronoun.'

Moresby smiled carefully. 'You are most obliging, your – that is, I shall endeavour to follow your wishes.'

'You'd better,' Giles said, smiling in return, 'or I might go to Tuke. Now, what is this urgent business of yours?'

Moresby took a moment to assemble his words, and Giles did not like him less for that. He was a scientist, and liked accuracy. 'It is customary for the will to be read immediately after the funeral, and usually the whole family assembles to hear it. But I don't think that will be appropriate today. You see, about a year ago, my father went to see your father to tell him – no, to *remind* him, because it was a subject that had been discussed before – that the estate was in poor financial health.'

Giles sat forward. '*How* poor?'

Again Moresby hesitated, then said, 'To give it to you with the bark off, there is no money left. Only debts.'

Giles sat back, feeling it like a blow. He had not expected this. The money had not much interested him, given that he had had his own adequate provision, but he had always assumed it was there. 'Go on,' he said at last.

'My father urged your father to undertake some retrenchments, and your father agreed to do so, though without enthusiasm. My father, thinking to urge him on, said, "As things stand, if anything should happen to you, there would be no point in reading your will. There is no money to honour the bequests."'

'That's plain speaking,' said Giles, absently.

'I'm not sure my father used those exact words, my lord.'

'Well, go on. Were there retrenchments?'

'I'm afraid not. Nothing changed – except that a few

46

days later, your father summoned my father to write hi
a new will.'

'Ah,' said Giles, sensing they had come to it.

Moresby was looking at him with acute sympathy. 'The
new will is very simple. All previous provisions are taken
out. It simply states that he leaves everything to his eldest
son Giles. My father tried to discourage it, but he was quite
determined. He said as he signed it – I'm sorry, my lord –
"Let the boy sort it out. I haven't the time."'

Giles was silent for a moment, absorbing it. 'He just
turned his problems off onto me? And went on as before?'

'That's it, in essence,' said Moresby.

'And there's no money?'

'The income from the estate just barely pays for the
day-to-day running of the Castle. The entail ended with
your father – I don't know if you knew that?' Giles shook
his head. 'And there are no other legal restraints, other than
your mother's jointure, which will have to be found somehow.'

There was a silence. Giles rubbed his head absently, staring
at the two dogs, which were sitting at his knees and staring
up at him, waiting for instructions. 'What am I to do?' he
said at last. Moresby seemed to take it for a rhetorical question, so he looked up and said, 'What am I to do, Moresby?'

'Nothing, today, if you'll allow me to advise you. It's not
the time or place. I can attend you at any time of your
choosing to go over matters in detail, and help you to devise
a strategy. For today, I think you need only tell your company
that there is no need to read the will because it contains
only one clause, leaving everything to you.'

'They won't like that,' he said. 'They'll think . . .' Yes,
what would they think? There must be some among them
who had been expecting something, even if only a token
remembrance. Some might be hoping for much more. It
would be damned unpleasant – embarrassing. What in God's
name had his father been thinking? He had come home

dreading the responsibilities he would have to face. Now he had to face them with nothing but debts in his armoury. 'I'll have to tell them something.'

'If you'll forgive me, anything beyond the plain statement will only attract more questions. And it would be a bad idea to allow any hint of the true state of affairs to escape this room. Creditors tend to get nervous and call in their debts if they think there's any doubt they will be paid. You could face a storm of demands. Confidence is everything. Everyone must believe there is nothing wrong. I do urge your lordship—'

'I understand you. I must be cold and arrogant and simply refuse to discuss it.'

'It is not without precedent, my lord. An earl is a king in his own castle.'

But I'm not like that, Giles thought. *I shall have to act a part. It was all right for my father . . .*

And then he wondered suddenly whether his father's untouchable arrogance had been his nature after all, or whether he, too, had adopted an act.

A matter of survival.

He summoned the family to the library, and stood with his back to the fireplace until they had settled. They stared at him, murmuring among themselves.

His first words cut through into silence. 'There will be no reading of the will.' Now they were listening. 'A year ago, my father made a new will, which is very short, having only one clause. It says, in essence, "I leave everything to my eldest son Giles."'

Now there was a clamour. Every sentence seemed to begin with the words, 'But what about—?'

He held up his hand for silence. 'I need to study the previous will to discover what provisions were named in it. I must also take time to learn the condition of the estate and where the various assets are disposed. I suspect all this will take me some time.' His mother's eyes were boring into him. Did she know? Or suspect?

There was more murmuring. Linda took half a step forward and said determinedly, 'But, Giles, you *must*—'

He interrupted her. 'I *must* understand fully before I act. Anything else would be irresponsible. And that is all I have to say to you today.'

The clamour broke out again, everyone wanting him to answer *their* question. His little sisters, at the back of the throng and nearest the door, were watching him silently, passively, as though none of this had anything to do with them. But it did, of course, didn't it? They ought to have dowries. His father ought to have set money aside for them. It was not a legal requirement, like his mother's jointure, but it was a *moral* requirement. Another responsibility his father had shrugged off onto him.

Something else occurred to him. He lifted his hand again, and the talking stopped. 'There is one more thing. This matter must not be spoken about beyond these four walls. You must not discuss it with anyone not present in this room.'

An indignant protest arose. But his mother stopped it. 'Would you have our affairs bruited about the neighbourhood, the subject of common gossip and coarse speculation?' They looked at her uncomfortably. 'I will not have my late husband's actions picked over by ignorant outsiders. You *will* keep silent.' She turned and looked at Giles. 'And my son *will* resolve everything. In his own time.'

The slight emphasis on 'will' made it sound more like a threat than loyal support. Giles met her eyes steadily but could not read her: she had a lifetime's practice in being impenetrable. But it bothered him – he could not say why – that she had called him 'my son' and not Giles, or even Ayton, as she had several times since he'd come back. Yet what should she have said? 'The new earl'?

49

He turned quickly to leave, before there could be any more argument, so quickly that he tripped over one of the dogs – they had crept up close to him again. It yipped, the sound of a trodden paw, and he muttered irritably, 'Get out of the way, damn you!'

At the door, Alice looked at him with reproach. He met her eyes questioningly. She said, 'Don't be horrid to them. They don't understand, poor things.'

Two girls, two young women, trembling on the brink of adulthood, the future shape of their lives in his hands. He felt the fragile weight of them settle on his soul. Everyone wanted reassurance. Who was to comfort him?

Dory was helping carry things back down – everyone had to help on a major occasion like this. She was following Rose with a tray of crockery when, approaching the door to the senior servants' sitting-room, she heard Mrs Webster say, 'Something's going on. I can tell. There's an Atmosphere. Something was said when they all went into the library.'

Mr Moss's voice replied, 'Well, don't look at me.'

Rose slowed, listening, and Dory, behind her, kept very quiet.

'Why didn't you go in as well? Then we'd know,' Mrs Webster said.

'I wasn't required,' said Moss, with dignity.

'You opened the door for them. You should have stepped inside before you closed it.'

'I can't intrude myself into private meetings.'

'Oh, they'd never have noticed you. We're just furniture to them. You pull out a chair for them and they sit without even seeing who did it.'

Dory heard Rose snort at that.

'It could be something that affects us,' Mrs Webster went on. 'If there's trouble coming, I want to know.'

'*I* know,' said Rose, allowing herself to appear in the doorway. Dory hung back, out of sight.

'You shouldn't listen to our conversation,' said Mrs Webster, sharply.

'You shouldn't talk when I'm listening, then,' Rose retorted.

Moss drew in a sharp breath. 'Impertinence,' he said.

But Mrs Webster waved down the rebuke. 'Not now, Mr Moss. *How* do you know, Rose?'

'How d'you think?' Rose said.

'Lady Cordwell?'

At the Castle, Rose maided Lady Cordwell, who always said there was no point in bringing her own maid when there were Castle servants with nothing to do; but Rose suspected, as did Mrs Webster, that Lady Cordwell didn't have a maid. Couldn't afford one? Or too mean? It could be either.

'She always tells me everything in the end,' Rose said. 'She does love to talk.'

'Don't gossip about your betters,' Moss said sternly.

'Just observing a fact, Mr Moss. She sent for a glass of milk, and when I popped up to her, she told me all about it. But you wouldn't want to hear gossip, would you?'

Moss hesitated an agonising beat, but then said haughtily, 'Certainly not. Go along with you.'

Rose grinned and passed on. Dory scuttled after her, and behind her heard Mrs Webster say, 'I'll get it out of her later.'

And Moss said, 'Not on my account.' But he didn't sound sure.

Before they reached the scullery, they met Mr Crooks coming the other way with a pair of boots in his hand.

'Thumb mark on the heel,' he muttered. 'Not mine, of course.'

'Of course not, Mr Crooks,' Rose said ironically.

Crooks seemed to take this for an invitation to chat. He lowered his voice. 'I must say, there's a very odd atmosphere Upstairs. I have the feeling that something unusual was said

51

when everyone went out to hear the will read. You don't suppose there's anything wrong, do you? Oh dear, they can't have lost it, can they? I've always heard Mr Moresby very highly spoken of. Though I believe it was *young* Mr Moresby who came, and we don't know anything about him. But still, they're the best firm in Ashmore, everyone says so.'

'Something's going on,' Rose said, with an air of enjoying herself, 'but that's not it.'

'You know something?' Crooks asked hungrily.

'I'm saying nothing,' Rose replied. 'Come on, Dory. Lots more to do yet.' They went on, leaving Crooks looking more anxious than ever.

Each day Giles shut himself in the library with strict instructions that no-one was to disturb him unless sent for. He spoke to the agent, Markham; the bailiff, Adeane; the head gamekeeper, Saddler; the head man, Giddins. The banker, Vogel of Martin's Bank, came with accounts and ledgers and a furrowed brow. Giles interviewed Moss and Mrs Webster. But most of all, he spoke to Moresby.

He breakfasted alone and early, took no luncheon, and did not appear in the evening until dinner was actually announced. At the table he sat grimly silent, and excused himself as soon as the dessert was put on. At least it meant he could keep out of the way of his relatives.

One day, however, Linda waylaid him. Tired of hoping for an interview, she hovered near the library door and caught him on his way back from the closet, jumping out from an alcove in front of him.

'I've *got* to talk to you, Giles,' she said. She actually stretched out her arms to block his way.

'Not now, Linda. Let me by.'

She stared him down. His mother was a great starer, from beneath half-lowered eyelids, with a cool menace. Linda had inherited the power, but her stare was wide open, her eyes like twin gimlets boring straight into one's head, hot and painful.

'You must listen, Giles. You can't keep avoiding your responsibilities by locking yourself in the library.'

Giles winced. 'It's my responsibilities that keep me locked in the library . . . Oh, what's the use? What is it, Linda? What do you want?'

'My allowance, that's all,' she said. 'Papa paid me an allowance. I want to know if it was in his will.'

'I told you, there was nothing in the will except the one clause, leaving everything to me. Do you think I'm lying?'

'I suppose not—'

'You *suppose*?'

'Oh, don't change the subject,' Linda said impatiently. 'Just answer me: are you going to pay my allowance?'

'*Why* was he paying you an allowance? Surely it's for Cordwell to keep you.'

Her eyes shifted away for an instant. 'Times are hard. Especially in the West Country. You have no idea . . . God, I *hate* that place!' It burst out of her. 'Damp and cold and crumbling round my ears. Nothing for miles around but fields. Green, green, green everywhere you look!'

He felt an unwelcome pang of sympathy, though he knew she was longing for shops and pavements and theatres and bright lights, while he was pining for the desert. Still, it made him answer more kindly than he might otherwise have. 'Linda, I can't help you at the moment. I'm still learning about the estate, trying to sort out—' He almost said 'the muddle' but stopped himself in time. 'You'll have to wait, like everyone else. And now, let me by.' He grew impatient. 'The longer you keep me from the books, the longer you'll have to wait for an answer.'

She let him by, reluctantly. As he opened the library door she called after him, 'I'm your *sister*, Giles! Remember that. Your *sister*!'

He thought she'd been going to say 'your only sister' but remembered just in time the existence of the two quiet girls whom everyone seemed to forget so easily.

There was so much to learn. Books and books and books, talk and talk and talk. The room filling with cigarette smoke, ledgers, accounts, and earnest men trying to make him understand matters that were simple and obvious to them. And outside, the low grey skies and the endless weeping rain.

The dogs lay at his feet and sighed. He took them out for brisk walks very early in the morning and late at night. They were not comfortable walks: dark, and cold, and frequently wet. The dogs didn't care, and after the first day, Giles had too much on his mind to notice. Old Frewing, the hall porter, had a lamp ready for him and never so much as tutted when he brought in mud or kept the old man from his bed. Frewing had a fair idea of how things stood. 'Twas surprising what folks'd say right in front of you when you was hall porter, just as if you wasn't there. And he'd been at the Castle all his life, since starting as a water boy aged eight. He'd seen his late lordship grow up, seen him come into his inheritance too young . . . Oh, he knew a thing or two, did Frewing; but it wasn't his place to talk about it. He gave the young master a kindly nod when he passed, and silently wished him luck. He was too young as well. Wouldn't be in *his* shoes, Frewing always thought.

Giles returned the nod politely each time, but it was automatic politeness. He didn't really see the old man. His mind was firmly elsewhere. Between them, Markham and Adeane had got him to understand that the problem was twofold, general and specific. Generally, there was an agricultural slump, prices were down, depressed by a flood of cheap imported foods. Specifically, the estate hadn't been looked after as it should have been.

'The land is in poor heart,' Markham said. 'And it's not

efficiently farmed. It could bear more, if improvements were undertaken.'

'I put a scheme before his lordship four years since,' Adeane said, 'for marling and drainage, but nothing happened.'

'And there is a long backlog of repairs. Some of the cottages are in poor order. All of them need improving. Roads crumbling, ditches blocked. Overgrown hedges,' said Markham.

'There's a lot of modern ideas that ought to be brought in,' said Adeane. 'Better breeding stock, f'rinstance. Not just getting your cow in calf with any old animal that's got balls – begging your pardon, my lord. But start improving your livestock and you improve your yields.'

'But you can't expect the tenants to pay for prize bulls,' said Markham. 'The estate would have to put up the capital to start with, and the estate's got no money. Rents are too low.'

'Can't the rents be increased?' Giles asked.

The two men gave each other a brief look of exasperation. Hadn't he *understood*?

'Rents depend on production. Raise production, you can raise the rent. The tenants couldn't bear any increase now. You'd end up taking the leases back in hand, and be worse off.'

Giles frowned. 'You're saying you can't raise the rents without improving the properties first? You can't make more money without spending more?'

'That's it, in essence,' said Markham.

'But there's no money to invest,' Giles said.

So he went back to Moresby. 'Where has all the money gone?'

It was a problem with a long history, Moresby explained. An estate made money, yes, but a lot of it had to be ploughed back in. Also, repairs need to be done promptly, because dilapidation is a growing expense. Fix a tile now, or the whole roof later. 'Things have been let slide,' he concluded delicately. It wasn't for him to point a finger.

'But there must have *been* income. I ask again – where did it all go?'

Maintaining the house and the family was an expensive business, Moresby told him. And, he added reluctantly, the previous earl had been extravagant.

'My *father*?' Giles said in surprise. He had always assumed, as far as he had ever thought about it, that his father spent his time hunting, shooting and fishing – particularly the former. In the hunting season he went out three or four times a week, and Giles had hunted often enough to know that after a day following hounds one had no energy for anything but dozing by the fire in stockinged feet.

Now he learned that his father had had another life, a Town life. There were his club subscriptions and expenses – several clubs, gambling clubs among them. His father had paid up all right, pay and play was his creed, but those clubs would not survive if the members were not losers overall. There were tradesmen's bills – tailors, hatters, bootmakers: his father had dressed surprisingly expensively. Giles had not taken him for a dandy.

There were several London properties, not bringing in income, but on which rent was being paid out, plus a house in Bloomsbury and a flat in St John's Wood on which the estate paid the leases. 'What for?' Giles asked, and Moresby said he didn't know, implying it was not his business to ask.

And his father had been a large spender of cash. Giles wondered how he could have got through so much. The usual things – theatres, restaurants, taxis, cigars – could hardly account for it. Vogel was careful to make no comment when he allowed Giles to glimpse, among the other bills, accounts for women's clothing and jewellery. Had there been, Giles asked himself, with a cold sense of shock, *women*? It is always difficult to see one's own parents as sexual beings, but – and here Giles glanced at the portrait in the alcove beside the fire – his father had been a very good-looking man in his youth. Perhaps – and a man of twenty-six might well find this a struggle to accept – a man of fifty-two could still be attractive to women. But surely one should not give in to temptation.

It was pointless speculation. The question now was, what must he do? What *could* he do?

'Retrenchment, my lord,' said Moresby. 'My father urged it on your father, and had it been undertaken ten years ago, you might have inherited a very different estate. The longer it's put off the harder it becomes. I don't conceal from you that it will be a long and painful road. But the alternative would be bankruptcy.'

'Couldn't we sell something?' Giles asked.

'I'm afraid the valuable paintings have already been sold,' said Moresby. 'And the antique silver.'

'Isn't there some family jewellery?'

'I don't know how much it would fetch, but we could look into it if . . .'

'If?'

'Her ladyship – your mother – as the person most closely affected—'

'She'd be more affected if we're forced into bankruptcy,' Giles said.

'Very well, my lord. But I doubt the jewellery could do more than tide us over.'

'That's something, at any rate. What about selling some of the land?'

'Mortgaged.'

Giles stared at nothing for a moment, gathering himself. 'Retrenchment, then,' he said. His father's London life, he determined grimly, should be dismantled. 'Cancel all memberships and subscriptions. Get rid of the rented properties. Sell the leases – I suppose they'll bring in something?'

'Yes, my lord. But do you wish me to look into—'

'I *wish* you to cut out London entirely,' Giles interrupted angrily. 'Enough has been wasted there. I won't waste any more. It's Ashmore that matters. Whatever he was spending in Town, it stops at once. If anyone from the Castle wants to go to London they can stay with my aunt or my grandmother.'

'Very well, my lord.'

'And retrenchment at home. I'm sure there must be a lot of waste.'

'I would advise against wholesale reductions – it would spread unwelcome gossip, and as I said before, confidence is everything. Luckily, if I might put it like that, your bereavement means you will not be entertaining for some months, which allows you to exercise a certain austerity without attracting notice.

'Indeed,' said Giles, drily.

'And the stables are a large expense. You might usefully cut down there.'

Moresby enumerated: his late lordship kept six hunters, with two youngsters being brought on. Aside from them there were her ladyship's and the young ladies' horses, six carriage horses, two road horses, four grooms' horses, and two ponies – in all, twenty-five head eating their heads off. To care for them there were seven grooms and four boys, in addition to Giddins, Archer and Josh Brandom, and two coachmen.

'I can sell the hunters,' Giles said. 'Even if I were to be hunting this season – which obviously I'm not – they wouldn't suit me.'

'Then you should sell them now, my lord, with some of the season still to go. You'd get a better price.'

'I'll see it done. What else?' Moresby was shuffling papers, evidence of embarrassment, or a reluctance to go on. 'Out with it, man. I think I'm past shocking now.'

Moresby looked up. 'Nothing shocking, I assure you, my lord. Perhaps – delicate.'

'Oh, Lord, what now?'

'Your mother's jointure,' Moresby said. 'If it is asked for, it must be paid, and the only way I can see for such a sum to be procured is through a loan. Reluctant as I am to suggest taking on more interest payments—'

'*If* it is asked for?' Giles queried.

'The jointure, as you know, is for the maintenance and comfort of the relict. But if her ladyship remained at the Castle with all her present comforts, she would not immediately need it. The issue might be passed over for a few valuable months, or even years.'

Giles was faintly amused, though in a sour way. 'You mean, if I send her to the Dower House, I'll have to pay up, but if I let her stay here, she might forget about it?'

Moresby winced at the plain speaking. 'In essence—'

'Does she know?' Giles interrupted.

'Know, my lord?'

'How things are.'

'I really cannot say, my lord. It is entirely up to you how much you reveal to her, but if she *doesn't* know . . . The fewer people who know, the better.'

But if his mother wanted her jointure, he would have to borrow, and put the estate deeper into debt. And what about his sisters? There had never been any money set aside for their dowries – presumably his father had thought he would cross that bridge when he came to it – but they were Giles's responsibility now. He would have to do something.

'I feel like a rabbit in a snare,' he said. 'It's a miserable mess, and there seems no way out but years of austerity or more reckless borrowing – or both.'

Moresby paused for a moment before saying hesitantly, 'There is one other way out, my lord. It may not be a solution that appeals to you, but it has a long – and, may I say, respectable – precedent.'

'Tell me,' said Giles.

CHAPTER FOUR

At Miss Thornton's School for Young Ladies in Kensington, Kitty Bayfield sat in the far window-seat of the drawing-room, her knees drawn up and her arms locked round them. It was the last day of term, and girls had been trotting in and out in ones and twos and groups, but they did not notice her there in the shadow of the curtain.

The house was alive with running footsteps, and down below in the street, under a soft damp sky, the grey of pavement and road had almost disappeared in an excitement of movement and colour. Carriages and hackney cabs were coming and going, trunks and valises cluttered the pavement, footmen were carrying out bags and parcels, servants and mamas and the occasional papa were collecting their daughters, extracting them from a confusion of hugs and kisses and flying curls, forgotten items, lost gloves and a good many tears. It was the last day of term.

The room was light and modern with big windows and comfortable, chintz-covered furniture. So different from home, Kitty thought. Bayfield Court in Hampstead was Tudor, with small leaded casements and a warren of dark rooms that always smelt faintly of mould. There was dark oak panelling and polished wood floors, and the furniture was Jacobean and punitive – hard upright chairs and settles with tapestry covers. It always made her think of a church: cold, musty, and a temple of rectitude.

It was lonely, above all. She had been lonely all her life. Her father, Sir John, was a baronet, a well-bred man with impeccable manners. His one passion was genealogy: he spent hours every day studying in his private room and had published several well-received monographs on the bloodlines of the great houses of England. Her earliest memories of him were of being taken to his room to say goodnight, feeling awed and apprehensive. Sir John was not an unkind man, but he had been brought up in a strict and formal age and did not unbend easily. To Kitty, he was an impressive but forbidding figure: Papa must not be disturbed, Papa demanded this, Papa would not like that, Papa forbade the other.

Kitty's mother, Catherine Harvey, a jam heiress from Cambridgeshire, had brought a considerable fortune to the marriage. (Kitty felt a little thrill of connection every time she saw a pot of Harvey's Jam. Sadly, Miss Thornton's school favoured Chivers'.) She had died of complications a few days after Kitty's birth. Kitty was named for her, but knew her only from her portrait over the drawing-room fireplace, by Sargent, in a white satin evening gown with a pale pink chiffon stole. She had a sweet but rather tense expression, and her heavy eyelids made her look as though she'd been about to cry. Kitty had studied it often, trying to find something in the face that spoke to her. The first Lady Bayfield had had a heart-shaped face and pointed chin, as did Kitty, and the same smooth, arched eyebrows, but her hair was light golden brown and wavy where Kitty's was black and curly, and her eyes were hazel where Kitty's were blue.

Nanny had told her that her mother had gone to a better place. 'She's in Paradise and better off out of it, if you ask me,' Nanny had said sourly. She was a stout but hard woman, bosoms and stomach rock-like inside uncompromising corsetry. She was hard of face, hard of hand and, most of all, hard of mind. She read the Bible a great deal,

61

but the God she spoke of to Kitty was also hard: watchful and critical. She seemed to view life as a difficult and unpleasant task to be completed before the big Bedtime of death. Then it would be Paradise – or the Other Place, depending on how you'd done.

'Will I go to Paradise like Mama when I die?' Kitty had asked.

'If you're good,' Nanny had answered.

To be good mainly seemed to require Kitty to be quiet, to sit still, and not to dirty her clothes; but there was always an unspoken sense that some other kind of goodness was required, the secret of which was not divulged. Kitty feared she must always fall short, because she did not know how to do better.

When Kitty was six, Sir John married again. Nanny disapproved. She explained loftily to Kitty that girls couldn't inherit titles, so her father needed a son to be baronet after him. Kitty gathered from the tone that Nanny felt this was merely an excuse for some more frivolous purpose. 'Half his age,' she sniffed one evening over her mending. 'Some flighty piece of fancy-work, leading him by the nose.'

'I've seen her. She's pretty,' said the housemaid, who had just come in with a pile of linen.

'Handsome is as handsome does,' Nanny said sourly. 'We shall have all sorts of shenanigans, you mark my words.'

Kitty, on the other side of the room with a book and not supposed to be listening, liked the idea that she would have a new mother who was young and pretty. And shenanigans was what Nanny called things she didn't approve of, like singing, dancing and laughing. When the barrel-organ man stopped in the street outside their house she would complain about his 'blamey shenanigans' and ring for the footman to send him away. Kitty thought some shenanigans around the house would be rather nice. And perhaps a stepmother would love her, as her own mother had never had a chance to do.

Jayne D'Arcy duly made her appearance, and at first sight she seemed more likely to please Nanny than Kitty: a tall, thin lady, elegant and smart, but with a pointed nose and thin mouth, and a sharp voice that demanded obedience. Her brisk footsteps, rattling on the bare boards, could be heard approaching from a distance – a useful warning. She took the house in hand, shook it up and remade it to her own requirements, new furniture, new hangings, new routines, a new cook, more footmen. A great deal more cleaning went on than under the previous, mistress-less regime, and a smell of lavender wax partly obscured the odour of mould. Kitty heard her declare, when the changes were in place, that Bayfield Court was now an establishment worthy of a baronet and his lady. They became very social, entertaining or dining out most days of the week, going to plays and concerts in London, going away for Saturday-to-Mondays.

The new Lady Bayfield never came up to the nursery – which pleased Nanny, who did not like 'interference' – but Kitty was summoned into the presence every evening to be inspected. The inspections were brief, and Kitty sadly learned that there would be no more smiles and embraces from this mother than from the previous one. Kitty was instructed to call her 'Mama', and was quite willing to do so, but she seemed more like Nanny's watchful and critical God, always on the look-out for anything about Kitty that might 'disappoint your father'.

But she did do one thing for her stepdaughter: when Kitty was seven, there was a period of prolonged, suppressed excitement in the house, with everyone exchanging knowing looks. When Kitty asked what was happening she was told, 'Nothing that concerns little girls.' This turned out to be untrue, because one morning Nanny woke her early and dressed her in grim silence, then told her to come and meet her new brother.

Peter, Sir John named him, after his own father. Kitty

was just the right age to believe that Peter was a present meant especially for her. She adored him from the moment she first hung over his crib, enchanted by his little face and tiny fingers. She had always been fond of her dolls – a child has to love *something* – but now she had a living, breathing one.

Lady Bayfield handed him over to the nursery staff, and took herself off to resume her social life, satisfied to have him brought to her once a day, clean and beautifully dressed. Kitty heard her say once that babies were ugly things, and that he would be more interesting when he was older. It surprised her: from the beginning he was a pretty baby, never red and crumpled, but smooth and luminous as a pearl.

Her father talked a great deal about Peter's future: what school he would go to (Eton), what club his father would nominate him for (White's), what tailor he would patronise (Poole's). There was talk of cricket, rowing, a grand tour. Papa sounded very happy when he spoke of these things, and his voice was warmer than Kitty had ever heard it. But he also never went near the nursery. When once she mentioned it tentatively to Nanny, Nanny replied that men were not given to noticing their sons until they went into trousers.

So she continued to believe that Peter was *her* baby. It was she who steadied his first steps, marvelled at his first words, taught him to handle spoon and pusher, told him the names of things, taught him games. In return, he adored her. His face lit at the sight of her. He watched the door for her if she went out of the room. And as soon as he could get up on his hind legs he staggered after her everywhere, crying, 'Kitty-Kitty-Kitty!' And when he was tucked into bed, it was she who read him a story until he fell asleep, his hand wrapped around one of her fingers.

When he was four, and Kitty was eleven, he caught diphtheria and died.

It seemed to Kitty, in retrospect, that nothing at all happened after that for a long time. The routines of the house continued drearily from day to day but there seemed no point to them. After a time, Sir John and Lady Bayfield took up their social life again. Her father had grown older and graver, Mama seemed to have grown smarter, more glamorous, more glittering, but there was no change in their attitude to Kitty. Or to her empty, do-nothing life. Except that she was lonelier than ever. After the wonder of Peter, her dolls no longer had the power to charm. She longed for someone to love – anyone at all. Once in the garden she tried to befriend a stray cat, but it crouched suspiciously, and scratched her when she tried to stroke it.

Then one day Lady Bayfield summoned her to the morning-room. 'Has it occurred to you, Catherine, that your father has plans for you?'

'No, Mama,' Kitty said, startled. She didn't think her father ever thought about her at all.

'You are fourteen years old. The day will soon come when you will be launched into society.'

'Yes, Mama,' Kitty said doubtfully. She wasn't really sure what that meant.

'And when that time comes, you must *shine*, Catherine. *Shine!* You must lead society, and you must make a good – no, an *excellent* marriage. You must never forget you are Sir John Bayfield's daughter, and whatever you do will reflect on him. And on *me*. We want to be proud of you. We *will* be proud of you.'

It was not a sentence to which 'Thank you' was an appropriate response. Mama had not said 'we shall' but 'we *will*' – an expression of determination. Kitty must not disappoint, though, from the way Mama was inspecting her, it seemed all too likely that she would. She said nothing, waiting.

'You are pretty-ish,' Lady Bayfield said at last, 'and I have the taste and knowledge to make the best of you. I shall make sure you are introduced to the right people. But you lack polish.'

Kitty bit her lip and looked at the floor.

Lady Bayfield drew an exasperated breath. 'Hold your head up, Catherine, and do not dare to cry. You must cultivate a clear, steady look when people speak to you, and a light, confident walk, not this head-hanging, shuffling mien.'

Kitty wanted to say, 'I'm sorry,' but knew if she opened her lips to speak she would start crying.

'And there is your ridiculous shyness,' Lady Bayfield went on. 'You cannot show to advantage when you are too scared to open your mouth. Perhaps,' she allowed grudgingly, 'you have been left too much alone. You see too little of anyone outside this house. So I have decided – *Sir John* and I have decided – to send you to school. What do you think of that?'

Kitty had felt an instant fear of the unknown, of being pitched into a strange environment with new opportunities to fail. But immediately afterwards she felt a surge of hope. To go to school, with other girls – away from this gloomy house – a new place, new activities . . . Perhaps she might make a friend. Someone to love, who would love her. At all events, it would be a change from the aching boredom and isolation of her life. She could hardly be *more* lonely than here.

'I'd like it, Mama,' she said, and ventured an upward glance and a shy smile which quite surprised her stepmother, but seemed to please her.

And she did like it. She had loved her three years here. And she *had* made a friend.

There was an awkward stage in the life of a girl when she was no longer really a child but was too young to be married. Good governesses were notoriously hard to find, and few mamas had the time or inclination to have their daughters with them all day. In response to the problem, schools for young ladies, where they could be kept out of harm's way for a few years and given a little polish, sprang up in all the major capitals. Miss Thornton's was considered to be one of the best. Girls were taught the usual things – how to walk and sit, manage a train, get in and out of a carriage; how to dance, play cards, pour and hand round tea; the correct way to lay a table, the proper precedence of guests and the right way to address anyone from a monarch to a rural dean. Miss Thornton's 'special pupils' had a little more: they were schooled in current affairs, fine art, music and classical literature; they had a few words of French and Italian; those with the aptitude played musical instruments, sketched or painted. They were conversable. Everyone agreed that Miss Thornton's chosen girls, whom she taught herself, had an extra polish; but you couldn't *make* her take on your girl. She chose them herself – and it wasn't a matter of money, because she had even been known to lower her fees if she took a fancy to someone.

Nina came into the room and roused Kitty from her thoughts. 'Oh, there you are! I was looking for you in our room.' She came across to the window. 'I wish it would snow. This weather's so dreary.' She leaned over to peer down into the street. 'There's Nancy Brevoorte leaving. Goodness, what a lot of luggage she has! And that must be her papa. He's wearing a fur coat, all the way down to the ground! Doesn't it look queer?'

'It must be an American fashion,' Kitty said. 'It looks warm, though.'

'Yes, and I don't see why men shouldn't wear furs as well as women,' Nina said. 'I expect they do in Russia.'

There was a sharp explosive sound, making the horses at the kerb throw up their heads, then a rattling, rumbling noise that had them wanting to bolt.

67

'What on earth—?' Nina said. 'Goodness! It's a motor-car! Do look, Kitty!'

Kitty got up on her knees, craning to stare along the road 'It must be Mr Brevoorte's. It's a Packard. I heard her telling Cora Van Dycke about it – she's going to spend Christmas with the Brevoortes because her family's in New York.'

The motor-car was painted a dull red, with yellow wheels and red leather upholstery, deeply buttoned. It was open, but with a canopy fixed across four uprights to cover the seating area. There were two seats in front, the one behind the steering-wheel occupied by a liveried chauffeur, and two in the back.

'There absolutely won't be room for all Nancy's luggage,' Nina said, 'leave alone Cora's.'

But when Mr Brevoorte had handed the girls into the back and taken the front seat, and the motor-car had roared away, a horse-drawn brake pulled up and the luggage was loaded into that. 'All is explained,' Nina said. 'I can't help thinking a motor-car's not very practical if you have to have a separate vehicle for your luggage. You can get just about everything into a growler.'

'But they were very excited about riding in it,' said Kitty. 'I've never seen one close up. Mama says they're vulgar.'

'They're certainly noisy,' Nina said. 'I should like to try one, though. Cora's lucky. But American girls always stick together.'

'I expect it's lonely, being so far from your own land,' Kitty said. 'And their brothers went to school together, I heard them say. So they're bound to be friends.'

Nina left off staring out of the window and sat down beside Kitty. 'I can't believe it's all over,' she said. 'After today, we'll never be girls at school again.' It wasn't just the end of term, but the end of their stay at Thornton's. Kitty had just turned seventeen and Nina would be seventeen in January. They were young ladies now. Nina observed her friend's expression. 'Oh, Kitty, don't look so blue! It isn't a tragedy, you know – it's the beginning of real life.'

'I don't want real life,' Kitty said. 'I wish we could stay here for ever.'

'But you've got everything to look forward to,' Nina said, encouraging her as she had done for the last three years.

On the first day, when all the new girls had been standing around in the drawing-room waiting to be told what to do, she had drifted over to Kitty, attracted by something about her – perhaps by the contrast with herself. Kitty was little and delicate-looking, and though not strictly pretty she gave the impression of it. With her pointed chin, large eyes, and a cloud of dark curls, people were always put in mind of a kitten, and since most people liked kittens, they were prepared to think she was pretty without actually analysing her features.

And she was so terribly, desperately shy, it gave her almost physical pain to be obliged to talk to someone she didn't know – even to be looked at upset her. Nina couldn't understand it, but she had felt immediate pity, and had instituted herself Kitty's champion. The two girls had been close ever since, sharing a bedroom and doing everything together.

Nina's background was very different from Kitty's. She did not come from a titled or rich family, not even from the *ton*. Her father had been an army officer, her mother the daughter of a country rector of moderate means. Both were well educated and shared a love of reading and conversation. Nina's mother's name had been Antonia, and it was she who had suggested, almost as a joke, that her baby girl should be named Antonina, on the Roman diminutive principle. Her father had laughingly agreed.

It was a love-match between them, so when Captain Sanderton went abroad, Antonia went with him. Nina was born in India, where she spent the first years of her life. It was a happy marriage, between two well-matched people, and Nina's had been a happy childhood, full of love, laughter, conversation, encouragement and activity – everything Kitty had lacked. Only in being without siblings were they similar. The Sandertons would have loved more children, but it hadn't happened.

When Nina was nine, this happy scene was ruptured. The climate did not agree with her mother, and Antonia's health was suffering so much that the now Major Sanderton decreed she should go back to England, taking her child with her.

'It was awful leaving Papa behind,' Nina had told Kitty. 'And my dear pony. And the servants. But it was even more terrible for Mama. They'd never been parted before. She cried and cried on the boat going home. She tried not to let me see, but I couldn't help knowing it.'

They went to live with Major Sanderton's older sister, who had married an academic, but was now widowed, and had room in her tall, narrow red house in Draycott Place for the wife and child of a brother of whom, in her understated way, she was very fond.

Antonia's health improved a little, but she was missing her husband dreadfully. Nina fared better, missing him too, and missing India, which was all she knew, but she had an enquiring mind and boundless energy and quickly found things to please her. And she soon learned to use her aunt as a source of both information and diversion.

Aunt Schofield had no children and had never wanted them. As well educated as her brother – unusually so for her time – she had married into academia and relished the life of the mind and the intellectual opportunities furnished by her sympathetic husband. He had been considerably older than her, and from the beginning they had both realised she was likely to be long a widow. She had a pension and the leasehold of the house, and with a circle of bluestocking friends, she had not anticipated any difficulty in

70

occupying those years. She had never minded solitude – indeed, rather preferred it – but she did not shrink from her duty to her brother and his family. And the large brown eyes of her little niece, turned up to her in the flattering assumption that 'Aunt' knew the answer to every question, were endearing.

After the initial rally, Antonia's health declined again, and only a year after her return to England she died. While Kitty had lost her mother before ever knowing her, Nina had lost warmth and love and intimacy, the sort of mothering Kitty had always craved.

'Aunt Schofield wrote to Papa that she would take care of me for as long as necessary,' Nina had told Kitty. 'I don't suppose she imagined it would be for ever.'

The major got leave at last, and started the long journey home. But he contracted a fever in the Suez Canal, and died before the ship reached Marseille. When Nina had told her this part of the story, Kitty had been silent, unable to express how awful she thought it must have been for Nina to become an orphan.

From what Nina had gathered about Kitty's family, she felt her friend had always been an orphan, despite having two parents. *She* at least had *known* love, and still did, though Aunt Schofield's was not expressed in caresses. She was brisk and practical with a sharp intellect, and she showed her love by tending Nina's mind, like a prize garden. She undertook Nina's education, gave her books that never normally came a girl's way, and involved her various academic friends in the scheme: Nina had teaching from some of the best in each discipline. Some of her aunt's character rubbed off on her: she was practical, sensible, not given to complaining or brooding. The loss of her dear parents left a dark place inside her, but she shut the door on it and always looked resolutely forward.

She was surprised when her aunt interrupted a lesson

one day to say, typically without preamble, 'I am going to send you to school, Nina.'

Nina frowned. 'But why? They just polish girls up to get married. I'm going to be a teacher.'

Mrs Schofield was unmoved. 'Nevertheless, you shall go. You spend too much time with old people.' She raised a hand to stop Nina protesting. 'You need to make friends of your own age. But I have chosen a school where I believe you will have many opportunities to extend your education.'

Nina was doubtful, but she was always willing to try a new experience, and supposed it might be fun. 'Will I be boarding?' she asked.

'That is an important part of the experience. But you will come home for holidays, of course.'

Nina thought, *It will only be for a few weeks at a time. I'm sure I can put up with that.* And, as it happened, she had met Kitty on the first day and taken her under her wing. So she had a friend and a project – bringing Kitty out of her shell – and since her aunt's dictum was 'Never miss the opportunity to learn something new', she threw herself into school life and found she enjoyed it. She was sorry it was over.

Kitty asked now, with trepidation, 'What do you suppose is going to happen to us?'

Nina said, 'I know exactly what will happen to you. You'll have a splendid come-out, you'll be the belle of the Season, you'll fall in love and marry your handsome prince.'

Kitty didn't speak. She longed for love and marriage, though the idea scared her too.

'Miss Thornton says we're lucky to be finishing now instead of December last year,' Nina went on, 'because court mourning cast a shadow over the Season. But next year's Season will be brilliant.'

The old Queen, Victoria, had died in January. Everyone had been very sad – it was like your own grandmother dying

– and though court mourning had been over at the end of April, the mood had continued to be dampened for some time. It was not helped by the continuing bad news about the war. When the main towns in South Africa had been captured in 1900, everyone had thought the war was as good as finished, but it was still dragging painfully on with no end in sight. The newspapers complained bitterly that a quarter of a million disciplined British soldiers seemed unable to conquer just twenty thousand unruly Boers.

But despite the war, everyone was looking forward to a new era beginning with the new year. People said things would be much livelier, because King Teddy would be a very different kind of monarch from old Queen Vicky. Rules would be relaxed. He liked to eat and drink; he encouraged conversation at dinner; he attended the races and the theatre; he dined at subjects' houses. He even included commoners among his closest friends.

Nina didn't quite understand how the tastes of someone as remote as the King or Queen could affect lowly people like them, but Miss Thornton said the country always took on the character of its monarch.

At any rate, it would affect Kitty, whose father was a baronet and, she gathered, very wealthy, and would bring her out in the first style.

But Kitty sighed. 'I dread coming out. I'm not like you. I hate people looking at me. And having to talk to *men*!'

Nina was amused. 'You won't need to. All you'll have to do is smile. The men will do all the talking. Miss Thornton says one can be either pretty or charming – one needn't be both.'

'*You*'re both. You're much prettier than me.'

Nina knew that she was blessed with good looks. Her features were classically handsome – a straight nose and firm chin – and her brown eyes made an unusual contrast with thick fair hair the colour of harvest wheat. But she had no vanity about it. Her aunt valued only the things of the mind, and it had rubbed off on Nina. And from her school days, she had learned that though prettiness *did* matter for females, when it came to marriage other things mattered more: money, and family.

'You know I won't have a proper come-out like you,' she said lightly. 'We're not high society. And I've no fortune.'

'But won't you have *any* dancing, or parties, or anything?'

'Aunt Schofield might take me to a public ball or two, but the people she knows don't have daughters to bring out, and that's how one gets invitations.'

'I'll ask Mama to ask you to mine.'

'Thank you, darling, but I don't suppose she'd want me there. Don't worry about me – I don't need to come out. I'm going to be a teacher.'

'You always say that, but will you be happy?'

'Look at Miss Thornton. Doesn't she seem happy?'

Kitty still doubted. She herself wanted love, a husband, and babies – particularly babies – to fill the empty place inside her, and as she couldn't imagine a contented life without those things, she wanted Nina to have them too.

'We will always be friends, won't we?' she asked, in a small voice.

'Always,' Nina said.

Lady Bayfield had not intended to fetch Kitty from school herself, but she had received a carefully worded letter from Miss Thornton, saying that when she did, Miss Thornton would welcome the opportunity of a brief word with her about Kitty's immediate future.

Lady Bayfield was inclined to dismiss the request as impertinence, but she remembered that Miss Thornton's was considered the best school in London and that her fees were extremely high, so perhaps she had something worth hearing. She sent a scribbled note, and on the day arrived in her carriage and a severe mood, ready to be offended if necessary.

In the comfortable private sitting-room – only too well furnished with books to be truly elegant – Miss Thornton offered refreshments, and when they were declined began. 'We have been privileged to have Miss Bayfield as a pupil here and I have grown extremely fond of her. I assume that you will be bringing her out when the new Season starts?'

Lady Bayfield assented.

'She is a most accomplished and, may I say, beautiful girl, but . . .' a quick frown tugged Lady Bayfield's brows at the word, and Miss Thornton hurried on '. . . she is shy and retiring, especially in the company of strangers.'

'Are you saying she won't "take"?' Lady Bayfield interrupted, with blunt readiness to be affronted.

'I am saying that a lavish debut and a full Season can be a considerable strain on a girl of such delicate sensibilities. I would like to think that everything possible would be done to make her debut enjoyable for her, as well as successful.'

'Kindly get to the point,' Lady Bayfield said frostily. She couldn't see where this was going, but she was suspicious.

Miss Thornton obliged. 'Miss Bayfield has a very particular friend in the school, a Miss Sanderton, and I have noticed that she's always more confident in her company. It can be a great comfort to a shy girl to have the companionship of a friend during her Season.'

Lady Bayfield's mind was working quickly. It was not infrequently done, two girls, friends, being brought out together. Miss Thornton would hardly have mentioned Kitty's shyness if she hadn't thought it might be a problem: awkwardness in company could certainly damage her chances. On the other hand, the last thing she wanted was for Kitty to be outshone by some other girl. If there was to be any arrangement of this sort, the other girl must be second to Kitty in every way and that must be clearly understood by the girl's parents.

Loftily, as though not much interested, she asked, 'Who is this Miss—?'

'Sanderton. She's a nice, well-behaved girl, well-spoken and refined, from a most respectable family. Unfortunately, her lack of dowry will prevent her making as brilliant a marriage as we all expect for Miss Bayfield. But they are very fond of each other, and I feel she would prove most useful in bringing out Miss Bayfield's fine qualities and helping her to shine as she should.'

Lady Bayfield considered. This Miss Sanderton sounded rather middle-class. She didn't want some indigent hanger-on lowering the tone of Kitty's debut. On the other hand, if she brought out the best in Kitty, as Miss Thornton suggested . . . and provided she *was* well-behaved and could take instructions . . . The image of Kitty cowering tongue-tied at her own come-out was one to make Lady Bayfield shudder.

'What is her family?' she asked abruptly.

'Her father was an army officer, of a good Northamptonshire family. Her mother was a country rector's daughter. Both are dead, and she is being brought up by her paternal aunt, a widowed lady who has a private income and no children of her own.'

Lady Bayfield liked the sound of the last part. If there was Sanderton money for the girl to inherit, that would make her more acceptable. There must be no whiff of poverty, however genteel. 'Very well,' she said. 'I will consider what you have said, and if Sir John and I decide it would be in Miss Bayfield's interest, I will ask the girl's aunt to come and see me.'

Miss Thornton inclined her head gracefully, and rang to have Lady Bayfield shown out. She had done what she could for Kitty – and for Nina.

Nina had come to her school as one of her special pupils, at a reduced fee, for though there was clearly intellect in the family, there was no money. But even at the initial interview, she had so loved Nina's mind, she would have taken her for no fee at all. Kitty was no more than average, but she had a great capacity for trying hard when affection was involved, and seeing how attached she was from the beginning to Nina, she had taken her in hand too – though at the full fee. Lady Bayfield was the sort who believed the more she paid for something, the more it was worth.

So the girls had been taught together, by her. She was fond of them both, and felt each in her way had the possibility of success within her grasp. Together, they ought to do better than apart. She hoped Lady Bayfield had taken the bait; and she hoped – for she had met her – that the intelligent and independent Mrs Schofield would see past Lady Bayfield's arrogant manner and fashionable appearance and consider her niece's best interests.

CHAPTER FIVE

Dory was settling into her new home. The sewing-room was on the first floor, next to the linen-room, in a good position to see everyone who went to fetch clean sheets or towels, or went past to the back stairs. People who popped in with small sewing jobs – a button off here, an apron string coming loose there – usually stayed to chat. And she was sent here and there about the house to do running repairs, so she was always in the way to hear the latest gossip.

She was learning about her new family: that Mr Moss's great passion was his stamp collection, over which he brooded with magnifying-glass and tweezers whenever he had the chance. That James was sharp and pushing and ambitious to get on. Mrs Webster was an enigma. She hadn't been long at the house and no-one quite knew what made her tick, but they said she saw everything – it was no use trying to put one over on her. You did not speak to Miss Taylor until spoken to. Mrs Oxlea the cook had a melancholy secret, and was given to bouts of weeping and, more inconveniently, occasions when she got too drunk to do her work. Rose, the head housemaid, was a care-for-nobody but so good at her work she got away with it. Daisy, who attended the young ladies, loved to gossip, though most of her stories had no basis in fact.

Two topics dominated the conversation: what changes would come about as a result of the old lord's death, and what Christmas would be like this year. They already knew there would be no entertaining, and the traditional servants' ball was cancelled.

'Mean, I call it,' said Ellen, the pretty housemaid. 'We don't get much fun as it is.'

'I heard they're going to have one at the Grange instead,' said Daisy.

'Rubbish,' said Rose. 'You've got to stop making things up, Daisy. Your tongue'll turn black and drop out.'

'*I* didn't make it up,' Daisy said, with a flounce. 'Someone told me.'

'Someone!' Rose scoffed. 'That post boy, I suppose. He'd say anything to get inside your bodice.'

'Ooh, Rose, don't say such awful things!' Mabel, the fat, plain housemaid exclaimed.

'What's the servants' ball?' Dory asked.

'Didn't they have one where you worked last?' Mabel asked. 'It's a Christmas thing. All the servants and the families from the local big houses come, and the gentry have to dance with us. Rose danced with his lordship last year, didn't you, Rose?'

She gave an enigmatical grimace. 'Much good it ever did me. Anyway, there's not going to be anything this year. No visitors – not even any presents, far as I can tell.'

'I s'pose it's mourning,' Daisy said, 'but I think it's rotten.'

'Mean, I call it,' said Ellen.

'You'll have to find some other way of running after that footman from Ashmore Court,' Rose said. Ellen couldn't think of a sharp response, and stuck out her tongue instead.

Dory was pondering all this later over her work when William, the second footman, came to her door, fidgeted until she looked up, and said, 'I've – er – I've got a button off. Can you – um . . . ?'

'Give it here,' she said kindly. She almost had a soft spot for William: after James, who was frankly sinister, and Cyril, third footman, who was sly and cocky and modelled himself on James, his hero, William was a relief. He had no ambition, he was mentally rather slow, lazy in his work, and too fond of his food, but he never spoke ill of people or made trouble.

He sidled further into the room, handed her a button – it was warm and damp with sweat from his hand – and shrugged off his striped waistcoat.

'You're the third this morning,' she said. 'There must be a curse on buttons in this house.' She examined the place where the button was missing, and frowned. 'This looks as if it's been cut off. Has someone been playing tricks on you?'

She looked up, and saw him blush scarlet, his eyes shying away from hers. It came to her in a flash – he had cut it off himself, so as to come up and see her. It was not the first time in her life a male servant had taken a fancy to her, but with William, his shyness seemed to make liking her more a pain than a pleasure. In sheer pity she tried to put him at his ease.

'I can fix this for you in no time,' she said. 'What d'you think about not having the Christmas ball? They all seem quite upset downstairs. Was it fun?'

'Yeah, sort of,' he said. 'There was lots to eat, anyway, and you got to talk to servants from other houses.'

'And dancing,' she said, concentrating on threading the needle. 'I like dancing. You a good dancer? I bet you are. You're quite light on your feet.' He mumbled something incomprehensible. 'What's that?'

'I'd dance with *you*, if there was a ball,' he muttered, staring at his feet. 'Ask you, anyway. Don't 'spec' you'd . . .' His voice trailed away. He looked as if his head had been dipped in hot water, but he still managed to go a shade redder.

'You're a nice boy,' she said.

'My mum says I have to be.' William swallowed an Adam's

apple that had grown twice its normal size. 'She says do-as-you-would-be-done-by.'

'I bet she's proud of you,' Dory said, biting off the thread. She gave the waistcoat a shake and handed it to him. 'There, all done,' she said.

'Thanks,' he said. 'Thanks ever so.' He stood holding it and staring at her speechlessly, until she waved him away – not unkindly, but with a little flutter of the fingers.

He bumbled off, thinking of her white teeth between her pink lips biting the thread – *his* thread! He wanted to get round the corner quick and kiss where they'd been, before the magic wore off.

In light of what Miss Thornton had said, Lady Bayfield decided to expose Kitty to all the society possible for a girl not yet out, and observe her. Bayfield Court always entertained during the Christmas season, and Hampstead was a genteel place with a lot of good families.

Sir John was startled at the scale of the entertainments planned. 'It is for Catherine's sake,' Lady Bayfield told him. 'She needs to become used to being in company.'

'I thought that was why you sent her to school,' he objected.

'School can only do so much. And it was a *girls'* school, Sir John. She needs to be comfortable in male company.'

He sighed, but only a little. 'Whatever you think necessary, my dear.'

'You wish her to be well settled,' Lady Bayfield urged.

'Of course. But there's no hurry. She's only just seventeen, no need for her to marry for a year or two.'

Lady Bayfield held her tongue, but privately she had no intention of allowing Kitty to linger on the market. To get her married in her first year would reflect well on Lady Bayfield; a second- or third-season daughter was verging on shameful.

Kitty was thrilled with her first floor-length gowns and pinned-up hair; and since Mama had not told her she was to be on trial, she entered the Christmas celebrations with quiet pleasure. But she was too quiet for Lady Bayfield. With guests of her parents' age, she was meek, polite, and never ventured an opinion of her own: that was just as it should be. The verdict of that generation was that she was 'a nice, well-behaved girl'. But with the young people Lady Bayfield had gone to such trouble to acquire, Kitty behaved no differently. She smiled and listened, but did not join in. And with the young men, the smile disappeared, and she seemed almost apprehensive, as though faced with a strange dog that might bite. Lady Bayfield was exasperated.

'You must not be so stupid in company,' she berated Kitty, after one evening party. 'You hardly said a word last night.'

'I'm sure I spoke to several people, Mama,' Kitty faltered. She hated to be told off.

'Young Mr Woods sat beside you for ten minutes and could not get a word out of you.'

'He's very . . .' Kitty began, and stopped. She hardly knew what – very *male*.

'He's just the sort of young man you will meet at your come-out. What will become of you if you can't be agreeable like other girls? Surely they taught you how to make conversation at your school.'

Kitty hung her head.

Lady Bayfield saw tears beginning to gather. 'Don't cry, Catherine, for Heaven's sake!' she said impatiently. 'We'll say no more now. But you must try harder. Go to bed. You're tired.'

Kitty hurried away, and Lady Bayfield sat down to think. A few more parties might harden Kitty and bring her on, but if they didn't, perhaps she might, little as she wanted to, have to consider Miss Thornton's suggestion.

★   ★   ★

Aunt Schofield did not believe in God. She was a rationalist and a Benthamite, but England was a Christian country and she felt it was important for Nina to be brought up in the Christian tradition. She had taken her to church regularly, so that she knew the forms of service, and had read the Book of Common Prayer and the Bible with her extensively. They were not only texts of literary beauty, they were the foundation stones of so much of English culture that an educated Englishwoman ought to be as familiar with them as she was with Shakespeare.

Christmas in Draycott Place was cheerful, much like a pagan midwinter feast. There was no Christmas tree, which Aunt Schofield dismissed as a German innovation of Prince Albert, but they decorated the fireplaces with holly and ivy. There was no mention of the star, the manger, the wise men and so forth, but there were big fires and lots of mince pies and mulled wine.

Aunt Schofield kept a small establishment – just Cook, the house-parlourmaid Minny, and Haydock, who had been butler and valet to the late Professor Schofield and now took his position as man of the household very seriously. With a live-out char for the heavy work, they lived pleasantly but economically for most of the year. But on Christmas Day no expense was spared. All the extra leaves were put in the dining-table and a very grand seven-course dinner was given for Aunt Schofield's oldest and dearest friends – bachelor dons and spinster bluestockings, people who were not obliged to spend the day with their families. It was hard work for the servants, but the guests all tipped generously, and there were lavish left-overs to eat up.

Nina loved it too. Her aunt's friends were highly educated, so the conversation round the table was lively and wide-ranging; and, having no children of their own, they spoke to her just as they did to each other. They listened to her seriously, disagreed courteously, and corrected misinformation diffidently, taking her new, tentative ideas and running with them, showing her a wider world and more diffuse applications.

There was no dividing after dessert, and coffee was taken at the table, because it was easier to converse sitting around the board facing inwards than when scattered around a drawing-room. The party went on until, late and reluctantly, the guests dragged themselves up from their chairs and took themselves away.

It was the perfect celebration, Nina thought, and the only shadow over it was wondering where she would be next Christmas.

On a raw day in January, Giles pushed away the ledgers he was trying to make sense of. Sickening suddenly of the confinement and stale air in the library, he decided to go out for a ride. At the stables, Giddins hurried towards him, alerted to his presence by one of the boys, and eager for conversation. But Giles was not in the mood for a chat. He asked curtly, 'What is there for me to ride?'

Giddins's eyes lit up. His new lordship had not been across a horse since he arrived, and apart from selling his late lordship's hunters, had not shown any interest in the stables. Gloom had prevailed among the mangers – but perhaps this was the start of better times.

'Well, my lord,' he said warmly, 'it's certainly time we started to think about buying horses for you. You won't want hunters yet, but a couple of hacks – and I do know of a very nice chestnut for sale—'

Giles stopped him. 'I want to go out for a ride *now*. Any plain road-horse will do – you must have something.'

Giddins swallowed his disappointment and eyed him professionally. 'What does your lordship ride these days? About ten and a half stone? Well, my lord, let's see. Dexter would carry you – he's quiet. Or if you wanted something more lively you could have Archer's Abelard. He's not going out this morning.'

'I won't deprive Archer. Dexter will do. I shan't go far.'

'No, my lord. It's a nasty-ish day all right,' Giddins said. He had the air of settling in for a chat, so Giles walked away to the other side of the yard to wait for his mount to be brought out. Dexter was a fifteen-two brown, docile, but fresh enough. The dogs had followed him, hoping for a walk, but when he rode up the hill they lagged behind, and soon turned back to make their own way home.

When they got out onto the hillside, Dexter indicated his readiness for a gallop, which certainly blew away the cobwebs. It was a dark day, clammily cold, with low clouds like hanging fog that soaked as effectively as rain. He was not surprised to have the hill to himself – it was not a day for pleasure jaunts.

When he'd had his head-clearing spin, he rode through the woods for relief from the mizzle, and coming out on the other side found he was not alone in the world after all. Shapes in the murk resolved themselves into Alice, coming along the crest on her liver-chestnut Pharaoh, followed by the groom Brandom. Dexter whinnied a greeting, and Alice saw him, stopped, and waited. When he rode up, she looked a little apprehensive, as though she expected trouble.

'I didn't think anyone else would be riding today,' he greeted her. 'It's a nasty sort of day.'

'I go out every day,' Alice said, eyeing him nervously. 'Mama said I could, though she said we can't hunt while we're in mourning.'

'Quite right,' he said. 'You're riding alone? Where's Rachel?'

'I'm not alone. I've got Josh. Rachel thinks she's got a cold coming.'

He sighed. 'I'm not looking for reasons to scold you. Don't be so nervous. May I ride along with you?'

She relaxed just a little. Being asked permission seemed to please her. 'Yes, of course,' she said, and lowered her voice to add, 'Josh isn't much company. He's very disagreeable today.'

Giles glanced back. The groom was hunched into his collar, his face reddened with the cold, except for his nose, which was purple. 'I expect he doesn't like the weather.'

'Where are the dogs?'

'They went home. They don't like the weather either.'

She gathered her courage to converse. 'We've hardly seen you since you got back. You're always locked up in the library.'

'There's a lot to do.'

She slid a sideways glance at him. 'Are things very bad?' she asked.

'Who said they were?' he countered.

'Everybody's whispering about it. Daisy – she does our rooms – says they think a lot of them will be dismissed. She says Mrs Webster's furious, because she needs more housemaids, not fewer. Some of them are looking around for other places.'

How the devil did these things get about? He'd been doing everything he could to allay fears – but he supposed it was impossible to stop servants talking.

'You shouldn't listen to gossip,' he said automatically, and then was sorry because she shut her lips and turned her face away at the rebuke. He sought a way to open her up again. 'That's a nice gelding,' he said. It was the right approach. She turned back to him, her face lighting. 'Bred, is he?'

'Three-quarters. Papa bought him for me. I thought I'd have to ride a pony for another year, but Papa said I was a good horsewoman, and deserved something that could keep up in the hunt. He goes like the wind. I miss hunting, don't you? Wasn't Christmas *grue!*'

'Grew?' he asked, puzzled.

'Gruesome. No ball, no visitors, no Boxing Day meet. Oh dear, I suppose I shouldn't think about that, only about poor Papa. It isn't that I forget, but being in mourning's so *dull*. I say, Giles, was it strange that Mama went to visit Aunt Vicky? I thought you weren't supposed to go visiting or have fun or anything.'

Every year, Lady Stainton was accustomed to spend January and February with her other sister, the Princess of Wittenstein-Glücksburg, in her winter palace in Germany. She had departed two days before in all the grandeur of trunks, travel valises, hat-boxes, furs, rugs, her maid, and a courier.

'I don't think visiting relatives counts,' Giles said, and added, 'And I wouldn't imagine there's ever much fun to be had at the Wachturm. The word *trostlos* barely does justice to the Wachturm in winter.'

'Oh, *Giles*!' Alice concealed a guilty smile with her gloved hand. She raised enquiring eyes to him. 'Is it wrong to laugh when you're in mourning?'

'Not when you're fifteen,' he reassured her. 'Though perhaps not in public.'

'It's strange,' she said, turning a wind-stirred lock of Pharaoh's mane back the right way. 'Papa was so – *grand*. Not like other people's fathers. I mean, Ena and Clara Brinklow, our friends, their papa chats to them and makes *jokes*. They really love him. If he died, they'd cry like anything. Is it wrong that I don't want to cry for Papa?'

'You keep asking me if things are wrong,' Giles protested mildly.

'Well, you're old – grown-up at least. I haven't anyone else to ask.'

'You don't have a governess, do you?'

'Not for years. We had one when we were little. We don't need one now. Rachel will be old enough to come out next year.'

'So you don't have lessons? What do you do all day?'

'Well, we ride. And hunt. And visit friends.' She racked her brains. 'We go poor-visiting in the village. Mama makes us.'

'What about when you're indoors, at home?'

'Oh, I don't know. I suppose we chat. We play cards sometimes.'

'Read?'

'Mm, not really. Not very much.' She thought again. 'I like to draw. I copy out of Bewick's *Birds* sometimes, and I draw Rachel. She likes to sew. She embroidered hand-kerchiefs for everyone last Christmas.' Giles was struck by the emptiness of their lives, and felt a vague determination to do something for them as he listened to her. She made a downward *moue*. 'Last Christmas was different,' she mourned. 'You weren't home but Richard was and it snowed on Christmas Day. Have you heard from Richard? Is he coming home?'

'He's a soldier, and there's a war going on,' Giles said. 'He can't just drop everything and leave because he wants to.'

'But *does* he want to?' She didn't wait for an answer. 'That old war seems to have been going on for ever. Everyone was so excited about Ladysmith and Blom – Blum—'

'Bloemfontein.'

'We thought the war was over. But that was years ago, and it's still going on.'

'It has entered a new phase,' Giles said. He looked at her, to judge how far she was seeking information, and decided not to try to explain the finer points of guerrilla warfare to her. She really just wanted information about her brother. Richard, the lively one, had always been the favourite. He, Giles, being grave, studious and, moreover, never in favour with their father, had not had the temperament to make fun for his little sisters and win their affection. 'I expect he'll have leave soon, and then you'll see him.'

Alice had been studying him while he studied her. She said, with an abrupt change of subject, 'You're really worried, aren't you? Is it about the estate?'

He hesitated. What to tell her? 'Things are in a bit of a muddle,' he admitted.

'Are we poor?'

He smiled. 'Not *poor*.'

'Will we have to leave the Castle?'

'It won't come to that. Should you mind, then?'

'It's home,' she said simply.

'You'll have to leave one day. When you get married.'

'I shall never get married,' she said firmly. 'I should hate it.'

'Wouldn't you like to have babies?' he asked, amused.

'Absolutely not. We've always had to coo over Linda's when she comes visiting and, honestly, Giles, they were just awful when they were tiny, like horrid little baby mice, all naked and wrinkled. And they're not much better now – always crying and making a fuss. I'd far rather have horses and dogs. Rachel wants to get married – it's all she talks about – but I heard some of the maids say neither of us will be able to get married if there's no money left. Did—' She looked up at him earnestly. 'Was Papa very bad?'

'It's not like that. Things are complicated. I can't explain it to you so you'd understand.'

'I bet I would. I'm good at understanding things,' she assured him.

He shook his head. 'Just don't talk to anyone about Papa being bad, or there not being any money. It's not the done thing. And it would make my job much more difficult.'

'I won't, then. I won't say anything to anyone except you. But, Giles, if there's anything I can do to help you . . . Rachel said you were cross and strict, but I don't think you are, not really. And I'm good at listening.'

'I bet you are,' he said, smiling. 'But don't worry about

things. They'll work out. Shall we canter along here? It doesn't look too muddy.'

Alice's mind was easily distracted. 'I'll race you,' she said, with an impish grin, and Pharaoh took off, leaving Giles to catch her up, and Josh to tut in disapproval.

Giles's grandmother Victoire lived in a tall, narrow house in Bruton Street, with a staff of lady's maid, butler, cook and two housemaids, an establishment that might have been termed modest, except that her cook Durand was Escoffier-trained, and her butler Chaplin was such an archetype of butlerhood that her neighbour, the Earl of Strathmore, had several times tried to poach him.

At the age of seventy, she still had an active social life and rarely went to bed before midnight, so Giles curbed his impatience and did not present himself at her door until almost noon. As a favoured caller, he was admitted, and shown to her small sitting-room adjoining her bedroom on the second floor, where he found her drinking linden tea, into which she dipped the macaroons her chef was famous for, and reviewing the morning's crop of invitations and letters.

At his entrance she put all aside and rose to her feet with graceful ease (if it cost her any effort she would never let it show) to step forward and embrace him.

'Grandmère,' he said, kissing her scented cheek. 'You look blooming.'

'You look tired,' she said. She patted his cheek. 'Fagged to death, *chéri*. One is not surprised. Sit. Chaplin will bring coffee. You will not care for my slops.'

'You are the best advertisement for them,' he said. 'No-one would believe you were a day over forty.'

'You cannot conceive how much work goes on in the morning, to bring me to look even this good. If Simone ever leaves me, she can get a post as curator of a museum, restoring ancient, cracked vases.'

90

'*You* are not ancient or cracked.'

'You, however . . .' she returned. '*Mon pauvre*, what did my son leave you, aside from cares? Dragged back from your desert, where I dare say you were on the brink of wonderful discoveries.' He smiled and shook his head. 'But I must tell you, by the by, that dry desert air is the worst thing for your complexion. You have not suffered any harm yet, but it is as well you are recalled to soft English dampness, before you begin to resemble your own leather portmanteaux.'

He laughed. 'It's good to hear you talk nonsense! I was afraid I would find you—'

'Plunged in gloom?'

'You have lost your only son,' he said seriously.

'At my age, one expects to lose people. And it is a long time since Willie and I shared any warmth. He was not a man to inspire *tendresse*. Of course one must feel it, to lose a child at any age, and it was a shock. But I am not broken, my dear. I am more concerned that *you* should not be.'

He sighed. 'Things are very difficult. The more I find out, the worse it gets.'

He had received a further shock the previous day. The enquiries made of Garrard's about the value of the family jewellery had received an answer: all the important pieces had been copied over the years, and the originals sold. His mother had been wearing paste and base metal – he didn't know, and couldn't ask, whether she knew.

Conversation paused as Chaplin entered with a tray bearing coffee pot and cup, and a plate of Durand's *moulinets*, delicious little savoury pastry circles. Giles was particularly partial to them. 'You must have known I was coming,' he said.

His grandmother was incurably honest. 'It is a delight to see you. But, no, Sir Thomas is to take me to luncheon, and he likes a glass of champagne here first. *Moulinets* are perfect with champagne.'

'Sir Thomas – is he well?'

Sir Thomas Burton was twenty years her junior, the scion of an industrial family (Burton's Little Liver Pills were found in every home). He had been a pianist and studied music at the Conservatoire in Paris, where he had first met Victoire on one of her twice-yearly visits. Some years later they had met again in London, by which time he had become a conductor, and was using his fortune to stage concerts and operas. She was by then a widow, but he was married, and the *affaire* they had embarked on had shocked society. However, it had been going on for so long now it was spoken of openly. His wife, Lady Violet, had made ill-health a lifelong hobby, and the unspoken assumption was that she was glad to have the vigorous, irrepressible Sir Thomas taken off her hands.

'Tommy is always well,' Grandmère said. 'He only has too much energy and not enough to do. He talks now of founding his own orchestra, so that he shall never want for someone to conduct.'

'That sounds like a good idea,' said Giles. 'London is thin of musical life.'

'And thin of concert halls also,' said Grandmère, severely. 'The Queen's is so dreary, and the Albert's acoustics are so dreadful. He will have to build his own concert hall too, and then he can play in it to his heart's content.'

'You make him sound like a child in a sandpit,' Giles said, smiling.

'He is very child-like,' she agreed. 'He keeps me young. But, Giles, enough of me, tell me how things are with you. Maud is in Germany, I understand. Is that why you have come – to discuss things without her knowledge?'

'You are very astute,' he said. 'The trouble is, I don't know how much she knows about anything.'

'Very little, I imagine. She has always been one to look straight ahead and refuse to see what is to either side. You know your father had *affaires*?'

'No,' Giles said. He had suspected, since seeing his father's London expenses, but to suspect was not the same as being told in plain words. He felt absurdly shocked. It was one thing for his grandmother to entertain an elderly lover (a man of fifty, his father's age, must seem elderly to him, and it was beyond him to imagine that Sir Thomas and his grandmother did anything more now than keep each other company) but for his father to betray his mother in that way was something else. 'I didn't know, until now.'

'No, I suppose you would not,' Victoire said thoughtfully. 'Maud's guiding principle always was "Never complain, never explain." She is so English.'

Maud was the eldest of the three Forrest girls, daughters of the 8th Earl of Leake. She was also the plain one, but had never allowed that to affect her in any way. To be a Forrest was to have reached the pinnacle of civilisation. The family motto, carved into the ancient, pitted stone lintel over the door of their Northumberland fastness was *Manners Mayketh Manne*, which they took to mean that you should behave exactly the same to all people – and indeed they did, since a Forrest looked down on absolutely everyone, including the Royal Family (who were, after all, parvenus.) To a Forrest, the Prince of Wales and a coachman were of equal unimportance, and both should be treated with the same chilly courtesy.

All three girls had made good marriages. Victoria, the prettiest, had married the Prince of Wittenstein-Glücksburg, with a winter palace and a summer palace and full access, through the vast network of cousinage that linked them, to all the Continental royal courts. Caroline, the youngest, had married Sir James Manningtree who, though only a knight, had been extremely wealthy. She had been widowed young, and had no children, and now lived in a lavish way in a large house in Berkeley Square. Maud had set her heart on marrying a duke, but when Stainton offered for her, the match had been thought good enough. The title was an old one – the barony went back to the seventeenth century, the earldom was late eighteenth – and the property was good.

Maud's Forrest chilliness and disdain for all other human life might have been mitigated by a different husband, Victoire thought – after all, Caroline was a perfectly pleasant and agreeable woman. But she had to admit that her son Willie had had a self-sufficiency and arrogance that did nothing to soften his wife.

'They say the children of lovers have a hard time of it,' Victoire said now to Giles. 'My William and I were so much in love, I fear we neglected poor Willie. He was left to nannies and tutors, who fed his self-consequence. He grew up thinking he could have whatever he wanted just for the taking. He and Maud – well, they each did their duty, but there was no *connection* between them. It was as if one lived on the moon and the other on . . .' She paused, at a loss for another planetary body.

'Jupiter?' Giles offered.

'Just so. And you children were all far away on earth and might as well have been orphans. My poor Giles! *En résumé,* your father did just as he pleased always, and I don't suppose he told your mother anything.'

'There is,' Giles said, with delicate hesitancy, 'the question of her jointure.'

His grandmother understood at once. 'All spent?' He nodded. 'Hmm. Well, if she demands it, something will have to be done. But unless her sister the princess brings up the subject – she always was mercenary, you know – I don't suppose she will think about it for some time. Is that what is worrying you?'

'Not only that.' Giles hesitated again.

'Giles, don't be so English! Tell me everything, without disguise. I cannot be shocked. And I am so old, I must have some wisdom. Perhaps I can help you.'

94

So he told her. She listened attentively, quietly, and he poured out everything.

'I have been tearing at my hair for a solution,' he concluded, 'and the only one that has been suggested is something quite distasteful to me.'

'To sell the land?' she ventured.

'No, I couldn't do that,' he said. 'It would be to betray the family. And in any case, land prices are depressed, and there are mortgages. No, I need a completely fresh source of money.'

'Then it is clear what you must do,' she said dispassionately.

'Is it? Markham says I must marry an heiress.'

'*Bien sûr.* That is exactly what I was going to say.' She made a sound of impatience. 'What is it? What is your objection?'

'To marry a woman for money . . .' he began.

'But you cannot be so delicate! It is a thing well understood. You have a title, an old name, an estate. You find a girl whose father has money and who wants these things for her. What can be wrong? It is a fair bargain on each side. And, believe me, the girl will be of one mind with her papa.'

'It seems so – cold. So heartless.'

'Giles, you are not sentimental, I hope? I thought better of you. This is the way the world goes. Love matches are not for the likes of us. We have responsibilities.'

'You loved my grandfather.'

'But I would have married him even if I hadn't. Caroline loved her James – but *after* they were married. To marry for love sounds pretty, but unless there is more to it, it rarely works out well. Now, put all this nonsense out of your mind, and think like a rational man.' She examined his expression, and laughed. '*Chéri,* don't look so *triste*! We shall find you a nice girl who will not only bring you a fortune but will adore you into the bargain. *Pourquoi non?* You are a handsome young man that any girl would want

95

to marry. Now, we must go and see your aunt Caroline. She is the one to find out which girls are on the market this year.'

'On the market?' he groaned.

'Enough! No more complaining. Caroline and I shall put our heads together. I'll ask her to—' She was interrupted by a knock at the street door downstairs, such a heavy, impetuous knock it was clearly heard all the way up here. '*Oh, tiens!* I had forgotten Tommy. He is here. *Chéri*, I will scribble you a note, and you shall take it round to Caroline at once. We shall not let the grass grow under our feet. Hand me my writing-case.'

She was a quick writer and Chaplin was a slow climber, and she was folding her note and thrusting it into an envelope as the door opened and Chaplin announced, 'Sir Thomas Burton, my lady.'

Burton was not a tall man, but he had an important figure, a very upright carriage, and rather piercing dark eyes. His hair was parted in the centre, brushed straight back and, like his large moustache and trimmed beard, was dark and so without grey threads that Giles wondered if he dyed them. He projected great presence, which Giles supposed was necessary in a conductor, impresario and all-round Great Man, but there was something endearing about the boyish smile he bestowed on Grandmère, and the air of shy eagerness with which he clasped her hand in both of his and stooped to kiss her cheek. The *affaire* had been going on for twenty years, he reflected, so there must be love of some kind between them.

'Tommy, dear, look, Giles is here. You remember Giles? Is it not shocking that I have a great, grown grandson like this?'

Burton shook Giles's hand cordially and said, 'You've been out east, I believe?'

'With Carter, sir, at Thebes.'

'Ah, the temple fellow! Must have been a shock to you, to be recalled in this way. Tragic thing, your father's accident. My condolences. Fixed in England now, I imagine?'

'Yes, sir.'

The dark eyes scanned him. 'A great deal of business, I expect. Sudden deaths cause a great deal of work for everyone. But don't let it overwhelm you, my boy. This, too, shall pass, as the philosopher says. I dare say your life dealing with antiquities has taught you about the fleeting nature of human concerns. Mine with music, too. Music lasts. Little else does.'

'No, sir,' said Giles.

He didn't think the words particularly comforting, and presumably Grandmère did not, either, for she said, 'Tommy, don't stand there talking nonsense. Ring the bell for Simone. As you see, I am not dressed yet. Giles is just leaving. Take that note to your aunt at once,' she told him, kissing him and pressing it into his hand as she turned away. 'Tommy, you shall play the piano while I dress. I shall leave the door half open so that I can hear you.'

'What shall I play?' Burton asked, looking pleased as he stepped across to the piano.

'Schumann. You know I love Schumann,' she said, as she disappeared through the door.

Giles smiled to himself as he took his leave. A pianist herself, Grandmère had always said that of all piano works Schumann's were the most exacting. She was intending to keep her lover fully occupied until she was ready for him.

Lady Manningtree's house in Berkeley Square was just round the corner. When Giles presented himself, his aunt was on her way out to luncheon with Lady Vaine – her carriage was actually at the door – but whatever Grandmère had written was so powerful she instantly had it sent away, and scribbled off a note of excuse to Lady Vaine instead.

Then she placed herself on a settle in the elegant drawing-room, made Giles sit beside her, and said, 'Now, what is all this? Victoire says you must be persuaded to marry. But, Giles, you must have known you would have to. You must have thought about it.'

'I haven't, not really,' he said ruefully. 'I supposed that one day I would meet a suitable girl and—'

'Fall in love? Please do not let me hear anything so vulgar from your lips.'

'Not exactly, but I supposed that . . .' He hesitated. Yes, what *had* he supposed? '. . . that my marriage would be a matter for me alone to decide. And not for a long time yet, in any case.'

She shook her head. 'I blame William. Maud, too. Your parents should have seen to it that you were married off as soon as you reached your majority, not waited until you developed fanciful ideas. And then for William to go and get himself killed!'

'I don't think it was his idea,' Giles said mildly.

'The estate is all to pieces, I gather.' He nodded. 'Then, my dear, it is as Victoire says. You must marry an heiress. I will find you someone. She shall be a nice girl whom you will like, and she will like you, and you will trot along very well together.' A sudden thought came to her, and she shot him a sharp look. 'You haven't formed an attachment already?'

He smiled at the idea. 'I've been in the desert, Aunt Caroline. The only women there are four thousand years old and carved in stone.'

'Well, that's a relief.' She looked suddenly animated. 'This will be such fun! I was thinking it would be just another Season, but now I shall have an interest! I shall visit all the hostesses and find out who's coming out, and you shall have your choice. I'll make you a list, and you'll meet them and dance with them—'

'I am in mourning,' he pointed out to her.

She paused for a moment, but then flipped her fingers. 'I don't think that signifies. The rules are not followed as strictly as they used to be. And there have always been exceptions in cases of need. By the time the Season starts you'll have been in deep mourning for four months. No-one will think anything of it if you begin to attend respectable balls. By the end of May six months will be up, and you can marry in June quite properly.'

'June!' he said, dismayed.

She gave him a sympathetic look. 'No sense in putting it off, my dear. Every month you delay just adds another month's interest to the debts.'

That, Giles thought, was one way of looking at it.

CHAPTER SIX

In the past when Lady Stainton had gone to Germany, the earl had held hunting and shooting parties, and Linda had always offered to be his hostess, moving in for the whole period, leaving her husband and children at home in Dorset to enjoy practising economy.

But with the earl dead and the house in mourning, there were no parties, and no invitation for Lady Cordwell.

'It's like a mortuary, this place,' Rose complained.

'It's a chance to catch up on the cleaning,' Mrs Webster countered. One of the housemaids, May, had left – 'Gone to a better place,' Moss had remarked, which made it sound as though she had died – and Mrs Webster had been wondering if she should hire a replacement without direct permission from her ladyship. In the end, she didn't quite dare. At least with no-one Upstairs but the new earl, Mr Sebastian and the two young ladies, there wasn't so much to do, and with relish she set out a programme of deep cleaning that she had been longing to get her teeth into.

Dory had often heard the piano being played somewhere in the house, without paying it much attention. But one day, when she was carrying a silk counterpane she had been mending back to the Jade Room, she heard it much louder and, roused to curiosity, followed the sound. It came from the small drawing-room (small in this case being a relative word – it was smaller than the state drawing-room). She paused in the open doorway and looked in, to see Mr Sebastian at the piano. A ripple of music held her entranced for a few moments, until his fingers stumbled, the music stopped and, afraid she had disturbed him, she tried to back away out of sight. But he looked up at her calmly, as though he had known she was there, and said, 'Out of practice. Trouble at my age, the old fingers get stiff if you don't keep it up.' He reached for the cigar resting in the ashtray on top of the piano and said, 'Come in, don't be scared.' She took a few steps forward. 'Dratted thing's gone out,' he muttered, putting the end in his mouth and patting his pockets for matches. She saw a silver match-case on a small table and carried it over to him. 'Thank you,' he said, and she stood, obedient to his previous summons, while he struck a match, and got his cigar going again.

He was looking at her, examining her carefully, not the way Upstairs folk usually looked at you, but as if he could actually see her. 'Fond of music, are you?' he asked.

She liked his voice – it seemed rich and plummy, as though mellowed by years of expensive cigars and fine wines. 'I don't know,' she said. 'I haven't heard much, not that kind of music. But I think I could like it.'

'Well done,' he said. 'Scarlatti.'

'Sir?'

'That's the name of the composer. Scarlatti. Wrote lots for the piano, all very good for keeping the fingers moving.' He began to play again, but obviously from memory, as he continued to look at her. There seemed no danger here – she began to relax. 'What music *have* you heard?' he asked.

'Oh, not your sort, sir, not good music. People playing in public houses. And in the street. Squeeze boxes and barrel organs. Jiggy tunes for dancing. And music-hall songs.'

He nodded, sucking on his cigar, and the music under his hands changed to 'A Bird in a Gilded Cage'. Dory smiled, and began to sing the words under her breath. It had been

101

the most popular song of 1900. He joined in the last line, managing somehow to sing through a cigar, and finished with several decorative runs and arpeggios. She pretended to clap, but without making a sound.

'All music is good, if it brings people pleasure,' he said, putting the cigar in the ashtray again. 'Nothing wrong with a jolly tune. What have you got there?' He nodded towards the counterpane folded over her arm.

The abrupt change of subject didn't trouble her. Upstairs folk were like that. 'Bedspread, sir. I've been mending it.'

'Show me.'

It was a command, so she obeyed it. He stood up, and helped her partly unfold the material on the piano top. Close to, he was taller than she had expected, and though he was untidy, with unruly, bushy hair and ash sprinkled down his front (her hand wanted badly to brush him down) and a spot of some kind of food on his cuff, he smelt very nice, of clean linen and soap.

She showed him where she had mended a tear in the old silk, and restitched the embroidered peacock whose body had been separated from his tail by the injury.

'That's very fine work,' he said. 'You are an artist.'

'Oh, no, sir,' she demurred automatically.

'What's your name?' he demanded.

'Dory, sir.'

'Well, Dory, as one artist to another, I advise you to accept a compliment when it's offered. As long as it's just, and not empty flattery. Your stitchery is wonderfully fine. This peacock says you are an artist – and so do I.'

'Thank you, sir,' she said. When he smiled, you could see he must have been handsome when he was young. 'I liked your playing, too.'

'Then stay and listen,' he said, sitting down at the piano again.

'Oh, no, sir, I must get on. Mrs Webster—'

'I understand. Off you go. But you're welcome to come and listen to me any time.' His smile became a boyish grin. 'I love an audience.'

Since his mother had gone away, Giles had been having a tray in the library instead of going down to dinner, so that he could keep working, and since the girls took their meals in the schoolroom unless summoned to dinner, Uncle Sebastian had been fed at the small table in the morning-room. It suited Mrs Webster not to have formal dinner to arrange, meaning she could divert the servants' energies elsewhere. She was as surprised to get orders from Mr Sebastian as Giles, Rachel and Alice were to receive hand-written invitations to dinner in the dining-room, with 'Dress: formal' at the bottom.

Sebastian was waiting to receive them, his hair sleeked back for once, his coat brushed, his face wreathed in genial smiles.

'Interesting,' Giles said, as his hand was formally shaken. 'To be invited to dine in my own house.'

'I despaired of getting you to a civilised table any other way,' said Sebastian. 'Sherry?'

Rachel and Alice arrived a little late, flustered, but excited. 'Is it a game?' Alice asked.

'Just dinner,' said Sebastian.

'It's so *late*,' Alice gloated.

'We weren't sure what to wear,' Rachel apologised. 'We don't have dinner gowns.'

'Daisy said our velvets would be all right,' said Alice. 'They're our best.'

But Rachel was anxious. 'Only Alice's is brown, not black.'

'*Mesdemoiselles*, you look charmingly,' said Sebastian, and bowed over their hands in turn. 'May I offer you a glass of orgeat?'

'What's that?' Alice cried.

'You'll love it,' Sebastian promised.

Giles looked at his little sisters in their frocks and hair

103

ribbons, saw their eyes shine with pleasure, and felt guilty. Eating on a tray suited him, and he preferred solitude, but he realised uncomfortably that their entire lives consisted of solitude, and the chance to put on the best frock and eat at a different table was a welcome break in the monotony.

He turned to Sebastian. 'I am properly rebuked,' he said. 'I have been thoughtless.'

Sebastian smiled kindly. 'No-one is rebuking anyone. We all need a little company from time to time – even you! And I haven't entertained in years. High time I did.'

It was a successful evening. Sebastian was charming, drawing the girls out so that they chattered and laughed. Dinner was slightly better than usual, thanks to Sebastian's having given very detailed instructions – and was certainly better than the nursery fare the girls usually faced.

And after dinner, in the drawing-room (he decreed no dividing), Sebastian organised some games, and concluded by going to the piano and playing some sweet, sentimental tunes that the girls could sing to.

At last he rose, clapped his hands, and said, 'Off to bed with you now, chickies!'

Alice gave him a grave look. 'We're not chickies. Rachel will be seventeen next year.'

He bowed. 'You are right to remind me. Then, good night, ladies, good night, sweet ladies, good night, good night.'

When they had gone, Sebastian fetched the cigar case and proffered it to Giles. He refused. 'I'll have one of my own cigarettes.'

'You don't care for these?' Sebastian asked, taking a long draw.

'I haven't developed the habit,' Giles said.

'You should do. A great deal of important talk goes on after the women leave. And fellows don't warm to fellows who don't share their customs.'

'I don't—' Giles began, and stopped. He supposed that

getting on with other 'fellows' of his uncle's sort would assume an importance in his life it had never had before. He knew how to get on with academics; he had avoided the world of the landed gentry.

Sebastian examined him for a moment, then said, 'Master of the house now, eh, Giles? Strange world for you, I suspect.'

Giles was startled. It was as if he had read his thought. 'It – will take getting used to,' he said.

'For me, too,' Sebastian said, smiling. 'Having to remember to call you Stainton.'

'My mother doesn't remember. As often as not she calls me Ayton.'

'Yes. Well, difficult business for her. Women don't like to be widowed, you know. Interferes with their plans.' Giles couldn't think of a useful response to this statement, and kept silent. 'Bound to wonder what'll happen to her when you marry. House can't have two mistresses, eh? You'll be marrying soon, I imagine?'

'I've taken some first steps,' he said reluctantly. 'Consulted my grandmother and aunt.' Sebastian nodded. 'I hadn't thought there was any particular hurry,' Giles went on, 'but there are considerations . . . Some urgency to the matter has arisen.'

Sebastian was watching him closely. 'Have you ever wondered why I'm not married?'

'Er – no, I can't say I ever have,' Giles said, a little embarrassed.

'I know what you're thinking. But I wasn't always queer old Uncle Sebastian frowsting by the fireside, you know. I was handsome enough when I was young, I had a comfortable house and a decent independence from my mother – there was no reason I shouldn't marry.' He examined the end of his cigar, decided the ash could hold on for a little longer, and went on. 'In fact, my father – your great-grandfather – was quite anxious that I should marry. He

105

already had a son to carry the title, of course, but wanted a little insurance. He even found the girl for me, decent family, decent dowry, the right shape for breeding.'

Giles looked up with a frown, and Sebastian said, 'You don't like that, I see. Customary or not. Well, neither did I. There was a young woman I had a fancy to. Lived in the next village. Daughter of a major in the Foot Guards. Hero of Sebastopol. No money, though. No name. M'father didn't approve. Talked to me like a Dutch uncle. Imagine my dilemma. There was my duty on one side, and there was little Phyllis on the other. I hesitated. And while I was hesitating, she caught putrid fever and died.'

'I'm sorry,' said Giles, awkwardly. He was not used to such confidences.

'So was I. Still am. I always blamed myself. If I'd married her and taken her away from the village, she wouldn't have caught the fever. I see her eyes in my dreams. Reproaching me. They were grey, like rainy skies.'

'So you never married.' It was not a question, but a prompt.

'Couldn't do it,' Sebastian said. 'It seemed like a betrayal. In the end, it's yourself you have to live with the longest.'

Giles sighed. 'But, you see, it's different for me. You weren't the earl. I don't see that I have any choice. My father—'

Sebastian tapped the ash off his cigar. 'I'm well aware of the way the world goes. Your father was a perfectly normal beef-witted country man. But you are not in that mould. You have thoughts and feelings a fellow in your position can't afford. As an outsider myself, I recognise it in you. You will not be happy doing what you don't feel is right. And this – quest,' he waved his hand to indicate that he knew it was not the right word, 'makes you uncomfortable. I just mention, while there is time for you to change your mind.'

Giles thought for a long moment. 'I'm afraid there isn't. The time has run out.'

'As bad as that, is it?'

'Every bit as bad.'

'Then, my boy, you must do your duty, but do it with a whole heart. Don't repine. Don't sulk—'

'Sulk?' Giles was indignant.

'—or you will poison not only yourself but all those around you.'

Giles pressed his lips together, resisting. He did not like being told what to do. Sebastian looked at him cannily, knowing what was in his mind. *You can lead a horse to water* . . . he thought. *Time to lighten the atmosphere.*

'One more piece of advice I must give you, Giles. About marriage. Something you may not have thought about, but it's damned important.'

'Sir?' said Giles coldly. *Now what?* he thought.

Sebastian leaned forward and placed both hands on his knees to emphasise his words. His blue eyes bored into Giles's. 'Get a new cook,' he said. 'A man has to be comfortable at his own table, and you're not a good doer anyway. I've seen you losing ground since you got here. Overrule your mother and get a new cook – *before* you bring a bride home. Don't want to poison the poor girl before she's had a chance to whelp.'

Crooks was fond of music, and liked to remain after Sunday service to listen to the voluntary, while the other servants from the Castle hurried from the church as soon as possible. When the organ fell silent, he walked out, hat and prayer book in one hand, gloves and stick in the other, into a mild grey February day. The ancient paving stones inside the porch were worn and uneven, and as he juggled with his burdens while trying to put his gloves on, he started to drop his cane, grabbed for it, struck his foot against the raised edge of a flag, and fell forward. For a breathless moment he saw himself crashing face-first into the ground in humiliation, pain and blood, but a large hand grasped his upper arm, while his other outflung hand caught hold of a sleeve under which a forearm was firm and strong as rock.

Startled, he looked up into the face of a Greek god. Below a thick crest of red-gold hair were golden eyebrows and eyes of cerulean blue, a straight nose, sculpted lips and a firm chin. It was a brown face, but light brown and smooth, with a blush of youth over the cheekbones.

'Wh-wh— Thank you! Thank you!' Crooks stammered.

'Are you all right, sir?' the young Apollo asked, in a soft country accent.

'I think so. Thank you so much. You saved me from a very nasty fall.'

'Glad I could help, sir.'

The large, hard hand released Crooks's upper arm, and reluctantly he let go of the stranger's forearm. 'May I know to whom I am indebted?' he said. And seeing the stranger did not quite understand the question, rephrased it: 'May I know your name?'

'Axe Brandom, sir. Assistant blacksmith, along the forge at the end of the high street.'

'Brandom?' said Crooks. 'Any relation to—?'

'My little brother Josh, sir? He's a groom up at the Castle.'

'That's where I live,' Crooks began.

The young man smiled, a thing of particular beauty, and said shyly, 'I know who you are, sir – his lordship's valet. I seen you many a time, in church and in the carriage. And one time you come looking for his lordship in the stable-yard when I was there. His late lordship, I mean. I go up the Castle now and then to see to the horses.'

Crooks had never paid particular attention – the stables were not his natural milieu – but when he thought about it he was aware that, like many great houses, the Castle had its own forge at the end of the stable-yard, though not its own blacksmith. A smith, he supposed, could easily be

108

summoned when there was work to do, but there was not sufficient work to justify employing one full-time.

Crooks stooped to pick up his hat, gloves and stick, which had all gone flying when he thought he was falling. At the same time, Brandom stooped to pick up his prayer book for him, and caressed it briefly with one gentle finger as he handed it over. 'It's a beautiful thing, sir,' he said.

It was indeed a lovely thing, leather-bound and beautifully tooled, with a filigree brass binding to the spine. Crooks loved it. 'It belonged to my father and grandfather before me,' he said.

'It must be a wonderful thing,' said Brandom, 'to be book-learned. I learned to read and write at school, but I'm no scholard. It must be grand to . . .' He hesitated, as if unsure how to express it.

'To read for pleasure?' Crooks suggested. 'Yes, it is the finest thing in the world. It opens up such vistas, like being able to travel the whole world without rising from your chair. The thoughts and visions of all mankind are laid before you, at your fingertips.'

Brandom gazed down at him, seeming transported by the words. Two stragglers came out of the church door behind him and said, 'Excuse me,' as they edged past on either side, breaking the spell.

Crooks recollected himself, his duties, and the hour, juggled again briefly with his belongings as he donned his hat, and said, 'Well, I must be off. Thank you again for your prompt assistance. I am very much in your debt.'

'Oh, no, sir,' Brandom said. 'There's no debt.'

Crooks met the wide blue eyes for an instant, then dragged away his gaze. 'Good day to you.'

'Sir,' said Brandom.

Crooks went past him and hurried down the path, aware of eyes fixed on his retreating back. But when he glanced back, Brandom was gone, presumably having passed round the corner of the church to leave by the west gate.

Kitty was aware that her stepmother had taken a house in Berkeley Street, and lived from day to day in dread of being summoned to take up residence there – which would mean that the frightening Season had begun. But, at first, nothing changed. Lady Bayfield went up alone, and Kitty continued her dull, peaceful routines in Hampstead. She gathered that the house had to be put in order and suitable servants engaged; and then there would be a process of leaving cards and paying morning calls so that when the Season began, the hostesses would know Kitty existed and would send her invitations.

Kitty's presence would not be required until it was time to assemble her clothes. 'When fittings begin,' Lady Bayfield told her, in a rare burst of communication, 'I shall bring you up to Berkeley Street, and you shall accompany me on calls.'

Kitty looked so frightened at the prospect that Lady Bayfield almost snapped at her, but desisted, knowing it would only make things worse. The child seemed to be growing more, not less nervous. In truth, she was starting to worry not about whether Catherine would 'take', but about whether she would cope at all. The whole Season could be an expensive disaster. Her mind returned to the suggestion of Miss Thornton, but she looked at it with disfavour. The girl who had been suggested – would she bring Catherine any credit? And yet *something* must be done. Restlessly, she tossed the idea about in her mind, and finally decided that she should at least inspect the girl's aunt, and see what sort of a person she was. She acquired the address from Miss Thornton and sent a note, summoning her to Berkeley Street.

Mrs Schofield came, but while she must have wondered why she was there, she would not give her hostess the satisfaction of asking, which seemed to Lady Bayfield to demonstrate too sturdy an independence of mind for a

110

female not of the *ton*. Mrs Schofield had nothing of fashion about her, though her clothes were of good quality – indeed her fur was very good and her pearls looked excellent. Her accent was quite pure, and she spoke with sense, but Lady Bayfield would have preferred some air of deference, some evidence that she understood the social distance between them. Her manners were proper, but not ingratiating. It gave rise to the spectre of a niece who would be *too* confident, *too* sure of herself, perhaps even – horrible thought! – *pert*. Catherine needed a confident companion, but not one who would have an opinion on every subject and be unafraid of airing it. There was nothing gentlemen liked less than being *challenged*.

Mrs Schofield departed and Lady Bayfield was just concluding that she need go no further in the matter, when another visitor was announced. She was as pleased as surprised: Caroline Manningtree was an extremely elegant, wealthy woman who moved in the best circles, but they were no more than acquainted. Lady Bayfield could not help wondering what she wanted. She did not have a daughter she was bringing out: the Manningtrees were known to have been childless. Could she perhaps be sponsoring a niece or other relative?

Her first words, on being shown into the drawing-room, were, 'I beg your pardon, but was not that a Miss Sanderton I just saw leaving? She was coming down the steps from your house as my carriage drew up.'

'It was a Mrs Schofield who was calling on me,' Lady Bayfield corrected her, surprised by the question.

'Ah, of course! That was her married name. She married a gentleman of letters – an interesting choice. She and I were at school together, you know, though not in the same year. She was above me, and was much admired by all, I may say. Quite the most popular of her year. A beautiful girl, but with a formidable intellect.'

111

'Too much schooling,' Lady Bayfield said cautiously, not knowing how her visitor felt about it, 'can be a handicap to a girl's prospects.'

'Indeed!' Lady Manningtree laughed. 'You should hear my sister Stainton on the subject. I was one of three sisters, and the only one who went to school. My sisters married a prince and an earl between them, and when I married no better than a knight, they blamed my education! But mine was a happy marriage. And I don't believe I was changed by my time at school. I should have turned out pretty much as I am, with or without it.'

'I'm sure you are right,' Lady Bayfield said. 'With a very few exceptions, education makes little mark on females. It slips off them like—'

'Water off a duck's back?' Lady Manningtree suggested.

She was easy company, and the regulation quarter-hour passed quickly. But Lady Bayfield really wanted to know what she was doing there. Conversation on these occasions was rather like playing whist, where you had to try to work out what your opponent's hand contained without revealing your own. Lady Bayfield was extremely good at whist, which was something of a passion with her. Lady Manningtree appeared to be good at it too, and the conversation circled elegantly on hints and suggestions and effortlessly deflected probes. Lady Bayfield suspected Lady Manningtree was concealing a queen, but it emerged that in fact it was a king she held. And it emerged, Lady Bayfield realised afterwards, not because she was better at whist, but because Lady Manningtree had wanted it to.

Not a niece, but a nephew.

The newly succeeded Earl of Stainton was looking for a bride. Lady Bayfield had to take several deep breaths. What a thing that would be for Catherine! An old title, a castle and a large estate! But there would be competition. Lady Manningtree, she supposed, was going about whipping up interest so as to have the most lucrative possible auction when the time came. Girls with determined mamas would be shoved to the front to display their qualities, while Catherine languished at the back, like a frightened fieldmouse.

Her mind turned again to Mrs Schofield. This visit had added a new dimension: Lady Manningtree not only knew Mrs Schofield but had admired her. If Mrs Schofield moved in the best circles she had no need to court approval – might even be mildly eccentric without being regarded as *blue*. And the girl, Miss Sanderton, might attract attention from a better circle than Lady Bayfield had supposed. In short, it was a connection worth having.

She thought a little more, then crossed to the walnut desk in the corner and sat down to write a letter.

Aunt Schofield was no advocate of idleness. To keep Nina busy she involved her with her current scheme to open a Free Library in the East End: dictating letters to her, taking her with her when she went to drum up support and collect donations, sending her on errands to printers and estate agents. In addition, she required Nina to read or study for several hours every day, as well as practising her drawing and music. Nothing had been said yet about her becoming a teacher. Nina supposed that when the library scheme was further along and she could be spared, arrangements would have to be put in hand.

For the moment, she was content to stay on at home. She was curled up on the window-seat in the morning-room with a book when her aunt came in, late one morning, with a letter in her hand.

'Put that aside, Nina. I have something to discuss with you.' Nina obeyed, and waited as her aunt seemed to inspect her thoroughly. At last, she began, 'I suppose you would not have any particular objection to coming out this Season?'

Nine felt a quick rush of excitement, which showed in

her face. 'I hadn't really thought about it,' she said. 'I didn't think anything of that sort was planned for me.'

Aunt Schofield had seen the look: she had her answer. She said neutrally, 'It would cost a great deal of money, and I have always doubted the benefit to you would be worth the expenditure. However, there is now a possibility of doing it without great outlay, and if it would give you pleasure, I shall consider it. It is only a few weeks, after all,' she added, as if to herself.

Nina surveyed her expression, wondering how she should answer. For all her education, she was only seventeen, and the thought of gowns and balls and parties had a certain power over her. But she believed her aunt disapproved of society and its ways. Was this a test?

While she was hesitating, her aunt went on, 'I have here a letter from Lady Bayfield with a proposal. I called on her yesterday at her request, but she didn't mention it then. I suppose I was summoned on approval,' she concluded, with disdain. 'She seems now to have decided I am suitable to be condescended to. But her proposal is not in itself objectionable. She writes quite feelingly of her daughter Catherine—'

'Kitty,' Nina said, a smile breaking like sunrise on her face. 'My best friend at school, Aunt, and the dearest, sweetest girl. You would love her if you met her.'

'I'm glad your affection for her is all that Lady Bayfield claims. She says that Catherine – Kitty – is very shy and nervous, and would benefit from having a more confident friend to support her through the strain of what sounds like a very *ton*nish come-out. To that end, she proposes that she brings you out alongside her daughter and chaperones you to all the same parties and balls. Would you like it? Would it give you pleasure?'

'Oh, yes, Aunt, *please!*' Nina said urgently. 'If you don't dislike it too much.'

'My dear, I shall have nothing to do in the matter. Once we have acquired your clothes, you'll stay with them at their house and go with them everywhere. I shall hardly see you until the Season ends.'

'But you disapprove,' Nina ventured anxiously.

'It wasn't something I ever wanted for you. We do not move in those circles. But I don't disapprove.' The examining gaze was back. 'However, I do want to be sure that you won't have your head turned by it. You must remember that it is a holiday from reality, and not reality itself. You will come back to the life you have always known. Nothing will have changed. If you understand that – if you are ready to undertake it rather like a foreign expedition—'

'To observe and make notes of all the curious customs?' Nina suggested mischievously. 'And not get myself eaten by cannibals.'

Her aunt smiled. 'Especially the cannibals. The fashionable world can gobble up young women, if they are not level-headed.'

'I shan't have my head turned, I promise,' Nina vowed.

'Don't take this warning lightly, Nina. You may be sorely tempted. But I know you *are* a sensible girl, and mature for your age.'

'I want to do it for Kitty,' Nina said. 'Oh, I'm sure I *shall* enjoy it, but poor Kitty is so shy, and dreading it so much, and I do love her. If I can get her through it, and perhaps show her she doesn't need to be afraid, isn't that a good thing to do? A charitable thing?'

'Very charitable,' Aunt Schofield agreed solemnly. 'Very well, I'll write to Lady Bayfield, and then I suppose we had better think about clothes.' She started to leave, then turned back. 'You will be in a position where some men may pay you a great deal of attention, and given that you are not of that order in society and will not have a dowry, their attentions may be mischievous. It is often the case that the worst of them are the most plausible and charming—'

'I understand,' said Nina. 'I shan't be taken in, I promise.'

115

CHAPTER SEVEN

Giles was not particularly surprised that his mother had extended her stay in Germany. There was no pressing reason for her to come back, and the sympathy of a sister might be a balm she did not expect at home.

He had taken the first steps in unpicking his father's affairs – the London properties had been disposed of, the subscriptions cancelled. After brief consideration, he had retained his own diggings there for the time being – much cheaper than either a club membership or a hotel room, and while he could, of course, always stay with his aunt, it was somewhere of his own, where he might be anonymous and unaccountable. For a man who had enjoyed a large degree of freedom, it was a consideration.

The sale of the hunters and the London properties allowed Giles to pay off some of the most pressing debts. Aunt Caroline had told him firmly that he must invest in some new clothes for the Season, and Crooks, more gently but with urgency in his eyes, had seconded that. Aunt Caroline had expected him to go to London and be fitted out in style, but impatient both of the time and the expense, he had called in local men, Frean the tailor and Silverson the bootmaker. Crooks had taken them both quietly aside and menaced them, so Giles would be got out at least decently, and at a fraction of the London price.

His mother arrived home in the middle of March in a

thoroughly bad temper. She had not been long back at the Castle before Miss Taylor, taking her shoes down to be cleaned, came back up with the latest talk. Lady Stainton actually sought Giles out in the library to berate him.

'What's this I hear about your intending to get married?' she demanded.

'Oh, you've heard that, have you?' he said, a trifle wearily.

'It was the first thing Taylor heard when she went downstairs. And yet, you have not spoken a word to me about it.'

'I haven't had the—' he began, but she cut him off.

'You cannot have made a new attachment in the few weeks since you returned from Egypt. Therefore it must be a long-standing one, which you have been too *undutiful* to tell me about. That my own son should think to marry without even the courtesy of mentioning the woman's name to me, let alone introducing her! One would almost think you were ashamed.'

Giles roused himself to stem the flow. 'There is no name to tell you, no attachment, new or old. I have not yet met anyone. But I must look for a bride. You can't be surprised. You of all people must want me to get an heir and secure the title.'

She would not give up quite yet. Anger sustained her. 'So now you are concerned with the future of the family and the title, are you?'

'Circumstances have changed,' he said shortly. 'Please, Mama, I'm very busy—'

'What circumstances? What can provoke you to seek a bride with such unseemly haste? Not even out of mourning! You will give the impression that you had no reverence for your father, that you care nothing for the decencies. You will shame us all!'

His temper slipped away from him for just a few words. 'If anyone brought shame on the family it was my—' He managed to stop himself, but it was too late.

117

She bristled with anger. 'You had better tell me plainly what you mean. No more innuendoes. What is going on?'

So there was no alternative but to tell her how things really stood. As he spoke, quietly and calmly now, the flush of anger drained from her face. She was first disbelieving, and then grew pale. She reached behind her for a chair and sat down.

'Is this really true?' she asked at last. It was a protest rather than a question.

'You didn't know any of it?' Giles asked more gently.

'I knew your father was extravagant, but there was never any suggestion that we could not afford it.' She raised her eyes to him. 'Are we ruined?'

'Not quite,' he said. 'But it's a close-run thing.'

'Why did you not tell me before?'

He hesitated. 'I am in the process of finding out the true extent . . .' He paused and resumed. 'There is the question, among others, of your jointure.'

'All gone?' He assented. 'But what are you saying? That you didn't tell me in case I demanded the money? What must you think of me?'

That shamed him. 'I'm sorry. This is all . . . It has been a shock to me too.'

She stared blankly for a moment, and spoke out of memory. 'There was a crisis some years ago . . . Stainton had to tell me, because the important pictures were sold, and I noticed their absence. But I thought it had been resolved.' Her mouth tightened and she seemed to come to a decision. 'There is a great deal of jewellery, my own and the family's. You must have it – sell it—'

He hardly knew how to interrupt. 'Copies,' he said. He saw the shock hit her. 'The originals are long gone. I'm sorry.'

She made a little gesture of repudiation, and was silent in thought, which appeared not pleasant to her. At last she roused herself. 'Very well. What do you propose to do?'

118

There was no sense in flowery words. 'Marry a rich girl. As soon as possible.'

'I see. Well, you will not be the first. Such marriages can work out as well as any. Have you someone in mind?'

'Aunt Caroline is making a list,' Giles said, wincing slightly at the word. He hurried on, 'Now that you know, I can tell you that in the mean time, we ought to make economies, wherever we can.'

She disagreed. 'That would be fatal. To let the world know we are in difficulties? You would find every debt called in and every tradesman withholding credit.'

'That's what Markham said.'

'Do not undertake any reductions without consulting me.'

He didn't reply to that, and she said, in a milder voice than any she had used to him for years, 'I will *help* you, Ayton. I am your mother.'

He gave a rueful, slightly twisted smile. 'It might help if you could remember not to call me that.'

Her eyes hardened again. 'It is difficult for me to call you Stainton.'

'I know. But I have a name, Mother,' he said.

'You mean – call you Giles?' She considered the proposal with faint surprise. 'Very well,' she said. 'In private, perhaps.' He felt a tentative thread of warmth reaching out to her from him, but her next words made it shrivel. 'It was your father's choice of name. I never cared for it.'

March was mild and damp, as February had been mild and wet. 'We haven't had any proper winter,' Rachel complained, as they drove in the trap along a winding lane from the hamlet of Ashmore Carr. 'No snow at all.'

'I don't like snow,' Alice said.

'But it's so beautiful. It makes everything sparkle.'

'Frost is better. A good, hard frost to kill the pests is what you need.'

'Kill the pests? You're so unromantic.'

Alice was unrepentant. 'Snow means hardship, 'specially if it goes on a long time. The poor people suffer . . . And the animals, the sheep dying in snowdrifts, the birds falling from the branches.'

'Can't I even think about a pretty snow scene without you spoiling it? You didn't mind the snow last winter when you did that painting.'

'Oh, that was— *Look out!*'

A bicyclist had come round the blind bend they had just reached, riding fast. Biscuit, the dun pony, had been daydreaming, trotting along with his eyes half closed. Startled awake and nearly collided with, he flung up his head, snorted and backed. There was a terrible lurch, and the nearside wheel of the trap went down into the drainage ditch that ran alongside the road.

Fortunately he was a sensible pony, and feeling at once that things were awry, he did not try to bolt, but stopped dead, ears back and eyes rolling white. Alice had scrambled down from her side, dropping the last foot into the ditch to the detriment of her boots, and ran to the pony's head. The cyclist had skidded to a halt just past them, and now freed himself from his machine, propped it against the hedge, and hurried back, snatching the cap from his head.

'I'm so sorry! Entirely my fault! The hedges are so high, I didn't see you coming. Are you all right, ladies? Please tell me you're not hurt.'

'Of course we're not hurt,' Alice said stoutly, though Rachel, still in her seat, clutching the front rail, was looking shocked.

The cyclist was a young man, warmly and suitably dressed in a tweed Norfolk and matching knickers, thick lovat-green stockings and good stout shiny boots, the outfit completed by the tweed cap he had doffed, and a lovat-green woollen scarf wound round his neck. He was of slim build, and had a rather thin face with a prominent nose, but he was still attractive, with large blue eyes and curly brown hair, and he spoke like a gentleman.

He had only glanced at Alice: Rachel took all his attention. *He probably thinks I'm just a child*, Alice thought. Her sister, she realised, was looking rather lovely, with a healthy blush to her cheeks, her Scotch bonnet, worn at a rakish angle, revealing her long, soft fawn curls. *Rachel is the pretty one.* She had heard that all her life, and didn't resent it. So far, the world of men and love and so on had seemed distant and unimportant, and she much preferred animals to most humans, especially males. But Rachel was almost of an age to come out, and might be expected any moment to start being 'soppy'. Alice looked at the cyclist critically, then back at Rachel, who, she was alarmed to see, had begun to smile at him in a tremulous fashion.

'I'm – not hurt,' Rachel managed to murmur.

'I'm so glad to hear it,' the young man said warmly.

'You were going much too fast,' Alice said sternly.

He turned his smile on her. 'I know. I'm so sorry. But what a remarkably sensible pony, not to bolt.'

Alice was placated. 'His name's Biscuit, and he's a wise old cove, Josh says – he's our groom – only Biscuit isn't old, really, only nine.'

'What a good name for him,' the young man said.

'*I* chose it,' Alice said proudly.

'Well, ma'am,' said the bicyclist, 'if you could go on holding his head, I'll have a look at what's happened to your trap.'

Alice quite liked being called 'ma'am'. 'I can see what's happened,' she called, as the man disappeared behind it. 'The wheel's gone down the ditch.'

He reappeared, and said, 'I don't think anything's broken. If your friend would be so good as to climb down—'

'My sister,' Alice corrected, and Rachel gave her a minatory look.

'The trap doesn't look very heavy. I think if I lifted the body a bit, the pony could pull it out.'

That sounded like a good scheme to Alice. 'Get down, Ray,' she urged. 'You'll have to get down and lighten the load.'

'Would you permit me to assist you?' the young man said, coming close. Rachel had been scrambling in and out of the trap unassisted for years, but she looked sweetly helpless as she placed hesitant hands on the young man's shoulders. He grasped her firmly at the waist – Alice couldn't see his face from where she was standing, but she knew he looked up at Rachel, and that Rachel blushed – and jumped her neatly down. Rachel was released, and the young man peered into the trap. 'Anything else that's heavy?' he asked, eyeing a large basket.

Alice answered. Rachel was taking care of her blush. 'Oh, that's empty now. We took some things to old Mrs Clay in Ashmore Carr – goosefat and soup and some woollens. She has an influenza, poor thing.'

'All right,' he said. 'We'll give it a try, shall we? When I say "go", lead him forward slowly.'

Alice felt a twinge of conscience. 'I hope your boots won't be spoiled.'

'I'm prepared for it,' he said, muffled by the trap's body. 'A cyclist expects to get muddy. Ready now? One, two, three – go!'

It was probably heavier than he had thought, Alice reflected, for she could hear him grunting, but the ditch was not very deep, and he only had to raise the body enough for the rim of the wheel to clear the edge. Biscuit obeyed her voice and her tug and stepped forward, the nearside wheel found purchase and the trap was free. Alice led the pony on a few steps and safely into the middle of the road, and the young man came scrambling out, brushing his hands together. His boots were no longer shiny.

'All's well, it seems,' he said, approaching Rachel again.

He doesn't see me at all, Alice thought. 'Though if I might presume to advise, it would be as well to have a blacksmith look at the wheel, and make sure there's no damage.'

Rachel, still in high colour, brought out a sentence she had been practising for minutes. 'May we know to whom we are indebted?'

'My name's Lattery – Victor Lattery. I've just come to stay in Canons Ashmore with my aunt, Miss Eddowes. She lives in the stone house at the far end near the church, Weldon House. She's a philanthropist.' He looked for reciprocation, and as Rachel seemed to be tongue-tied again, Alice stepped in.

'I'm Alice Tallant and my sister's Rachel. We live at the Castle. How do you do?'

'How do you do?' he replied. 'The pleasure of the meeting, I suspect, is all mine, but I hope you've taken no real hurt. May I help you up again?'

'We can get up all right,' Alice said, and went round to the near side to scramble up, but Rachel let him take her hand and help her, though it was quite unnecessary. 'I'll drive,' Alice said firmly, gathering the reins.

Lattery was still at the other side, gazing up at Rachel, one hand resting on the trap's side. 'Don't forget to have the wheel checked,' he said earnestly.

'We won't,' Alice said. 'Goodbye.' She clucked to Biscuit and drove briskly away. 'Don't look back!' she whispered urgently to Rachel. But it was too late – she already had. 'What will he think?'

'He did us a kindness,' Rachel said, facing front again. 'It would have been very awkward otherwise.'

'I expect someone else would have come along. And it was his fault in the first place.'

'Oh, Alice. Don't be so hard.'

'He seemed nice, though, didn't he?'

Rachel didn't answer that. 'I wonder how long he'll be

here,' she said instead. 'He said "staying with" his aunt, but that could be just a short visit. What's a philanthropist?'

'Isn't it something to do with stamp collecting?' Alice said vaguely. 'I wonder if Giles knows him, or Richard.'

'Richard would be more likely. Giles has hardly ever been here to make friends. Oh, I wish Richard would come home. I wish the war would be over.'

'Giles is more likely to be interested in stamp collecting than Richard,' Alice observed. 'Do you think we ought to go round by way of the forge? It would be awful if the wheel collapsed on us.'

When they reached the forge, the blacksmith, Eli Rowse, was working on a large, placid Shire horse tethered out front. He looked up and nodded to them as Alice halted, his large hand full of hoof while he pared the horn. The horse was dozing comfortably, ears relaxed and pouched lower lip quivering with its breaths.

'Hullo, Mr Rowse. He's almost asleep,' Alice called with amusement. 'Mind he doesn't go down!'

'Ar, he's a soft 'un, all right,' said Rowse. 'Likes to put all his weight in my hand.' At the sound of voices, his assistant, Axe Brandom, came out of the forge, wiping sweat from his brow with a grubby cloth, blue eyes squinting at them as a stray beam of sunlight broke though the grey cloud bank. 'Something I can do for you, my ladies?' Rowse asked, dropping the hoof and straightening up.

'We had a little accident,' Alice said. 'Wheel went down a ditch. I thought p'r'aps you'd have a look and make sure it's not broken or anything.'

Both smiths came forward. The girls jumped down. 'Nearside,' Alice said, going to Biscuit's head. The carthorse craned round to see what was going on.

'How'd you come to do a thing like that, miss?' Rowse asked.

'Oh, a bicyclist came round the corner too fast and startled poor Biscuit. He helped us out of the ditch afterwards, though.'

Rowse squatted to examine the wheel. Axe, bent over him, raised his head to say, 'Bicyclist?'

'A young man. In tweed knickers. He said his name was Victor Lattery.'

'Oh, ar, I saw him go by earlier on,' Axe said. 'Come to live with his aunty, I did hear tell. Miss Eddowes.'

Alice and Rachel exchanged a glance. *Live with. That sounded permanent.*

Examination over, Rowse eased himself to his feet. 'Bit of a crack here, in the axle arm.'

'Is that bad?' Alice asked, wondering whether they would get into trouble.

'Oughter be fixed,' said Rowse. 'Might go any time, specially if you was to bump over a rock or summat.'

'But we can drive home?'

Rowse shook his head. 'Wouldn't risk it. That road up to the Castle's in a state. Wouldn't want you ladies taking a tumble.' He gave them a small smile, a whiteness in the blackness of his face. 'My reputation'd take a tumble if I was to let you.'

'But how shall we get home, then?' Rachel asked, too anxious to laugh at his joke.

The two men exchanged one of those looks in which questions were asked and answered without words. 'We got a little cart out the back,' said Rowse. 'Axe here'll drive you home.'

The cart was shabby and old, but Axe laid a clean blanket over the seat. 'Don't want to mess up your nice frocks,' he said shyly. He harnessed up an elderly brown pony, attached Biscuit to the back with a rope halter, and invited the girls to get in. Rachel climbed up, and as Alice prepared to follow, a stout little Jack Russell bitch came bustling out and demanded her attention.

'She's sweet!' she exclaimed squatting to scratch behind the ears. 'Is she yours? What's her name?'

'Dolly,' Axe said. 'She's in pup.'

'Oh, how wonderful.'

'Daft old thing,' he said, smiling at the dog. 'Never likes me out of her sight.'

'Oh, then can't she come with us?' Alice pleaded.

''Fyou don't mind. She mid have dirty feet.'

'I'm already muddy from the ditch. My coat can take it.'

So they drove off, with Axe at the reins and Dolly enthroned on Alice's lap, facing forward with an air of intense interest. Axe was too big for the trap, like an adult in a child's pull-cart, and his hands, Alice noted, were enormous – the reins just disappeared in them. But there was something very gentle about him, and he kept a light contact with the pony's mouth, not jerking or pulling as she had often seen men do.

The forge was a place of interest to the girls, particularly to Alice, who had often had long conversations with Mr Rowse while one of the horses was shod. So they knew Axe Brandom by sight – he was one of a large local family, and the elder brother of their own groom Josh – though had never had occasion to talk to him. Alice looked at him sideways now under her lashes, impressed by the size and presence of him. She noted the fine golden hairs over his cheekbones, illuminated by that same stray sunbeam, the nice straightness of his nose, like something architectural, the curve of his lips . . . She shivered suddenly.

He glanced sideways at her. 'All right, miss? Hope you didn't take cold, waiting about?'

'No, not at all,' Alice said, and suddenly wanted to keep him talking. 'Do you know Miss Eddowes?'

'Seen her at church,' he admitted. 'Never spoken to her. Mended her gates once,' he remembered. 'New hinges.'

'Oh, I know – those tall, fancy ones with the bird thing in the middle.'

He nodded. 'Phoenix,' he offered.

'What's that?'

'Bird that rises from its own ashes,' said Axe. A slight blush touched his cheeks. It was not often that he was the purveyor of knowledge – especially to one of the gentry. 'Rector had it in his sermon one time and I asked Mr Arden,' he explained.

Mr Arden was the choirmaster. 'Do you sing in the choir?'

He nodded, still blushing. 'Tenor,' he admitted.

'I'll look for you next Sunday,' Alice said. She had never particularly noticed the choir. So he sang, she thought. Somehow, despite his massive frame – or even because of it – it fitted. She remembered someone, long ago – could it have been their governess? – saying that when birds sang in their innocence, they sang to God. It was a nice thought, Axe Brandom, innocent too in some essential way, singing to the Maker.

But there was the question of the phoenix still to be settled. 'Why would it rise from its own ashes? How did it get to be ashes?' she pursued. She liked to get to the bottom of things. But Axe only shook his head – either didn't know, or didn't want to tell her. Rachel nudged her and frowned, telling her not to converse so freely with strangers, she supposed. But Rachel had asked the cyclist's name, so she was in no position to object.

'Do you live in the village?' Alice asked next. Perhaps she could get him talking about himself.

He shook his head. 'Got a cottage over the other side of the Carr,' he said.

'Is it nice there? I bet you see lots of birds.'

She'd said the right thing. He actually looked at her. 'Any amount,' he said. 'Ducks and moorhens and coots. Woodpeckers, nuthatches, chaffinches. I had a starling last year – fox'd injured its wing. I kept it in my kitchen a month till it healed. Got tame as a Christian, it did, sit on my hand, take food from my fingers.'

'Oh, I wish I'd seen it!' Alice said. 'Have you still got it?'

'Let it go once it could fly. You can't keep wild things – 'taint right. Aaron Cutmore, he had a vixen once – had it from a cub.'

'Who's he?'

'Woodsman.'

What a good name for him, Alice thought. 'Was it a pet?' she asked.

'Tame as anything. Lived in his old dog's kennel at the back door. But it broke its chain one night, bust into the brooder pens and killed two dozen pheasant chicks. Mr Saddler nearly had a fit. Said it'd have to be shot when it come home. But no-one never saw it again.' He shrugged. 'Musta died somewhere out there – couldn't hunt, you see, trailing that old chain.'

'Oh, the poor thing!' Alice cried.

'Can't keep wild things,' Axe said again. ''Specially foxes – they always turn back to the wild.'

'Have you got any animals now? Apart from Dolly?' She caressed the soft ears, and the little bitch sneezed.

'One or two. I got two cats. Hare with a broken paw – he's nearly mended. Two young hedgehogs I took in last year, orphaned. They'll go soon. And a jackdaw. Had him three years.'

'I thought you said you couldn't keep wild things.'

He shook his head, smiling. 'Can't get rid of him. He's not in a cage or nothing, he can come and go as he likes. Seems like he chooses to stay.'

'I bet he does,' Alice said. *I would.* 'What's his name?'

'Captain.'

'Does he talk?'

'*He* thinks he does. Lot a gibberish. Clever, though. He can open boxes and find things.'

'Oh, I *wish* I could see him!' Alice cried.

She was sure Axe was on the verge of inviting her, but at

the last minute he must have thought better of it, because he clucked to the pony instead to hurry it. Rachel pinched her hand, and when she looked round, she was scowling and shaking her head. So the rest of the drive went in silence. They were delivered to the stable-yard at the Castle, explanations were exchanged with Giddins and Josh, Biscuit was untied, the basket swapped for the rope halter, and Axe drove off without a backward look, comically too large for the shabby little trap – except that Alice didn't feel at all like laughing at him.

There were more explanations at dinner. With no company, Lady Stainton allowed the girls to dine down. Unlike Giles, she would never have contemplated a tray, and since Sebastian had gone to his own house for a few days, having her daughters there was preferable to a tête-à-tête with Giles – or, more likely, long silences, because he did not seem to have developed any social small-talk. Thank goodness, she thought, that Easter was approaching, when family members would come and stay to break up the monotony.

The girls had to explain first about the damage to the trap. Giles's first thought was *More expense*. 'How did you come to put it in a ditch?' he demanded crossly.

'Not all of it – only one wheel,' Alice said. 'And it wasn't Ray's fault – Biscuit was startled when the bicyclist came round the bend.'

The rest of the story followed. Lady Stainton paid little attention until it got to the part about Victor Lattery staying in the village with his aunt. 'What's a philanthropist?' Rachel asked.

'Someone who does good works,' Giles answered her.

'Oh, then she must be very respectable,' Alice said, with a glance at Rachel, 'and so must he. He said she's called Miss Eddowes.'

The dowager's face stiffened. 'We don't know her,' she said, in an icy voice.

'He said she lives—' Alice began, but was quelled by a positively glacial look from her mother.

'We *do not* know her.'

There was a brief, awkward silence. The girls exchanged a glance, and seemed on the verge of disastrously pursuing the subject when there was an interruption. The second footman, William, came in with a telegram on a silver tray, which he handed to Moss, who examined it loftily, then stepped in stately mode across the room to Giles.

'A telegram has just come for you, my lord,' he said – *As if*, Alice thought, *we didn't know that!*

Giles read it, and looked up. 'It's from Richard. He's coming home tomorrow. Wants to be picked up at the station – the nine-fifty.'

'Richard! Hooray! Oh, Giles, can we be the ones to fetch him?'

'I don't see why not.'

'Moss, tell Mrs Webster to prepare Mr Richard's room,' said the dowager, neutrally. But even she looked pleased.

'And send word to the stables to have the carriage ready to meet the train,' Giles added. 'I suppose it's compassionate leave,' he added to his mother.

'Not *very* compassionate,' Rachel said, 'all these months later.'

Victor Lattery and Miss Eddowes were forgotten.

Richard Tallant was a little shorter than Giles, a little stockier in build, and was handsomer and more charming. He was 'the spare', the sole reason for his existence being to guarantee the title should Giles die untimely. But he had never minded that. He had inherited not only his father's looks but his lack of introspection, while Giles had more of his mother's reserve. Not having to be serious and steady and take responsibility suited Richard perfectly. He could enjoy life and leave Giles to stand the nonsense. A second son traditionally went into the army, and that suited him too. He loved horses and good company, and the army had not been engaged in any dangerous actions when he first got his commission. He was a little put out when the second South African war broke out, but he anticipated no danger or hardship from being sent overseas. And while he met, in fact, with both, it never dented his sanguine assumption that everything would turn out all right: the world, he believed without thinking about it, was designed specifically to ensure his happiness. On the whole, he had been proved right.

He was pleased to see his little sisters waiting for him on the platform as the train pulled in. Rachel was starting to be very pretty – she would break hearts, he thought – and Alice had grown tall. He climbed down, leaving his servant, Speen, to see to the luggage, and enjoyed their excited greetings and their concerned cooings over the sling on his left arm. 'It's nothing, just a scratch,' he assured them, then winced as Alice hugged him. 'Not that much of a nothing! 'Ware the wing, old thing!'

'Oh, sorry – but it's so lovely to see you!' Alice cried. 'I don't think you've changed a bit.'

'Only you're very brown,' Rachel added.

'It's hot out there in South Africa,' he assured her solemnly. 'I thought you knew.'

They walked to the gate, where Giles was waiting. He, Richard thought, looked older, and even more grim than the last time he'd seen him, as if the earldom wasn't bringing him much jollity.

The brothers shook hands. 'Wounded?' Giles said, scanning Richard's face anxiously.

'Just a nick. Almost healed.'

'So it's sick leave? You'll have to go back?'

'Not me,' Richard grinned. 'My tour's finished, and I've declined to sign on again. I'm out and clear.'

'But . . .' Giles began, wondering how Richard was going

131

to support himself. Or did he believe the estate would do it?

Richard went on quickly, before anything else could be said, 'I calculated that you'd need me here. Must be a lot to do. I'm yours to command, brother of mine. I'm here to help.'

Giles frowned, but this wasn't the place to pursue it. Richard processed to the carriage, with people smiling and greeting him, and many hands to shake – a bit like his own homecoming, Giles thought, except that there was no element of duty in it: these well-wishers simply liked Richard and were glad to see him again. *I wish I could do that*, Giles thought. A young woman held up her baby to Richard, and he kissed its cheek, then kissed hers as well, and made everyone whoop and laugh.

'Mr Richard's handsome, isn't he?' Dory said, as she walked with Rose down the long basement corridor they called Piccadilly, towards the dining-room and the servants' dinner.

'Yes, and good-natured too,' Rose answered.

James, overtaking them with his rapid, jerky walk, said, 'You've already got William following you like a little dog. Isn't that enough?'

'No-one was talking to you,' Rose spat back.

'And I wasn't talking to you. Miss Dory here seems to think every male in the house has got to drool over her.'

'You're just sore because she doesn't fancy you,' Rose said.

He snorted in derision, and, having passed them, turned and walked backwards for a few paces so that he could say to Dory, 'Don't you get mixed up with Mr Richard. He's limed a lot of little birds in his time, and they all ended up dead.'

'What *are* you talking about?' Dory said, but he'd turned and hurried on.

'Pay no attention,' said Rose, and then, curiously, 'Are you really William's sweetie?'

'No. I just feel sorry for him,' Dory said.

Neither noticed the half-open door of the china room as

they passed it, or William just inside about to come out with a tureen in his hands.

Dinner that evening was lively. The girls were chatty as they rarely were in their mother's presence, and Richard regaled them all with stories, some of which might even have been true. It was a pleasant interlude.

Later, when the ladies had gone to bed, Giles and Richard sat together by the fire in the library, with a decanter of brandy and Richard's cigarillos, which he preferred to cigars or cigarettes. Giles, who was not much of a smoker, tried one and quite liked it. The dogs stretched out between Giles's feet and the hearth, groaning occasionally with the double pleasure.

'I see you've got Father's hounds,' Richard remarked. 'Are you fond of dogs? I can't remember.'

'You know I am. I had a spaniel when I was a boy – don't you remember Buffy?'

'Good Lord, yes, now you mention it. He was gun-shy and Papa was going to knock him on the head.'

'I didn't endear myself to Father by pleading for the dog. Soft-heartedness was not a trait he wanted to see in his heir.'

'It all seems so long ago,' Richard said pensively. The firelight, throwing his face into relief, showed up lines that hadn't been there before.

'You *have* changed,' Giles said. 'I thought you were just the same old Richard, the court jester, when you were telling those outrageous stories at dinner—'

'True, every word, I assure you!'

'But underneath you're more serious. You've seen things, I suppose.'

'Too much death,' Richard said, his mouth turning down. 'Nobody dies easily in a war. And too many of them were women and children.'

'It's not finished yet?' Giles asked.

'All but,' Richard said. 'The Boers are licked, though they

133

won't admit it. "Bitter-enders", they call themselves, and they're not wrong. Bitter it certainly will be. But it can't last much longer. They're only hanging on by keeping on the move, keeping out of our way. They're achieving nothing. If you like a wager, put money on a peace treaty by the end of next month.' He gestured with the wounded arm. 'I wasn't entirely sorry about this. Excuse to get out. Not,' he said, rousing himself to smile, 'that it wasn't a good lark most of the time. Galloping about the veld. Chance to broaden one's horizons. Good horses, good fellows.'

He stopped, and smoked reflectively for a while.

The dogs sighed and turned over to toast the other side. Giles said, 'Now you're back, what do you mean to do?'

Richard roused himself. 'I told you – help you.'

'But how will you support yourself? I hope you don't think the estate can support you. Our father left things in a bad way.'

Richard grinned, waving his cigarillo. 'All that will pass away, old boy, when you hook your heiress. Marrying a rich girl for her money – you old dog!'

Giles was angry. 'Who told you that?'

'Keep your hat on! My man Speen got it out of old Crooks that you were looking for a wife with some urgency, and having a fair idea of how my father ran things, I assumed the rest. Your reaction tells me I've hit a nerve. How do you come to have Crooks as your valet, by the by? I wouldn't have thought he was to your taste.'

'I didn't have a man when I came back from Thebes. He was there with nothing to do, and I haven't got time to go looking for a replacement. He does his work well – but if he's going to be gossiping about my private affairs to strangers—'

'Oh, Speen can get anything out of anyone. It's his one talent. Don't fret, old dear. All Crooks said was that you wanted a wife. I told you, I guessed it was the rhino you were after

– what else? You never were a great man for the ladies, were you?' Giles still looked angry, and didn't reply. Richard went on, 'I think it's an excellent idea. I might even try it myself.'

'You don't have a title to exchange for a fortune,' Giles pointed out harshly.

'Ah, but I have so much else to offer,' Richard said lightly. 'Looks, charm – and the entrée into society. I know everyone worth knowing – and, better than that, they like me! You would never take the trouble to please people and, of course, with the earldom to come, you didn't need to. But things might be different now. You could do worse than have me at your shoulder, telling you how to go on.' His grin widened,. 'Better still, I can show you! I'll find a wealthy industrialist who wants to move his daughter up a rung on the social ladder, and promise to get her in everywhere. She'll fall so much in love with me, her pa won't mind that I'm only an honourable.'

'You're serious about this?' Giles asked, frowning.

'Why not? Oh, don't worry, I'll be good to her once we're married. I'm not a monster! She'll be happy, I'll be rich – and if some accident or disease should carry you off before you've managed to get an heir, I shall have the title too. Everyone wins.'

For an instant Giles's mouth hung open with outrage, until he realised his brother was roasting him, and he laughed awkwardly. 'Don't do that!'

'What? Tease you? I know I shouldn't – it's too easy,' Richard said. 'But I'm serious about helping you. People can't help liking me, and some of that will rub off on you. And if there should happen to be *two* heiresses, well, you wouldn't begrudge me the crumbs from under your table, would you? I promise to let you have first pick.'

'You're incorrigible!' Giles exclaimed, still laughing.

'Ah, but you love me all the same,' said Richard, with assurance.

CHAPTER EIGHT

A butler opened the door of the house in Berkeley Street to Nina, and she was admitted into a large hall, with a marble floor, a huge chandelier and a grand staircase. At school, she had not thought much about Kitty being an heiress, but the size and splendour of the house and the butler brought it home to her. She felt suddenly very small, and very young. Still, the butler seemed to have expected her. He said, 'This way, if you please,' and conducted her upstairs.

She had expected to be taken straight to Kitty, but she was shown instead into a small, stiff parlour, and left to wait. She was shivering by the time Lady Bayfield arrived. Kitty's stepmother was tall and thin, beautifully dressed, and wearing *eight* rows of pearls – Nina had time to count them while she was being coldly examined.

'Attend, please, Miss Sanderton,' Lady Bayfield said at last. 'Before you go to your room, I want to make sure you understand the terms on which you are here.' The tone was stern, the eye unfriendly. Nina's stomach felt hollow. 'You will be receiving,' Lady Bayfield resumed, 'a very great advantage from your stay here. You will go to all the parties, balls and other entertainments that Miss Bayfield attends. Few girls of your station in life will ever have such an opportunity. I hope that you are grateful.'

'Yes, ma'am,' Nina said humbly.

'And I hope you will always remember,' Lady Bayfield

went on, 'that you are here for Catherine's benefit. You are to be at her side and at her service. You will support her spirits, encourage her, reassure her. She is Miss Bayfield, and she must always come first. You, Miss Sanderton, are nothing and no-one. You will not put yourself forward, or try to usurp *any* part of her consequence. Do you understand me?'

'Yes, ma'am,' Nina said.

'Very well. Ring the bell, and you will be taken to your room.'

Nina's room was large, and a door led into an adjoining bathroom, which was nothing like the one at home. It was as big as a bedroom, and there was an old, faded Turkish carpet on the floor, and an enormous fireplace with two deep, comfortable armchairs in front of it. On the far side a further door led into Kitty's bedroom. The girls were delighted with the arrangement, which meant they could come and go to each other's room.

'I'm so glad you're here at last,' Kitty cried. 'I've been feeling so nervous.'

'You mustn't be. We'll practise together before every occasion, just like we used to at Miss Thornton's. I say, have you got lots and lots of gorgeous dresses?'

Kitty laughed and nodded. 'Any amount! And Mama's hired a real lady's maid to dress us both and do our hair. She's French, and called Marie. What do you think about that?'

For once, Nina had no words.

'I've made a list of girls for you,' said Aunt Caroline, with a notebook in one hand and a small gold pencil in the other. 'Some big families start coming back after Easter, but the important balls and parties don't start until May, except for the Wansborough House ball at the end of April. That's always the first main event of the Season. It will be a dreadful crush but at least you won't be noticed among the crowds, so you can look at the girls I've picked out for you without being seen to do so.'

'It sounds horribly like a—'

'If you say "cattle market" I shall slap you! Honestly, Giles, I've gone to a great deal of trouble – because, plainly, your mother can't do anything while she's in deep mourning – and I'm not going to have my efforts go to waste because you're stupidly squeamish!'

'Squeamish?' he protested.

'How on earth do you think girls find suitable husbands? Everybody understands the rules. Now, let's have no more of your silliness.' She put her little notebook on the table in front of her. 'I've made a list of ten, but I think you had better concentrate on the first five to begin with, because I'm not sure . . .' she gave him a doubtful look over the top of her glasses . . . 'that you'll be able to keep more than five in your head at once.'

'I can remember the Roman emperors and their dates, in order, down as far as Caracalla and Geta,' he pointed out mildly.

'That's because you *want* to,' Aunt Caroline said. 'Now, there are two useful American girls coming out this Season: Nancy Brevoorte's father is in hotels and railways – rail*roads* I think they call them – and very rich indeed, though I suspect he may want something higher than an earl. I believe Rockport is looking around for a wife, so you'd be in competition with a duke's son. Then there's Cora Van Dycke – the family makes some kind of patent foods, I believe. American girls are so lively.' She looked at Giles with some doubt. 'You will have to exert yourself, dear, to engage their interest. They will like to be amused. And they're much less *dutiful* than English girls. Their fathers indulge them to a degree we would think foolish.'

'Be lively,' Giles repeated, like a dull student. 'Engage them with witty epigrams and light chatter.'

Lady Manningtree frowned. 'Are you being *satirical* with me, Giles?'

'I'm sorry, Aunt,' he said,

'Now, among the English girls there is Honoria Everingham – she's Lord Rayleigh's daughter. She came out last Season but didn't *take*. She'd probably suit you better than an American, being rather dull and quiet. Plain, too, but that's nothing to the purpose. But I'm not absolutely *sure* about the fortune. Rayleigh is playing his cards very close to his chest. That may just be a ploy to excite more interest – I shall make more enquiries, but of course it's a delicate matter.'

'Of course,' Giles said.

'But he wants her off his hands because he has another in the schoolroom, so if you did make an offer, you'd be well received. Then there's Toria Scott-Mackenzie – landed people, very big estate in Perthshire. They have their own grouse moor so you'd never want for shooting. Salmon and trout fishing too, I believe, in the River Tay.'

Giles, who had never cared for either shooting or fishing, smiled gamely.

'And I've put down Catherine Bayfield,' Aunt Caroline went on. 'Nice old family, father's a wealthy baronet, mother was a jam heiress, very large fortune. She's the only child so she'll come in for everything. I haven't seen the girl yet – she's just out of school and they're working her in quietly. I suppose I should mention Sofie Uffenheim-Bartstein – they're acquainted with your aunt Vicky, dripping with money, but I think they might be looking for a royal. There's Russian imperial blood a couple of generations back. Otherwise I'd have put her at the top of the list. Girls from those German principalities, even the minor ones, know what's expected of them. So there it is. What do you think?'

'I don't know any of them,' Giles said blankly.

'Of course you don't,' said Aunt Caroline crossly. 'Apart from Rayleigh's girl, they're all debutantes. *Nobody* knows them. For Heaven's sake, Giles, what do you want? Should I have had their portraits painted for you to inspect?'

He smiled apologetically. 'That didn't work out very well for Henry the Eighth, did it?'

'Didn't it?'

'He picked Anne of Cleves but the portrait turned out to be over-flattering. He couldn't bring himself to consummate.'

She removed her glasses sternly. 'He was a horrible fat old man, as I recall, and didn't deserve a wife at all.'

'Quite. She didn't like him, either.'

'But you are very pretty, my dear, and when you exert yourself you can be charming. Just do as I tell you, and you'll do finely. We'll set you up with a nice girl with a good dowry. You do pay for dressing, I will say – and Crooks knows what's what. It was very sensible of you to take him on.'

'I hadn't the heart to turn him off,' Giles admitted.

She smiled and patted his hand. 'You're a good boy. I never understood why your father had such a down on you. Richard was his golden child, and Richard was never anything but trouble.'

Richard stood in a fitting-room at Henry Poole's, cigarillo clenched in his teeth, while Batty did the thing with the chalk, marking the set of the jacket. Richard turned a little this way and that to examine himself in the long mirror. He patted his stomach.

'Not too bad, eh, Batty?'

'Very trim, sir,' said Batty. 'If I might say so, you cavalry gentlemen always have a very pleasing, upright carriage. Marks you out from the crowd.'

'Ah, yes, that's what I want – to stand out. In an appropriate way.'

'You'll do that, sir. His lordship is a fine figure of a gentleman, too. Rather on the thin side, but not what you'd

140

call weedy. Excellent shoulders and legs. It's a pleasure to make for him. Very happy, we all are, to see you both back from Abroad, safe and sound. Not but what the sad circumstances . . .'

'Quite, quite.' Richard did not want to get on to the subject of his father, in case that led to the subject of the very large tailor's bill his father had left behind. Poor old Giles had been greatly exercised over acquiring more clothes from Poole's in the circumstances, but Richard had endorsed Markham's rationale, that the best way to prevent Poole's from asking for settlement was to order more things. 'It's not as if you mean to bilk them,' Richard had pointed out. 'You'll pay up whenever you get the money. Though if you'll take my advice, you won't clear the whole account. Leave a little bit on the books to keep them interested.'

Now he said, to distract Batty, 'Thinking of getting married, you know.'

'Indeed, sir? Who is the lucky lady?'

'I haven't decided yet. But I'm told there's a fine crop of debutantes coming on the market this year. Everyone says it'll be a brilliant Season.'

'Yes, indeed, sir. Our new king will have quite an enlivening effect on the festivities.'

'You make for him, don't you?'

'His Majesty has been a valued client of the company for many years,' Batty affirmed, 'though of course Mr Cundey attends to him personally. But I have been privileged to work on royal garments from time to time.'

'And now we have the coronation to look forward to,' Richard mentioned. It had been fixed for the 26th of June.

'Yes, sir. His majesty will no doubt ensure it is very sumptuous, in every way. The lapel, sir – are you satisfied with it?'

'If you're satisfied, I'm satisfied,' said Richard, happy

that he had turned Batty's thoughts far from the late earl's account. 'Are the sleeves a trifle long, should you say?'

Stepping out onto Savile Row a while later, he stopped to light a fresh cigarillo. It was a pleasant day, dry, with fast-scudding clouds and gleams of sunshine. He consulted his pocket-watch, and decided to stroll back to Aunt Caroline's. He had no luncheon engagement, and though no-one would be at home, there was always grub available.

When he turned into Berkeley Square, he did not pay attention to the two female figures standing on the pavement outside his aunt's house, apparently engaged in some discussion. But as he reached the steps, they looked at him, and his hand rose automatically to his hat.

The gesture seemed to reassure the elder of the two, for she smiled a troubled, hesitant smile, and said, 'I beg your pardon, sir—'

He stopped, thinking she was going to ask for directions. She seemed to be a woman in her forties, extremely good-looking still, and dressed neatly, though not in the first style. The other was a young woman of perhaps eighteen or nineteen, and she was quite unusually beautiful, with golden hair and blue eyes and soft lips that he would wager had never yet been kissed. He glanced at her appreciatively.

'May I speak to you for a moment?' the elder woman said.

It wasn't the first time he had been accosted in the street by a strange female. However, their clothes and manner were not those of a lady of the night and her keeper, though now he looked more closely, there was something a little worn about them, as though they had fallen on hard times. He was intrigued, but wary.

'I believe I have not had the pleasure . . . ?' he said cautiously.

The woman coloured slightly. 'We have not been introduced, but I believe I know who you are. Are you not Lord

Stainton's son? You have very much the look of him, and I understand he is staying in this house at the moment.'

'You knew my father?'

She looked more than ever troubled, and her confusion reassured him: this was not the bold approach of someone out to diddle him. 'I— Yes. You – are you Lord Stainton?' she managed.

'I'm his brother,' he said. 'Richard Tallant. Is there something I can do for you?'

'I am Mrs Sands, and this is my daughter, Chloë. It – it is not to be supposed that you ever heard of us, but I did know your father. Oh, this is very difficult! A matter of great delicacy.'

He began to have a horrid suspicion. 'Then you had better come in.'

'It was your brother I really wanted to speak to.'

'He's out. Everyone's out,' Richard said. 'Perhaps you can tell me what it is you want. I'm very discreet, I promise you. And there'll be no-one else around to embarrass you.'

'You are very kind. Yes, I am embarrassed,' she admitted. 'But I think a mistake has been made, and I am forced to see if I can rectify – that is, I can no longer . . . If I could explain . . .'

Richard held up his hand. 'Inside,' he said. 'Not here.'

The butler was evidently putting his feet up somewhere, for it was a footman who came into the hall, and looked surprised at the incursion – a surprise that only increased when Richard said, 'I am taking my guests up to the drawing-room. I'll ring if I want anything.'

In the drawing-room, he apologised for the lack of a fire and bade them sit. He said, 'Please won't you tell me plainly what it is you want? I am much more approachable than my brother. How did you know my father?' Mrs Sands seemed even more wretched, studying the carpet. He added gently, 'Or can I guess?'

143

She looked up and sighed. 'I suppose you can. I am a very private person, Mr Tallant. I lived in the shadows and was content to do so. I would never, never have approached any member of the family, I swear to you, if it hadn't been that I am sure there must have been a mistake. He would never have left me in such difficulties.'

'You were my father's mistress,' Richard said.

She straightened her back. 'I was,' she said, with a touch of defiance. 'I am sorry if it shocks you—'

'It doesn't shock me. I know what my father was. And it's the sort of thing that happens all the time. I would have been more surprised if my father *didn't* have mistresses.'

She seemed not to like that. There was a touch of reproach in her voice as she said, 'Ours was a loving relationship, Mr Tallant. After such a long time, we had passed into calmer waters. We were almost like an old married couple.' She seemed to realise that was not tactful. 'I'm sorry, I shouldn't be talking like this to you.'

Richard raised a hand. 'Don't apologise. You can be frank with me – I shan't be offended. My father and I weren't close, and I've been abroad for many years. You must feel his death more than me.'

'I loved him, and I believe he loved me. And now . . .' She gathered herself. 'I am a widow, Mr Tallant, but I was an independent person. I am a piano teacher, and was able to keep myself and my daughter on what I earned. Your father helped, from time to time, with gifts. Most importantly, he provided us with a house – small, neat and modest – where we could live respectably and where I could take my pupils. One of whom is my daughter – she has extraordinary talent, sir, and will be a great performer. But our quiet life came to an end when I read in the obituaries column of your father's sudden death. And then, without warning, they came to tell us we must leave our house, that it had been sold from under us with no means of appeal.'

'Ah,' said Richard. 'I understand.' He had gathered from conversations that Giles had undertaken economies, including selling his father's London properties. It was possible he had not realised the house was occupied. More likely he had not even thought about it.

'Do you?' she asked, with a touch of bitterness. 'We were made homeless, Mr Tallant. We now live in a single room, all I could afford – one bed, one washstand, sharing a common privy. It is hard to keep oneself decent in such a place. There is no piano, so I cannot teach. My small savings are gone. I am reduced to doing such menial work as I can find.'

He leaned forward, not unsympathetic. 'What is it that you want?'

'Justice!' she said, in a voice that quivered with intensity.

He sat back again, thinking. The common cant would say that this woman deserved her fate: she was a sinner. But he had been a sinner too, and had never expected any consequences from it. He thought of his suits, making at Henry Poole's, his shirts at Turnbull's, his shoes, his cigarillos – all on credit. The estate would pay, when Giles secured his heiress. He would never be homeless or destitute: there was always the estate to fall back on. He was attached to the civilised world by a strong cord that allowed him to bob freely in the wind but never be blown quite away. In a piercing moment of clarity he understood what it meant to this woman to have to share a privy with strangers. He only wondered what 'menial work' meant.

Automatically he reached for his pocket book. 'I haven't much about me,' he said.

She recoiled. 'I did not come here to beg,' she said woodenly.

'I know. But a little something to tide you over . . .' He held out a bank note, discreetly folded. 'All that I have comes from the estate. Look on it as a gift from my father.'

145

She took it, after a hesitation. 'You are very kind,' she murmured unhappily. The next words seemed to burst out of her. 'It is the house, you see! Without a decent place to live, without a piano, I cannot work, I cannot support myself. And my daughter cannot practise. Her ability – her wonderful gift – will wither! We need a place to live. It needn't be much, but it must be respectable enough for my pupils to come to. Oh, you do *see*, don't you? He would never have left me in such difficulties! He promised I would always be taken care of. I am no mendicant. I ask only for – for my independence.' The last three words were spoken on a downwards cadence, as though she had realised the contradiction of what she was asking. 'I'm sorry,' she said. 'I should not have troubled you. I'll go now.'

He stood as she did, and with a gesture stopped her. 'I am sorry for you, truly,' he said. 'But I'd advise you not to approach my brother directly. He is not – shall I say? – as *understanding* as me of the ways of the world. And he has a great many worries at present. His patience is limited. His first reaction, were you to speak to him, might be harsh.'

She said nothing. Her daughter sighed, and looked down at her folded hands. He felt uncomfortably like an executioner. At last she said, in a dead voice, 'Thank you for your kindness,' and was turning away.

The words seemed to jump out of him without his volition. 'I will speak to him for you.' A questioning look. 'I can choose the right moment, put it to him in the right words. There *has* been an injustice – he will see that. I will – I will do all I can.' He couldn't promise more. 'Give me your direction.'

She gave it, and then, to save them any more embarrassment, he saw them out himself. The butler, roused presumably by the puzzled footman, arrived just as he closed the door on them, and stared at him with reproach. Richard raised an eyebrow, daring him to speak. Wisely, the man remained silent, and Richard said, 'Send me up a light luncheon, Forbes. And the newspapers.'

'They are already in the morning-room, sir.'

'Then I'll have luncheon there.'

He went away, up the stairs, thinking about the situation, suppressing an unruly impulse to laugh. Oh, good Lord, to think of his father's middle-aged mistress coming to Aunt Caroline's house to confront Giles! It was as comical as it was tragic. But, then, most good comedy had its feet in cold water. The girl was a stunner. It would be a shocking waste if she was to dwindle in a slum and perhaps come to a bad end. (The idea of her being a concert pianist he dismissed unpursued, not being himself of a musical bent.) As to whether Giles would relent – he could not guess. There *were* pensioners of the estate – former employees who were taken care of when they could no longer work. Aged nannies and valets, those who had been close personal attendants, were often treated quite generously. And, though he had no personal experience in the area, he supposed men of substance took care of their discarded mistresses in some way. Did they leave them money in their wills? He didn't know. That might cause a scandal, surely. But he felt confident it did not usually fall to the son to pay for his father's doxies. Oh dear, oh dear! He chuckled. It had been a good fiver's worth of entertainment, that was a fact!

'What was Adam Grisedale talking to you about?' Kitty asked, as she and Nina lay in bed together, analysing the evening they had just spent. It was her favourite part of the day.

'We were talking about our pets. He was telling me about a parrot he had when he was a boy, so I told him about a monkey I had when I was little.'

'You had a monkey?'

'Not for very long. It got sick and died – and it did have very dirty habits. The servants were always grumbling.'

Kitty sighed. 'I was never allowed to have a pet. Mama didn't like animals in the house.'

'Oh, poor Kitty! But just think, when you're married, you can have all the pets you like. What would you choose?'

Kitty pondered. 'A dog, perhaps. But I wouldn't mind, really – just as long as it loved me.' Nina didn't reply, and she went on, in a small voice, 'You think I'm silly to want so much to be loved.'

Nina roused herself. 'Not at all. It's what everybody wants.'

'*You* don't. You're so strong, you can face the world on your own.'

'If I have to, I suppose. Doesn't mean I want to. And you're getting better. I'm sure you're more confident. And you're enjoying it all more than you expected, aren't you?'

So far there had been lunches and teas, visits to theatres and exhibitions, and evening parties, but no formal dinners or balls. Lady Bayfield was acclimatising her stepdaughter by degrees.

'Yes,' said Kitty. 'I like the five-o'-clock teas especially. And when we play games. I never had anyone to play games with at home.'

'In India when I was little, we used to play carrom. Everyone plays it out there. We had a beautiful lacquered board, and carrom men made of polished ivory. I wonder what happened to it.'

'Who did you play with?

'Mama and Papa.'

'It must have been lovely to have the sort of parents who play with you,' Kitty said.

'It was,' said Nina. *Only then it's worse when they die*, she thought. 'But my parents weren't grand like yours.'

'When *I* have children, I shall never be too grand to play with them.'

148

'Do you like any of the men we've met so far?' Nina asked. She felt Kitty shrink.

'They seem so rough and loud,' Kitty said, after a pause. 'And – big. When a great tall man looms over me, I feel as though I should be crushed.'

'I saw you talking to Jock Galbraith,' Nina said. 'You seemed to like him.'

'Yes, he's nice,' Kitty admitted.

Jock Galbraith had a stammer, and Nina knew many girls hadn't the patience to listen to him. But Kitty would always rather listen than talk. 'And what about Lord Hornsea? I thought he seemed interested in you. He's very handsome.'

'He's . . .' Kitty didn't know how to phrase it. Vernon Hornsea *was* handsome, but he knew it too well. When he spoke to Kitty, there was a demand behind every word. She felt pinned by it, like a butterfly to a card. 'There's just too much of him,' she said at last.

Nina laughed. 'You can be so droll, Kitty! If you could only be like that with other people!'

'But I never shall be.'

'Then we'll just have to find someone who understands that, and brings out the best in you.'

'I'm sure men aren't like that,' said Kitty.

'I'm sure some of them must be,' said Nina.

149

CHAPTER NINE

The Cordwells had come to the Castle for Easter, and Linda and the children had stayed on afterwards to be company for her mother. And since Linda's economies included not having a governess for her children, she frequently called on the girls to look after Arabella and Arthur.

'I don't mind it some of the time,' Alice said, as they escaped down the stairs one April morning, 'but not every day.'

'Poor little things,' said soft-hearted Rachel. 'Nobody wants them. They're rather sweet.'

'They're rather dull. Daisy can have them – she doesn't mind.'

'Daisy has her own work.'

'Well, I don't see why Linda shouldn't look after them herself. She's nothing else to do.'

'Comforting Mama?' Rachel suggested.

'Mama doesn't want comforting. She hates having anyone hovering about her. Like a bluebottle, I heard her say to Linda yesterday. Anyway, we're out of it for now. Let's go and watch the smith.'

Every six weeks, the smith, Eli Rowse, came up to the Castle to do routine removes. Alice and Rachel had seen plenty of horses shod before, so it was no novelty, but their lives were so lacking in amusements, it was something to do. Alice brightened when she saw that it was Axe Brandom who had come, and not his master.

'Now, Lady Rachel,' Josh said, as they headed towards the forge, 'I told you you couldn't have your horses this morning. Smith's here.'

'Where's Mr Rowse?' Alice asked.

'Got a kick on the wrist from a horse yesterday,' Josh said. '"Taint broken, but he can't do much one-handed. Yours'll be done this morning, and you can ride this afternoon if you like.'

'We know,' said Rachel.

'We just came to watch,' said Alice.

'Well, don't you go getting in the way. Stand over that side, and don't be asking a lot of foolish questions.'

'My questions are never foolish,' Alice said, with dignity.

Axe had removed the shoe from the off-fore of one of the grey carriage horses and, with the hoof comfortably nestled on his leather lap, was paring and shaping the overgrown horn. He looked up as the girls approached, and blushed slightly under Alice's ready smile. The mare nuzzled reflectively at his fair hair, wondering if it was good to eat.

'Hello,' Alice said. He nodded shyly in response. She glanced around. 'No Dolly today?'

'Back at the forge,' he said. 'She's getting too big to walk far.'

'You must miss her.'

'Ah,' he assented. He picked up the shoe and laid it on the hoof to assess, then put it aside and picked up the rasp. After a bit he said, 'She's getting near her time.' He tried the shoe again, was satisfied, and started to nail it on. The mare lowered startlingly white eyelashes over her dark eyes and dozed. So much trust, Alice thought. He had that effect on animals.

'How is the hare?' Rachel asked.

'Died,' he said.

'Oh dear! How sad!' Rachel's eyes filled with tears.

Axe glanced at her with alarm. ''Twas the shock, I expect. They can't take much handling, hares.'

'But I expect it knew you were helping it,' Alice said, for her sister's sake. Rachel turned away and blew her nose. Alice almost didn't dare ask, but after a pause she said, 'And your hedge-hoglets?'

'Gone,' he said. 'Back in the woods. Once they started eating proper – beetles and such – I could let 'em go.' He finished with the hoof, and turned his attention to the off-hind, drawing it up to rest in his lap, and pincering out the nails. This put him in the perfect position for the mare to lash him across the face with her tail.

'Shall I hold it for you?' Alice said, stepping closer.

He met her eyes properly for the first time, and now *she* blushed a little. 'Kind of you, m'lady,' he said. 'You don't want to get your hands dirty, though.'

'I can always wash them,' said Alice, sensibly. Holding the tail meant she was standing very close to him. She could smell his sweat, and the leather of his apron, and a tangy whiff of the forge fire, which reminded her of railway stations. Rachel had wandered off to talk to one of the stable cats, so she had Axe to herself. It felt very cosy – and also a little bit thrilling.

For a while she watched him working in silence, but she wanted conversation. She asked something she had been vaguely wondering for a long time. 'Why are you called Axe?'

He seemed to consider, but she guessed he was just assembling his words. Probably, she thought, with a sense of discovery, he didn't usually talk much to anyone – living alone, and working in the forge. He didn't seem to mind her presence, or her questions. She sensed no reluctance from him.

'My ma,' he said at last, 'she favoured Bible names for us childer. She called my eldest brother Seth. Then there was my sisters, Ruth and Esther, and my brother Job. When

152

I come along, she was a bit poorly, not in a way to think about names. So she told my dad to pick something. Well, Dad, 'twasn't a job he relished. Got in a bit of a state about it.' He paused while he contemplated the fit of the shoe.

'Go on,' she encouraged him.

He glanced up at her briefly, then down. She could have sworn he was smiling. 'He couldn't read, couldn't Dad, so it was only what he heard, like. And the 'pistle the Sunday previous'd been from Axe of the Apostles.'

'Oh, my goodness!' She laughed.

'He thought "Axe" was a good name – sounded kind of strong.'

'Like a mighty warrior?' Alice said.

'Like that,' he acknowledged. 'Time he found out the mistake, everyone'd got used to it. So I always bin "Axe", ever since.'

'I think it's a fine name,' Alice said. 'It suits you.'

'Don't know about that,' he mumbled shyly. When the hoof was finished, he let it to the ground and straightened up. 'That's her done,' he said, patting the shiny rump. 'Thank you for the tail.' He stood looking down at her, as if prepared for more conversation.

She racked her brain for a subject, and remembered the jackdaw. 'How's Captain?'

'Just the same.'

'Still talking nonsense?'

He nodded, then said, 'Learned a new trick.'

'What's that?'

'He fetches me a teaspoon to stir my tea. I say, "Spoon!" and he flies over to the dresser, and brings me one back. I leave the drawer open a bit,' he admitted.

'Oh, how clever! I'd love to see that!' Alice cried.

'Call by my cottage some time, when you're passing, an' he'll show off for you. He likes company. He's got a few little tricks I taught him.'

They were interrupted by Josh, who came over to say, 'Now, Lady Alice, you'll get all mucky standing there. And you're in the way. Let the smith get on with his work, and don't keep him chatting. He's not paid to talk.'

Axe was his own brother, but he gave him a disapproving look. Alice didn't want to get Axe into trouble, so she gave him a warm farewell smile and backed away. Josh had been their groom since her first pony, so he had a lot of authority, and they were accustomed to obeying him. But he was very different from his brother, she reflected, as she went to join Rachel. He talked a lot more than Axe, but there was no warmth in his words. He looked after her and Rachel and she trusted him completely, but she never got the feeling that he actually *liked* them.

Improving weather, and the April breezes drying the tracks, made walking down to the village an acceptable outing on one's afternoon off. Dory was walking along Canons Ashmore high street, idly looking in the shops, when suddenly James appeared at her side.

'So,' he said, slowing his stride to hers, but staring straight ahead, not at her, 'new maid joined us.'

Now that her ladyship was back in residence, Mrs Webster had made her plea for May, the housemaid who had 'gone to a better place' to be replaced; and Lady Stainton had said, 'You had better recruit an additional maid while you're at it. I'm sure there is a great deal of spring cleaning left to do.'

Rose had told Dory (they were fast becoming friends) that Mrs Webster had almost fallen over in surprise. 'She's wondering what else she can ask for while her ladyship's in the mood.'

The new maids were Tilda, a stocky, gingery girl with strong red hands and not much to say for herself, and Milly. Milly was extremely pale, and with thin, limp hair so fair it was almost transparent. She had a long, pointed nose, and the rims of her nostrils were always a little pink, as though she had been crying, or had a cold. Dory and Rose had agreed together that she looked like a white mouse, but she seemed a pleasant enough girl.

'What about it?' Dory answered James, though she guessed where he was going.

'William's stuck on that Milly – mad about her. You didn't last long, did you?' he jeered. 'Coupla months, that's all. She stole him from right under your nose.'

'He'd already gone off me,' Dory said indifferently.

'Gah! All heartbroken, aren't you, losing your sweetheart?'

'Don't talk so daft,' she said briskly. 'I was only being nice to him.'

'So why aren't you ever nice to me?' he asked, looking down at her insinuatingly.

'Because you're not a nice person.' The words seemed to shock him, and for an instant she was sorry she had spoken them.

'I'm nice,' he protested. Then he thought for a moment. 'I *could* be – if people were nice to me.'

'You see,' she said patiently, 'it doesn't work like that. It's not a trade. Not everything's got a price-tag on it.'

James, who thought exactly the opposite, considered. It was a ruse he had never considered before – tricking people by being nice to them. Was there a return to be had? What were the odds? Would it be too much of an effort, being friendly?

They had reached the haberdasher's. 'I'm going in here for some wool and silks,' she said. 'Goodbye.'

He made a decision. Right next door was the Three Corners café. 'Come and have a cup of tea,' he said. 'My treat.' She looked at him doubtfully, refusal on her lips, and he added, managing a slightly pathetic note, 'Go on! I'm trying to be nice. You got to give me a chance.'

155

In fairness, she thought, *I suppose I have to.* 'Oh, all right, then.'

He bought a pot of tea, and two slices of cake as well, and it was actually quite an enjoyable encounter. James had been at the Castle a long time so he knew a lot about its history and the family. He tried to quiz her on her previous jobs and childhood but she didn't care to have her private life probed, and managed to deflect him with questions of her own – he was a born talker. After tea, he even came into the haberdasher's with her, and bought himself a pair of fancy garters.

When they came out onto the street again, she wondered how to get rid of him – she didn't want to walk all the way back with him. But his attention was elsewhere.

'Isn't that Rose?' he said. He recognised her back view even in an overcoat. He'd watched her from behind for years, because he liked the effect of a large apron bow on a neat female backside.

Dory was about to say it couldn't be, because Rose had told her she was going to soak her feet, then lie on her bed all afternoon to rest them. But it was her. Before she could say anything, James said, 'See you back home,' and stalked away, following Rose's diminishing figure.

Dory shrugged. 'Thanks for the tea,' she called – which was only good manners. But James gave no sign of hearing her.

According to Lady Manningtree, the Wansborough House ball at the end of April was even more of a crush than usual. Giles knew only that there could be no inspecting girls from a discreet distance. All his aunt could do was to point out some of the patronesses as they passed – bedecked with jewels and clad in magnificent colours, they were easily distinguished from the pastel-clad debutantes.

As they eased their way through the crowds, Aunt Caroline

paused to talk to an acquaintance, and Giles was carried onward. When he looked round again he could no longer see her. He did not make any effort to find her. The main thing now was to seek a pocket of relative space so that he could breathe. This whole business was exhausting to a man used to solitude.

He pushed his way slowly around the perimeter of the ballroom and took in the scene. The lights, the colours, the movement, the music were a saturation to the senses. At times, nothing could be seen of the dancers but the feathers in the females' headdresses, twitching with their movements. Occasionally the wall of people watching would disgorge a couple, like otters popping up for air. The flutter of fans everywhere was like a distraction of pigeons.

When he had worked his way to the short end of the room, he found a little more space. There was a young woman standing on her own – he noticed, because it was an odd circumstance, when debutantes were closely chaperoned at all times. She was wearing a simple gown of a pale apricot colour, and a single strand of pearls, and he immediately liked the look of her, because she had an air of detachment. Her expression of faint amusement was not what you expected of debutantes. Those he had met so far were never at ease: they seemed either nervously too shy, or nervously too forthcoming.

Then he realised that he recognised her: Aunt Caroline had already pointed out to him Lady Bayfield, mother of one of her candidates, and this girl had been standing beside her. Therefore, he assumed, she must be the daughter who was being brought out. He couldn't remember her name, but remembered that Aunt had said she was a considerable heiress. The thought cheered him. He had been supposing all along that marrying was going to be nothing but a grim duty – certainly on his side, and quite likely on both – but she had the air of someone he could like.

157

She became aware of him staring and turned enquiringly. He was embarrassed. He couldn't now pretend he *hadn't* been looking. He would have to say something.

'Not dancing?' he said. He groaned at the inept question. But she smiled pleasantly and said, 'I have been. Now I'm watching for my friend – she's out there somewhere, but I can't see her at the moment.'

'It's a dreadful crush, isn't it?' he said. He only said it because Aunt Caroline had said it, and he couldn't think of what else to say. He hadn't much experience of talking to girls he was expected to marry.

'Do you think so?' she said. 'Well, it *is* a crush, which makes it difficult to get about, but I wouldn't call it dreadful.'

'What would you call it, then?'

'A kaleidoscope, perhaps. It's so pretty, all the different colours of the dresses whirling about and changing places. Or – what's that kind of picture called, that's made of little fragments of colour?'

It was very odd, to be talking to a strange girl in anything other than commonplaces. To have his banal question taken seriously, and answered as if he had meant anything by it. Of course, he had very little experience of young women, but from things he had heard – not least from Richard – this was not the way they usually were. But now he had to answer her seriously, as she had answered him. He thought for a moment. 'Pointillism?' he hazarded.

'Oh, you mean like Seurat? No, not that.' She thought, and then the frown cleared. 'A mosaic, that's what I meant! But a magic mosaic that keeps changing pictures.'

He smiled. There was definitely something *about* Miss Bayfield. 'Have you ever seen one?'

'A mosaic? Only in books,' she said. 'Have you?'

'Yes, lots. There are some particularly fine ones from Pompeii and Herculaneum. And the Knossos of Crete: dolphins and bull-leapers – beautiful!'

'You've been to those places? How lucky you are!'

'I suppose I am,' he said. 'Have you never been abroad?'

'Not since I came to England. I was born in India, and lived there until I was nearly ten.'

His aunt hadn't told him that. It might explain her differentness. 'I've never been to India. What's it like?'

'I don't remember a *great* deal,' she said regretfully. 'I remember the rain – oh, so much rain! The sound of it, drumming on the roof, everything green and wet and dripping. Rain was noisy, but when it was hot, it was silent – no sound except the cicadas, and the fan swishing back and forth on the verandah.'

'Yes, I know that silence,' he said. *The silence of heat* – she had brought it back to him.

'When I first arrived in England I was frightened of all the heavy boots that made such a noise indoors. I thought I should be trampled. In India the servants had bare feet. Just a soft padding sound.'

He smiled. 'In Egypt it's the scuffing of heel-less slippers.'

'You've been to Egypt too?'

'Yes. And Italy and Greece. But never India. Tell me more about it.' He wanted to listen to her, not talk. He was charmed by her confidence, which had nothing brash about it. She simply seemed to like to talk, as though it were a natural thing to do. It did not occur to him that he was doing a wrong thing, conversing with a girl to whom he hadn't been formally introduced, and without the presence of her chaperone.

'Goodness, where to begin!' she said. 'There were the horses. I loved the horses. Polo ponies are so gentle and intelligent.'

'Do you ride?'

'I was put into a basket saddle when I was two and led about by the syce. Dear Namgay! He was from Bhutan, where they're practically born on horseback. Bhutan horses

159

are small, but they're very strong and intelligent, and they make wonderful companions. I suppose they must have lovely horses in Egypt, too? All those Arabians!'

The music had come to an end and the crowd on the floor was breaking up. 'Would you like to dance?' he asked abruptly.

For the first time she seemed uncertain. 'Oh dear, I would like to, but I think you have to ask Lady Bayfield first.'

'Yes, of course,' he said. 'I'm sorry – we haven't been introduced—'

She smiled, a swift, ravishing smile, and said, 'I know, I shouldn't have spoken to you at all! But I won't tell if you don't. And I *must* go and find my friend right this minute – I'm sworn to take care of her, you see.'

He bowed and let her go, secure of finding her again. He turned, and pushed through the crowds the other way until he met Aunt Caroline, who was evidently looking for him.

'Oh, there you are! This crush is intolerable. You'll have no chance of inspecting anyone this evening.'

'But I've met one of them. Lady Bayfield's daughter – and I liked her.'

'Oh, Giles, I'm so glad! The family is unexceptionable, and the fortune is very good. And I'd *really* prefer you to marry someone you like, if possible.'

'I only exchanged a few sentences with her, but she seemed agreeable. And pretty.'

'Oh, yes, she's considered very pretty. And, thanks to her mother, very well dressed. Lady Bayfield has excellent taste. But if you liked her, you should dance with her and get her to like you. Make your move early. Because I think there may be a lot of interest in her. She's quite an heiress. Just a shame she can't inherit the title.'

'I don't need another title,' Giles said.

'I know, but it's an old one, and it's a shame when they fall into abeyance.' The music had started up again. She tapped his arm with her fan. 'Well, what are we waiting for? Let's go and find Lady B and you can ask for a dance. For all you know, the wolves may be circling already.'

Lady Bayfield was pleased when she saw Lord Stainton approaching. She had done her research, too, and knew it was a respectably old title, that the family's connections were more than good, that there was a fine old castle with considerable land. She also knew that the earl was looking for a wealthy bride and, on the whole, that was a good thing. A man looking for a dowry would be more likely to overlook Catherine's shyness.

'Lady Bayfield, might I introduce my nephew to you?' Lady Mannngtree said. 'Giles Tallant, Earl of Stainton.'

'I'm honoured to make your acquaintance,' Giles said, and bowed.

'Lord Stainton,' she said. He had a good voice, warm and rich, she decided. And she was woman enough to be affected by his good looks and charming smile. She wanted grandchildren for her husband's sake; she wanted pretty ones for her own. So she gave him half a smile. 'How do you do? I am well acquainted with your aunt, of course.'

'I have come to solicit the honour of a dance with your daughter.'

Lady Bayfield was pleased. It was quite correct of him to ask her first. When people abided by the social rules, you knew where you were. There were no unpleasant surprises. Casual manners could lead to all sorts of complications. There were good reasons why girls only danced with men their mothers presented to them.

'She is dancing at the moment, with Lord Lansleigh,' she said, dropping the name with an air of indifference that intended to impress. Caroline suppressed a snort, Lansleigh being a well-known trap, a confirmed bachelor who liked to flirt but would never be tamely noosed; but Giles had been out of England so long, he did not know his rivals. 'But when the dance ends,' Lady Bayfield continued, 'you may have the next one.'

'Thank you, ma'am.'

It was necessary to carry on some small-talk while the music lasted. 'I believe your mother is not in Town,' Lady Bayfield said to Giles. 'She is in mourning, of course. A most unfortunate accident – in the field, I hear. Do you hunt?'

'I haven't, for some time. I've been out of England on and off for several years.'

'But you are back for good, now?'

Giles hoped not, but he knew where that question tended. If he married her daughter, he was not to park her in the country and disappear. 'I have no plans to leave England again,' he said truthfully. No plans, only wishes.

She let him go, and the ladies exchanged commonplaces until the music stopped and the floor broke up again. 'Ah, here they are,' said Lady Bayfield.

Giles knew Lansleigh by sight – a tall, thin, good-looking man in his thirties. He was leading a dark-haired girl towards them. Giles was momentarily puzzled – hadn't she said Lansleigh was dancing with her daughter? This girl was small and slight, with dark curly hair and blue eyes and an air of soft prettiness, and was dressed in delicate white chiffon over pale pink taffeta. She advanced towards Lady Bayfield with an apprehensive look. Some kind of protégée, he supposed.

Lady Bayfield took the dark girl's hand from that of the man, and turned her to face Giles. 'Catherine, my dear, this is the Earl of Stainton. He would like to dance with you. Lord Stainton, my daughter, Miss Bayfield.'

Giles struggled with the blankness of his surprise and stitched on a smile. *What on earth . . . ?* But Lady Bayfield could hardly not know her own daughter. Yet the girl he had spoken to had definitely said he must ask Lady

Bayfield if he wanted to dance with her. Or had she? Had he misheard, in the din? Had she said some other name – Mayfield or Hayford or Baynton or—

His inner babble ceased abruptly as the girl in apricot silk appeared out of the crowd, led towards their group by a very young-looking man in military blues. Her eyes leaped straight to Giles's face, and she blushed. Lady Bayfield turned her head to see what Giles was looking at and, with a slight air of impatience, she said, 'Lord Stainton, my daughter's friend, Miss Sanderton, whom I am chaperoning.' From the sketchiness of the introduction, it was clear that Lady Bayfield did not think her of any importance.

'I—' Giles began, but a look of alarm on the girl's face reminded him that he could not acknowledge their previous conversation. Lady Bayfield, he felt instinctively, would not approve of Miss Sanderton's talking to him before they had been introduced. 'Miss Sanderton,' he said instead, and bowed.

The music began again, and he straightened, somehow found Miss Bayfield's hand on his arm, somehow gathered enough wit to lead her towards the floor. One glance back showed the fair-haired girl watching them with an expression of resignation. He felt desperately uncomfortable. He had asked her to dance, and was dancing instead with her friend; he hoped she did not think he had used her to get to Miss Bayfield. What were Miss Sanderton's circumstances? Who was she? There was no polite and decent way he could quiz Miss Bayfield about her. He must finish this dance, and perhaps he could dance with Miss Sanderton later. Now he had been introduced, it would not look too particular.

But then he remembered that Miss Bayfield was one of the favoured top five on his aunt's list, and that Miss Sanderton hadn't been mentioned at all. He was not here to enjoy himself, he was here to find a rich bride. He felt like an ass, and a cad.

He must pay his partner proper attention. He smiled down at her. 'There's a tremendous crowd here tonight, isn't there?' It was the conventional opening: *Il y a beaucoup du monde à Versailles aujourd'hui.* King's pawn forward two. Necessary start to the game.

Miss Bayfield flicked a glance up at him – a flash of blue that was startling in its intensity – then veiled her eyes behind dark lashes. It was not a look of coquetry, he realised, but one of nervousness – almost panic. Her hand trembled in his.

And she said – or, rather, whispered, 'Yes.' And that was all.

Richard laughed. 'Lord, what a pickle! I really should never let you out of my sight!'

'Difficult, when you didn't even bother to go to the Wansborough ball.'

'I never do. I knew how foul it would be. But, oh, Giles, how delicious! Chatting away and making famous progress with entirely the wrong girl! I wish I'd been there to see your face when the real Miss Bayfield appeared!'

'I couldn't get a word out of her during the dance,' Giles said gloomily. 'She was so nervous, I thought she might faint. The only time she even looked at me, it was the way a lamb looks at a butcher holding a very sharp knife.'

'That's rather the point,' Richard said, making himself comfortable. He offered his cigarillo case. 'Smoke?' Giles shook his head. 'Miss Bayfield is apparently terribly shy, so they're bringing her out with a friend to bolster her confidence.'

'How do *you* know about it?'

'I got it out of Aunt. Miss Bayfield and Miss Sanderton were at school together and formed a close attachment – you know how girls are.'

'No,' said Giles drily, 'evidently I don't.'

'You don't?' Richard blew out a fragrant cloud. 'Look, old boy, you and I haven't had much to do with each other for the past few years, so I really don't know . . . What, exactly, *is* your experience with women?' Giles did not answer, staring away over Richard's shoulder. More gently, he asked, '*Have* you any experience with women?'

'Of course I have!' Giles scowled. And then he looked away again. 'Just not—'

Richard got down to brass tacks. 'Have you ever kissed a girl? Come, come, I'm trying to help. Be frank with me.'

'There was my housemaster's daughter at Eton. I kissed her once. In the garden.'

'Once?'

Giles was nettled. 'There've been moments at house parties when I almost . . . The sister of one of the other fellows at Oxford – one Christmas in the conservatory . . . And a girl – the publican's daughter, at the Royal George—'

'Yes, I know her,' Richard said, effectively silencing him. 'So you've kissed two girls and had a fumble behind the Royal George.' He considered. 'Did you like it?'

Giles reddened. 'What are you implying?'

'Nothing, brother dear. Don't be so sensitive. Any little adventurettes abroad? Any Florentine beauties, Athenian goddesses? Any sultry dark-eyed Cleopatras in Cairo?' Giles didn't answer. Richard went on, 'So, in summary, you know nothing about women.'

'I have the benefit of a classical education,' Giles said. He seemed to realise this sounded feeble, and hurried on, 'I've been busy. I haven't had time to spare for any of that romantic business. I suppose *you*'ve—'

Richard held up his hands. 'We're not discussing me, vast though my experience is. But I think it's plain that you need me to guide you, or you'll end up leg-shackled to entirely the wrong person, and that won't help either of us. From now on, we work together. I shall be always at your shoulder,

165

advising you, pointing you in the right direction, writing your lines for you, bringing you suitable candidates and shielding you from predatory females.'

'Predatory?'

'What females want, the only thing they want, is to get married, and they hunt down husbands, like lionesses hunting deer.'

'Oh, come! You don't mean it.'

'In fact, it's worse than that,' Richard said solemnly. 'Women are like those insects that consume their mates. We men are helpless victims.'

It occurred to Giles at last that Richard was teasing him, and he laughed. 'Fool!'

Richard laughed with him. 'But, seriously, you need my help.'

'Seriously, you may help me.'

'Thank God for that! Now, attend: even when they're not as shy as Miss Bayfield, girls are always happier in pairs. Also, mamas don't worry so much about foursomes as they do about a tête-à-tête. So we'll hunt together, and I'll occupy the attention of the one you *don't* want while you make your number with her miraculously relaxed and receptive friend. And if we come across the Bayfield-Sanderton complication, you shall work on the Bayfield while *I* keep Miss Sanderton occupied. If what you say is true, it won't be any hardship.'

'No,' said Giles, despondently. 'She's very conversable.'

Crooks had frequently visited Berkeley Square in the service of the old earl, so he knew his way around below stairs. Lady Manningtree kept a decent establishment of well-trained servants, and everything was done in form, which he found comforting. The only discordant note was the presence of Mr Richard's manservant, Speen, who was a stranger to them all, having only just been taken on.

Speen was a Londoner, a thin man of middling height with slicked-back dark hair. He seemed to know his work well enough, but when Crooks asked him, in a friendly way, where he had served before, he only tapped the side of his nose and said mysteriously, 'Luke eight, seventeen.' And walked away.

Crooks had had to look it up, and found the words, 'For nothing is secret, that shall not be made manifest; neither any thing hid, that shall not be known and come abroad.' Which was all very well, but it told him nothing, except that Speen had a good knowledge of the Bible. That was reassuring, to an extent – one did not want to work with Godless people – but on the other hand, it struck him, when he thought about it, as not quite right to be using the Holy Scriptures to avoid answering what was, after all, a perfectly civil question.

Having seen his master off for his evening engagements, Crooks carried the boots he had worn that day downstairs to clean them, and was brushing them, his mind a pleasant blank, when Speen came into the boot-room and said, 'This is dull work, Mr Crooks! Moping in here when all London lies spread out for our delight.'

'Eh?' said Crooks, coming out of his reverie.

'This fair city hangs against the black of night, like a rich jewel in an Ethiop's ear.'

'What are you talking about?' Crooks asked warily.

'The Bard, Mr Crooks. Shakespeare. *Romeo and Juliet*.'

Crooks wasn't acquainted with *Romeo and Juliet* but he had the idea it wasn't quite proper – something about forbidden love? More evidence of Speen's education – but in a servant, it could even be a mite dangerous if improperly applied. He shifted ground to one he was more sure of. 'You shouldn't call me Crooks. While we are here, I am Mr Stainton and you are Mr Tallant.'

Speen made a gesture of impatience. 'Oh, I know all that

malarkey. Don't you worry, I won't make a slip-up when there's anyone else listening. I'm a man of many tongues, believe me, and I trim my cloth to my customer. But it's just you and me here now, refugees from the Castle. We ought to stick together. What say we join forces?'

'To do what?' Crooks asked, bludgeoned by words. The Bible, Shakespeare, talk of tongues – he stared at the tongue of the earl's boot, and felt even more confused.

Speen stepped closer. 'To have a bit of fun, that's what!' His accent had changed, slipping from the fluting tones of a trained servant to something more 'of the people'. 'Our guv'nors are out, won't be back before the wee hours – now's the chance for you and me to sample the delights of the greatest city on earth. What say?'

'But – but I've got things to do. These boots to clean. His suit to brush.'

'Plenty of time for all that tomorrow morning. They're having fun – why shouldn't we? Come on, old man. Keep me company – two Castle valets together! I don't want to have to go out alone. Be a pal.'

Crooks was strangely tempted. In London, he didn't usually go out in the evening, feeling obscurely that it wasn't his territory. When he had done his legitimate chores and fiddled about in the dressing-room inventing things to do, he usually retired to his room and read. He had two books with him, Gibbon's *History of the Decline and Fall of the Roman Empire*, and Mrs Gaskell's *Cranford*. He didn't really enjoy either of them, but they were very effective in making him drop off to sleep. 'Dull work', indeed! And Speen was looking at him so pleadingly – he didn't like to let a fellow servant down. He could imagine that going out alone wouldn't be much fun. 'What exactly had you in mind?' he asked.

'There's a little place just along the road, the Coach and Horses—'

'A public house?' At home he sometimes took a glass of ale on a summer evening in the private bar at the Dog and Gun in Ashmore Carr, but London pubs, he believed, were rough and dangerous places steeped in vice.

'Oh, highly respectable,' Speen said. 'Proper as a deacon. There's a back room where senior servants go from all the big houses round here. Decent fellows like us. For a bit of conversation, a glass or two, and they do a cracking ordinary, as well. We could have supper, meet some congenial chaps, perhaps play a hand of cribbage. Suitable entertainment for two men of refinement like ourselves.'

'It does sound . . . rather nice,' Crooks said hesitantly.

Speen clapped his shoulder. 'That's the dandy! Hustle along now, old man, and we'll be off. I'll just tell Mr Forbes we won't be eating with them.' He gave a ghostly wink. 'Make sure they don't bar the door before we're back.'

Thus it was that Crooks found himself for the first time in his life in a London pub, crammed at a wooden table with six other servants in a throbbing atmosphere of talk, cigarette smoke, and the smell of spilled ale and roasted mutton. It had not been so crowded when they first arrived, but more and more people had since come in. Speen had introduced the six as first footmen and valets from this and that establishment, and they all seemed to know him, greeted him heartily as 'Edwin!' and 'You old devil – back again, eh?' Now all the tables were full, the rest of the floor-space was packed with men standing, quaffing ale (he was sure 'quaffing' was the right word) and talking nineteen to the dozen. Everyone seemed to know everyone else, and people were constantly stopping on their way to the serving hatch or back to lean over and exchange pleasantries with Speen and his companions. Crooks could not imagine why his presence was needed. He had thought Speen would be lonely without him, but he obviously knew everyone in London.

169

The ordinary of roast mutton, pease pudding and cabbage was good and cheap, but so plentiful he could not make any inroads into the jam duff that followed. He had asked for a half of ale but Speen had brought him a whole pint, and when he had managed with some difficulty to reach the bottom of the glass, another appeared before him. He felt bilious, anxious, and out of place. But then one of the others leaned across the table and patted his arm and said, 'Don't look so blue, old man. They ain't coming to hang you!'

And Speen leaned over and bellowed in his ear, 'Glad you came! Wouldn't have felt comfortable without you here! Great little place, ain't it?'

And suddenly, for no reason he could think of, he began to enjoy himself. The second pint of ale seemed to go down more good-naturedly than the first. The faces around the table were all beaming. They were good fellows – companions in arms, he thought sentimentally. Only another servant could understand the difficulties and sacrifices of a servant's life. And the loneliness. The isolation. Imprisoned in a great house, far from the companionship of his own kind. Never to – never to—

He leaned forward. 'Good fellows!' he said. 'All jolly good fellows.'

The man opposite him grinned. 'He's away! Crooky's away!'

'Crooky! That's me,' Crooks said. He'd never had a friend before. He'd been an only child, an outsider at school, had gone into service so young there had never been the chance to make a friend. It seemed a blessed thing to have a nickname. 'Crooky!' he shouted.

'Crooky!' they bellowed back. They were all beaming at him. His face felt like a full moon, round and smiling and warm. But not silvery. Red, it was. Red and smiling.

Speen put his arm round his shoulders. 'Enjoying yourself?'

170

'I am,' said Crooks, eagerly. Someone put another pint glass in front of him. 'But got to go to the – to the—' He didn't know what it might be called here. He leaned in to Speen and whispered, or thought he whispered '—privy!'

'Out the back. Turn left out of the door. Here, I'll go with you – you might get lost.'

'Kind of you,' Crooks said when he had got to his feet and found his balance. 'Kind.'

Speen's arm was round his shoulders again. 'That's what friends are for. And we're not finished yet, Crooky. The night is still young.'

'Like a precious jewel,' Crooks agreed solemnly.

It seemed a long way to the privy and a longer way back, and after the darkness out in the yard the light and noise and smoke hit him hard. He reeled, and might have fallen if Speen hadn't been there. Reaching the table again, he saw to his surprise that there were women among the footmen.

'Here, Studs, give Crooky your chair. He's older and grander than you,' Speen commanded. Somehow Crooks found himself sitting at the near side of the table, Speen next to him, but the chairs had been turned outward to face the room. And there were two women, young women in evening dress – at least, they were showing a lot of décolletage, and they seemed young, with the red lips and red cheeks of youth. One of them sat on Speen's lap. Crooks stared owlishly at the phenomenon. Speen grasped Crooks's shoulder and shook it gently. 'Not falling asleep, Crooky? Here, this one's Susie, and she's all yours. Enjoy yourself! You only live once!'

To Crooks's immense surprise, the second young woman plonked herself down on his lap, put her arms round his neck, and said, 'What's your name, love? Can't call you Crooky!'

Round, soft bosoms were pressing against him – his nose was practically in the cleft. He smelt perfume, and powder,

171

and behind it, a whiff of sweat. She jiggled softly on his lap, and said, to his bewilderment, 'Hullo, hullo! What you got in your pocket? Oh, you're a card all right, Crooky! It's always the quiet ones you got to watch!'

Suddenly the red lips were pressed down on his, and he tasted waxy lip paint and brandy. Bosoms, red lips, cheap scent, bare arms round his neck, insinuating words . . . One of her arms left his neck and her hand was sliding into his lap, fumbling about . . . He panicked. He couldn't breathe. He pushed her back, gasping. Next to him, Speen was fully engaged with the other woman, their faces joined together and making a noise like a carthorse freeing its hoof from thick mud. And Speen's hand was deliberately rucking up the woman's skirt, exposing her ankle, her leg . . .

'Oh, no, no, no!' Crooks cried.

'What's up, love?' Susie asked with mild concern.

'I can't! No, really, I can't! Please, please don't!' He pushed at her increasingly wildly. 'Please get off! Get off me!'

She pulled herself to her feet, annoyed. 'Well, pardon me, I'm sure! I know when I'm not wanted! Here, Eddy, you got a right friend here! Thanks for nothing!'

Speen had emerged from his lady-friend's face in time to witness her dismissal. He sighed. 'What's up, Crooky? Don't you like girls?'

Crooks stood up, shock having sobered him enough to be able to stand without swaying too much. 'My life,' he said. 'My whole life has been dedicated to beauty. To order, to elegance. Not – not *this*!'

Speen's lady-friend was not pleased. 'Who are you calling "this"? Are you saying we ain't elegant?'

Speen didn't seem too put out. 'Never mind him, love. He's a bit of a choir boy. I'd better get him home.' He pushed the girl off his lap, and slapped her rump. 'Don't go anywhere. It'll only take half an hour, then I'll be back.'

'What about me?' Susie complained.

172

Speen winked. 'I'll take on both of yer. Stay right here, ladies, I'll be back.' He took Crooks's arm just above the elbow. 'Come on, then, my old pal.'

'I don't need help. I can make my own way,' Crooks said, pulling free.

Speen examined him, judging his condition. 'Fair enough,' he said. 'I don't want to leave the party. Know the way, do you?'

'Certainly,' said Crooks. And then misgave: Speen had been trying to be nice to him, trying to give him a good time. His tastes might be horribly low, but he had meant well. 'Thank you,' he said, pulled himself up straight, and departed with a dignity that was only slightly marred by stumbling over the doorstep onto the street and having to grab a stranger to keep himself upright.

CHAPTER TEN

It was a fine May night, and Richard and Giles had decided to walk home from the ball at the Uppinghams' mansion in Bedford Square. Giles had said he needed the fresh air, and Richard had gone along with it. He wasn't a bit tired. At the ball, he had put his 'foursome' scheme into action by engaging the attention of the two American heiresses, who seemed in any case to like to stick together. It had worked very well, he thought. Through his expert manoeuvrings they had taken them into supper and, by managing to occupy the end of one of the tables, had been able to engage them in conversation without too much distraction.

'So which did you like better?' he asked. 'For my money, Van Dycke is slightly the prettier, though there's not much in it, but from all accounts the Brevoorte fortune is larger. They're both nice girls.' His brother had not said anything. 'Giles? Which did you prefer?'

Giles came out of a reverie. 'Isn't the question rather, which of them preferred me? As far as I could tell, it was neither. They both liked you better.'

'Oh, you needn't worry about that. They're after a title. Your being rather a dull old stick is nothing to the point. Which did you like?'

'Neither,' said Giles. 'Oh, I suppose they were nice enough in their way. But they talked so much, they gave me a headache.'

'You praised the Sanderton girl for talking.'

'That was conversation. Theirs was empty chatter, like the noise in an aviary.'

Richard looked at him in alarm. 'Lord, you do sound in a bad way! I know what the problem is – you haven't had enough to drink. You hardly downed a glass all evening.' He looked around. 'There must be a public house somewhere, where we can get a brandy. Where are we?'

'Golden Square,' Giles answered. 'The Crown is the nearest, but it will be closed.'

Richard gave him a quizzical smile. 'How so knowledgeable?'

'My rooms are just over there,' he said. 'I sometimes ate in the Crown when I was staying here.'

'I didn't know you used to have rooms.'

'Not "used to". I still have them,' Giles said.

'But you sold all Papa's London places to save money,' Richard said, remembering with a pang of guilt that he had promised to raise Mrs Sands's problem and hadn't.

Giles threw him a distracted glance. 'I paid for my rooms out of my own income. And they cost so little, I thought I'd keep them on, in case.'

'In case?' Richard queried, raising an eyebrow.

Giles reddened. 'Why must you make everything sound disreputable? I'm used to coming and going unannounced. One might want to get away on one's own.'

Richard raised defensive hands. 'I've no quarrel with that, old dear. I merely wondered. Which house is it?'

'That one. I have the first floor. Nothing grand – just a bedroom and a parlour.'

Richard stared thoughtfully at the neat, brown-brick house with the white trim. 'Can we go in? I'd like to see. And I'm willing to bet you have a bottle of something up there.'

'I believe there's sherry. But it's very late.'

'You mean the housekeeper will be in bed?'

'I have a key,' he admitted.

175

Richard grinned. 'Then there's no excuse. Show me your secret hideaway, old boy – or I'll tell.'

Giles smiled. 'I believe you would. But I don't mind showing you.'

The rooms, being on the first floor, had the high ceilings and long, lovely windows of the typical Georgian townhouse. There was a handsome fireplace in each room, and the furniture, while old and plain, was solid and decent.

'This is cosy,' Richard said, dropping into a chair, while Giles searched the fireside alcove cupboard for bottle and glasses.

'I always thought so,' Giles said. 'It was enough for me, when I was in London, near enough to the university, but not too out-of-the-way.'

'Gas lighting, I see – most convenient. What do you do for a bath?'

Giles handed him a glass of sherry with a surprised look. 'There's a closet behind the bedroom, with a tin bathtub. The girl brings water up and takes it away.'

'And how did you feed?'

'Mrs Gateshill, the housekeeper, provides food if you give her notice, but I often ate out.'

Richard looked around appraisingly. 'And there's room for a piano.'

'Piano? What are you talking about? And why all the interest?' Giles asked.

Richard watched as Giles half-drained the sherry glass and, judging him to be reasonably mellow, told the sad story of Mrs Sands.

Giles listened in silence, but his expression underwent a number of changes: suspicion, disapproval, anger – and, finally, a faint shame.

'I didn't know,' he said, when Richard paused. 'Obviously.'

'Quite,' said Richard. 'No-one would blame you.'

176

But Giles was thinking. 'I ought to have found out whether the properties were empty or not. I wonder about the others . . .'

'Don't. It seems to me that was Markham's job. You gave the order, he had to carry it out, but the details were for him to advise you about.'

'You say she's – respectable?' Giles asked, frowning in thought.

'Eminently,' Richard said. He shrugged. 'Very well, I know she engaged in sin and wickedness with our father, but you know and I know that it happens all the time. Our beloved monarch has an extremely respectable mistress who even accompanies him to dinner-parties, and nobody thinks any the worse of him – or her. Well, hardly anybody.'

Giles waved all that away. 'All the same, I don't see why I should be responsible for supporting her,' he said, but Richard could hear from his voice that he did. Their father had died suddenly, and Giles had inherited everything, including his debts, financial and moral.

'As I understand it,' Richard said casually, 'she wants to support herself—'

'By giving piano lessons?'

'It's a living,' said Richard. 'Modest, but it seems to be all she wants. She's not asking for a pension, just a place to live and work. Papa had provided her with that.'

'And I sold it,' Giles said disconsolately. 'Well, I can't get it back.'

'No,' said Richard. 'But she'd settle for less.'

Now Giles understood the remark about the piano. His eyebrows went up. 'You want me to install her *here*?'

'Why not? It's already paid for. And I can't see you'll have the chance very often to use it. Seems to me you're keeping it for sentimental reasons.'

'But here! In *my* rooms! A woman and her daughter. What on earth would people think?'

'Why on earth should you care?'

'When I'm in the middle of hunting for a wife? No, no, that won't do.'

'Look here, you need never meet her,' Richard said. 'I'll sort it all out for you. I'll talk to your Mrs Gateshill, spin her a good story, and if you never come here again, she'll know there's no funny business going on. The Sands woman comes across as very respectable. I'll arrange for your personal belongings to be packed up and sent to the Castle. Just give me the key. Oh, and some money to buy a piano. How much would a decent upright cost, do you think?'

'I haven't the least idea,' Giles said. He felt disgruntled. His bolt hole was being taken away, and he was fond of it. But . . . Unease about his father's mistress fidgeted him like grit in an omelette. And now that he had talked about it with Richard, he felt he couldn't back down. After all, looked at dispassionately, it was the *right* thing to do. 'Send the bill to Vogel, ask him for any money you need to cover expenses, and tell him the rent on the rooms is to be paid automatically. And I hope,' he added, with a scowl, 'that I'll hear no more about any of this.'

Richard grinned. 'A simple "thank you" would be appropriate. I'm going to considerable trouble for you – and you know how I hate exerting myself.'

'If you hadn't got involved, I'd never have known about it, and so much the better,' Giles said. But he didn't sound convincing.

'Have some more sherry,' said Richard. 'No sense in transporting a half-empty bottle all the way to the Castle.'

Lord and Lady Leven were friends of the King, some of the new sort of person he had favoured when he was Prince of Wales. They were extremely rich and cultured. They had a large house in Portman Square, where they hosted an art exhibition every year. It was held before the Royal

Academy's Summer Exhibition, and great names often lent their pictures ahead of it, knowing that the cream of society would be there.

The Levens had a long gallery at the top of the house, where the walls were crammed with paintings and drawings for the occasion. A string quartet played quietly at one end, and trim servants circulated with champagne and the most delicious canapés. Lady Manningtree, who cared nothing for art, thought that a gathering that served *hors d'oeuvres* without ever getting to the main meal was a sad excuse to save pennies, but it was always a very popular occasion and invitations were greatly prized.

'And it's better for your purposes,' she told Giles. 'At a dinner you can only talk to the girls on either side, and the hostess chooses them for you. At the Levens', you can wander and mingle at will.'

So it proved. The atmosphere was easier than at a ball, and the usual fierce chaperonage was relaxed. Everyone moved between paintings at their own pace and according to their fancy, and discussing art was the perfect camouflage for flirtation.

Giles had had orders from his aunt to inspect two girls from further down her list – she had regretfully struck off the names of the Americans, as the Marquess of Rockport was aggressively courting one, and the other seemed to be favouring Lord Hornsea. But Richard nudged his brother and guided him towards Miss Bayfield and Miss Sanderton, who were standing in front of an Alma-Tadema.

It depicted bowing maidens scattering rose petals before a bearded man robed in red and gold. Both girls seemed completely absorbed, but they glanced round as the men came up to them.

'What do you think of this gorgeous piece?' Richard divided the question impartially between the two girls, but it was Miss Sanderton who answered, and Giles she looked

179

at. Miss Bayfield only peeked from under her eyelashes – but it was also Giles she peeked at.

'It *is* gorgeous,' said Miss Sanderton. 'I love all his work – so rich and delicious you want to eat it! Like one of the French gâteaux in Gunter's window.'

'I know just what you mean,' Giles said. It was always such a relief to talk to her after the other debutantes. Each time they met, they seemed to be resuming a conversation that had been going on between them for years, as if they had always been friends. 'Was there a "but"? I sensed a "but" in your answer.'

'Not about the painting, but the subject. Women scattering petals for a man to trample on. Things never change, do they?'

'I don't remember anyone ever scattering petals for me,' he said, amused.

'I wasn't speaking literally,' she said.

'Oh, but what man doesn't dream of lounging like a sultan,' Richard put in, 'while a dozen handmaids wait on his every whim?'

'Now you've shocked Miss Bayfield,' Giles said.

For a wonder, she looked up, her cheeks pink with her own daring, and said, 'I'm not shocked. I know men do like those things. Besides, women like to look after men. When they really care for them.'

The blush suited her, Giles thought – which was just as well, since she blushed so often. But he knew by now that she responded better to a softer tone of voice. Liveliness, raillery, unnerved her. He said, 'It is not called the gentle sex for nothing. Women are naturally kind. And men should not take that kindness for granted.' She lowered her eyes, but he thought she was pleased with his answer. 'Do you like the painting?' he asked.

'It's very pretty,' she said, 'but—' He had to coax the rest of her answer out of her, and was surprised when he heard it. 'I think it's too easy to like. As Nina says, like a rich cake.'

'What sort of paintings do you prefer?' he asked.

'I think, the impressionists,' Miss Bayfield answered. 'They – they make you work harder.'

Giles had thought her a timid, kitten-like creature, and had assumed she would like pretty, kitten-like things. He could not fit this opinion into his picture of her. And she, confounded by her own boldness, had now retreated into silence. To Miss Sanderton, he therefore addressed his next remark. 'I remember we once spoke of pointillism. It seems you and Miss Bayfield are both connoisseurs of art.'

'We did look at a lot of paintings when we were at Miss Thornton's school,' Nina said. 'She believed an educated female must have a good grounding in the arts. And she made us think about *why* we liked them or didn't.'

'She sounds very enlightened,' Giles said.

Richard laughed. 'I'm surprised she hasn't been run out of the country! Education for females? The old guard won't approve of that!'

Miss Sanderton leaned in to look at the label for the Alma-Tadema picture. 'Caracalla,' she read. 'I don't know who or what that is.'

'He was a Roman emperor,' Giles said, remembering how, by coincidence, he had mentioned him to his aunt not long ago.

'I've never heard of him,' said Miss Sanderton. 'We only did Julius, Augustus, Tiberius and – which were the others, Kitty?'

'Caligula and Claudius,' Miss Bayfield answered, without looking up.

'Caracalla was one of the later ones,' Giles said. 'Son of Severus, brother of Geta.' He saw Richard looking at him with raised eyebrows that said, *Can't you think of anything better to talk to girls about?* But Miss Sanderton seemed interested. 'When I was a boy I was made to recite the names of all the emperors and their dates, in order,' he explained apologetically. 'I never managed to get past Caracalla.'

'I had to learn the kings and queens of England. All the way back to those Edwys and Eadreds and Edgars.'

'Despite living in India?'

She smiled. 'You remembered that?'

Her eyes were dark brown. It fascinated him. Everyone in Egypt had dark eyes, of course, but he didn't think he'd ever encountered them paired with such fair hair. 'I remember everything you said.'

There was a moment of such tension in the air, it was as though they were generating electricity between them. And then he remembered where they were, and what his business in London was. He came down to earth with a bump.

Richard stepped in – quite literally, between Giles and Miss Sanderton – and said, 'You obviously know much more about art than I do, Miss Sanderton. Come and tell me all about this next picture, Sargent's portrait of Mrs Leopold Hirsch. I know Sargent is supposed to be the best, but you shall tell me why I'm to like it.'

She obeyed him with a polite smile, and Giles offered his arm to Miss Bayfield, on the 'foursome' principle – so that the chaperones would not come and interfere.

'Nina is so clever,' Miss Bayfield said.

'You prefer the impressionists,' Giles said. 'I've never before met a young woman who had any opinion on them.'

'We learned a great deal at Miss Thornton's,' Miss Bayfield said, and added, with an air of having just discovered it, 'without really knowing we did.'

'Did you read poetry?'

'We had to recite *The Pied Piper of Hamelin*,' she said. 'But I think that was to improve our memories and diction. It isn't,' she added in a low voice, 'a very good poem.'

'I had to recite "Casabianca" when I was a boy. And *Hiawatha.*' She nodded, as if she knew them too. 'One of the great things about growing up is no longer having to read things one doesn't like,' he went on, hoping to amuse her. But she didn't smile. The other two had moved on from the Sargent, but she seemed to want to stand and look at it. He racked his brain for something to say. 'What about Shakespeare? I'm sure your Miss Thornton made you read Shakespeare?'

It was like drawing teeth, trying to get conversation out of her.

In front of the next painting, Richard and Nina were talking easily. He glanced back to see how Giles was doing, and sighed. 'Your friend,' he remarked, 'is very shy.'

She frowned, as though it were a criticism. 'Kitty is the *dearest* creature. And very clever, only she doesn't know it. She only wants drawing out.'

'She's lucky to have such a loyal friend,' Richard said, examining her. She was really very lovely, he thought – those eyes! That hair and skin!

She looked at him with a shrewd amusement, as if reading his thoughts. 'I'm no-one,' she said abruptly. 'You shouldn't be wasting your time on me.'

'Don't worry. I'm just the younger brother. No estate. No fortune. We're not allowed to fall in love.'

'I've sworn not to,' she confided.

He was amused. 'Is that a thing you can swear? I thought all you girls believed falling in love was involuntary.'

'I was brought up by my aunt, and she believes in Higher Thinking. You control everything with your mind, even your emotions – she would say, *especially* your emotions.'

'"Tell me where is fancy bred? Or in the heart, or in the head?"' he quoted, slightly surprising himself. Of course he was grounded in Shakespeare, like any English gentleman, but he couldn't remember quoting any to a female before.

'My aunt would say the heart is nothing but an organ that pumps blood,' said Miss Sanderton, with a gleam in her eye.

'Your aunt sounds formidable. And you, Miss Sanderton,' he added seriously, 'strike me as a very dangerous young woman.'

'Oh, no,' she said dismissively. 'I told you, I'm no-one at all.'

Richard had not been brought up to consider anyone but himself. Selflessness and philanthropy were alien concepts to him. He had simply never been asked to practise them. But he found he had actually enjoyed helping Mrs Sands and her daughter, and liked the sensation of helping Giles by making all the arrangements.

Mrs Sands, he had told the housekeeper, was a respectable widow, who had a claim on the benevolence of the Stainton estate. Mrs Gateshill had listened at first with a tight mouth and the hard eyes of suspicion, but when Richard returned Giles's key and mentioned that the earl would be too busy ever to call on his protégées, she relaxed a little; and once he mentioned that the rent would be paid by the estate, directly from the bank, she was all co-operation.

So it was Richard who brought Mrs Sands and her daughter the good news, and received the first flood of their gratitude. It was such an agreeable sensation that he decided then and there to help them make the move. Supported by the knowledge that he could apply to Vogel for any expenses incurred in the business, he hired a growler and went to collect them and their luggage in person, and supervised their reception by Mrs Gateshill. By the time he had conducted them over their new home, he felt a proprietary interest in them, and took personal charge of acquiring the piano. Robert Morley & Company was the place to go to, said musical acquaintances, and having left the choice of instrument to Mr Edgar Morley, he had only to make sure he was on hand when it was delivered to feel the full pleasure of successful benefaction.

'It is so very, very kind of you,' Mrs Sands said, with tears in her eyes.

In justice, he felt obliged to murmur that the estate was paying.

She said, 'But I know who has taken the trouble to make it happen. You have exerted yourself on our behalf and we are truly grateful.'

Well, he *had* exerted himself, that was a fact. He smirked a little. 'Won't you try the instrument?' he asked Miss Sands.

She needed no more encouragement, but sat quickly as though only a thread of politeness had been holding her back. Richard watched in amazement as her fingers ran across the keys so fast he could hardly see them, releasing a flood of sound such as he'd never heard before. He'd had no interest in music until then. He never went to concerts, and though hostesses sometimes held 'musical soirées', there was no need for a guest to listen. Flirting and whispered conversation beguiled the performances, and one could always slip out of the room for a smoke if particularly bored. Little girls like his sisters learned to thump out 'pieces' on the piano as part of their training for marriage, but he had never heard playing like this. The rippling tune – he had no better word for it than 'tune', though he knew it was much more complex than that – poured and tumbled and sparkled like a mountain stream rushing downhill, and only when she abruptly stopped playing did he discover he had actually been holding his breath.

Mrs Sands had been watching him. 'She is good, isn't she?'

He groped for a word. 'Miraculous,' he said.

She smiled, satisfied. 'It's a very nice instrument,' she said, 'and we are more grateful than I can say. I shall be able to teach, and Chloë will be able to practise. But I wish you could hear her play on a concert piano – a grand. Then you would really know how good she is.'

He didn't know what to say. He thought of all the grand pianos he must have walked past in his life, in the great houses of relatives and acquaintances. To him they had been merely large items of furniture, no more significant than a marble-topped console on which he laid his hat; and to judge by the array of silver-framed photographs and bowls of flowers they so often carried, their owners probably thought the same. He wished, suddenly and foolishly, that he could conjure one from its forgotten corner of a drawing-room for Miss Sands to work her magic on. But even if he had the power, there would be no room for it here.

She had stood up now, and turned to him with a shy smile and said, 'Thank you, sir. With all my heart.'

'Oh, it's nothing, nothing at all,' he mumbled. 'Well, I had better be going.' He felt obscurely disappointed to have come to the end of his association with them.

Mrs Sands held out a hand to stay him. 'Oh, Mr Tallant,' she said, 'would you – is it too much to ask? – would you do us the honour of dining with us one evening?' He hesitated, thinking of his engagements with Giles, which took up most evenings. She went on, 'It would only be a simple meal and we eat rather early, I'm afraid – at six, usually . . .'

That would enable him to be on hand for Giles at nine or thereabouts, and evening engagements rarely started earlier. 'I should like that,' he said.

May brought fine weather and long, light evenings, and with them more freedom for Rachel and Alice, who could be out of doors all day, as long as they arrived clean and dressed for dinner. Amusing Linda's children was easier to do outside. Long walks, fishing for sticklebacks, collecting wild flowers, spotting birds and butterflies, paddling in the Ash – all kept them busy and tired them out, so that their fretfulness and whining diminished and they became more agreeable companions.

Rachel decided to teach them to ride, using Biscuit, the trap pony, and Goosebumps, the flea-bitten grey pony that pulled the lawn mower and roller, both very quiet. Alice helped her, but one Sunday after church, feeling restless, she left Rachel to it, and took Pharaoh out for a ride. It was Josh's day off, and the grooms were all absent (probably asleep somewhere, she thought) when she reached the stable-yard, but she told the boy on duty that she didn't need to be accompanied. If she had to dismount for any reason, she could find a gate or stile to remount from.

It was glorious to be out alone. Pharaoh was fresh and wanted to gallop, so she let him, revelling in the freedom from Josh, whose disapproval ground her down, like an over-sharpened pencil. Galloping was an easier pace at side-saddle than cantering, and she adored the wind rushing past her face, and the sound of Pharaoh's pounding hoofs and snorting breaths. She let him run until he slowed naturally, then pulled down to a walk, and idled along, enjoying the clean air, the smells of grass and leaves, and the birdsong.

She rode without thinking about her destination, but finding she had almost reached the hamlet of Ashmore Carr, she wondered suddenly about Axe Brandom, and where his cottage was. He had said 'out past the Carr', which meant on this side of it. He'd invited her to call in and see his animals, and he should be at home on a Sunday. Seeing a boy just disappearing into the trees with a home-made fishing rod and jam jar, she called to him, and when he came lounging reluctantly up to her, she asked if he knew where Axe lived.

'The blacksmith?' he said. He pointed. 'Down that way. Go on a bit, and there's a big ole bush and a track along of it what goes right to his house.'

'Thank you,' she said.

187

He looked at her doubtfully. 'He don't have a smithy there. 've you lost a shoe, miss?'

'No,' she said. 'I just wondered where he lived. I knew it was somewhere hereabouts. Go along now.'

She watched him go, until he reached the trees, then sent Pharaoh on. She found the big old bush and the track easily enough, hesitated a moment, then turned onto it. He'd *invited* her, after all. He couldn't be cross.

The track did lead straight to the cottage, and ended there, in a beaten yard. It was a stone cottage, with a slate roof, and several wooden outbuildings tacked on. The front door stood open, and as soon as she arrived, Dolly came bustling out, barking officiously. 'It's only me,' she said to the dog; and Axe appeared at the open door, wiping his mouth with a dishcloth. 'I'm sorry,' she called to him. 'Did I disturb your dinner?'

'Just finished,' he said. ''Twas only a bit o' pie.' He advanced and took hold of Pharaoh's rein, looking up at her with, she thought, some reserve.

'You did say I could call in if I was passing,' she apologised. 'To see your animals. But I can go away again if you're busy.'

'No,' he said. ''Tis all right. Surprised, that's all. D'you want to get down?'

She needed no further invitation. She freed her legs and let him jump her down, enjoying the feeling of his big hands on her waist. It surprised her, because she had never even noticed when Josh did it. Without a word, Axe led Pharaoh to a ring fixed in the cottage wall, tied him with a piece of rope and loosened his girth. He went into one of the outhouses and came out with an armful of hay, which he put down in front of the horse, patting his neck as he began happily pulling at it.

All the while, Alice watched him, while crouched on her haunches petting Dolly, who leaned against her knees, eyes closed in bliss. When Axe finished with Pharaoh he turned to look at his visitor. 'She'll stand there all day for that.'

'She's got her figure back,' Alice said. 'She's had the pups?'

He nodded. 'In the scullery. Made herself a nest under the sink. Four on 'em.'

'Oh, could I see?' Alice cried.

He said, as if it were a caveat, 'You'll have to come inside.'

'Do you mind?' she asked bluntly.

'*I* don't,' he said. 'But it's not grand.'

'Well, nor am I,' she said. He grunted and turned, and she followed him in, with Dolly pushing past her to hurry on ahead.

Inside it was dark, and it took a moment for her eyes to adjust. She smelt a bit of coal from the range, a bit of dog, a bit of leather, and the sharpness of lye soap. Underneath all that there was the faint whiff, like mushrooms, of the damp that you always got in cottages like this, where the brick floor was laid straight on the earth. She had entered any number of cottages, in the course of the poor-visiting her mother insisted on, and they generally had a whole lot of other less pleasant smells, of dirty bodies and privies and sickness. All the smells of Axe's cottage were clean ones.

Now she could see, and it was just one room. The range was straight ahead of her, in the long wall opposite the door, alight, of course, but banked low, with two high-backed wooden chairs flanking it, and an open door to the left through which she could glimpse the scullery. A big table occupied most of the space. A narrow bed, with a patchwork counterpane, was pushed up against the right-hand wall, and a dresser occupied the whole of the wall to the left. There were two windows, one either side of the yard door, with window-seats under them, covered with red cloth, and lockers underneath. Everything looked clean and scrubbed and bare, the house of a man who spent little time in it. On the table a plate, knife and pewter mug were evidence of his meal; on the chimney shelf were more mugs, a tea tin – black with a pattern of pink roses – and a single ornament, a figurine of a shepherdess, about six inches high. It intrigued her – it seemed an odd thing for such a large, masculine man to have – and she wanted to ask where he'd got it from, but felt it wouldn't be manners to ask such questions so soon.

'It's not much,' Axe said, watching her look around.

'It's very nice,' she said, embarrassed to be caught looking.

'Scullery,' Axe said, and led the way. There was Dolly, in a box under the sink, with three squirming puppies tugging at her teats, while she gave her master a martyred look.

'You said she had four,' Alice said.

'One died right off. Runt,' he said. Alice squatted by the box. 'Best not touch 'em,' he warned. 'She's a fierce little mother.'

'I won't,' Alice said. Dolly gave her a careful look, then turned away to lick her pups. 'What's this?' she asked, picking up a small, very grubby and much chewed rag doll that was lying by the box.

'It's her doll,' said Axe. 'Dolly's dolly. She don't care about it now she's got the pups, but once she gets tired of 'em, she'll want it again.'

She stood up. 'Where's Captain?'

'Out back somewhere.' The rear door was open onto another beaten yard surrounded by wooden sheds, with the dark woods beyond. Axe stood and whistled. In a moment, there was a whir of wings, and a black bird with a grey neck flew down onto his outstretched arm and gave a sharp cry.

'Oh, he's handsome,' Alice cried, as it tilted its head and examined her with a pale eye. 'Will he come to me?'

'C'n try,' said Axe. But as he brought the bird towards her it hopped up his arm to his shoulder and then onto his head. 'Shy,' he said. 'He'll get used to you.'

'Can I see his tricks?'

'Once he settles.' Axe considered. 'I was just going to mash some tea. Will you have a cup?'

'Yes, please,' Alice said shyly.

'Go and sit you down, then,' he said.

She sat at the table, and watched as he made the tea, his movements quiet and sure, a creature at home in its element. The bird hopped down onto his shoulder, and after a while, onto the back of the chair opposite Alice. It examined her, first with one eye, then the other, then let out a stream of 'words' that made Alice laugh, because it sounded so close to human speech. When Axe sat down at the table with the tea, the bird hopped again to his shoulder, and chattered to him with its beak poked into his ear, as if to make sure he could hear.

Axe poured a cup for Alice, and then said, 'Oh, look, I went and forgot the *sugar*.'

He said the last word sharply and distinctly, and the bird cocked its head, and flew over to the dresser, where there was a bowl of roughly broken sugar. It picked up a lump in its beak and flew back to Axe, dropping it on the table beside him. 'Two lumps,' Axe commanded, and it repeated the action. Then he said, 'Spoon!' and it fetched a spoon from the half-open dresser drawer.

Alice applauded, and the bird cocked its head at her and reeled off another sentence. 'How clever!' she said.

Axe looked pleased. 'Tea all right – my lady?' He added the last as an afterthought, but with a faint blush that he had forgotten it before.

'Oh, you needn't call me that,' Alice said hastily. 'Yes, thank you, the tea's good. Nice and strong. It's always so weak at home. Mama has Earl Grey, and it's awful, like dish-water.'

'I've never drunk dish-water,' Axe observed, and she realised he was joking, and laughed.

'Do you do all your own cooking?' she asked.

'Mostly,' he admitted. 'Not that I'm much good. Stews

and such, they're easy, and there's plenty of good stuff in the woods to go in 'em. That bit of pie, Mrs Rowse gave me that,' he explained. 'She thinks I don't get enough to eat, makes me pies and cakes. I don't stop her.'

'What do you put in your stews?'

'Pigeon, rabbit, game when it comes my way. Mushrooms from the wood. Herbs. Veg from me patch out the back.'

'Sounds lovely. Food is so dull at home. It never seems to taste of anything – except when it's burned.'

'I like things tasty,' he admitted. He looked at her for a moment – rather, she thought, like the bird, a sort of considering look – and then said, 'Got some baby rabbits. Orphans – fox got their ma. Want to see 'em?'

In a shed in the rear yard he showed her the four little rabbits in a box of hay, protected by chicken-wire. The cats came stalking daintily in to visit, and the jackdaw kept them company and conversed, and at last consented to hop onto Alice's shoulder and even press its beak to her ear. It was surprisingly hot. And all the while, she watched Axe move about in his own familiar world, astonishingly graceful for so large a man – and, she began to notice, astonishingly beautiful. When his blue eyes turned to rest on her, she felt it like warmth in the pit of her stomach; when he spoke to her, she felt a quake as if his words were physical touches, little feet running on her spine. He seemed at ease, as though he was glad of her presence. No-one in her life had treated her like that, and she loved the sensation. She felt she would like to stay there for ever, and never leave; but eventually she became aware that she needed to use the privy, and she didn't like to ask to use his: it would be too embarrassing. So at last she had to say, 'I must go.'

He seemed taken aback for an instant, and then at once became more formal, as though he realised he had forgotten himself. She wanted to say, *No, don't be like that, don't make me Lady Alice again*, but she couldn't, quite. So in slight stiffness they went back through the scullery, where Dolly was resting in her bed, her pups asleep, and declined to get up to see her off, though she wagged her stumpy tail.

They passed through the cottage to the front yard, where Pharaoh had finished the hay and was half asleep. Axe untied him, tightened the girth, and stood waiting to leg her up. She came up close, keenly aware of his presence, his smell of clean man – soap and leather, with an under-hint of musk. Their eyes met for an instant and she gave a little shiver. His lips parted as if he was going to comment on it, but closed again. She gathered her skirt, cocked her knee, and he threw her up neatly. He held Pharaoh while she arranged herself, then as she gathered the reins, let him go and stepped back.

'Thank you for the tea,' she said. 'And for showing me everything.'

'Thank you for coming,' he said. 'I don't get many visitors out here.' Their eyes met again. 'You can come any time.'

She couldn't hold his gaze. She looked down at her hands and felt herself blushing, hastily turned Pharaoh, and rode away.

Aunt Caroline's list was showing the signs of age. Names had been crossed out, others added, notes and question marks littered it. The paper was growing soft with use.

'What are you *doing*, Giles?' she said, one morning at breakfast. 'Are you even taking this seriously?'

'Of course I am,' he answered automatically, then added, 'I *do* know the whole future of the estate rests on my marrying.'

'But you reject girl after girl, for no reason that I can discern. Do you think there is an unlimited supply?'

'Of course not.'

'You seem to me to be determined not to like any of them. All perfectly nice, good girls.'

'But they're so difficult to talk to,' he excused himself. 'I try, but there's so little response—'

'You're not supposed to talk to them,' she interrupted testily. 'You're just supposed to marry one!'

'And spend the rest of my life with someone who bores me? With whom I can't share a single interesting conversation?'

She looked at him with exasperation. Then her expression softened. 'Giles,' she said, quite kindly, 'the trouble is that you've had so little contact with women. School, then university, then off on your digs in foreign places. Nothing but men around you, all the time – tutors and dons and academics and so on. You can't expect a relationship with a woman to be like that. Men and women lead quite different lives. You have your interests, and we have ours. There's no common ground for conversation.'

'Then what's the point of marrying?' he said bleakly.

'It's different after marriage. There's the home, and children, and social events to discuss. Common experiences. Even so, husbands and wives lead separate lives. We meet in the bedroom and at the dinner table.' He looked morose. 'Come, my dear,' she said, smiling, 'I didn't expect you of all people to be foolishly romantic! It's not Romeo and Juliet or Antony and Cleopatra. It's a simple matter of mutual comfort and providing heirs. Choose a healthy, good-tempered girl – that's all you need to do.'

'A healthy, good-tempered, rich girl,' he amended.

She sighed. 'Will you never get over that? *Yes*, in your case. Her fortune for your title. I assure you she won't feel hard-done-by. But, for goodness' sake, cease this obsession with *conversation*,' she said the word witheringly, 'and get on and *choose* somebody. The more you think about it,' she added wisely, 'the harder you'll find it. Don't think. Just pick one and be done with it.'

'Thank you for your advice, Aunt Caroline,' he said tonelessly.

She couldn't tell whether he was employing irony or not. She hoped it was *not*.

CHAPTER ELEVEN

Dinner with the Sandses was indeed simple, and there was no wine. It was a long time since Richard had sat down to a meal without the lubricant of alcohol. Not since nursery days, he supposed. They ate around a gateleg table, which had been set up in the centre of the drawing-room, and Miss Sands brought each course up in turn from downstairs: curried eggs with lettuce, stewed veal with mushrooms and peas, and a savoury of herring roes with biscuits.

'Is this Mrs Gateshill's cooking?' he asked.

'My daughter and I did it together,' said Mrs Sands.

He was impressed.

'We were quite accustomed to cooking for ourselves in our last home,' she explained. 'But we had a kitchen there.'

There was no sweet or dessert, but by that stage, deep in conversation, he hardly noticed.

Miss Sands, he discovered, was not shy so much as reserved. There were many subjects on which she had no opinion, and would merely listen, answering, if pressed, in monosyllables, eyes averted. But on a subject she cared about, she could be eloquent, and would meet his eyes frankly. As he observed her through the evening, he was astonished again by her beauty, and her long, eloquent fingers in particular fascinated him. But it was Mrs Sands with whom he had the majority of the conversation.

She told him that she had already given some lessons.

'Some of my old pupils who haven't yet found a new teacher – I contacted them as soon as your lovely piano arrived. And two new ones, recommended to me by an acquaintance. It feels good to be independent again.'

They talked about the war, Richard tempted into eloquence by Mrs Sands's intelligent interest. Since the beginning of April, it had been clear that the Boers *had* to come to terms. 'Conditions on the veld are terrible for the women and children,' he said, 'and it takes the stuffing out of the fighting men, knowing their families are suffering.'

'I thought the women and children were put into camps,' Mrs Sands said. 'I read a report in *The Times* . . .'

'Yes, we did round them up in the beginning,' Richard said, 'but last December Lord Kitchener ordered that they were to be left alone. It means the Boers have to take care of their own, you see. It slows them down. And now we've learned to fight like them – living on the veld, making lightning strikes – we're better at it than them. We live harder and move faster. We chase them from pillar to post, never letting them rest. They've got nowhere left to go and no hope of winning.'

He did not mention the other thing they had learned from the Boers – not to take prisoners. In that kind of warfare, holding prisoners used up manpower and hobbled a unit's effectiveness. It had become standard practice to shoot them, as the Boers did, though this could never become official policy: it was not the British way. Just this February there had been a show trial of two officers, Handcock and Morant, for shooting prisoners, and they had been executed as an example, not to the army but to the watching world.

It took its toll, that kind of warfare, and underneath his flippant, devil-may-careity there was a strain and weariness Richard had been at pains to hide – from himself as much as others.

But now all the Boer leaders were in Pretoria where peace talks were going on.

'So the war is over?' said Mrs Sands.

'It will be, when they sign a treaty,' said Richard. 'I suspect there'll have to be a lot of talking first. They do love to jaw, your Boers. But the fighting is over. I'm guessing there'll be a treaty by the end of the month.'

'And then we'll have the Coronation to look forward to,' said Mrs Sands, changing the subject to his relief. Introspection was not the soldier's way, and Mrs Sands's sympathy had brought him closer to it than was comfortable.

'Strange to think of having a king,' said Richard. 'We're so used to talking about "Queen and country".' He sang a phrase, '"It's the soldiers of the Queen, my lads, who've been my lads, who've been my lads . . ."'

'I think he'll be a good king,' said Mrs Sands.

'You've met him?' Richard asked, from something in her tone.

'I used to hear about him from—' She stopped abruptly, colouring.

It was the first awkward moment: he knew what she had been going to say. He was forced to remember for the first time that this pleasant woman had been his father's mistress.

'My father was a close friend of the Prince of Wales,' he observed.

Chloë looked from him to her mother and back, apprehensively. Would there be unpleasantness?

Richard roused himself to speak cheerfully. 'I imagine he'll be a jollier monarch than the old Queen, at all events. He does love to laugh. Do you know the story that Frederick Treves, the surgeon, told him?'

'Do tell,' Mrs Sands invited.

'Well, one of our officers in South Africa was shot in the head, and was sent back to England to be treated by Treves. It was such a bad wound that Treves was surprised the man survived the operation. He'd had to remove a large part of his brain, and he told him he might have difficulty in following his profession in future. The officer said, "Thank God my brain is no longer wanted, sir – I've just been transferred to the War Office." When Treves told the story to the King, he laughed until he cried.'

Mrs Sands also laughed; Chloë smiled politely. To Richard's amazement, he found himself thinking he would sooner spend the evening with the mother than with the daughter, no matter how beautiful she was, or how talented. Mrs Sands was still a very handsome woman, besides being intelligent, well-read and witty. And the understanding warmth of her eyes when she smiled at him made her very attractive . . .

He was almost sorry when he had to go. 'An evening engagement,' he apologised. 'I wish I might cancel it, but I really can't.'

Chloë fetched his hat, gloves and cane from the other room. As he shook hands, he said, 'I've enjoyed this evening so much. Would you allow me the honour of taking you out to dinner one evening? I don't cook,' he added lightly, 'so it would have to be a restaurant, but I promise to choose a respectable one.'

Chloë, he noticed, looked grave, and Mrs Sands said hesitantly, 'You are very kind, but you do not need to have us on your conscience. There is no need for you to trouble yourself with us any further.'

He felt a moment of pique that they could even consider turning him down – him! But then he made himself remember the sensitivity of their position. 'I don't ask out of duty. It would be a great pleasure to entertain you, if you could think it proper. The obligation would all be on my side.'

She said quickly, 'I'm ashamed to make you beg when you are offering us such a treat. We accept gladly – don't we, Chloë?'

198

Chloë thanked him, but he did not feel there was any great warmth in it. Beautiful, but cold, he thought, as he walked off round Golden Square. And then he corrected himself – not cold, precisely, but . . . What? Living in another world altogether, he decided at last. Only the visible part of her was present. The rest of her was elsewhere.

As May tilted over into June, the Season reached full speed. Engagements came thick and fast, and Nina was made aware of an essential difference between Kitty and her. Kitty had started off with a large wardrobe, and Lady Bayfield was still adding to it, while Nina had to wear the same gowns over and over. She had been dazzled in the beginning by her lovely new things, but now she realised why 'coming out' was such an expense. However logical she meant to be about it, she could not help the occasional pang of envy. Also Marie, the French maid (at least, she *said* she was French) whom Lady Bayfield had hired for them, had a way of looking at her . . .

Kitty, though she never spoke of it, was aware of the situation, and did what she could by lending Nina little things here and there – gloves, sashes, hair ornaments – and would have given her whole dresses, had they not been too small for her taller friend. And had it not been for fear of her stepmother. Lady Bayfield was happy to have a distinction maintained between her daughter and the indigent friend. That was as it should be. She had not appreciated at the beginning how *very* good-looking Miss Sanderton was . . .

But when they were invited by the Earl and Countess Wroughton for a Saturday-to-Monday at Dene Park, their country estate in Hertfordshire, Nina wrote with the greatest reluctance to Aunt Schofield asking if it was at all possible for her to have a new evening gown, because the Saturday evening would be very grand indeed. Lord Wroughton was a close friend of the King, and His Majesty was expected to look in.

Aunt Schofield had expected an application before this. She knew something of the sartorial demands of the Season. She took Nina to Derry & Toms and bought her two new day dresses and an evening gown. 'But this must be the last of it,' she said, with a sternness she did not entirely feel. 'I hope you are not being spoiled, Nina. I want you to enjoy yourself, but you know the fashionable world is not your sphere, and never can be.'

Nina, whose expectations were modest, was delighted by the new clothes. 'I don't *think* I'm being spoiled,' she said. 'But, oh, I *am* enjoying it, Auntie. It will be lovely to look back on, when—'

She faltered. It wasn't just the fun and frolic, but the new friends she had made: the other debutantes, and the jolly fellows they danced and flirted with, and dear Kitty – would she ever see her again when their lives threw apart? And Lord Stainton – how close they seemed to have grown over these past weeks. At every social occasion, he seemed to veer straight to her and Kitty and they talked like old friends – about music, books and art, current events, and often about archaeology and ancient civilisations. She loved the fact that he deemed her worth talking seriously to. All that would end when the Season did, and she and Kitty were parted, for his world and hers were a universe apart. She would never see him again, and she was horribly afraid she would miss him.

She came back from her thoughts. 'There is bound to be an adjustment to go through afterwards,' Aunt Schofield was saying, 'but there are great satisfactions to be found in our world too, and you will appreciate them in time.'

'I know. I *do* know,' Nina said, eager to reassure her.

Her aunt patted her hand. 'Yes, you're a good girl. Enjoy your jaunt while it lasts.'

* * *

Dene Park was a grim-looking square mansion with massive columns on the front ('the purest Georgian architecture in the south of England', said the guidebook – they had looked it up in preparation). It was set in a park of lavish summer greenness, dotted with fine old timber and affording the odd glimpse of a deer. The Saturday-to-Monday featured a more elderly crowd than the girls were used to, for the Wroughtons' two sons and one daughter were still in the schoolroom. But they had invited some young people too, for the sake of a niece who was staying with them, who had come out in the year 1900 and had not yet had a suitable offer. So there would be a ball on the Saturday night, and Nina and Kitty found many of the same crowd they had been mixing with in London.

The King did come, bringing with him a party of four gentlemen, who seemed to the girls very elderly and dull, though they were brushed at first with the glamour of being the King's friends. The King himself was tall, stout, grey-bearded, and unnervingly familiar from a thousand illustrations. He, too, was elderly, but that didn't matter in a king, especially one who smiled and seemed pleased with everything. Though the girls did not get very close to him, he had a big, booming voice and they could hear a great deal of what he said. His party arrived after dinner, having dined at another great house, and had come by motor-car, about which he was very enthusiastic.

'Forty miles in two hours – not bad, not bad! But the dust is prodigious! I swear we were as white as millers when we arrived. Lucky we had dust coats on, or we'd not have been admitted to the house – eh, Wroughton?'

'It is generally thought to be the great disadvantage of motor-travel,' Lord Wroughton said cautiously.

The King clapped him on the shoulder. 'You're a horse-lover, I know. So am I, man. But the motor-car is the transport of the future. Horses are finished. It had to come.

Rothschild was telling me some American feller has calculated that in ten years from now, horse manure in New York will be as high as the second-floor windows!'

Nina put her fingers over her mouth to hide a giggle, mostly at the suppressed outrage on Lady Wroughton's face at the introduction of dung as a topic. Across the crowd, she caught the eye of Lord Stainton, who gave her a sympathetic smirk. Lady Wroughton repaired the situation by asking in a loud voice if they had His Majesty's permission to begin the ball. The music struck up. The King did not dance, but having been conducted to a sofa at one end of the ballroom, he stayed for a while, talking genially to various Wroughton guests, before passing into another room for bridge, which was his passion. Two of his party went with him, but Prince Ludwig of Fürstenstein and Mr Cowling stayed to dance.

At the first interval, the young ladies were conducted upstairs to the designated bedroom to re-powder their shoulders and fan their overheated faces. Kitty and Nina found a place together on an ottoman out of the way while they waited their turn at the dressing-table.

'The band is very good, isn't it?' Nina said. 'Here, let me.' She took Kitty's fan from her and plied it more effectively.

'Oh, thank you,' Kitty said. 'My corset is *so* tight, I'm sure it pushes all the blood up into my face. I wish Mama didn't insist . . .' She didn't finish the sentence. Nina knew anyway – that Lady Bayfield was determined her daughter should be the most fashionably dressed of the debutantes, which entailed having the smallest waist.

'I'm so lucky,' Nina said. 'I've danced every dance. It's a very grand ball, isn't it? What did you think of Prince Ludwig?'

The ball had been opened by the Wroughtons' niece, Lady Jane Harcourt, with the prince, who was the highest ranking of those dancing, but the second dance he had had with Kitty.

'It was quite an honour to be chosen, wasn't it?' Nina said.

'I suppose so – Mama seemed pleased. But I didn't like him. He's so *old*. And he smells funny.'

'Tom Massingberd says he's like a lizard,' Nina said, quoting one of her partners. 'So wrinkled – and the way he pokes the tip of his tongue out and quickly licks his lips. Like this.' She imitated it.

'Oh, don't!' Kitty shuddered. 'It's true!'

'He said Prince Ludwig is all to pieces. He's had to sell his palace, and he's going round his royal relatives hoping someone will give him a pension.' She didn't repeat the other thing Massingberd had said – that as well as a pension the prince was looking for a rich wife. 'Miss Bayfield had better beware,' he'd said lightly. 'It would be a shame to see her swallowed up by that horrid old mendicant.'

'But you had nice partners after that,' Nina went on. 'Mr Freehampton and Lord Richborough and Lord Stainton.' Kitty nodded. She was more comfortable in company by this stage in the Season, especially as the other debutantes were nicer to her now. All had their admirers, and as there were enough to go round they did not begrudge Kitty her share. 'I think you like Mr Freehampton, don't you?' Nina said.

'Yes – he's so gentle, and doesn't speak much. He seems almost sad.'

'Sad because he'd like to marry you but hasn't enough money,' Nina said. She knew the backgrounds by now of all the young men. People liked to talk to her: it was the great benefit of not being important. 'But you're so nice to everyone, Kitty, I can't tell if there's anyone you really fancy. Are you in love with anyone yet?' Kitty looked grave and didn't answer, and she went on, 'You can tell me. You know I would never repeat it.'

But Kitty shook her head. She had an obscure feeling that it would be unlucky to state her preference aloud. She couldn't tell if he liked her, still less if he would make an offer, but at night in bed, in the twilight moments before sleep, it was his face she saw . . . Instead of answering, she asked, 'Who was the man from the King's party that *you* danced with?'

Nina allowed the subject to be changed. 'Oh, that was Mr Cowling. He's what they call an industrialist, I think. He's very rich, and the King is always looking for people to lend him money and invest in his plans.'

'You seemed to be having a long talk with him.'

'He was telling me about his business. He makes boots and shoes.'

Nina thought about Mr Cowling. It had been an odd beginning to a conversation for, having asked her to dance, Mr Cowling had led her to the floor, then looked down intently at her feet. 'Very nice,' he'd pronounced. 'Amaranth morocco, lined with roan, with false pearl rosette buttons. Hardings in Sloane Street?'

Nina, astonished, said, 'Goodness, how did you know?'

He chuckled. 'You can also buy them from Howell's in Endell Street, so it was a fifty-fifty chance I'd get it right.'

The music started and they began to dance. He danced properly, a little stiffly, holding her as though she might explode. She had grown used to more flexible young men, but adapted herself to him, and examined him covertly from under her eyelashes. It was hard to guess how old he was – she was not good, in any case, at judging the age of grownups. The King was sixty, she knew, so perhaps he was that age; but unlike the King he wore no beard, which always made a man look younger. His hair – which was plentiful – was grey, but his face, though rather brown, was firm and not wrinkled. He might be anything from forty to eighty, she thought with generous inclusion.

'But tell me, how did you know about my shoes?' Nina had asked, after a few moments.

'Why, it's my business to know,' he said. He had a flat accent that she thought must be from the north somewhere. 'I made those slippers of yours, and there's only two places in London I sell them to.'

'*You* made them?'

'Not with my own hands,' he said, 'though I could if I wanted. That's how I started, making shoes, in a little village called Wigston that you won't ever have heard of. Now I've two factories in the city of Leicester and one in Northampton, making all manner of shoes and boots. Cowling & Kempson, footwear to the gentry.'

'I know that name,' Nina said. 'I've seen it in the shops.'

He looked pleased. 'I've come a long way, I don't mind admitting. When I was a boy I was prenticed to the village cobbler in Wigston, but handling all those shoes I saw how they could be made better, so I took a mind to try making a shoe myself. My master let me have a go – and he laughed himself to fits over the first pair I made. But I'm a quick learner, and he didn't laugh at the second. By the time I'd finished my prenticeship, people were coming from miles around to order my shoes, and since my master was happy to stick with the cobbling and mending, I set up my own shoe-making business right across the street. Never looked back. Made my fortune by it. Then I bought Kempson's, which makes boots for the military, and made a second fortune. Which is how come I'm a friend of the King. His Majesty's got a lot of expenses so he needs rich men around him.'

Nina was surprised at this frankness. The *ton* in general thought it vulgar to discuss money.

He looked as though he had read her thought. 'Have I shocked you? But honest work is nothing to be ashamed of. I dare say you'd find my shoes on many a foot in this very room.' His eyes twinkled. 'Whatever they might say contrary! For a machine-made shoe, if it's well designed of good leather, will wear as well as a hand-made one, and cost a fraction as much.'

Nina laughed. 'This is the oddest conversation I've had on a ballroom floor.'

'Aye, I dare say it is,' said Mr Cowling. 'People of fashion don't like to admit where things come from, if there's a machine or a pair of dirty hands in it. You'd think gowns and shoes and furniture and food all came down from the sky in a shower of fairy dust!'

'I'm afraid you may have made a mistake,' Nina said. 'I'm not a person of fashion. I'm only here as a companion to one. I expect you won't want to carry on dancing with me now you know,' she added mischievously.

He gave her an appraising look. 'Do you talk to all the young men that road? You'll never get wed if you do.'

'I don't expect to get wed, sir.'

'Well, well. I'm happy dancing with you. You seem a nice young lady to me. And I like plain talking. The King's a straight one, too. He takes a man as he finds him, and judges him for what he's worth – not by the handle to his name.'

Nina, accustomed to making her partners comfortable, inserted a question about how Mr Cowling had first met the King, which turned out to have been at the Leicester racecourse. The King, as was well known, adored the sport and kept his own racehorses. Mr Cowling, encouraged by Nina, who loved horses, was happy to expand on this story, and the conversation lasted until the dance ended.

Nina brought herself back to the present. There was a vacancy at the dressing-table, and their maid stepped into it and beckoned them across. They sat down together on the wide upholstered bench. Kitty looked sideways at her friend, at the vivid, confident face, and wished with all her heart she could swap lives with her. What use was the huge dowry that made her 'a catch' when she couldn't speak intelligently to the man she was so in love with? She wanted to be loved – she longed for love with all the desperation of her cramped, cold upbringing. In her mind, Nina's childhood had been conducted in glorious colour, while hers had been in sorry shades of grey. There must be love for her, or she would die.

Back in the ballroom, Nina danced with Mr Courtlandt, taking his turn with her while he waited for Miss Vesey to be free. Nina liked dancing, so she never minded being a fill-in.

'Who was that rum old fellow you were dancing with earlier?' he asked idly.

'Not so very rum,' Nina said. 'He's a friend of the King.'

'The King has many rum friends – my mother's always complaining about it. But who is he? He seemed very taken with *you*, Miss Sanderton. Perhaps you should fix him.'

'I'm sure he *isn't* interested in me,' Nina said. 'He's very rich, so he can have anyone he wants.'

'How do you know he's rich?'

'He told me so himself.'

Courtlandt curled his lip. '*Did* he, indeed? Good Lord, what a clod!'

'Oh, I thought it was rather charming,' Nina said lightly. 'In return, I told him I haven't any money at all, so we were on terms of equal frankness.'

Courtlandt laughed, and looked at her admiringly. 'If I weren't obliged to look elsewhere, Miss Sanderton, I should find you dangerously refreshing.'

'I assure you, Mr Courtlandt, you are in no danger from me whatsoever,' Nina said.

He began to reply, then realised there was more than one way in which to take her words, and lapsed into silence while he thought it out.

* * *

207

At the supper interval, Nina lost sight of Kitty in the press around the door, and as she stood alone for a moment, found herself accosted by Mr Cowling, who asked if he could take her in to supper. She wanted to say no – she had no desire for such a potentially dull supper partner. But as she was clearly not engaged, and didn't know how to refuse politely, she allowed him to take her on his arm, install her at a table, and forage for her. While she waited for him to come back, she spotted Kitty across the other side of the room with Lord Stainton, at a table with Courtlandt and Miss Vesey, so she was satisfied Kitty was in good hands and that Lady Bayfield would not berate her for abandoning her post.

Cowling came back with champagne and various eatables. 'Good wine this,' he said, taking his seat. 'I will say for Lord Wroughton, he knows his wine – or his wine-merchant does. Do you like champagne, Miss Sanderton?'

'Very much.' Nina felt languid after all the dancing, and as she was hungry too, she preferred him to do the talking while she ate. So she plied him with questions, and once she had got him started, he went on quite freely. He had interesting things to say about the King's problems. 'He thinks Buckingham Palace is in a shocking state and wants a whirlwind going through it. Waste everywhere, daft rules about who does what. Can't so much as get a fire lit without applying to the master of this and comptroller of the other. One feller brings the coal, but he's not allowed to touch the matches.' He shook his head at the folly. Nina made an interested sound to keep him going. 'His Majesty wants to modernise everything, but it's like trying to shift a mountain. Everyone's got their own interest in keeping things as they are. Like Osborne House, you see – there's the King and Queen, don't like the place, never go near it, can't afford to keep it up, and what do they need it for anyroad, when they've got Sandringham? But can he get rid of it? Not on your life! The rest of the family throw up their hands in horror – what, sell dear Osborne? With all its precious memories?'

This, Nina realised, was sarcasm. 'I suppose,' she said cautiously, 'they were all children there, and the old Queen—'

'Aye, you've put your finger on it,' said Mr Cowling. 'It's his brothers and sisters. Want the place for free lodgings. The fact of it is, they mean to live off him as much as they can. Well, I've told him – don't you let 'em!'

It was an exciting conversation to Nina, concerning such high-up royal personages. It gave her a feeling like falling through the air – exhilarating, but potentially dangerous. 'The King relies on your advice?' she prompted.

'He likes me to speak my mind. And I do. Mind, I don't say he isn't everything a king should be, and there's no doubting when you're in his presence that he's as grand as our old queen was – more so. You wouldn't dare speak out of turn, not without he asked your opinion particularly. He's a very great man, our king,' he assured her. 'And he's that full of energy, he's wearing 'em all out, all those silk-lined courtiers. They've had it easy for too long. Why, he's up till one in the morning, playing bridge, then back in his office at eight reading despatches. Lord knows when he sleeps! I have to say, Miss Sanderton, that I can't get by without a decent night's sleep. I like my eight hours. But I'm not the King.'

'You must work very hard, though,' Nina suggested, 'with your businesses to run.'

'You're right,' he said, seeming pleased. 'Hard work, that's been my watchword. Along with honesty and fair dealing. That's how I've made my fortune – not by rooking folk with shoddy goods and deceiving words, like some I could mention. But,' he seemed to recollect himself, 'this is a poor way to be entertaining a young lady. You must be bored to tears with my nonsense.'

'Not at all,' Nina said, and meant it.

He looked at her closely. 'I must say, I find you very easy to talk to, Miss Sanderton. I don't know how it is, but when I saw you, when we first arrived, I sort of liked the look of you. The fact is, I've never had much to do with young ladies, so you must forgive me if I'm a bit awkward. I knew my wife from childhood, you see, she was like an old friend, and I never had to do much in the way of courting her. We married very young.'

'Is your wife back in Leicester?' Nina asked politely.

'Aye, that she is – in Welford Road Cemetery. She died five years since.'

'Oh, I'm sorry,' Nina said, embarrassed.

'Well, *I'm* sorry – sorry as can be. But there's no need for you to be,' he said. 'And here I am, still not talking about things a young lady'd like to hear.' He clapped his hand to his brow. 'What kind of a noddy must you think me? You'll go back to dancing with your friends after supper and tell 'em you were stuck in a corner with a complete nodcock.'

'No, no,' she protested politely. 'It must have been a dreadful shock for you to lose your wife, when you'd been married such a long time.'

'Well, it was,' he acknowledged. 'She was sixteen and I was twenty when we wed, and such a sweet pretty thing she was. She had a look of that young lady over there, the one with the glacé sarcoline pumps.'

'Miss Bayfield,' Nina supplied, from the direction rather than the shoe description.

'Aye, as pretty and fresh as a bunch of violets,' he said admiringly. He was silent a moment, gazing at Kitty, then went on talking about his late wife, a topic that lasted until people began to move.

Kitty came past on the arm of Lord Stainton. 'We're going back in, Nina. I'm dancing with Mr Courtlandt next,' she said. Her cheeks were flushed and her eyes bright – Nina guessed she had been enjoying her supper conversation just as much as Nina had, but for very different reasons.

Mr Cowling stood up. 'I should deliver you to your first partner,' he said. 'Who are you dancing with next, Miss Sanderton?'

Carriages were provided on Sunday morning to take everyone to church who wanted to go, which, as Lady Wroughton was known to be a stickler, was everybody. The service was a long one, and the night before had been strenuous, and many a young lady had difficulty in keeping her eyes open and her mouth shut all the way through.

When they stepped out into the sunshine, some people stood and chatted, while others got into carriages in different combinations from the journey out, with the result that there were not places for all. Several people said they would like to walk back through the park on such a lovely day, rather than wait for the carriages to go to the house and return, and Nina was one of them. She felt stiff and stuffy and wanted fresh air and movement to clear her head. She had seen Kitty climb into a carriage with her parents, presumably summoned for an inquisition on the night before, so she knew she wasn't needed.

Eight of them started off together, but by the time they turned in at the park gates they were well strung out. Nina, a good walker, was in the van with Lord Stainton – they had come together quite naturally and comfortably, like old friends. Mr de Grey and Miss Courtlandt started out with them, but soon began to lag behind, absorbed in a tête-à-tête. For a while Nina and Stainton walked in silence – one of the comfortable things, she thought, about real friends was being able to be silent together. Nina enjoyed the movement of her limbs, the verdant view and the sounds and smells of nature. The green of the park was decked in bridal white, hawthorn and chestnut, moon daisies and kex.

'Who was that queer old fellow you went in to supper with last night, Miss Sanderton?' Stainton asked at last.

'Mr Cowling. He was one of the King's party.'

'So I saw. But he seemed to have a great deal to say. He quite monopolised you.'

He sounded almost peevish about it. Nina glanced up at him. 'He was telling me about his wife, who died five years ago. He misses her.'

Stainton's expression softened. 'You were good to listen to him so patiently. But I believe you are always kind.'

'No-one is *always* kind,' she said. 'And Mr Cowling was interesting when he talked about his business.'

'Then to interest you I should talk about *my* business? Unfortunately, I'm only just starting to learn it.'

'You mean your estate?' He nodded. 'Don't you love it? I mean, I suppose you grew up there?'

'I've never had much to do with it. My father and I didn't get on – one of the reasons I spent so much time abroad.'

'Oh, I'm sorry.'

He shrugged. 'I believe it's a matter of chance whether a son likes a father and vice versa. There's no rule about it. Mine disapproved of my academic bent. Now I find the estate's in a bad way. My father left matters much involved, and I have to straighten them.'

'You sound as though the job is not to your taste,' Nina said.

He was silent a moment. 'I confess that I felt very resentful when I was summoned home to take up the . . .' He hesitated.

'Burden?'

'Yes.' He looked around him. 'I even hated England – all that wetness and greenness.'

'I suppose you'd got used to a very different landscape,' Nina said. 'Your estate – Ashmore, isn't it? Is it like this?'

'No, not at all. Dene is the archetypal English park, laid

out around all sides of the house. Pretty much flat, so it was an empty canvas to whoever designed it.'

'Humphry Repton,' Nina supplied. He was amused that she knew. 'I looked it up before I came,' she explained.

'How thorough of you,' he said.

'You didn't have Repton at Ashmore? Or Brown or Bridgeman?'

'We didn't have anyone. It just evolved. It has a long history – perhaps I may have time to tell it to you one day. But it's built on quite a steep hillside, so there's no room for "improvements" of the Repton sort. No park in the accepted sense. There's a walled vegetable garden and small area of what you might call pleasure grounds to either side of the house, but apart from that it's just the untamed hillside all around.'

'It sounds rather nice.'

'Oh, so you prefer the picturesque movement to the classical? More Emily Brontë than Jane Austen?'

She laughed. 'You do like to put a neat label on people, don't you? Put them in this box or that one, all nice and tidy.'

He looked at her with pretended shock. 'Are you mocking me, Miss Sanderton?'

'No, how could that be? You are the Earl of Stainton and I'm Miss No-one-at-all.'

'I think you are very much a someone,' he said seriously.

Almost for the first time with him, Nina felt self-conscious. She had to deflect him. 'I'm just Miss Bayfield's friend,' she said. 'Tell me more about your estate. Do you still hate it?'

'Not hate. I . . . resent it, perhaps. It's like a great boulder I have to roll uphill.'

'And, unlike Sisyphus, you haven't deserved it?'

'Perhaps I have,' he said thoughtfully. 'We're none of us without sin. I haven't been as dutiful to my father and mother as I should. I've been determined to go my own way and do what *I* wanted. That's why I stayed abroad so long. I have two younger sisters I hardly know, who now depend on me. Perhaps this is my punishment – to take up my father's boulder and push it for the rest of my life.'

She was distressed by his melancholy. 'But life is not all boulders,' she said. 'I'm not from your world, so I don't know what it's like to be you, but every life has responsibilities, just as every life has joys and pleasures. Isn't Ashmore beautiful in its own way? Wuthering Heights rather than Mansfield Park, perhaps, but still beautiful and worth preserving?'

'Yes, it's those things. I suppose what angers me most is the measures I have to take to repair matters. I feel like a cad and a villain to be searching for a wife on the basis—' He stopped short, with a heightened colour.

She started to say, 'Won't you feel satisfaction in caring for it and passing it on to your—' And then she stopped short too. He was looking at her intently. She blushed, her fingers became nerveless, and she dropped her prayer book.

Dipping hastily to retrieve it, she bumped shoulders with him as he went down at the same instant. Their hands collided on the book; and his closed over hers. The world went still.

They both rose slowly. He was very close to her: she could feel his breath on her cheek. His face was inches from hers. Terrified, exhilarated, she thought *What just happened?* She was used to looking at him, knew every feature of that face, had often traced its lines with her eyes, admiring them in the abstract. But now it was different, and she knew with a blind instinct that the change was permanent. Those familiar features had taken on a significance that made looking at him a thing of agonised joy, a food for the spirit that she would crave from now on. He was no longer merely Lord Stainton, a man she enjoyed talking to: he had become simply *him*, the one person that the mind and the heart and the soul never needed to name.

He said, very quietly, 'Oh, God!'

What is it? she thought. *Is it love? Is this what it feels like?* It wasn't what she had read about, or heard other girls discuss. They talked about 'falling' in love, but there had been no falling. She had been struck by some force – a jolt, it had seemed, like a silent, painless earthquake that had shifted all her perceptions an inch to the left and into another dimension. This feeling, this difference, was where she lived now, an entirely separate place, and there was no going back. She had seen girls in love giggle and blush and whisper to each other, but she had no urge to do anything of the sort. This feeling of hers was profound and rather solemn. She needed to discover first if she could still breathe.

'What—?' she managed to say.

'I didn't mean—' he said.

She looked at his mouth and had an overwhelming desire to kiss it; and she knew, somehow or other, that he was thinking the same thing.

Voices drifted towards them from the people following and, at the same time, they realised what a spectacle they were providing. Nina glanced back. Fortunately it was still Miss Courtlandt and Mr de Grey, whose attention was all for each other. The others were even further behind.

'We had better walk on,' she said, and was amazed to hear her voice sound quite steady, though distant.

'Yes,' he said. He released her hand, and she felt a rush of hollow coldness as if life itself were being withdrawn from her. He was Lord Stainton and she was Miss No-one-at-all, as she had said lightly in the world Before. The irony was not lost on her. He was still Lord Stainton, but now he was also *him*. And she was host to a passion that, like a parasite, she was afraid would consume her, because there was nothing she could do either to feed it, or end it.

215

CHAPTER TWELVE

The day passed in a dream: luncheon; a walk round the walled gardens for the ladies, and a visit to the stables for the gentlemen. Conversation, music, cards. She was not at any time particularly near him, but she knew where he was in the room. She chatted with other people, listened, lubricated the conversation as she always did, but was not really aware of what anyone said. She knew without looking when he went out of the room to play billiards, saw without seeing when he came back. She knew, without having to verify it, when he was looking at her: his eyes on her face were like a physical touch. And when their eyes met, it caused a pang deep in her stomach.

Tea-time. More conversation.

She found herself alone on a settle with Kitty, balancing teacup and plate. For the moment, no-one else was nearby.

Kitty said, 'I envied you your walk back from church.'

'Were your mama and papa difficult?' Nina asked. The words seemed to arrive at random, as though some other Nina – the one in the Before world – were sending them through.

'They asked me about the people I danced with last night. That's all. Wanted to know what they'd said to me. Really, they want to know if anyone wants to marry me,' she concluded abruptly.

'My Mr Cowling admired you greatly,' Nina said. 'He said you reminded him of his wife, whom he loved.'

'Oh, Nina, don't,' Kitty said, hurt. 'Don't make fun.'

'I didn't mean to. *Does* anyone want to marry you?'

'If they do, they never say so, not to me. I don't even know if they like me. They like *you*. They're so easy with you. Why are you so different?'

'It's because I don't matter,' Nina said, 'so they can say anything they like. But they *do* like you, Kitty, only I suppose they have to be careful what they say, because marriage is an important thing for people like them, and like you.'

'I *hate* being people like me,' Kitty said passionately. 'I wish I could swap lives with you. You'd be so good at mine. What use is all this money to me if I can't have the person I want – or even speak to him?'

'So there *is* someone you fancy?' Nina said.

'I don't think he even knows I'm there. When I dance with him, I can't think of a single thing to say, and we go round and round in silence. But you – I've seen him talking to you. He's like a different person. Annabel Courtlandt said you never stopped talking all the way back from church.'

Nina felt a cold chill on the back of her neck. 'Lord Stainton?' she said in a faint voice. 'You're in love with Lord Stainton?'

'You see? You say it as if it's the silliest thing ever,' Kitty said bitterly.

'No, no – just that you've never said anything.'

'What would be the point?' Kitty said. She stood up. 'I'm going up to dress.'

'The bell hasn't gone yet,' Nina said automatically.

'I just want to be alone for a bit,' Kitty said, and was gone.

Nina sat for a moment, rigid. Why should she be surprised that it was Stainton Kitty preferred? Wasn't he the most worthy of being loved? And hadn't he always been kind to Kitty – gentle and thoughtful of her – when they were all together?

Kitty loved Stainton. Something twisted bitterly inside

her. She might have enjoyed her newly discovered love for a while, even if it was hopeless, thought about him secretly, talked to him when opportunity arose. But Kitty loved him, and loyalty to Kitty dictated that she must not think of him at all, not any more. She was only here for Kitty – otherwise, she would never have met him.

She couldn't remain where she was, with the danger that someone would join her. She felt she simply could not bear to talk to anyone else just then. She put down her cup and plate, and drifted casually away. The orangery was likely to be empty at this time of day, and if anyone came in, it would not raise eyebrows that she should choose to wander there alone to refresh herself.

It *was* empty, and she walked between the pots and plantings, breathing the intense scents of damp earth, moss, gardenia and orange blossom. Her mind was tense with trouble but her thoughts were completely locked and wordless. She couldn't even think what it was she wanted to think about. And before she'd had the chance to sort it out, she heard footsteps approaching, and felt almost tearful at being interrupted. But then the hair stood up on the back of her neck and she turned to see Lord Stainton.

'I saw you leave,' he said. 'You looked troubled. I . . .' He paused, seeming at a loss.

She moved away, deeper into the foliage, and he followed. In a bower of ferns and palms, hidden from sight, she turned and looked up at him, and caught her breath. Just to be this close to him . . .

They were silent a long time. At last she said, 'What do you want of me?'

He let out a shaky breath he had been holding. 'Nothing. Everything,' he said. 'I didn't believe . . . I hadn't expected ever to feel like this. You feel it too, don't you?'

'Yes,' she said. It was a relief to have the words said. 'But it's no good, is it?' she added unhappily.

He looked pained, as though at a blow. 'I can't—' he began, and had to try again. 'I am in a hateful situation. I feel like the worst, the lowest—'

'Don't,' she protested quietly.

'I can't marry where I want.'

'I know.'

'If I could . . . But I have – responsibilities. To the estate. My mother. My sisters. So much depends on me.'

'The boulder.'

'Yes.' He clenched his fists, a movement of frustration. The words burst out, 'I wish I could run away with you. Never come back. Go where no-one knows us.'

Just for an instant she allowed herself to imagine it. The heaven of it! To see Abroad – with *him*. But the flash of glory fizzled out all too quickly. 'It wouldn't work,' she said at last. 'You'd think about it all the time – the thing you should have done and didn't. You'd be miserable.'

'What makes you so wise?' His voice sounded strange.

'I'm not,' she protested, shocked that he was agreeing with her. *Don't make me make your decisions*, she wanted to cry out. *I'm not wise. Not even sensible. You're older than me, you're a man!*

'I have to marry for money,' he said bitterly. 'That's the sort of cad I am.'

'You're not—' she began, and stopped. When he had followed her into the orangery, a small part of her hoped he might be going to claim her in spite of everything. But he was going to let her go. She saw it as clearly as she saw him standing there. Being in love didn't matter. In the world of the grown-ups, other things were more important.

Well, she could be grown-up too. *I'm just Miss Bayfield's friend*, she thought.

'Kitty Bayfield is very rich,' she said. Her voice seemed to be coming from a great distance.

'I know,' he said, and added bitterly, 'She was on my aunt's "list" of suitable girls.'

'Marry *her*, then.' He looked shocked, and she said, 'She likes you. I care about her, and I know you'd be good to her. Some of the others, I wouldn't want her to end up with them. They'd trample her, crush her. Marry Kitty. Let some good come out of it.'

He shook his head. 'How can you talk like that?'

She didn't answer. She didn't know. She was drowning.

He took her hands. She was astonished at how much it meant, that touch. They both heard the distant bell.

'Dressing bell,' he said.

'I should go,' she said, wishing with all her heart he would defy the world and say they would run away together. But she didn't know what it was to have people depend on you. Perhaps the world felt very different from that place.

He stepped closer. 'Just this one time . . .' he said. 'If I can never be with you like this again, let me kiss you, just this once.'

She had no words. She wanted it just then more than breath or life. He bent his head towards her. Their mouths met. It was a joy shot through with such pain. It went on for ever, and lasted less than an instant.

She rocked as their lips parted, and he set her tenderly back on her feet and held her until she had her balance. Then he released her. *Never again*, her mind said. She would never kiss him again.

'I'll go first,' he said. 'You wait here until you're ready.'

'Yes,' she said. It was all she could manage.

'Oh, Nina,' he said, by way of goodbye. And was gone.

Nina stood staring at nothing, waiting for life to start up again. Whatever sort of life it would be for her now.

Dawn comes early at the end of May. After a largely sleepless night, Giles got up and put on his dressing-gown, went to sit in the window and watch the long light slip across the night-chilled grass. His mind was full of Nina, like a song and a river of tears intermingled. But when the first blackbird fluted, tentatively, then strongly, his thoughts hardened. He knew what he had to do. His feelings changed nothing. He must put her from his mind and never think of her again.

Crooks came in, surprised to see where he was sitting. 'Is everything all right, my lord?' he asked anxiously.

'Is *any*thing all right?' Giles replied bitterly. 'Will it ever be again?'

'My lord?'

'How does one go about proposing, Crooks? To a very young lady barely out of the schoolroom?'

Crooks settled his weight carefully, as though he feared that somewhere down the line his master might swing at him. 'Well, my lord,' he said, 'there *are* forms and precedents.'

'I knew you would know,' Giles said, but not as though it were a compliment.

Crooks blinked, but continued, 'It would probably be tactful, my lord, given the financial circumstances, for you to approach the young lady's father first, and ask permission to address her. Less embarrassing than gaining her approval only to have her parent forbid the match.'

Giles stared at his manservant in a way that would have unnerved a lesser man. 'Tell me, Crooks,' he said at last, 'does everyone in Town know about my "financial circumstances"? I suppose they're all talking about it.'

'Oh, no, my lord,' Crooks said, and seemed surprised at the question. 'I imagine one or two intimate friends of his late lordship might have had some inkling, but even if they did, they would never speak of it. And no-one else would have any way of knowing. I am sure society in general knows nothing.'

'Hmm,' said Giles. Then, abruptly, 'Miss Bayfield is the one. I suppose you knew that?'

Crooks did not say, either way. 'A very nice, modest young lady,' was his comment. 'And pretty,' he added, as an afterthought.

Giles shrugged that away. 'And rich.'

'So I believe, my lord.'

'Her parents – do you think they know I'm in Queer Street?'

Crooks winced at the expression, but said, 'I'm sure not, my lord. Sir John and Lady Bayfield, they're people of fashion, and received everywhere, but not what I would call in the *first* rank.'

Giles frowned. 'Then how come they were invited to Dene Park as house guests? And for such an important weekend, with the King expected?'

Crooks cleared his throat nervously. 'Er – I believe, my lord, that it may have had something to do with her ladyship . . . Lady Manningtree.'

'Good God! My aunt arranged it?'

'She is, as you know, an old friend of Lady Wroughton, my lord, and her maid, Cecile, happened to mention to me that her ladyship took tea with Lady Wroughton just before the invitations arrived.'

'That proves nothing,' Giles said, still frowning.

'Indeed not, my lord,' Crooks agreed. Which was a well-trained servant's way of saying the opposite.

'But how could she know?' Giles muttered. 'I didn't know myself until—'

Crooks cleared his throat. 'I believe,' he said, looking carefully into the distance, 'that there was – ah – a process of elimination, my lord. That certain other possibilities had been, as it were, crossed off. That is to say . . .'

Giles rescued him. 'Thank you, Crooks. Hot water now, if you please.'

So, he thought, as his manservant went away, Aunt Caroline had seen how much time he spent talking to the

222

Misses Bayfield and Sanderton, had decided the former was his last chance. Hoped to bring about a conclusion by confining him at a country house with her. How ironic!

She could not have known, of course, that anything else would transpire to persuade him of the hopelessness of his position and the need to do something that was still, in spite of all his relatives said, abhorrent to him. And if Nina was right, and Miss Bayfield liked him and would be willing to marry him, did that make it any better? No, he thought, on the whole, it made it worse.

Richard had not been invited to Dene Park. In fact, he had no engagements for once. It would have been easy to pick a gathering – single men were always welcome at balls and parties – or to run down a friend at a club for supper and a game of billiards; but he did not quite want to do any of those things. He found himself instead, almost without volition, drifting towards Golden Square, rehearsing in his mind excuses for turning up on the doorstep.

He found Mrs and Miss Sands at home, and no excuse proved necessary. He was welcomed with the readiness of people whose lives are confined. He was amusement, distraction, entertainment. He enjoyed the novelty of it – company with no ulterior motive. It amused him to step out after an hour and purchase a bottle of sherry at the Crown, because they had no liquor in the house. It amused him to share a simple supper of bread and cheese and cold beef, and to play childish games, sitting on the hearthrug with spills stuck in his hair saying, 'I'm a genteel lady, ever so genteel,' or with pencil and paper playing Consequences.

And at the end of the evening, there was cocoa (when had he last drunk cocoa?) and Chloë played on the piano, a complicated piece, which at any other time or place would have had him yawning or sidling to the door. But he listened with his brain tingling, and a sense of being opened up, like a skilfully shucked oyster, to something new and extraordinary.

When he took his leave, he shook hands with them both and thanked them, and Mrs Sands's smile filtered deep through his rock layers into his heart as she said, 'We've enjoyed it so much. Please come again, any time. You will always be welcome.'

On Sunday morning he woke unprecedentedly early, after his sober Saturday night, and found himself thinking again of the music. Too restless to stay in bed, he sent for Speen, and while he was being shaved, he said, 'You're a Londoner, Speen. What would be the nearest church to Golden Square?'

Reassuringly, Speen took time to answer. 'Depends what you're after, sir. There's one in the square itself, but it's Our Lady of Something so it must be Catholic. For genteel folk, I suppose it would be St George's, Hanover Square. Very posh, that is.'

'Would there be music?'

'Oh, yes, sir, famous for it! It's got a massive great organ, thousands of pipes. They say Handel – the composer, sir – used to worship there regular, on account of the organ was so grand and the acoustics were so good for music.'

'How do you know these things?' Richard asked in wonder.

Speen tilted his head over to get at the spot beside his ear. 'Used to know this woman, sir, Dottie Hanks, who played piano in a pub in Brewer Street. Loved music. Told me about it one time in—' He stopped abruptly.

'In bed?' Richard guessed.

'Well, sir, you know how it is.'

'Thankfully, I do.'

'You planning to go to church this morning, sir?'

'I thought I might. A grand, massive organ, eh? I'd like to see that.'

All the same, he established himself before time behind

a newspaper on Regent Street opposite the end of Beak Street, the route they would almost certainly take if they were going to St George's, because he saw no point in putting himself through a church service if they *weren't* to go. And was rewarded by the sight of them walking briskly, side by side, in what he judged to be their best hats and coats. He followed at a discreet distance. When the service was over, he lingered near the door and allowed himself to be discovered, apparently so absorbed by the Recessional he did not see them until Mrs Sands spoke.

'Mr Tallant! I didn't know you worshipped at St George's,' she said, with no apparent suspicion. 'We come every Sunday.'

He rose, bowed over their hands, and said, with perfect truth, 'I don't attend every Sunday. But the music here! The organ! Did you know Handel used to worship here?'

'Yes, we did. The acoustic is particularly good for baroque music,' Chloë answered.

'So I believe,' Richard said, and before he could get any further out of his depth, he changed the subject. 'Are you ladies engaged for luncheon, or might I have the pleasure of taking you out somewhere?'

Mrs Sands looked worried. 'You do so much for us. I'm sure you must have many engagements . . .'

'As it happens, I'm at a loose end. All my usual friends have been invited to country-house weekends, but somehow or other I was missed out.'

Mrs Sands was instantly concerned. 'Oh, what a shame! Well, if our company can be any recompense . . .'

'It would give me great pleasure. The Imperial is just a short walk away. Will you?' He offered one arm to each of them, comfortable in the knowledge that the estate would reimburse him. Giles had given him *carte blanche* where the Sandses were concerned. He might not have realised it at the time, but he had.

* * *

Giles was not a man who put off necessary visits to the dentist. He sought an interview with Sir John Bayfield as soon as he got back to Town on Monday. He felt obliged to be honest, but it was horribly humiliating. Sir John listened gravely, only toying now and then with a pen, and frowning occasionally. He did not, as he might have, interrupt the dismal narrative to order Giles indignantly from the house. But towards the end of his exposition, when he had got on to the future prospects of Ashmore, Giles surprised himself with his own eloquence. Ashmore, once brought up to standard, would flourish, and repay the investment, he said. He heard his own enthusiasm as he described the improvements he planned in creating a model estate. He had not thought until then that he actually cared so much.

When he finally stopped speaking, all Sir John said was, 'Have you spoken to my daughter about your wishes?'

'No, sir,' said Giles. 'I did not think it would be proper, in the circumstances, to address her without your permission.'

Sir John thought a moment, then said, 'Lady Bayfield has mentioned you as a suitable – er – suitor. I know she would like Catherine to marry into the aristocracy.' Giles winced inwardly. Sir John was evidently not a card-player. 'For myself,' the baronet went on, 'I only desire her happiness.'

'Indeed, sir,' Giles said.

'You will excuse me for a few moments while I consult with Lady Bayfield. A mother's understanding . . . her point of view . . .'

'Of course, sir.' Giles rose as Sir John left the room, and spent the interval pacing up and down, trying not to imagine what might be being said. The approval of the mother might be worse to bear than the disapproval of the father. He half hoped to be thrown out of the house after all. But, eventually, they came in together, Sir John still grave, and a little bewildered, Lady Bayfield terrifyingly wreathed in smiles.

It was she who spoke. 'Sir John tells me you have been admirably frank, Lord Stainton. We honour you for that. For myself, I believe my daughter has developed a *tendresse* for you, and it would go against a mother's natural feelings to deny her the chance of happiness. You will remain here, and I will send her to you.'

Only the last sentence, issued with a general's expectation of being obeyed, rang true to Giles. *Oh, God, what have I got myself into?* he thought. And how in God's name did one propose in these circumstances? *I need your money, and your mother wants you to be a countess. Will you marry me?*

Perhaps, he thought, with equal hope and despair, she would reject him.

Kitty and Nina had been feeling languid after the excitements of the weekend. They had no engagements until the evening, and had been yawning over the periodicals in the small sitting-room reserved for them. Unusually for them, they had hardly spoken. For once, Nina could not do her job: though she saw Kitty was not in spirits, she was too preoccupied with her own troubles to encourage or comfort her.

Both girls rose automatically as Lady Bayfield came in. 'We have a visitor,' she said. Nina wondered a little over the expression on Lady Bayfield's face, and realised with surprise that it was meant to be a smile. 'The Earl of Stainton is here and wishes to speak to you.'

For an instant, Nina's heart jumped so hard it actually hurt her. Her hands went to her chest. But Lady Bayfield was looking at Kitty – indeed, she hardly seemed to know Nina was there.

Kitty had turned so pale, Nina thought she might fall, and instinctively stepped closer.

'He wishes to marry you,' Lady Bayfield said briskly. 'Sir John and I have given our consent. He came to us first, just as he ought, and now he wishes to propose to you in person.

Stand up properly. What have you been doing? Straighten your skirt. And pinch your cheeks – you are too pale.'

'What must I do?' Kitty asked falteringly.

'You will listen to what he has to say,' Lady Bayfield said impatiently. 'And then you will accept his offer. You may thank him if you wish, but there is no need to be too grateful – your fortune is an uncommonly large one. You will be married in your first Season, Catherine, and Sir John and I are very pleased. You will be Lady Stainton. Your son will be an earl. Come, now,' she concluded, 'and I will take you to him. Don't stand there like a ninny!' she added impatiently, to her frozen stepdaughter. 'It won't do to keep him waiting.'

'Can Nina come too?' Kitty whispered through dry lips.

Lady Bayfield cast a first glance in Nina's direction, in which there seemed to be contempt and triumph mingled. 'Of course not. Don't be ridiculous!' *She doesn't need you any more*, the look said to Nina, *and good riddance!* 'Come, Catherine – at once!'

And Kitty, bred to obedience, followed her stepmother out.

The scene: Sir John Bayfield's study. Kitty, shoved in like a reluctant dog into a rat pit, smelt dusty books, tobacco, her father's bay rum. She heard the door close behind her, and saw a man's dark shadow against the sunlight from the window.

It took Giles a moment to realise she could not see him where he was standing, and he moved away to the bookshelves opposite the master's desk. Kitty's head followed him round, but she stood where she had stopped as though further movement were impossible.

'Miss Bayfield,' he said. She was staring at him with wide eyes, like a victim. Had Miss Sanderton been mistaken? Were her parents bullying her into this? Sympathy was as unwelcome as it was novel. He had so hated the whole business

228

of finding a wealthy bride that he had never thought of the females on Aunt Caroline's list as people, just objects. And Richard, the authority on women, had represented them as rapacious hunters bent single-mindedly on catching a mate. But what if Richard was wrong, if the whole of society was wrong? What if women were no different from men? His few weeks of friendship with Nina Sanderton made it easier to believe that. They had talked together – at least, until the end – like two equal people. But had that just been her? Or would any woman be the same?

He must not think of Nina any more.

He began again: 'Miss Bayfield, your parents seem to believe that you are willing to – to receive my addresses. I assure you that I have no wish to press you into anything you don't like. If they are wrong, you have only to say the word and this interview will end at once.' Still she stared. He said, 'Do you want me to go away?'

She licked her lips. 'No,' she said. He raised an uncertain eyebrow. 'I – I am – I wish you to go on,' she managed.

Well, then, he thought. How to proceed? He supposed, from the little fiction he had read, that it was traditional to talk of love. *I have never believed in 'love', and even now when I suspect it may exist, I don't love* you. That was the truth and it wouldn't do. And in any case, he thought, examining her expression, even if he lied and said he loved her, he did not suppose that she could believe it. He had never given her reason to suppose it. So why did she want to marry him? *Because*, said some inner voice, *she has to marry someone, so it might as well be you.* But why me? *Because she likes you. Miss Sanderton told you so.*

Yes, he saw now why she looked like a victim, and felt a vast pity. She had to marry someone. Why Miss Sanderton did not look so he could not at present consider. His task lay before him, and he had to tackle it. Truthfully, but tactfully.

229

'Miss Bayfield, I am here to ask you to marry me. Though my resources are constrained at the moment, I believe they will improve. I have the wherewithal to make you comfortable, and I hope I can make you happy. I promise at least that I will do everything in my power to see that you are. Whatever you want, if it is within my gift, you shall have. Will you do me the great honour of accepting my hand in marriage?'

Large tears filled the wide blue eyes that gazed up at him, but he had just enough wit to realise they were not tears of grief. A tremulous smile was trying its best to occupy her lips. He smiled in return, and urged her gently, 'I believe it is traditional for you to answer.'

The smile had won. 'Yes, please,' she said.

He felt relief, and something like sadness. Something more was needed, he realised, for the ceremony to be complete. He stepped closer, took both her hands, and stooped to kiss her softly, briefly on the lips. He had to stoop further than he had the night before . . . Horrified with himself, he banned the memory from his mind. He must never think of that again.

'Shall we tell your parents?' he said, and she nodded. He would not have thought it possible to look both ecstatic and troubled at the same time, but apparently it was. He retained one of her hands as he led her towards the door. It lay passively in his, unlike another hand he had recently held, which he would not think about, but which had seemed to connect him with the vital force of life.

Richard was aware that his grandmother did not leave her bedroom until eleven o'clock, or twelve if she had been out late the night before. He was not an early riser himself, but on Monday, trusting that Grandmère had not been carousing on Sunday evening, he presented himself on the stroke of eleven, shaved as smooth as a pebble, dressed with meticulous neatness, and bearing a bunch of iris, which she loved.

All his care merely convinced her, when he was shown into her presence, that he was up to something. She sat at the small table in her sitting-room, dipping squares of toast into her delicate gold and white Limoges cup of linden tea, and eyed him narrowly. 'I suspect I am about to be asked for something.'

He gave her a wounded look. 'Can't a fellow bring his favourite grandparent flowers?'

'I am your *only* grandparent,' she said.

'But you see I thought about it carefully. I didn't bring you roses.'

'I give you credit for that. Roses must only come from lovers. Simone, put them in a vase.' But she held on to them for a moment, and ran a finger over their taut curves. 'God's flowers,' she remarked, with soft pleasure. 'Three, and three, and three. The flower that bears the Trinity always in its heart. Also Mary's flower – the sword-lily of Our Lady of Sorrows. All beauty wears sorrow on its other face.'

Richard nodded intelligently, feeling that his recent exposure to church had given him more sensitivity on the subject of religion. He wondered if he should tell her about his visit to St George's, then thought it would just remind her of how rarely he went. He'd been given credit for the iris – he shouldn't push his luck.

'You are up early,' she said, as she relinquished the flowers to her maid. 'Or have you not yet been to bed?'

'*Au contraire*,' he said. 'I have had a Saturday and Sunday of unparalleled virtue. Giles was invited for a Saturday-to-Monday at Dene Park—'

'Ah, yes, the Wroughtons,' Grandmère said. '*Not* people of the greatest refinement. Respectable, but dull.'

'Don't you find all English aristocracy respectable but dull?' he suggested.

'And some not even respectable. But they are better, at all events, than the French aristocracy, who can do nothing but complain about their lost treasures. *No-one* – remember this, *petit* – no-one enjoys self-pity. Not other people's, at all events. One's own is a different matter, *bien entendu.* That is always most agreeable.'

'You are especially mordant this morning, Grandmère.'

'Come to the point, *enfant*,' she said, growing brisk. 'Giles went to Dene Park and you did not. *Eh bien, ensuite?*'

'I was occupied in matters of philanthropy. And I come to ask you a great favour—'

'I knew it!'

'But not for myself. For a very worthy person, whose concerns you will understand and feel sympathy with.' He saw she was growing impatient, and hurried on: 'There is a woman, a very respectable widow, living in reduced circumstances, who has a daughter with a miraculous talent for music. I have heard her play the piano, Grandmère, and it took my breath away.'

'You?'

'Me!'

'*Tiens!*'

'But they only have an upright piano. And she longs to play on a better one. Her talent *deserves* it. You have a grand piano—'

'Two,' she reminded him in the interests of accuracy.

'Quite. The one in this room, and a very fine one in the drawing-room below that stands idle for most of the time.'

'I play,' she said sharply. 'And Sir Thomas plays for me, when he visits.'

'Not the one in the drawing-room.'

She shrugged that off. 'You cannot,' she said, with authority, 'expect me to give away my piano to a stranger.'

'No, no, of course not. Even if you did, there's no room

for one in their lodgings. What I'm asking is that you let her come here and practise, whenever it should be convenient to you.'

'Let a stranger into my house? Impossible. You cannot ask it.'

'Knowing how you love music, and how Sir Thomas nurtures talent, I do ask it. For her sake – for this very good, respectable young lady, who loves music as you do.'

Grandmère's eyes narrowed again. 'You are in love with her, this young woman.'

'No!' Richard said.

'She is your mistress. Some men take ballet girls. Sir Thomas is susceptible to young female musicians. Last year it was a flautist—'

'It's nothing like that, I swear to you,' Richard said.

'But you,' she said suspiciously, 'have *never* cared a jot for anyone but yourself.'

It was true, and he knew it, but it still stung a little. A fellow could change, couldn't he? 'It's different this time. I don't understand why,' he admitted, 'but somehow her talent has affected me, and I don't want to see it go to waste. I want to *help*. Please, Grandmère, only hear her play, and you'll want to help too.'

She was silent, considering, and he was wise enough to say no more. She disliked to be importuned. At last she said, 'I do not leave my room until eleven, as you know. The maid has finished with the drawing-room by nine. Let her come then. She can play until half past ten. She will leave the drawing-room door open, and I will be able to hear her from here. If she is as you say, she shall come every morning, from Monday to Friday, at the same time. If she is not, I will send a note round to you, and you shall tell her to come no more.'

'Thank you, Grandmère,' Richard said excitedly. 'I swear to you she—'

She held up her hand to stop him. 'Do not swear. I shall listen, that is all. I shall not see her or speak to her. She shall present herself at the front door and be admitted, and let herself out afterwards. No-one will bother her. If she is a true musician, she will prefer that. What is her name?'

'Miss Sands,' Richard said – and only as he said it, he felt a sick fear in his stomach that she would know the name.

But it seemed to mean nothing to her. 'I shall tell Chaplin to admit her. Let her come on Wednesday. Not tomorrow – I will have the piano tuned tomorrow. It is time in any case that it was done. She shall come on Wednesday, and we shall see.'

Richard jumped up and kissed her hand, then her cheek, and she brushed him off carelessly, like a fly. 'But I still do not understand,' she said, 'what you are about – why you should want this.'

'Quite honestly, Granny, I don't understand myself,' Richard said, with enough surprise to convince.

'Don't call me Granny,' she commanded.

Kitty would have preferred not to go out on Monday evening, but Lady Bayfield insisted. She wanted to parade her engaged daughter before the *ton*. Urged by her, Sir John had sent off the notice to *The Times* at once, and it should be in the paper tomorrow – not that she had any fear Stainton might withdraw. From what Sir John said, he needed Catherine's money badly. That did not trouble Lady Bayfield. Money she *had*. Status was what she wanted. She could never now be better than a baronet's lady, but her grandson could be an earl, with a seat in Parliament, and land. Ancestral acres. At Lady Bayfield's deepest core was the very English hunger for land that had sent explorers out through the centuries to find unclaimed stretches of it, no matter how bleak or remote. She did not know, of course, of Lord Stainton's reservations about his offer, and would have dismissed them if she had. Land was land: it endured when all else failed. It was a fair bargain.

She did not for a moment consider Catherine's feelings. A mother's duty was to get her daughter married as well as possible; and a daughter's duty was to obey. Had she known any *real* harm of Stainton – a hideous disease, say, or previous wives who had died in mysterious circumstances – she might have paused for thought, but he was a healthy-looking, pleasant-seeming man, so Catherine could have no objection. It annoyed her that the child did not behave in a more lively manner in Lady Vaine's drawing-room that evening. But it hardly mattered: Lady Bayfield supplied enough triumphant joy for both.

In the small hours of the next morning, Nina was lying sleepless, staring at the ceiling and waiting for dawn, as troubled people do the world and time over, when the communicating door opened, and Kitty came quietly in and got into bed with her.

'Your feet are like ice,' Nina discovered. 'Your hands, too. Are you all right?'

'Yes,' Kitty said, but there was a world of trouble in that small word. Nina gathered her friend into her arms and held her close, warming her, feeling her tremble. 'Do you hate me?' Kitty asked after a long time.

'Hate you? Of course not! Why on earth should I?'

'For marrying a man who doesn't love me.'

'Oh, Kitty!'

'I know he doesn't. Mama told me he's in financial trouble and needs my dowry.'

Yes, Nina thought, she could believe Lady Bayfield would be that honest.

'Do you think I'm wrong to accept him?'

Nina couldn't answer. Had her words to Stainton brought this about? *Let some good come of this.* Had she been trying through Kitty to keep him near her? Would he have proposed anyway?

Kitty spoke again. 'But I love him, you see – so much! And I can make him comfortable. Even if I can't make him happy, I can do that.'

'But will *you* be happy?' Nina asked.

'It is my dream,' Kitty said. 'To be with him – to be *married* to him!'

Yes, Nina could sympathise with that. Guilt racked her – and jealousy – and despair. Her aunt had warned her against the glamours of the Season. She had thought she was too sensible to be taken in. She had believed that the mind controlled the heart. Well, it should do so in future, she determined. This sickness would pass, and then she would be sensible for the rest of her life. At all costs, she must never let Kitty know how she felt.

'I'm glad for you,' she said now, putting all her warmth into her words. 'Didn't I tell you, back at Miss Thornton's, that you would fall in love and marry a handsome prince?'

'You do like him, don't you?' Kitty asked anxiously.

'Yes,' she said – all she could manage. 'Do you know when the wedding will be?'

'Mama says the twenty-eighth of June.'

'That's very soon!'

'She says there's nothing to wait for. And apparently, Lord Stainton wants to marry quickly. It's just a matter of my wedding clothes. It'll be hard to get everything made in such a short time, with the Coronation on the twenty-sixth. Mama says she might buy some ready-made things and have them gone over by hand. She says Higgins and Marie can do it so no-one could tell.'

The twenty-eighth. *So soon!* Nina thought. But better that it should happen quickly – like pulling off a plaster. He would be gone and married and out of reach, and she would return to her own world where there would be nothing to remind her. She would be a teacher, like Miss Thornton, and train young female minds to look to wider horizons than those of their mamas.

Still, there was a knot in her throat as she said, 'So, we'll say goodbye tomorrow, then, Kitty. I'll pack my things and be off, but I shall be thinking of you when the great day comes.'

Kitty was startled. 'What do you mean? You can't go!'

'You don't need me any more,' Nina said. 'I was supposed to help you through your come-out, and that's all done now.'

'But I'll need you more than ever! Oh, please, don't go! I shall be so scared, and Mama will be cross and difficult, and if I don't have you beside me I shall never get through it. Nina, please say you won't leave me!' Kitty sounded in an absolute panic.

'I don't want to leave you,' Nina said soothingly. 'I'll gladly stay until the wedding, if I'm allowed.'

'And you'll be my bridesmaid?'

'If I'm allowed.'

'Of course you will be! I'm sure your aunt will spare you.'

But I think your mother might have something to say about it, Nina thought.

There was much that demanded Giles's attention back at the Castle, and it was with relief that he cited business to his aunt to excuse his immediate departure from London.

'You haven't much time to make preparations,' she said sternly.

'It's the bride's family that does all the preparing,' he reminded her. 'Vogel will see Sir John about the financial settlements, and Markham can arrange the travel for the – the honeymoon.' The word sounded ridiculous coming from his own mouth.

'You will need a great many clothes,' said Aunt Caroline.

'Not a *great* many. And there are tailors outside London, Auntie, though the news may shock you.'

'*Local* tailors!' she said, with scorn. 'Well, if you want to appear at your own wedding looking a sketch—'

'I shall look a gentleman,' he said quietly. 'I can't do more.'

He could do a great deal more, she thought. He did not seem happy about or even interested in his upcoming marriage. But she knew that the marriage had been forced on him by circumstances, and though she had always thought his scruples overblown, she was uncomfortably aware that she had done more than anyone to push him into it.

'Giles,' she said more gently, 'you are doing the right thing. You mustn't regard this as some monstrous perversion of the natural order. Your duty was to marry, and you've chosen a very nice, suitable girl who will make you a good wife. You've let it all grow out of proportion in your mind. Everything will be all right. Indeed, it's all right already.'

He listened to her patiently, with an unmoving expression. Now he said, 'I know. Don't worry. I shall be back, but I do have a great deal to do at Ashmore, and there's no-one else to do it. So I must go.'

Which all sounded very nice and reasonable, Caroline thought, but it still felt like eating air. Nothing went down, and it didn't satisfy.

CHAPTER THIRTEEN

With their six months' mourning over, Rachel and Alice could accept invitations again. The first came from their friends the Brinklows of the Red House in Canons Ashmore, Ena and Clara, who were of an age with Rachel and Alice, and therefore not 'out'.

'A children's party,' Lady Stainton said. 'How very – quaint. Parlour games, I suppose, and tea. You wish to go?'

'Yes, *please*, Mama.'

'I suppose you wish to see your friends,' she said, as though plucking the least unlikely reason from the aether. She surveyed them with a critical frown. 'You had better wear your tarlatan plaids. And Taylor must do something with your hair. What an awkward stage you are at! Not out, but too old to be children.' She dismissed them with a wave of the hand.

The girls were eager for company and for change, and their pleasure was increased when the closed carriage was got out for them, drawn by the two bays and driven by coachman John Manley in livery.

'You didn't think you were going to walk, did you?' Daisy said, seeing them off. But they had thought just that. The carriage was the finishing touch for Alice, but it didn't quite overcome for Rachel the shame of the tarlatans. They were definitely frocks, not gowns, in a dark green-and-brown plaid, tied around the middle with a broad silk sash – Rachel's fawn and Alice's pale green. The simple skirts had no bustle, and ended at the ankle-bone. Furthermore, Miss Taylor had refused to allow them to wear their hair up. 'Not suitable at your age,' she snapped. She had brushed it until their heads hurt, and drawn the side pieces back into a knot, tied with a ribbon, but the rest of it fell loose behind in ringlets.

'We look like children,' Rachel fretted.

'We are children,' Alice answered.

'I'm *practically* seventeen. And I hate having to dress the same as you.'

'Oh, don't spoil it, Ray,' Alice pleaded. 'Let's just enjoy ourselves. We haven't been anywhere or seen anyone for months. I wonder who'll be here?'

Ena and Clara, and their younger brother Leopold, who was twelve and therefore beneath consideration, rushed to greet the girls.

'You'll never guess what! Ernie's here!' they cried. 'Isn't it splendid?'

Their elder brother was nineteen, and up at Oxford, and therefore very much to be considered, especially as he was also quite good-looking and very good-natured. In his honour, Mrs Brinklow had invited several other older 'young people', so it was not absolutely a children's party. In fact, Alice thought, with secret delight, if Mama had known who was to be there, she might not have let them come. There was Lord Bexley's younger brother and sister, Sydney and Eveline, and Mary Baring-Gould from Ashmore Court, all 'out' and proper adults. And the very first person she saw when they went into the drawing-room was the bicyclist, Victor Lattery.

He came straight away to greet them, but it was Rachel he looked at. 'I thought I was never going to see you again,' he said. Alice passed on to talk to other people. Lattery continued to gaze at Rachel. 'It's been months and months! I've looked for you everywhere, but I've never seen you,' he said, in a low voice that she found rather thrilling. 'Where have you been hiding yourself?'

'Nowhere,' Rachel said stupidly – she wasn't used to this sort of conversation. 'You could have seen us at church every Sunday.'

'Church?' he said vaguely.

'Don't you go?' she asked, slightly shocked. She thought everyone in the world went.

'You mean St Peter's, I suppose?' he said. 'Well, you see, my aunt's Catholic. We go to St Aiden's in New Ashmore.' This was the settlement at the top of the hill that had developed around the railway station.

'Oh,' said Rachel. She had never met a Roman Catholic before. She was sure her mother wouldn't approve. But it didn't seem important for the moment. The important thing was that he had looked everywhere for her.

'I hope you didn't take any harm from your tumble into the ditch that day?' he said.

'No, not at all,' she said. 'But the cart's axle was cracked and we had to have it mended.'

'And your splendid pony – what was his name?'

'Biscuit. Oh, nothing bothers him.'

'When you said you lived up at the Castle, you didn't mention that you were the earl's daughter. Rather naughty of you, *Lady* Rachel! I might have made an embarrassing mistake.'

'Why? Who did you think I was?' she said, puzzled.

'You must remember, I was new to the area. It wasn't until I mentioned your name to my aunt that I learned the truth.'

Ena and Clara were trying to organise everyone into a game, assisted by their governess, Miss Wylie, who was there to ensure propriety. 'Victor, Rachel, *do* come on,' Ena called. 'We're going to play Lottery Tickets.'

Lattery ushered Rachel to the table, pulled out a chair for her, and took the next one for himself. She had never

241

had so much attention, and was pleased and flattered. Lattery helped her with every hand, even cheating himself to make sure she did well.

To Rachel's surprise, even the older young people seemed to enjoy a romp. After Lottery Tickets, they played Crambo, and then Nebuchadnezzar. A very good tea was served; and after tea, on the suggestion of Ernie, the carpet was rolled back and Miss Wylie agreed to play the piano for some country dances. Rachel danced with Victor Lattery, Ernie Brinklow, Sydney Bexley, then out of kindness with young Leo Brinklow, and then with Lattery again.

He squeezed her hand and said, 'When shall I see you? I can't bear the idea of losing you when I've only just found you again.'

'But I was always here,' she said, a little bewildered.

'Do you bicycle?' he asked.

'I don't know – I've never tried.'

'Oh, it's a delightful exercise, so health-giving and wholesome. I'm sure your mama wouldn't object.'

Rachel rather thought she would – Mama seemed to object to just about everything – but she only said, 'I haven't got a bicycle.'

'Oh, that's no problem at all. They're easy enough to borrow. Look here, if I arranged a party to go out one day, would you come?'

'I'd like to,' she began – the rest of the sentence was, 'but I don't suppose I'd be allowed to.'

He didn't wait for it. 'I'll send you a note, then, when it's all arranged.'

Rachel didn't say any more. She wanted him to think she was as grown-up as him, and could do as she chose. She didn't really expect anything to come of his scheme; and the next day, the news arrived that Giles had chosen a bride, and it went out of her head.

★ ★ ★

Dory had been listening to Mr Sebastian play. He liked her to be there, and she had taken some sewing in with her, so she hadn't been doing anything wrong. All the same, she must have had some sense of guilt because she jumped like a startled hare when she came out of the room and James suddenly appeared beside her.

'I wish you wouldn't do that – creep up on me,' she complained, trying to walk away from him down the corridor.

But he kept up easily. 'You like that old man,' he said, as if it was an accusation. 'What's there to like about him? He's old and ugly. And messy. I have to brush his clothes – you should see the state he gets 'em in.'

'Go away,' she said.

'You can't talk to me like that. I'm first footman.'

'Go away, *please*,' she said, with irony.

'Answer me. Why do you like him and not me?'

'I've told you – you're not a nice person.'

'I could be nice. I *am* nice – didn't I buy you tea? I've got money. I could buy you a present. What would you like?'

'It doesn't work like that,' she said, with an unwelcome pang of pity for him. He wanted to be a real man, but he was incomplete, a human being with essential parts missing. 'Do you know the story of Pinocchio?' she asked.

James was distracted. 'No! What? What's that got to do with anything? Look, here, you ought to stick with me, because I've got ambition. I'm going places.'

'I wish you'd let *me* go places – I've work to do.'

'I'm not going to be a footman for ever. Either butler or valet, not sure which'd pay off best. There's a lot of extras you can lay your hands on as butler. But you travel more as valet. Our new lord—'

'Our new lord has already got a valet,' Dory pointed out.

James gave his least attractive grin. 'That old fool? I can see him off.' He looked at her closely. 'Would you like me if I was his lordship's valet? I could do things for you. Get you moved up. You're too good to be just a sewing-maid.'

'I wasn't always a sewing-maid,' she said mischievously, 'but it suits me just now.'

'What d'you mean? What were you, then?'

'I'm a foreign princess, in hiding from the revolutionaries. One day the call will come from my loyal subjects to reclaim the crown, and I'll be off.'

He had to think about that, and though it was only for a few seconds, it was enough for her to nip through the pass door onto the back stairs and have it swish shut between them.

Crooks was profoundly glad to be back at the Castle, not least because Mr Richard had stayed on in Berkeley Square, which meant he had got away from Speen. The man had been urging him to come out on the spree again, and Crooks couldn't help feeling that the invitations were issued simply to tease him. The horror of that night at the public house . . . the young woman with the plunging décolletage . . . There were nights when he woke, sweating, from nightmares about vast wobbling bosoms, where he was pursued, engulfed and suffocated. It had got so he hardly dared eat toasted cheese for supper any more.

Everyone at the Castle was interested, of course, in his lordship's engagement, and wanted more details than he was able to give. 'Very small. Almost like a child. Dark-haired. A very nice young lady,' he managed.

'You've met her, then?' Rose asked, for everyone at the dinner table.

'Not to say *met*. I've seen her. At Dene Park, we were allowed to look down from the gallery at the dancing, and I saw her dancing with his lordship. He took her in to supper, too.' He summoned imagination with an effort. 'I dare say that's where the damage was done, because the very next morning his lordship asked me how to go about proposing.'

'He asked *you*?' James said derisively.

'James!' Moss rebuked. 'Remember Mr Crooks is your superior.'

Cyril muttered something under his breath that sounded like 'superior ass' and Wilfrid, the house boy, sniggered.

'So he's mad in love with her?' asked Ellen.

'*Course* he is,' said Tilda. 'Must be, else he wouldn't be marrying her.'

Mrs Webster saw a minefield ahead and changed the direction. 'An early wedding, I believe?' she said. 'So much the better. Long engagements don't do anyone any good. In London, I suppose?'

'I believe the Bayfields are keeping the house in Berkeley Street for the wedding.'

'St George's, Hanover Square,' said Miss Taylor, with authority. 'That's where Mayfair gentry get married.'

'I'm sure you're right, Miss Taylor,' Crooks said politely, recognising an ally.

'Pity it can't take place here,' said Moss. 'We haven't had a wedding here since Lady Linda's. Now *that* was a wedding to remember. Everything done just as it ought. The wedding cake was four feet across, the bottom tier. And Lady Linda's train needed six bridesmaids to hold it up.'

'I thought Lady Cordwell'd still be in residence when we got back,' Crooks said. 'Do you know where she's gone, Mr Moss?'

'The Isle of Wight,' the butler supplied.

Mrs Webster provided more detail. 'Lord Cordwell managed to get an invitation to a friend's house on the island. Of course, it's quiet there now, Cowes Week not being until August. I don't suppose he'd have got the invitation in August.'

'It'll be nice for the children, playing on the beach,

sea-bathing and so on,' said Crooks, doubtfully, 'though it doesn't sound like Lady Cordwell's style.'

'No, but it's free,' Rose said caustically.

Moss asked, 'Was anything said about the destination for the honeymoon, Mr Crooks? I suppose we daren't dream they would come here?'

'Abroad,' said Crooks, with a touch of gloom. 'Paris first, then Italy, I believe.'

'Not Egypt, then?' said Moss. 'He won't be showing his bride the Pyramids?'

This alarming thought hadn't occurred to Crooks. 'Not as far as I know. Oh dear, surely he'd have said if that was the plan. Egypt? I don't see how one could keep up standards there. All that sand – it gets everywhere.'

'Just like on the Isle of Wight,' said Rose.

It startled Giles to discover that since he had last seen her, his mother had left off heavy blacks: she'd been wearing them since his return from Thebes, so he'd got used to the sight. She was still sombrely dressed, in a gown of purple-grey twilled shot silk. She noticed him looking, and said impatiently, 'Half-mourning. It's been six months – and you could hardly get married with me in deep mourning. Speaking of which, your aunt Caroline says the Bayfield girl is suitable, though her father is only a baronet. But it's an old creation. She looked it up in *The Baronetage* before she put the child on her list. Created in 1661. The Coronation honours of Charles II.' She frowned at him. 'Why are you back here already?'

'There's estate business I have to see to.'

'The decencies must be observed, if we are not to provoke gossip. The marriage will look improperly hasty if everything is not done to form. You must have her and her parents here for a visit.'

'Here?'

'As soon as possible,' Lady Stainton said implacably. 'I suggest Saturday – best to get it over with as soon as possible. They will come for luncheon, you will show them around during the afternoon, and they'll stay for dinner and overnight. You may leave all that to me. They will return the invitation, which we must accept, I'm afraid. What are you doing about a bride gift?'

'I didn't know one was required.'

'You had better find out what sort of thing she likes before the wedding day. Stainton gave me the four Corot souvenirs that used to hang in my dressing-room. You might not remember them – they were sold during the crisis. I never liked them much – rather dreary, I thought them. I'd just as soon have had a dog, but Stainton didn't ask.'

The dogs had greeted his return with profound but largely dignified joy. It was his sisters who bounced around him, like excited puppies.

'Oh, Giles, tell us all about her! Is she pretty?' Alice cried.

'Is she nice?' Rachel demanded.

'Are you madly in love with her? Does she like horses? When will we see her?'

'On Saturday,' Giles answered. 'Mama is to invite them all here. Yes, she's pretty. She's very shy. And I don't know if she likes horses. But,' he dredged up from the meeting in Lord Leven's house, 'she knows a lot about paintings, so you'll have something to talk about.'

'Does she paint?' Alice asked.

'I really don't know,' he had to admit. Alice gave him an odd look, but Rachel hurried on with the next, more important question.

'Are we going to be bridesmaids?'

'I think it's for her to decide, isn't it?' Giles said. 'She may already have chosen friends or relatives of her own.'

'Her sisters?'

'She doesn't have any sisters, as far as I know.'

'Oh, good,' Alice said. 'I mean, sad for her, but we'll be her sisters once she's married, and she's bound to ask us to be bridesmaids if she hasn't any of her own.' She giggled suddenly. 'To think of you being married!'

'Why is that funny?' Giles asked.

'I don't know,' she admitted. 'You just don't seem like a *husband.*' And she giggled even more at the word.

James came upon Crooks in the boot-room, contentedly polishing his lordship's dress boots. He leaned in the doorway and watched him until Crooks's content dissolved under the scrutiny and he threw him a nervous glance.

'Difficult times ahead for you, Mr Crooks,' James said, oozing sympathy.

'What? Why?' Crooks felt a prickle of fear. James had that effect on him.

'Well, this honeymoon for a start. Like you said, how can you keep up standards in foreign parts?'

'Oh! But I believe Paris is quite civilised,' he said nervously.

'Civilised?' James hooted. 'The French? They don't even have proper privies, not like England. Dreadful smells – and the diseases that go with 'em.'

'Really? I thought—'

'And Italy's worse, not to mention all those *banditti* roaming the streets, cutting people's throats.'

'Surely one is safe inside the hotels,' Crooks said.

James shrugged. 'In London you would be. But these foreign hotel clerks . . . I've heard they take bribes from the criminals to turn a blind eye while they ransack the guests' rooms. And if anyone should disturb them at their wicked crimes, or happen to be in the room when they burst in, well, dead men tell no tales.' He passed a finger across his throat in dreadful mime.

Crooks paled, but he said bravely, 'I'm sure the best hotels must be safe, or one would hear about it.'

'One does, all the time,' James said solemnly. 'There was a piece in the paper only last week.'

'*I* didn't see it.'

'But you don't read that newspaper, do you? Only his lordship's *Times*. And then there's the food. That greasy foreign stuff, and you with your delicate digestion! I pity you, Mr Crooks, really I do. Insolent porters, dirty sheets, fleas, food that's close to poison . . . So much to put up with, and at your age. But you've always been one to do your duty, no matter what it costs you.'

He pushed himself upright and stalked away, leaving Crooks staring blankly at the space where he had been, the evening boot forgotten in his hand.

'What *is* the matter with you, Nina? You've been answering in monosyllables. Your mind is clearly elsewhere.' Aunt Schofield had been trying to engage Nina in conversation ever since she arrived, and finally lost patience at the end of luncheon.

Nina roused herself. 'Oh, I'm wondering how Kitty is getting on, that's all.' She had come back to Draycott Place to see her aunt while Kitty and her parents paid the visit to Ashmore Castle. The house seemed cramped after Berkeley Street, and too quiet.

'*Is* that all? You don't seem in spirits.' Nina didn't answer, fiddling with her butter knife. Aunt Schofield sighed. 'I hope you haven't been spoiled by your experiences.'

'How is the library scheme coming along?' Nina asked, with an effort.

'That's what I have been talking about for the last half-hour,' said Aunt Schofield.

After lunch she got straight down to inviting some of her friends for dinner. In the course of a lively evening of brisk, academic conversation, she was relieved to see Nina perk up and join in. *She sees now what she's been missing,* Aunt Schofield thought. *She'll have had no talk so satisfying these last weeks.*

But on Sunday morning she seemed down again, and breakfasted in moody silence.

'You had better not go back to the Bayfields,' Aunt Schofield said at last. 'I see your stay with them has made you dissatisfied. I was afraid of it when I agreed to let you come out with Kitty, but I *had* thought you sensible enough to come through unscathed.'

For an instant Nina looked up, and Aunt Schofield recoiled before the misery in her eyes. *This is not just dissatisfaction,* she thought. Then Nina looked away, and said, with an obvious effort to sound normal, 'I'm not spoiled, truly I'm not! And I *know* it's not my world. I don't want it to be, really. I enjoyed dinner last night so much. But I promised Kitty I would support her at her wedding. Please let me go back, just until then. It's only a few more weeks.'

'If you promised, then I suppose you must go.'

'Thank you,' Nina said, but she didn't sound relieved by the permission. To go back was not the answer to whatever was troubling her.

A suspicion formed in Aunt Schofield's mind. 'Nina, you haven't—?' she began. *Fallen in love?* But at the last minute she realised she didn't want the answer to that question. Instead she said, 'You may go back, but you must buck up. I can't have you drooping about like a wilted flower. It's not seemly – and it's not helpful. Behave cheerfully, and you'll feel more cheerful. When you come back after the wedding, I shall see to it that you are kept busy. There are always plenty of good works to be done, and not enough people to do them. All this idle pleasure is sapping your moral fibre, and I don't like it.'

Nina said, 'You're very bracing. I wish you were with me all the time.'

'You must learn to do it without me. I shan't always be here, and you have the rest of your life ahead of you.'

Just then, the rest of her life looked like an endless desert, but she thought, *I have to be cheerful for Kitty, so it's a good thing to practise now*. And she managed a smile.

The peace treaty had been signed in Pretoria on the 31st of May and, with the war over at last, Richard began to see army friends and colleagues reappearing in London, some on leave and others, like him, out for good. It didn't take them long to find out where he was, and his two best friends, Bracegirdle and Keenswell, ran him down in Berkeley Square on their very first evening home, and took him out on a carouse that lasted until dawn. Over the first bottle, he saw the look in their eyes, the long stare of men who have been used to a different horizon, and who are still not entirely living in the here and now. More bottles followed, and the look gradually faded, as he supposed his had.

They wanted to know what he'd been doing.

'The Season,' he told them. 'Every ball, rout, dinner, card party and supper on the schedule. Exhausting! Hunting Boers across the veld was child's play in comparison. I was helping my brother find a wife.'

'Your brother that's the earl?' Bracegirdle asked unsteadily. His head was moving minutely as if he was having difficulty in keeping Richard in focus.

'That's the one. Haven't any other. Any amount of sisters but only one brother. Anyway, I've got him fixed up, getting married at the end of the month, and then I shall be free to do . . . whatever I like.' There was a slight hesitation before the last three words, as he realised he hadn't thought about what to do next.

251

'Brother getting married,' Bracegirdle explained solemnly to Keenswell.

'Important event,' Keenswell agreed. 'Going to be his supporter, I suppose?'

'That's the ticket,' said Richard.

'And then – *pfft*! Another good man gone.'

'Happens all the time,' Bracegirdle agreed.

'Not to me,' said Richard.

Bracegirdle concentrated owlishly. 'Sisters. You said you had sisters.'

'That's right.'

'Enough for both of us?' Keenswell enquired.

'Too young. Not out yet,' said Richard.

'Oh,' said Bracegirdle. 'Just as well, perhaps. Interfere with the fishing, women. They squirm, and talk about fish being slimy. And complain about water being wet.' He shook his head at the illogic of the other sex.

'Fishing!' said Keenswell, as if he had just heard of it for the first time.

'Scotland, that's the thing,' said Bracegirdle. 'Town's impossible this time of year. Too noisy. Salmon, trout – July's best for trout. We should all go to Scotland.' He managed to get Richard in focus again. 'Haven't you got an uncle in Scotland? Lord something?'

'My mother's brother. Earl of Leake,' said Richard. 'His seat's in Northumberland, but he has a place on the Spey for fishing.'

'We should go,' said Bracegirdle.

'We should,' said Richard. 'But I have to get my brother married first.'

'Right! Get the brother married. Then we'll all go and visit your uncle Leake.'

'On the Spey,' Keenswell added.

'For the fishing. Think he'd like us to come?'

'I'm sure he'd adore it,' said Richard.

★ ★ ★

The next morning, Speen roused Richard from a deep sleep with a cup of coffee and said, 'There's two gentlemen downstairs to see you.'

'What time is it?' Richard asked, struggling back to the world.

'Half past eleven. Her ladyship's at church, but I let you sleep in.'

'Two gentlemen?'

'Came in a motor-car. Very keen to see you, sir. Said something about plans made last night.'

Downstairs, Richard found Bracegirdle and Keenswell looking surprisingly alert. He commented on it.

'I think I'm still drunk,' Bracegirdle admitted. 'But that's all right.'

'What are you doing here so early?' Richard asked.

'Agreed last night,' Keenswell said. 'Don't you remember? We decided we'd borrow Farringdon's motor-car and go for a spin.'

'To Richmond,' Bracegirdle added.

'I seem to remember Richmond being mentioned,' Richard said, with a frown, 'but I can't remember the context.'

'Going for a spin, luncheon by the river, fresh air, et cetera. Are you ready?'

Richard grinned. 'Why not? Who is Farringdon? Never mind. I've never driven a motor-car. I've always wanted to. I suppose it must be easy.'

'Must be,' said Keenswell. 'Farringdon manages, and he's an awful fool.'

'Let's go, then,' Richard said, eagerly.

It was a 22h.p. Daimler, with two seats in front and two behind. 'Goes like the Dickens,' Keenswell promised. Bracegirdle took the wheel to begin with, but after he'd manoeuvred them at a modest pace through the narrow streets, Richard became ever more anxious to 'have a go'. Finally, when they got out onto the wider Oxford Street,

Bracegirdle agreed to let him take over. Having had the controls explained, Richard took the wheel with supreme confidence, and after a few mighty coughs from the engine, some stops and starts and one alarming passage of going backwards, he got the hang of it. 'Couldn't be easier!' he crowed, as they bowled along. 'Nothing to it! Let's have some fun.'

'Hang on to your hats, boys,' Bracegirdle said, grinning.

'Hang on to everything,' Richard said, and let out the throttle.

The journey down to Canons Ashmore by train was not long. Kitty beguiled the time by rereading the guidebook's description of Ashmore Castle. She had been studying it ever since the invitation came, following Miss Thornton's rule of being prepared.

Ashmore Castle, the first sentence said disappointingly, was not actually a castle, though the first Earl of Stainton, when rebuilding the house in 1780, had finished the parapet with crenulations to reflect the name. But there had once been a castle – a motte-and-bailey fortification built in 1080, and abandoned in 1202. It had been a little to the north-west of the present house, and the mound of the motte could still be discerned, though there were no stoneworks left above ground.

The stones of the bailey had been removed by local people over the years, many of them to build, in 1232, an Augustine priory in the valley, from which the village of Canons Ashmore took its name. In 1248 the canons had been given permission to alter the course of the river Ash to create fish pools. When the priory had been dissolved by Henry VIII in 1536, the pools had been abandoned, and subsequent flooding and encroachment of surrounding trees had created the present Ashmore Carr (a carr, the book explained help-fully, is a waterlogged woodland).

The Priory and its lands had been granted immediately after the dissolution by the King to his friend and courtier Henry Tallant, who had pulled down the priory house and used the stones to build a new house in a more elevated situation further up the hill. Local people had dubbed it Ashmore Castle because of the vaunting ambitions of its owner. He and his son showed remarkable agility in managing to thrive under both Mary and Elizabeth, and his grandson was raised to a barony by James I in 1620. The house was massively extended and altered in 1710 by the fourth baron, with a grant from Queen Anne, in whose favour he found himself after the fall from grace of the Marlboroughs. The earldom was granted in 1780, for services during the Siege of Charleston, and on his return home the first earl largely rebuilt the house in Georgian style, adding the famous battlements.

All this mention of historical figures and events (the third earl had been killed in the Crimea) made Kitty feel smaller and more unworthy than ever. She seemed to be about to marry into the entire history of England. She wished so much that Nina was there to comfort her. She wished even more that she could jump out of the train and run away very fast and very far. When she was roused from her reading by the shouts of '*Canons Ashmore! Canons Ashmore!*' as they pulled into the station, her heart contracted so hard she felt faint.

'Come, Catherine! Don't dither!' Mama's voice was sharp, and had the effect of galvanising her, but as she gathered herself together, she noticed Mama's hands were shaking – she actually dropped the magazine she had been leafing through. Could it be that *Mama* was nervous too? She wasn't sure if the idea gave her courage, or the opposite.

The station master himself came to open their carriage door, hand them down, and guide them towards the exit, and right outside there was an open landau, gleaming black with gold trim on the wheels, and drawn by four beautiful dapple greys. There was a coachman and two grooms in

255

livery, who bowed to her and helped her in and did not once betray any shrug or curling of the lip to suggest she was anything but a Very Important Person.

They drove through a pretty village, then across a bridge over a river (the Ash, she supposed) and up a hill of green pastures dotted with fine old timber and grazed by sheep. *All this will be yours,* she heard Nina's voice whisper in her mind. It was too much. She felt like crying. Surely she must wake up soon.

And then they caught the first sight of the house. It looked very large, a symmetrical oblong of many windows, a large portico with Corinthian columns covering the central third, and the roof hidden by the crenulated parapet.

'Palladian style,' said Lady Bayfield. 'I am glad, Sir John. There is something fine about Palladian houses.'

'Yes, my dear,' said Sir John. He stared at the house, then looked doubtfully at Kitty. 'You've done well, Kitty.'

It was rare indeed that she was called Kitty at home. She melted with gratitude, and gave her father a shaky smile.

CHAPTER FOURTEEN

Kitty was glad that she'd had the experience of staying at Dene Park, which had prepared her a little. It had been even larger and grander than Ashmore Castle, and the Wroughtons were loftier than the Staintons. The meeting between Lady Stainton and Lady Bayfield was almost comic, with each attempting to out-gracious the other with gritted smiles and stiff compliments, but Kitty was too frightened to be amused.

A tall, stout man was presented, who reminded her a bit of the King – Giles called him Uncle Sebastian.

Giles at least was familiar, though she felt more shy with him than ever, now they were engaged. But he was accompanied by two large dogs, which bowed politely, waved their tails and butted her hands with their big heads, and she could be at ease with them, at least.

'They were my father's,' he said. 'They adopted me when he died. That's Tiger and this is Isaac. They're very gentle.'

'Oh, I'm not afraid,' she said. 'I've always wanted a dog.' And he seemed pleased.

As well as the dogs, there were two very nice, cheery girls, Giles's sisters, who did not seem at all lofty and were dressed quite plainly. Nothing to daunt her there. They greeted her warmly.

'We're so glad Giles is getting married,' said Alice. 'Now we'll be your sisters.'

'It must be nice for you, to be always two,' said Kitty.

They looked at each other. 'We don't think about it, really,' said Rachel, 'because we're used to it. But it is, of course. Are you really only one?'

'I had a brother,' Kitty said, 'but he died.'

'Oh, that's so sad,' said Rachel, her eyes growing moist. Kitty's did too. 'It was a long time ago,' she faltered.

Luncheon was served at once. The food, to her surprise, was not very good. Sir John and Lady Bayfield only picked at it, but Lady Stainton, Uncle Sebastian and Giles's sisters ate as though there was nothing wrong. Giles ate very little. Kitty worked away as well as she could, swallowing what she didn't know how to spit out politely, pushing the most inedible bits together to make them look less. The conversation was all between Lady Stainton and Lady Bayfield, and between Sir John and Uncle Sebastian. The latter two seemed to be getting on better than the ladies, and chatted pleasantly about politics and the land.

After luncheon, Uncle Sebastian excused himself and the others were taken on a tour of the house. Lady Stainton expounded its history as if she had learned it by rote. There was no escape – even Giles's sisters were quiet and did not whisper together. But when they reached the picture gallery, and Lady Stainton led Sir John and Lady Bayfield firmly around the portraits to impress them with the achievements and royal connections of the family, Giles extracted Kitty and took her to the far end, where there were landscapes, still-lifes and many paintings of horses and dogs.

'These, I think, will be more to your taste,' he said. 'Other people's relatives, I always think, are of limited interest.'

The girls came hurrying to join them. 'Come and look.' Alice drew Kitty towards another wall. 'This is my favourite painting – Great-grandpa's horse, the one he rode at Crimea. He's called Buckingham. Isn't he splendid?'

'What happened to him?' Kitty asked.

'Buckingham? He was brought home after the war.

Great-grandpa died out there, you know, and a friend, Lord Tilney, took over his horse because they were so short of them. They both survived, and he brought Buckingham back here, to the Castle, because he thought Great-grandpa would have wanted it.'

'My father told me my grandfather used to go and see the horse every day,' Giles said. 'He'd take him an apple or a carrot and stand talking to him.'

Alice chimed in eagerly, 'Grandmère says Grandpapa always claimed he got more sense out of the horse than any of the humans he knew.'

'He lived to be thirty and died of old age,' Rachel said. 'Papa buried him and built a memorial over him. We can take you to see his grave.'

'I'd like that,' Kitty said. This sort of history was much more interesting.

Lady Stainton had finally bored herself with the grand tour, and invited Giles to show Kitty the gardens while she and the Bayfields took refreshments in the drawing-room. Lady Bayfield almost spoiled it by suggesting that Kitty would do better to sit quietly in the drawing-room and rest, but she protested that she was not tired, and Giles and his sisters hurried her away before any more objections could be raised.

'It's too nice a day to sit indoors,' Giles said, as he, his sisters and the dogs pattered downstairs. 'The gardens aren't very interesting – nobody has ever cared to do much with them – but the views are pretty.'

'Or we could go and see the stables,' Alice added beguilingly. 'I could show you my horse, Pharaoh. He's *lovely*!'

'Oh, I should like to see the stables,' Kitty said, and glanced nervously at Giles to see if it was all right to express a preference.

'Then we shall,' he said patiently. 'Do you ride, Miss Bayfield?'

259

'I did learn, as a child,' she said, 'but I haven't had much opportunity. There doesn't seem to be much riding in Hampstead.'

'It must be horrid, living in a city,' Rachel said.

Giles said, 'Londoners count Hampstead as the country – isn't that right, Miss Bayfield?' Kitty looked at her feet and blushed. *She thinks I'm making fun of her*, Giles thought, exasperated. He had meant it only as a gentle pleasantry. He felt hollow, realising that he was irrevocably tied to this very young person who did not understand him at all. Miss Sanderton would have laughed and said something droll in reply.

But he mustn't think of Miss Sanderton . . .

The visit to the stables, however, was a success. Giddins seemed to take an instant liking to Kitty. He instinctively lowered his voice and spoke more gently, but he did not mistake her timidity for fear of horses. He led her right up to them, introduced them, and produced horse-nuts from his pockets for her to give them. She admired and stroked them, even asked questions, and seemed relaxed for the first time.

They lingered there until a servant came out from the house to summon them for tea.

In bed that night, Kitty lay sleepless. The mattress was hard and lumpy and the blankets had a musty smell that was not vanquished by the lavender of the sheets. All the new impressions, the new people, and most of all being on her guard all the time against making mistakes, had worn her out. And this was just the beginning. After she was married, there would be flocks of people of the Staintons' sort to disappoint. What would her duties be, as a countess? She wouldn't know what to do and would be constantly in the wrong, running to catch up in a world she didn't understand.

She wept a little, like a tired child. Now that she was engaged to Giles, he seemed more, not less, daunting. She had noted his slight impatience with her. She didn't understand him, or know how to please him, but that did not stop her loving him. She loved him as wholly and helplessly as a flower turns to the sun. She could not withdraw from the engagement, not only because it was socially unthinkable but because she didn't want to. She *wanted* to marry him; but she did not suppose it would be easy, or that she would not often be unhappy.

But there was much she could do for the house, if she was allowed. Bathrooms, for instance. When she had asked her maid where her bathroom was, Marie had looked disdainful. There were no bathrooms in Ashmore Castle. If you wanted to bathe, a hip bath was placed in your bedroom before the fire, and cans of hot water were brought up the back stairs by toiling servants. It was all very laborious, and the unspoken thought seemed to be that you had to want a bath very much to initiate it.

And there were no wash-down water-closets.

The food had been very poor. She noticed that Giles didn't eat much, and thought he looked too thin. Surely something could be done about that. One of the first things Mama had done when she married Papa was to employ a new cook.

There was no electric light, or even gas. Lamps were such a nuisance. A lot of the carpets were in holes, and the curtains at many of the windows were faded and frayed. There was a good housewife deep inside her, somewhere in her real mother's blood. And if Giles was marrying her for her money, couldn't she spend some of it on making him more comfortable? Thinking about those things, she began to drift off to sleep at last, borne on visions of electric chandeliers, velvet drapes and modern plumbing . . .

* * *

Giles was also sleepless. He had learned, while on digs, to sleep on virtually anything, but he was also thinking with some dread of the marriage he was committed to. It had been a ghastly day. Except in the stables – there she had seemed happier, though she had still not spoken to him, only to Giddins and the horses.

He had been a solitary boy, and though in young manhood he had worked and co-operated with others in his field, it had been on an intellectual, not a personal plane. He had never really had any friends, or been close to anyone, and his inner solitariness had endured. He had always been alone, but it had been a natural state to him, and had not troubled him.

But he was to be tied on terms of intimacy with a very young girl, almost a child, who seemed afraid of him, and out of whom he could get scarcely a word, however hard he tried. He became aware of loneliness for the first time in his life. Now that he had been brought into a situation where one might reasonably expect companionship, he found he wanted it. The brief weeks during which he had shared thoughts and opinions and understanding with Miss Sanderton had given him a liking for such intimacy. To be alone and lonely was one thing, but it seemed to him just then that to be with someone else and lonely was much worse.

Yet he pitied her, having enough imagination to realise that shyness was desperately painful to the sufferer. He must curb his annoyance. And as a husband he must always do his best for her, however little comfort he took from the situation.

Richard dreamed he was back on the veld. His mouth was as dry as a desert, and the thunder of his patrol's hoofs hurt his head. He hurt all over, in fact, from being in the saddle sixteen hours a day. This kind of pounding was hard, but it was harder on the horses. They would endure for so long, then simply keel over and die. Now he dreamed his horse had fallen, and he was trapped under it. He couldn't move. He was racked with pain, struggled feebly, tried in vain to call for help . . .

He moaned, drifting upwards into consciousness. Opening his eyes a crack, he saw the sky a blank white above him. No, not the sky. Not the veld. He was in a bed. A strange bed in a strange room. The pounding hoofs were in his head. His mouth was so dry his tongue cleaved to the roof of it. He must have been very drunk last night to feel this bad. He tried to open his eyes fully, but it hurt too much, so he closed them and allowed himself to sink back into unconsciousness.

Giles, with Uncle Sebastian, his mother and his sisters, was standing on the front steps, seeing the Bayfields off for the station the next day. As the carriage pulled away, Moss came up behind him with a discreet cough, and murmured that there was a policeman to see him.

Waiting in the rear hall was the very tall, muscular young constable from the village – oh, what was his name? Something odd. Hollyhock, was it? No, Holyoak. He was darkly handsome and unshakeable, and stood looking about him calmly, his helmet was politely in his hand. His dark hair was curly as a ram's fleece, Giles noticed. Removal of the helmet had even pulled up two little tufts at the sides, like embryo horns.

'Yes, Holyoak, how can I help you?' Giles said, proud of himself for remembering the name in time.

'I'm sorry to disturb you on a Sunday, my lord, but there's been an accident. Your brother Mr Richard's been in a motor-car smash, and seeing he's not married, and you being head of the family, you'll be his next of kin, so it was thought you ought to be told.'

* * *

'Looking for your hat brush, Mr Crooks?' said James. Crooks, on his knees searching yet again every crevice of the valets' room, looked up with a face so creased by anxiety he resembled, James thought, one of those bulldogs.

James waggled the brush in his hand from side to side enticingly.

Crooks scrambled with difficulty to his feet. James darted forward and seized his elbow to steady him. 'Here, here, don't go damaging yourself. You're not as young as you were.'

Crooks ignored his words, his hands snatching the air for his precious brush. 'Where did you find it? I've looked everywhere for it,' he cried.

'It was on the shelf in the boot-room,' James said, relinquishing it. 'Right next to your special tin of boot-black.'

'It couldn't have been!' Crooks wailed, taking possession and examining it tenderly for damage.

'You must've got confused,' James said kindly. 'Mixed it up with one of your shoe brushes. It's easily done.'

'It is not! I've never done such a thing in my life! Besides, I looked in the boot-room this morning and it wasn't there.'

James shrugged. 'Well, that's where I found it. You couldn't have looked properly. I expect you're upset about Mr Richard – we all are.'

'I know perfectly well I didn't leave this brush in there,' Crooks said hotly. 'Someone must have taken it.'

'Now, who'd want to touch your old brush?' James said jovially. He patted Crooks on the shoulder. 'Reckon you're getting too old for this game, Crooky.' He strolled out.

Crooks's anguished voice followed him: 'Don't call me that!'

Richard drifted up again, this time with a sense of long absence. He opened his eyes cautiously and found to his relief that his head did not hurt much, though a slight movement told him most of his body still did. The ceiling above him – not his ceiling at the Castle or at Aunt Caroline's. The bed – certainly not one he remembered ever gracing. Without moving his head, he could just see to his right a window with voile curtains and heavy velvet drapes, and in front of it a dressing-table with a three-wing mirror and a plethora of bottles and boxes on it – a lady's dressing-table. *Oh, Lord,* now *what have I done?* But he didn't remember. He didn't remember anything.

There was movement, a shape came into his vision, a hand wiped a cool, damp cloth over his face, not tenderly, but firmly and with skill. A nurse? Then a hand slid under his head to lift it slightly and a cup was put to his lips. He drank eagerly. His head was restored to the pillow, and he saw his grandmother standing by the bed.

'Grandmère?' he croaked. 'Am I ill?'

'Don't you remember?' she asked.

'I . . . No. Was I drunk? I feel as if I was. But I've never been in this bed before.' He tried to sit up, felt a lance of pain, and realised his left forearm was in a plaster cast and strapped immobile to his chest. 'What's happened to me?'

'You were in a motor-car,' Grandmère said. 'You drove into a tree. You were lucky you did not kill yourself, or anyone else.'

'I don't remember a motor-car,' he said. 'Whose was it? How bad am I?' She didn't answer at once, and he went on peevishly, 'Why so stern? Shouldn't you be tender and loving when I'm hurt?'

'You are a bad, foolish boy,' she said, seating herself in the chair beside the bed. 'The policeman said you were driving much too fast down Richmond Hill, endangering the lives of all around. You are to be charged with reckless driving, when you are well enough to go to court. A Tallant in court! You have brought disgrace on the family. And only by a miracle were those other young men not hurt, or anyone else. Think if you had struck a pedestrian – a child, perhaps.'

'Wait,' he said. 'Richmond? I remember something about Richmond.' He screwed up his eyes, but it wouldn't come. 'What other young men?'

'A Mr Keenswell and a Captain Bracegirdle,' said Grand-mère. 'They were unharmed, but you might have killed them.'

Richard groaned. 'I'm remembering now . . . something about an outing. To Richmond. They'd borrowed a car. But I don't remember driving it. Or crashing.'

'That will be the blow on the head,' she said. 'The concussion, the doctor calls it. He said you might not remember the accident.'

'But I wasn't drunk, I promise you,' Richard said. 'Something must have gone wrong with the motor-car. The brakes failed, or the steering.'

She looked grim. 'The policeman on Richmond Hill said you were all laughing – "like hyenas" – as you passed him, and shouted something discourteous when he warned you to slow down.'

'That's not fair,' Richard said. 'I can't defend myself, can I, when I don't remember?' he said sulkily. She raised an eyebrow, and he hurried on: 'What's wrong with my arm?'

'You have broken your arm and your shoulder. Many bruises. A sprained foot. And the blow to the head, where you were flung out and hit the tree. Fortunately for you, the family living in the house across the road are decent people and took you in. Their gardener and his boy carried you up here and their daughter gave up her bedroom. They called in the doctor, and have been looking after you most kindly, since the doctor said you must not be moved until you regained consciousness. You owe them a great debt. We all do.'

'I'll be sure to thank them,' he said. 'But how come you're here at my bedside? I'd have thought Mama or Aunt Caroline . . .'

'They have been here. Giles, too. But they all have things

266

to do, so I am taking a turn.' She registered his puzzled expression, and said, 'You have been unconscious for four days, stupid boy. Today is Thursday.'

'My God,' he breathed, and finally grasped the seriousness of the situation. He paled, and felt sweaty and breathless.

Grandmère was up instantly, and held a small bottle to his nose. 'Sniff,' she said. 'More. A big sniff.'

The smell exploded like a grenade in his head, but the faintness went away. She gave him another drink of water, and her expression was now concerned. He remembered from his army days how a man who took a blow on the head could seem all right, but then drop dead quite suddenly days later. That she was afraid for him pleased him, and calmed him down. 'I'm all right,' he said shakily.

She laid a cool hand over his forehead, then sat down again, and he realised, guiltily, that for once she was looking her age. 'You must not frighten me, *méchant petit*.' He felt better, because she'd used French – serious tellings-off were always in English. 'It would break my heart to lose you. One is not supposed to have favourites, but I cannot be fond of Giles as I am of you, though he is a good boy and you are the *mauvais fils*.'

'Giles,' he said. 'Oh, Lord. Will I be all right for the wedding?'

'Of course not. Perhaps to sit at the back – we shall see – but not to be the supporter. He must find someone else. But do not think about that now. I have something to say to you. The young woman you sent to play the piano in my house, you were right. She is *éclatante* – gifted beyond the usual. I have sent a note to you to say that she shall practise *chez moi* whenever she likes. But I suppose you did not receive the note. What is this her name is?'

'Miss Sands,' he said, and groaned. 'Oh, Lord, I was supposed to go to supper with them on Sunday! What will they think of me? Not to turn up, not even a message! They'll think I've forgotten them.' Or, worse, he thought, they'd think him proud, believing himself too good for them. He couldn't bear the idea that Mrs Sands should be hurt.

'I will send them a note,' Grandmère said, 'explaining all.'

'Thank you,' he said profoundly. 'Tell them I'm sorry. Tell them I'll come and see them as soon as I'm able. When do you think that will be? Can I get up today? I don't have to stay here, do I?'

How much this Miss Sands means to him, Grandmère thought. *I believe he is in love and does not know it.* 'You must stay in bed until the doctor has seen you. Then, if he says you can be moved, we will arrange to take you back to Berkeley Square. We must not impose on the Thatchers any longer than necessary.'

'The Thatchers?' he said vaguely.

'The kind family who took you in.'

'Oh, yes. I must thank them. Can you send the note to Mrs Sands right away, today? I don't want them thinking badly of me.'

James, passing the door of the housekeeper's room, paused as Crooks hurried out past him muttering, then leaned in the doorway to ask, 'What's up with old Crooky? Nearly in tears, wasn't he?'

Mrs Webster's lips were pressed together. She wasn't afraid of James – she wasn't afraid of anyone – but she was wary. She was a woman who liked to control everything in her immediate environment, and James always gave the impression that he danced to a different piper. He had a ready tongue, so it was hard to get the better of him, but he was good at his job and Upstairs valued him.

'Must be something serious,' he went on. 'I can see it's upset you.'

Mrs Webster turned away, picked up a sheaf of bills from her desk.

James watched her insistently, like a cat at a mouse-hole.

'Go on, you can tell me. Someone touched some of his things? I bet that was it. I know how he dotes on his brushes and stuff. Move 'em an inch and you could drive him out of his mind. What there is of it.'

She had to take him up on that. 'Mr Crooks is a senior servant. You show him some respect.'

'Respect? He's a soggy mess. Go on, what is it this time? Maybe I can help.'

She relented a fraction. 'His lordship's lapis cufflinks have gone missing.'

'Stolen? Old Crooky wouldn't steal 'em!'

'Don't say that word! Of course not stolen – mislaid somewhere, but naturally he's very upset.'

'I'll tell you what, he's starting to fall apart,' James said thoughtfully. 'His lordship won't put up with it for long. I'll have a look for 'em – I'm good at finding things.'

'All right,' said Mrs Webster, reluctantly. 'But keep your mouth shut. I won't have trouble in my house.'

She was privately worried. Jewellery going missing was always a matter of concern, and something that ultimately you couldn't keep from Upstairs. Secretly, she thought Crooks was a tiresome old woman, but she was positive he was honest. An accusation of theft would just about kill him, but failure to resolve the matter would sow suspicion among all of them.

She was deeply grateful, therefore, when James returned half an hour later and dropped the links into her hand. 'Where did you find them?'

'On the floor in the laundry, beside the shirt basket. He must have had 'em in his hand when he brought the shirt down, and dropped 'em.' He gave her a straight stare. 'Like I said, he's falling apart. Ask me, it's worry about this honeymoon trip. He doesn't want to go, but he doesn't want to ask his lordship to let him off.' He shrugged. 'Natural enough. He'd be scared to lose his job if he did.'

Mrs Webster didn't comment. 'I'll see he gets these back,' she said, and only added, 'Thank you,' because she felt forced to. The whole thing was a minefield.

Richard had been eager to be moved, but when he discovered how painful it was, he understood why they were taking him to Berkeley Square and not all the way to Ashmore. He had not known how much broken bones hurt. The move, which had to be done slowly, took most of the day, and knocked him back severely. He was in such agony that Aunt Caroline's doctor, Dangerfield, prescribed morphine, and he lay comatose for several days, drifting in and out of unpleasant dreams, waking to cloudy thoughts, sweat, debilitation, and always the return of pain.

Dangerfield, examining his various injuries, said that it was not merely a sprained foot but small bones were broken, and he set it in plaster. There was not much to be done about a broken shoulder, he said, except to keep it immobile; and among Richard's many injuries were a bruised spine, which accounted for the pain whenever he tried to turn over. There were many weeks of recovery ahead of him: going to the wedding was out of the question. When he had gone, Richard wept a little from sheer weakness. He had never felt so helpless.

Giles visited. He came in evening dress and with wine on his breath, having just been in Berkeley Street for the return visit to the Bayfields.

'Was it hell?' Richard asked feebly.

'Not as bad as I feared,' said Giles. 'Aunt Caroline had paid a visit of congratulation, so they asked her as well. She can always talk.'

'Why did she do that?'

'It seems she went to school with Miss Sanderton's aunt,

so I suppose she felt a connection,' Giles said, trying to hide his discomfort at having to mention Nina.

'Ah, yes, Miss Sanderton,' Richard said. 'Was she there?'

'Yes,' said Giles. Then he realised he had been too abrupt, and with an effort, said, 'She and Aunt Caroline kept things going.' He hoped Richard would not ask anything more about her.

Richard was too weak still to sustain much curiosity. He lapsed into silence for a while, then roused himself to say, 'This accident of mine, the sawbones says I won't be able to make the wedding.' He looked up apologetically at his brother.

'I know,' said Giles. 'It's already been discussed. Don't worry about it. I'm sorry you won't be there, but it can't be helped.'

'But who—?'

'Will be my supporter? Well, I asked Uncle Sebastian, but he said he was too old and that he'd spoil the effect for everyone. Said they'd think the organ needed repairing if they heard him wheezing. You know how he talks.' Richard smiled. 'He suggested Uncle Stuffy.'

'Uncle Stuffy?' Richard said in surprise. Their uncle Fergus, the Earl of Leake, their mother's brother, had acquired the nickname Stuffy at school because of his love of eating, and it had stuck, in an affectionate way. He was much younger than their mother, a bachelor dedicated to middle-aged pleasures that made him seem older. 'Would he do it?'

'Mama thought he would, so I sent off a telegram. It took a while to find him – you know how he moves from house to house at this time of year – but he telegraphed back that he'd be delighted. I must say,' Giles added, 'that she was really pleased I was asking him. It's put her in a better mood than I've seen since Papa died. So I didn't tell her it was Uncle Sebastian's idea.'

'Well,' said Richard, feebly, 'I'm glad it's all sorted out.'

'You're tired. I'll go,' said Giles.

'Come again soon,' Richard said. 'I'm infernally bored tied to this bed.' It was only partly true. He was too weak and still slept too much to be often bored.

'I will,' said Giles.

Aunt Caroline's solicitor, Camberwell, called. 'I'm afraid the matter is serious,' he said. 'Your companions will only be charged with unruly behaviour, but things are much worse for you as the driver. Criminal law is not my field, so I have consulted a criminal barrister, on Lady Manningtree's instructions. He says there is not much point in trying to devise a strategy until we know when your case will come on, and before which magistrate.'

'Strategy?'

'The penalties for reckless driving range from fines to imprisonment. And magistrates have considerable discretion. Some are particularly harsh when it comes to motoring offences – the older sort who think motor-cars are the invention of the devil. Others take a lighter view. A more lenient magistrate might decide that as no-one else was hurt, and you have already suffered considerably, no further punishment is needed. He might let you off with a caution.'

'Can't we get one of those?' Richard begged.

'I'm afraid it isn't up to us. I wish it were.'

Linda visited. 'You really are a fool, Richard. What a mess you've got us into! I had to come back from the Isle of Wight—'

'You were coming back for the wedding anyway,' he protested.

'Yes, but I had to come back early because of worries about you.'

'You don't seem worried.'

'I'm more angry about the court case than anything. Dragging our name into the mud, just when things are at such a delicate stage for Giles!'

'It might not come to anything,' Richard said. 'If the beak thinks I've suffered enough—'

'*You*'ve suffered!' she snorted. 'And why Giles has to rush into marriage in this unseemly manner I don't know. Another month of engagement would surely not be much to ask. He doesn't seem to realise the difficulty of getting anything new made. With everybody in London for the Coronation, and foreign royalties hogging all the best dressmakers . . . If he'd chosen the end of July, they'd have been begging for work and there would have been discounts to be had. As for hats, the expense is ridiculous, and my allowance is all used up. I simply *can't* appear at my own brother's wedding – and in St George's, with the whole of the *ton* invited – in a made-over hat. Won't you ask him for a little extra for me, as it's a special occasion?'

'I won't even be going,' Richard pointed out.

'Exactly. He'll feel sorry for you and agree to anything you ask,' Linda said triumphantly.

'Damnation! *Crooks!*' Giles bellowed.

Crooks appeared at the dressing-room door, saw the blood, and hastened to grab a towel. 'You cut yourself, my lord?'

'What the devil have you done with my razor?' Giles growled. 'It's as blunt as a rusty ploughshare!'

'I sharpened and set it just as usual, my lord,' Crooks said, in a quavering voice. Giles examined the towel he had pressed to the cut. 'The alum block, my lord?'

'In a moment.' Giles rinsed off the razor in the bowl, and held it up to the light. 'God damn it!' he exclaimed. 'There's a nick out of it. Look there! Actually a nick.' Crooks must have been damned clumsy to spoil the edge like that. Let the strop get too dry – or dropped the razor and then forgotten that he had.

Crooks's hands were trembling. He looked pale, and damp about the upper lip, as he stammered: 'I don't understand how it could have happened, my lord. Never in my whole life . . . his late lordship . . . wouldn't have it happen for the world . . . setting razors for thirty years—'

Giles cut him off. 'You had better send it back to Truefitt's to be reground. Send it straight away, ask them as a favour to me to get it back before the wedding. Is the other one all right?'

'I will examine it carefully, my lord, but I'm sure it is. I really don't know how this could have happened—'

'Yes, yes, that's enough,' Giles said.

Crooks shuffled his way out, back into the bedroom where he had been laying out Giles's clothes. The old fellow didn't seem to be on top of things, and that was a fact. Of course, his master's death had been a shock to him. But yesterday a button had come off his waistcoat as he'd tried to do it up, and the day before – or was it the day before that? – a thumb mark on his boot heel. Giles was not a dandy, but in his position you had to take care of your appearance – and you expected a certain level of competence from those who served you. If you couldn't shave yourself without the damned razor chopping lumps out of you . . . ! Crooks had been upset, he remembered, that he'd insisted on shaving himself rather than letting Crooks do it. He shuddered at the memory, and imagined himself lying in a welter of blood from a cut throat while the valet dithered and wrung his hands ineffectually . . .

If only there were a kind way of getting rid of him . . .

Giles visited Richard again. 'I'm just on the way to the bridesmaids' luncheon.' It had been decided by the two mothers during the visit to the Castle that Giles's sisters

274

should be bridesmaids as well. Lady Bayfield had suggested it – two Stainton girls would do something to balance out the Sanderton nonentity – and Lady Stainton had agreed to it because the subject interested her too little to resist it.

Giles gave Richard a grim look. 'It's the groomsman's duty really, but you're *hors de combat*, and I couldn't inflict Uncle Stuffy on them.'

Richard gave a feeble grin. 'Isn't it traditional for the groomsman to marry one of them? He can't marry his own nieces, so it'll have to be Miss Sanderton. Do you think she'll like him?'

'Don't joke about it,' Giles said stiffly.

Mrs Sands visited. 'I was so worried about you, I plucked up courage and wrote to your grandmother, seeing she'd been so kind to Chloë, asking if I might visit. She seemed to think it was all right, and gave me a note of introduction for your aunt. And so,' she laughed nervously, 'at the end of a long explanation, here I am.'

'I'm glad you came,' he said, and made an instinctive movement of his hand towards her. She took it, and he felt a sweet shock in his stomach at the warm smoothness, combined with the strength of a pianist's fingers. 'How is Miss Sands?'

'Chloë is in seventh heaven, having access to a proper grand piano. Your grandmother's instrument is a very fine one, she says.'

'Sir Thomas Burton chose it for Grandmère, and he was a pianist before he became a conductor, so he ought to know a good one.'

'It only adds to the honour, for her to play an instrument he chose. And, I must tell you, your grandmother has taken to leaving pieces of music lying on the lid for her to try. Sheet music is so expensive – it is a wonderful kindness of hers to think of it.'

Richard smiled. 'Grandmère is as selfish as the day is

long. She will have put out the pieces *she* wants to hear, you can depend on it. It's the one trait I share with her – complete self-centredness.'

'I know that's not true,' she said, squeezing his hand – then seemed to realise she was holding it, and released it quickly. 'I was sorry to hear that you won't be able to go to your brother's wedding on the twenty-eighth.'

'How do you know what date it is?'

'He's marrying in St George's, which is the church Chloë and I attend, as you know. We hear the banns read out. And your grandmother said you were expected to be bedridden for three or four weeks more. Is it painful?' she asked, in a concerned voice.

'You can't expect an ex-soldier to admit it,' he said.

'There's such a thing as being too brave,' she said. She rose. 'I had better go and let you rest.'

'But you will come again?' he asked urgently. 'Come and chat – nobody's got time to chat to me with the wedding coming up. Tell me all about your pupils and what you and Miss Sands are doing. Please come.'

'Well, I will, then, if your aunt doesn't mind. Is there anything I can bring you? Do you need anything?'

'No, thank you. Fruit and books and all that sort of thing get sent in regularly – my aunt is very efficient. Company is all I lack.'

'You know,' said Mrs Webster, handing Crooks a cup of tea, 'I'm sure his lordship would think no worse of you if you were to ask not to go on the honeymoon tour.'

The cup clattered in the saucer as Crooks's hands shook. So this was why Mrs Webster had invited him to take tea with her alone. 'Has something been said?' he quavered.

'No, of course not – well, not to me. But I've just been noticing that you've been a bit upset recently, and I know you don't relish the idea of foreign travel.'

Crooks took a restorative sip. 'I don't, of course,' he said. 'I'm sure I don't know who does. But I'll do my duty, as I always have done. It's his lordship's comfort and convenience that must come first.'

'Well, you know,' Mrs Webster said, as if casually, 'I'm sure James could be persuaded to swap with you – you could stay here and valet Mr Sebastian, and he could go with his lordship.' James had asked her to make the suggestion as though she had thought of it herself, for Mr Crooks's pride would be hurt if he thought James pitied him. She'd been surprised that James could be so thoughtful. 'He's a younger man, so the travelling wouldn't tax him as much. Not to mention' – something James had urged her to mention – 'the nasty foreign food. You have a delicate digestion. James could eat nails.'

The foreign food made the teacup chatter again. But 'I couldn't think of deserting my post,' Crooks said. 'His lordship is the Earl of Stainton. All eyes will be on him. He must have the very best of attendance at all times.'

'Oh, I agree, in general,' said Mrs Webster. 'But Abroad people don't have such high standards as we do, and James is quite a good valet in his way, good enough for them. Better you take care of your health so you can serve his lordship properly when he gets home, where it really matters. Can I offer you a slice of cake, Mr Crooks?'

'Thank you, Mrs Webster,' Crooks said thoughtfully. The golden vision of not going abroad beckoned him – not going, and having a good reason that assuaged his pride – and when coupled with the thought of James, whom he disliked, having to eat foreign food instead of him it became almost irresistible.

The Coronation was to take place on Thursday, the 26th of June, but on the twenty-fourth, with London already decked in bunting, souvenirs packing the shops and stalls,

Coronation parties arranged, and hotels and houses full of guests from all over the country and the Continent, it was announced that it had been postponed, with no set date. The King had undergone an operation at Buckingham Palace. He had been in acute abdominal pain for ten days, but had bravely carried on with his duties. His surgeons had finally persuaded him that his life was in danger if they did not operate. No announcement had been made beforehand, because abdominal operations were themselves life-threatening; but now it was said that the surgeons had acted just in time, and that a large abscess had been successfully removed.

The following day, Dr Dangerfield came in to see Richard on a routine visit, and was full of wonder at the story. Richard being a captive audience, and glad of anything to relieve the tedium, encouraged him to talk.

'It was Treves who operated,' Dangerfield said, leaning against the mantelpiece and idly swinging his stethoscope. 'The King's favoured him ever since he told him a very good joke at a dinner one time. Personally, I don't like the man – too full of himself – but one has to say he has nerves of steel! Hard enough to operate when the patient is sixty years old, vastly overweight, and a heavy smoker who suffers from chronic bronchitis, but when the patient is also your king . . .'

'Was it really dangerous, then?' Richard asked.

'All operations are dangerous,' said Dangerfield. 'Abdominals especially so. All those organs potentially to damage, all those opportunities for infection. And when the patient might not even survive the anaesthetic . . . Death on the table was probably the likeliest outcome.'

'Then why would he agree to it?' Richard asked.

Dangerfield shrugged. 'As I heard it, the King said he'd sooner die in the Abbey than on an operating table, and Laking and Barlow – his physicians – told him that that was all too likely. So he submitted. And apparently Treves got to the abscess when it was on the point of rupturing. If it had burst, it would have meant peritonitis and probable death.' Dangerfield grunted. 'The worst thing is that Treves will be lording it over the rest of us for ever. There'll be no living with him. Expect to see him in every fashionable drawing-room very soon.' He straightened up. 'And what about you, young man? How are you feeling?'

'Absolutely bloody,' Richard said.

'Good, good,' said Dangerfield breezily. 'One thing – with the Coronation cancelled, your brother's wedding is promoted to being the most important event of the week. Pity you can't be there.'

'Is that what you call a bedside manner?' Richard said savagely, as Dangerfield advanced on him.

But with the stethoscope in his ears he couldn't hear. 'Don't speak, please . . . Hmm, heart strong and steady. Lucky you're a healthy young man – but I advise you not to knock yourself about like this too often.'

James appeared in the doorway of the sewing-room, and looked for an indulgent moment at the top of Dory's head before she deigned to notice him. He didn't understand why she had got under his skin so bad. She wasn't tops in the looks department – all right, but no Venus. As a matter of fact, he had never been that much interested in looks. The new housemaid Tilda was no great shakes, but he had taken her for a walk in the woods and she had let him have a feel, which was the point. He'd impressed her with his talk and his status. Now, of course, she'd taken to staring at him with her mouth open and going red when he spoke to her, just like daft William did when girls spoke to him. He was used to that. What he wasn't used to was Dory seeming so unimpressed with anything he said or did. He almost thought sometimes she was *laughing* at him. It wouldn't do.

She *should* be impressed. He was going to damn well make sure she was. Dory! What sort of a name was that, anyway?

'Did you want something?' she asked, looking up at last.

'You heard I'm going with his lordship on the honeymoon trip instead of Crooks?' he asked.

'I heard,' she said, with as little emotion as if he'd said, 'Have you heard it's raining out?'

'*I'm* his lordship's valet,' he said.

'For now,' she said.

'For good. Trust me on that. By the time I get back, his lordship won't remember he ever had anyone else. He'll be so dependent on me—'

Dory had put her hand over her mouth, *almost* as if she was politely concealing a yawn. 'Congratulations,' she said, going back to her sewing.

'Listen,' he said, 'I told you I was going places. Valet to an earl – that's a big thing! And it means a lot of pickings. In a few years, I can get out of service, start up a business of my own. And if I take you with me . . .' He paused temptingly, but she didn't look up. 'Wouldn't you like to better yourself? You could set up as a dressmaker, make posh clothes for all the nobs. I could get you started. I'd manage the business, buy the cloth, handle the customers, all that sort of thing. We'd end up with twenty working for us.'

Now she looked up and smiled at him, but it wasn't the smile of awe and gratitude that he craved. It was – well, sort of indulgent. 'Big dreams,' she said. 'You let me know when it's happening.'

'You don't believe me?' he said, his nostrils flaring.

'Oh, I believe you mean it,' she said. 'Off you go, now – I'm a bit busy. And you should be, too, with all his lordship's clothes to look over before the wedding.'

He turned away, trying to do it with dignity, as though he'd been going anyway. 'I'll show you,' he muttered, under his breath.

CHAPTER FIFTEEN

In the afternoon of the twenty-eighth, Mrs Sands visited Richard again. 'I've come to tell you about the wedding.'

'You were there?'

'We stood outside. There was a huge crowd. We saw everyone arrive, and we could hear the music. And we saw them come out at the end. The bride looked beautiful. And your brother appeared very distinguished. There were so many photographers, it was like an electrical storm! There'll be pictures in all the papers. But I thought you'd like a first-hand account.'

'Tell me from the beginning,' Richard said. So she did, with particular reference to the music and – being after all a woman – what everyone was wearing.

Nina knew that her stay in Berkeley Street would end with the wedding, but she had not expected to be hurried away so precipitately. No sooner had the bridal couple left for the station than Lady Bayfield's maid, Higgins, appeared at her elbow and said, 'I'll help you get changed now, miss,' and urged her away upstairs to her bedroom. There she found everything already packed, some day clothes laid out on the bed, and her trunk only waiting, as Higgins told her, for the bridesmaid dress to go in.

'You've been – busy,' Nina said, swallowing tears.

'Her ladyship had me pack your things while you were all

at the church,' Higgins said, her face a blank. If she felt any sympathy, she didn't show it. 'I'll help you get changed, and there'll be a cab downstairs for you as soon as you're ready.'

Nina turned her back towards Higgins to be unbuttoned, thinking about Kitty. In the last moment before she went out of the front door with her new husband, Kitty had darted over to Nina, drawn her close, and whispered into her ear, 'Thank you for everything, darling Nina! I'm so happy.'

And over her shoulder, Nina had met Giles's eye for an instant, before he looked away with a fleeting expression of pain.

That was all there was. It was over. To say she felt flat was an understatement. She felt hollowed out, empty, transparent, lost.

Perhaps it was for the best not to linger here. She should get back as soon as possible to what would be her life from now on. Real life, whatever that turned out to be. And much as she loved Kitty, she hoped just then that she would never see her again, because it would be too painful.

Higgins helped her into her day clothes, and she picked up her hat and gloves and said, 'Thank you. I'm ready.'

'I wasn't sure when to expect you,' said Aunt Schofield. 'I have people coming to dinner tonight, but it will be easy to lay an extra place for you. What did Lady Bayfield say when you said goodbye?'

'I didn't see her. She sent her maid to help me change, and then a taxi came.'

Aunt Schofield gave her a keen look. 'What an odd woman she is. But never mind. They're nothing to do with us. You're not going to mope, are you?'

Nina managed to smile, wanly. 'No. I'm going to be brisk and get on with things.'

'Good girl. There's a very nice young woman coming

tonight who I think you'll be friends with – Lepida Morris. She's been helping with the library scheme, and I'd like you to join forces with her and really make a push to get things going, before everybody goes out of Town for the summer. I'd like the library to open this winter if possible. Run and take off your things, then come and help me decide the place-settings.'

At dinner that night, Nina felt foolishly surprised that no-one was discussing the Stainton wedding, which had been the foremost subject in her circle for the last month. There was much discussion of the King's illness and operation, and the cancelled Coronation.

'They're calling it "appendicitis" now, not "typhlitis",' said Dr Broadbent – a doctor of philosophy, not of medicine. 'It's the word of the moment. The appendix, which we are all accustomed to thinking of as a scholarly addition to a book,' he looked around the company with a dry smile, 'is apparently some superfluous organ in the abdominal region. An evolutionary left-over, like an ox-bow, a cul-de-sac in which infection can collect, unseen and unsuspected until disaster strikes.'

Quintin Caldecott, professor of ancient history, said, 'I wonder how frequently this mysterious appendix has been to blame in cases of sudden death. Until now, an episode of acute abdominal pain followed by convulsions and death was likely to be ascribed to poisoning, and many a poor wretch has gone to the gallows for it. It would be interesting to know if they were all appendicitis after all.'

'The danger is that the opposite will now prevail,' said his wife, Mary. 'Wronged wives who poison their husbands will persuade physicians to write it off as appendicitis.'

'We shall all have to be kinder to our wives from now on,' said the professor, giving her an adoring look.

'I've heard it said,' said Mr Carnoustie, lecturer in

political history at University College London, 'that removal of the appendix is expected to become the most fashionable operation in Town. That fellow Treves is making the most of his sudden fame. Members of the *ton* are already queuing up for it.' He looked at Aunt Schofield with a mischievous smile. 'Anyone who still has an appendix by the end of the year will be condemned as sadly behind the times.'

'Which just goes to show the folly of having too much money and not enough to do,' Aunt Schofield said.

'It's all very well,' said Mrs Henry Morris, 'but the King really was in mortal danger.'

'And I believe a lot of businesses have suffered considerable loss,' said Mr Carnoustie. 'Hoteliers. Manufacturers of souvenirs – all their plates and mugs have the wrong date on them.'

'My own magazine,' said Henry 'Mawes' Morris, who was an illustrator, 'had to destroy thousands of copies of the latest issue. It contains a long and detailed article entitled, "How I Saw the Coronation, by a Peer's Daughter". You may laugh,' he said, as everyone did, 'but the expense was considerable.'

'Not least the expense of imagination by the peer's daughter,' said Aunt Schofield.

'An expense of imagination in a waste of fame,' Quin Caldecott murmured.

'My favourite story,' said Oswald Eagan, 'concerns the Coronation feast. An exquisite banquet for two and a half thousand guests suddenly not wanted. Mountains of caviar, forests of asparagus, three hundred legs of mutton, tons of strawberries and lakes of cream.'

'I expect the palace servants made up parcels for their families,' said Mrs Morris.

'Of course, but there was so much that not even they could account for it all. Apparently, the rest was packed up to be given to the poor. Just think, while the King was under the surgeon's knife, East End soup kitchens were serving *consommé de faisan*! I am quite charmed by the idea of ragged beggars in Whitechapel dining on sole poached in Chablis, garnished with oysters and prawns. Mawes, you could do an excellent cartoon on the subject.'

'I shall speak to my editor,' Mr Morris promised.

'We must hope the poor won't be spoiled by the luxury,' said Professor Caldecott.

'Well,' said his wife, 'if they baulk at sleeping on the casual ward, they can always go to the Savoy or Claridges – both empty, now the foreign royalty who booked rooms for the Coronation have left. The hotel staff who were expecting large tips must be devastated.'

'If they were expecting large tips from foreign royalty, they were foolishly optimistic,' said Mrs Morris.

The Lord Warden Hotel in Dover was the largest and grandest, and had always been the first choice of eminent foreign travellers, but it, too, had emptied suddenly as disappointed Coronation guests went home. So the Earl of Stainton and his new bride were especially welcome. Their room was exchanged for a lavish suite at no extra charge, and there was almost an embarrassment of staff to hover about them.

The dining-room was quite daunting: a twenty-foot-high ceiling with elaborate classical frieze, floor-to-ceiling mirrors, Corinthian columns, crimson drapes with bullion fringes, magnificent gasoliers. The table to which Giles and Kitty were shown had a silver-gilt stand in the centre laden with exotic fruit and topped by an enormous pineapple, which prevented them from seeing each other. Giles summoned a waiter and had it removed. Kitty was impressed. It would not have occurred to her that the hotel's arrangements could be challenged.

She was very tired, worn out by the strain of the day: the

long hours on her feet, the solemnity of the church service, the frightening number of people she had had to greet, the noise of conversation and the hundreds of eyes on her – all critical, she couldn't help feeling.

She had been unable to eat at the banquet, and a few sips of champagne had made her feel so dizzy she had left the rest. Higgins had helped her change – Marie, she told Kitty, was busy packing. Kitty was afraid of Higgins, and she was by then so tired and confused she hardly knew what she was doing. Only as she and Giles were being urged out of the door by the press of guests towards the carriage that was to take them to the station did she see Nina nearby – she had been seated very far away at the banquet. She had shaken her hand free from Giles's arm to run back to her, feeling as if she were being torn away from a safe rock into a stormy sea.

Marie, and Giles's new manservant, James, had travelled in the same carriage with them to Dover, so there had been no conversation – she was too tired and bewildered in any case to talk. So it was not until, having been changed into a dinner gown, she sat down in the Lord Warden's dining-room, that she was in a position to look at her husband properly. She gave him a rather wan, nervous smile.

Giles, who was tired to the bone, and a little depressed, roused himself to do his best for his very young wife. 'It seems strange to be sitting down to dinner when we had an entire banquet only this afternoon. But I must say I wasn't able to eat much of it. Are you hungry?'

'I am, quite,' she admitted.

'Yes, I don't think you ate much, either. What would you like?' She was holding a vast leather-bound, gold-tasselled menu as though it might bite her. 'Would you like me to order for you?'

'Oh, yes, please,' she said gratefully. He gestured to the waiter, and ordered a little *foie gras* with toast, a poached fillet of sole in sauce mousseline, the pheasant with salads of endive and tomato, and a strawberry mousse, hoping to please her with light, delicate dishes that would not over-power her. He ordered champagne to drink, but noticed that she only sipped it.

Conversation was sticky. He tried talking about the wedding, but she answered with an effort, agreeing with his comments without adding any of her own. 'You're tired,' he said at last. 'Perhaps we can manage without conversation.'

Kitty felt immediately guilty, and roused herself to say, 'Won't you tell me about the places we're going to? I've never been abroad.'

He'd have been happy to eat in silence, but he couldn't ignore her request. 'Paris first,' he said. 'Then Italy. It's too late in the year for Venice – it smells intolerably when it gets hot there. We shall have to do that another year.'

'Another year,' she murmured, pleased. The words reminded her that it was not just today, and this trip, that she would be with him but for years to come. It warmed her.

'But we'll visit Florence,' he went on. 'I have an acquaint-ance there. Perhaps Rome – perhaps Naples. I would like to show you Pompeii.'

'Is that the lost city?'

'Lost under a volcanic eruption, yes.'

'Where you said there were lovely mosaics?'

He was pleased that she had remembered. 'Yes. And then, perhaps, a few days in Sorrento, which is nearby. It is one of the most beautiful coastlines in the world. Lord Byron was a regular visitor. And Goethe. And Walter Scott.'

'Walter Scott? We read *The Bride of Lammermoor* at Miss Thornton's,' Kitty remembered.

'Have you seen Donizetti's opera?' Giles asked. 'The mad scene is quite an experience. Perhaps we might catch a performance somewhere in Italy.'

'I'd like that,' Kitty said.

And so the conversation limped on between two weary people doing their best; until the lateness of the hour released them, and they retired to their suite and their waiting servants.

Changing again, this time into a nightgown, washing face and hands, having her hair taken down by Marie – from being warmly sleepy Kitty became nervously wide awake. Marie, fortunately, was not talkative, and attended to her in rather grumpy silence, going away at last leaving her sitting up in bed and prey to her thoughts.

Two days before the wedding, Mama had summoned her, alone, to her private sitting-room, and after staring at her disconcertingly for some time, she had said, 'There are things I have to tell you, Catherine, on the eve of your wedding.' She had paused, again for a long time, staring into the distance, while Kitty wondered what she had done wrong. Then abruptly she'd resumed. 'When you are alone together, in the bedroom, your husband will want to do certain things. You will find it strange, perhaps unpleasant, but I assure you it is necessary to the creation of children. It is your duty to endure it. Do not question your husband, or protest. Make no sound – it would be most indecorous. Above all, do not cry afterwards – men hate that above anything.'

Kitty felt cold with fright. 'Wh-why would I cry?' she stammered. 'What—?'

'I do not propose to go into detail,' said Lady Bayfield, grimly. 'It is not something one speaks about. I will just say that if you experience pain, it will be brief. After the first time there is usually none.'

'But . . .' Kitty began, with a score of questions pressing on her.

Lady Bayfield stopped her with an upraised hand. 'Obey your husband, try to please him. It is a relatively minor thing to endure, but men find it important, so you must be agreeable about it, and try not to show distaste. That is all. You may go now.'

Kitty had not spoken to Nina about it. Nina was not going to be married, and presumably unmarried girls weren't allowed to know. In the whirlwind of the wedding she had half forgotten about it, but now – her anxiety tripped by Marie's grimness – she supposed that the strange ritual, whatever it was, was about to happen. Sitting up in bed waiting, she felt like a sacrificial victim. But it was silly: Giles was not going to cut her throat. Whatever it was he had to do to her, she would bear it bravely, for his sake.

The door opened and he came in from the adjoining room. Her stomach swooped sickeningly, and a cold sweat broke out on her back. She couldn't look at him. She stared down at her hands and felt herself trembling.

'Shall I put the light out?' he said, and his unexpected voice made her jump.

'Yes, please,' she whispered. She thought it would be better if she couldn't see him. But as soon as he did, her anxiety increased. Now she couldn't see what was coming.

The mattress moved under her as he climbed into bed. She swallowed hard. This was Giles, whom she loved more than anything in her life. Whatever he wanted, she wanted it too. She felt him lie down, and then he put his hands on her shoulders and drew her to him, and she went, trembling, frightened, willing.

Giles entered the bedroom wishing he could be anywhere else. She looked so pathetic and child-like in her white nightgown, her hair loose on her shoulders, that he felt like a brute by comparison, a marauding Goth. It was now his duty to – well, not exactly *assault*, but in the circumstances it was not far off it – to do *those things* to a very young girl who had, he was absolutely sure, no idea of what was coming. He had to do it, whether he wanted to or not. The responsibility for getting it done was all on his shoulders – and, as it happened, he had never done it before.

Oh, he had had the normal feelings from time to time. As he had told Richard, he had kissed girls, and there had been that little episode with Ippy Cobham, the daughter of the publican at the Royal George. But he had not done everything with her. There had been fumblings, certain areas of the body had been touched with mutual pleasure, an outcome had been achieved – by him, at least – but there had been no actual penetration.

He knew the theory, of course, but he had never completed the act. His life had always been so full of other things, there hadn't been time, and young women had hardly come in his way. Richard, as a soldier, had presumably had access to various sorts of camp followers. Well, he was not going to be *too* apologetic about it – he had always rather looked down on men who scattered their seed willy-nilly. And his adventure in the hay barn behind the Royal George had left him feeling rather grubby . . .

But now this. He felt too embarrassed to look at her, and asked if he could turn out the light. It was easier in the darkness. He shed his dressing-gown, felt his way into bed, and, summoning up all his will, drew her towards him.

She came to him fluidly, and her soft, slender arms going round his neck unlocked something in him. Carefully, slowly, so as not to startle her, he began to caress her. Her skin was soft and warm and silky. His body began to stir. Perhaps it would not be so bad after all. She let him manoeuvre her into the right position, seeming willing, ready to learn. The moment of penetration was difficult, but then suddenly all was smooth and easy, and the sensation was overwhelming, so different from anything felt or guessed at before. He was glad for a fierce moment that it was his first time, as it was hers. Then there was no more thought. It was a storm of almost agonising pleasure. Dimly he thought that he understood now why literature and poetry made such a big thing of it.

She had not made a sound. When his tumbling senses slowed enough for him to remove himself carefully from her, he could hear her rapid breathing, and was afraid she might be crying. 'Did I hurt you?' he whispered. He thought she said, 'No,' but the word was too small to be sure. He turned onto his back and drew her to him, and she came with that same fluid willingness, her body folding into the lines of him, and he heard her give a small sigh. He could not mistake that sound – it was a sigh of content. He was overwhelmed with gratitude and tenderness towards her, and fell instantly into a dead sleep.

Kitty woke to a sense of absolute happiness, something she'd never felt before. For a moment she was puzzled, not knowing where she was. Then she became aware of the unexpected bulk of a body in bed beside her, and memory came flooding back.

Mama had been right, it *had* hurt, but only for an instant. And after that, it was – oh, there were no words for it! She never could have imagined such bliss. And then he had taken her in his arms, and she had fallen asleep, her head on his chest, cradled and warm and protected and safe in the circle of him, so utterly happy that if she had died then she would not have thought her life wasted.

She felt his breathing change, knew he had woken. After a moment he loosened his grasp a little so that he could look down at her, and she looked into his face properly for the first time since they had been married. How she loved him! She was the luckiest person in the world. She smiled.

The smile seemed to surprise him for the fraction of a second. 'Are you all right?' he asked.

She knew – she didn't know how, some new womanly knowledge, she supposed – that he meant the *thing* they had done last night. Mama had implied it was something a man did to a woman, that the woman had to put up with, but that was not true. It was something they had done together; and she answered his question with a rapturous 'Oh, *yes!*'

He looked at her quizzically and freed one hand to push the hair back from her face. 'Really?' he said.

'Can we do it again?' she asked.

For an instant he was shocked, then he laughed, not at her but in happiness. Her nightgown was twisted up and rucked and he said diffidently, 'Can we get rid of this, do you think?' He helped her take it off, and now she experienced the new bliss of her naked skin against his. It was *astonishingly* good. She thought he felt the same, because he started to breathe faster, and in a moment stretched his body over hers and—

No words for it.

Afterwards, she felt agreeably sleepy again. She wanted to ask him what time it was, but it didn't seem terribly important. *I'm married,* she thought. *Married to Giles.* The idea impressed her as both impossible and wonderful.

'Now, a lot depends on your demeanour,' said the barrister, David Carson. 'We're lucky to get old Lewthwaite – he has a soft spot for the military.'

'I'm glad somebody has,' said Richard. He was feeling nervous. The prospect of prison was terrifying, and Carson's brisk, cheerful demeanour somehow didn't reassure him. It gave him the impression that he didn't care much either way how Richard's case went, that he was just enjoying himself.

'What we want from you is modest and manly. Nothing cocky or care-for-nothing. Show respect, but not obsequiousness. Don't smile – but don't look nervous, either.'

'Do you think I'm the Rubber-faced Man at the Alhambra?' Richard grumbled.

'And don't make jokes,' Carson said severely. 'If you're

asked a question, answer directly and simply. Don't elaborate. Don't offer opinions or suppositions. In fact, don't speak unless you're spoken to.'

'No, sir,' Richard said facetiously. He glanced round. 'I wish *someone* had come along to show me support. Doesn't it look bad that they haven't? I mean, isn't there a thing about attesting to good character?'

'I don't think we'll need that,' said Carson. 'I've an idea about how this is going to go. What we're showing Lewthwaite today is a simple soldier who served his country, returned wounded, and is facing up bravely to a false accusation, trusting in his own innocence to clear his name. He'll love that.'

'Innocence?' Richard said, with a worried frown.

Carson gave him a stern look. 'Were you driving the car at the time of the accident?'

'I don't remember,' Richard said desperately.

'Exactly. You have no recollection of driving the car. Say after me, "I have no recollection of driving the car."' Richard said it. Carson slapped his shoulder – the good one, fortunately. 'And trust me,' he concluded.

The police constable looked tired, and somehow vulnerable with his helmet off. He gave his evidence in the usual police sing-song, reading from his notebook.

Carson allowed an instant of silence at the end of it, during which the constable looked from him to Richard and back, as though wondering if that was all. Then he said, 'The motor-car, you say, was travelling fast, and downhill.'

'Yes, sir.'

'So it must have passed you in a flash.'

'That's right, sir. Going like a bat out of hell, it was.'

'Going too quickly, I think, for you to have more than a glimpse of the people in it.'

'I saw the three young gentlemen, sir.'

'I suggest you saw three male figures,' Carson said, 'but you would not have been able to discern their features. Not so as to recognise them again.'

The constable gave him a sturdy look. 'I saw them when I reached the crashed motor-car, sir. I saw them all then, all right. Close up.'

'Indeed, Constable. Tell me what you saw when you reached the site of the crash. What were the gentlemen doing?'

'Well, sir, one was wandering about, walking in circles, like. Holding his elbow, and cursing. He said—' He looked at his notebook and up again. 'It was pretty ripe language, sir.'

There was laughter in court. 'I'm sure it was,' said Carson. 'No need to repeat it. It was just general cursing, I take it? Nothing of substance?'

'Just as you say, sir.'

'And the others?'

'One was being sick, sir. The other was lying crumpled up on the grass. I went over immediately to look at him, and ascertained that he was unconscious but alive.'

'And is that particular young gentleman in court today?'

The constable indicated Richard. 'That's him there, sir.'

Carson settled his weight comfortably. 'One smashed motor-car. Three young gentlemen, all of them out of the car, one way and another. One walking about, one unconscious, one being sick. What made you conclude, Constable, that it was this gentleman here who had been driving the vehicle?'

The policeman looked puzzled for a moment. He opened and shut his mouth. Then he referred to his notes again, and his brow cleared. 'When I questioned them, sir, the other two gentlemen said they hadn't been driving.'

'Just to be clear, Constable, you asked each of them in turn, "Were you the driver?" or words to that effect. Is that the case?'

'Yes, sir.'

294

'And each of them said . . . ?'

The notes were consulted. 'Mr Keenswell said, "Go away, I'm dying. Oh, my God! No, it wasn't bloody well me." He was the gentleman being sick, sir. And the other one, Captain Bracegirdle, said, "Not me. Don't just stand there, you bloody clown, do something. I'm not responsible for this mess."'

'And what did Mr Tallant say?'

'He was unconscious, sir.'

'So you couldn't ask him.' Carson smiled encouragingly. 'Tell me, Constable – you are an officer of some experience, I believe?'

'Twenty-three years, sir. And four months.'

'Indeed. And you must on many occasions have confronted people on the scene of some misdemeanour or felony. Let us say, for example, a man climbing out of a window with a sack full of silver. If you confronted him and asked, "Did you just steal those things, my man?" would you expect him to say, "Yes, indeed, Constable, I did"? Or would he be more likely to say, "Not me. I didn't do it"?'

More laughter. The magistrate said, 'The officer is not required to speculate on hypothetical cases, Mr Carson.'

'Indeed, Your Honour. I withdraw the question. Constable, in your experience, is it usual for people, when you question them, to say they are innocent, whether they are or not?'

'More often than not, sir,' the constable admitted.

'So if Mr Tallant had been conscious, he would probably also have said, "It wasn't me"?'

'Speculation again, Mr Carson,' said the magistrate.

But the constable answered anyway. 'Young gentlemen always say it wasn't them,' he said sourly. 'Especially when they've had a few. I had one last week snatched my helmet off, told me to my face he hadn't got it when I could see it there in his hand—'

'Thank you, Constable,' Carson stopped him. 'To sum

up, then, you concluded that Mr Tallant must have been the driver simply because the other two gentlemen denied it was them?'

'Yes, sir,' said the constable, sulkily. He could see where this was going.

'But you had no opportunity to question Mr Tallant because he was unconscious.'

'No, sir.'

'And when the motor-car passed you earlier, it was going too fast for you to recognise the faces.'

'I bet it was him, all the same,' the constable muttered.

'I beg your pardon?' Carson said exquisitely. The constable said nothing. 'Please look at Mr Tallant, Constable, and tell me categorically whether you can swear on your oath that he was driving the motor-car as it passed you.'

The policeman looked at Richard with loathing, but was obliged to say, 'No, sir. I can't swear it was him.'

Carson looked at the magistrate. 'Your honour, we have all heard Mr Tallant say that he has no recollection of driving the motor-car. Indeed, he had never driven one prior to that day and so had no knowledge of how to go about it.'

Outside, Richard blinked gratefully in the sunlight of freedom, and thanked Carson. 'Nothing to it,' Carson said. 'Lewthwaite was right to dismiss the case. Always a pleasure to see an innocent man walk free.'

'But—'

'You have no recollection of driving the car, have you?'

'No,' said Richard.

'There you are, then.'

'I do wonder, though,' Richard said a little peevishly, 'that neither of them – Keenswell and Bracegirdle – has come near me since the accident. Not a note, not so much as a grape. They might at least have come today and given me moral support in court.'

'Possibly just as well for you that they didn't,' Carson said, with a cheerful grin, and scuttled off to another case.

James and Marie had a compartment to themselves on the train to Paris. Marie, to his surprise, was reading a book. He had never seen a servant, least of all a lady's maid, read a book, though he supposed, generously, that the odd one might do so in private. He had nothing to read, and crossed and recrossed his legs restlessly, until he realised it might make it seem as though he was uneasy. He didn't want Marie to think he had never been abroad before. So he made himself sit still and look out of the window. The scenery, he thought, was nothing special – very like England, really, except a bit flatter. And strangely empty of people.

He thought about home for a bit, and wondered what they were all doing, and whether Tilda was missing him. Was Dory listening to Mr Sebastian playing the piano again? Was old Crooks getting in a state? He didn't feel guilty about the tricks he had played on him, to make him look a blunderer, though he'd had a bad moment when ruining the blade of the razor – it was a fine instrument, after all. But it had been the last straw as far as his lordship was concerned.

He had a moment of alarm wondering whether his protégé Cyril was worming his way into Mr Moss's good books and trying to usurp his place. Then he remembered he was his lordship's valet now, not a footman, and Cyril was welcome to leapfrog daft William if he wanted.

And that used up all his thoughts, and he was desperate for conversation. He stared at Marie, willing her to put down the book. And when she didn't, he said, 'Well, here we are, then.' She did not react. 'The happy couple, eh?' he tried next, with a short laugh. 'She'll have found out last night what it's all about. Talk about lamb to the slaughter!' Marie gave him a brief, cold look and turned a page. 'He'll have taught her a thing or two, I reckon. His lordship.' No reaction. 'I bet you wouldn't mind changing places with her, eh? He's a good-looking bloke, our earl.'

She looked up with a weary sigh. 'Must you talk?'

'Oh, come on! We're going to spend a lot of time together. Might as well be pally.'

'What do you want?' she asked. It was not encouraging, but she closed the book, though keeping a finger in her place.

'Well . . .' he searched for a subject '. . . France, eh?'

'What about it?'

'I thought it'd look a lot more – well, foreign.'

'What did you expect? Elephants? Camels? The great Pyramids, perhaps?'

'Mountains, at any rate.'

'There are mountains. Just not here. France is much bigger than England.'

He felt that was vaguely insulting to England. 'To you, maybe,' he said, and seeing her curl her lip, hurried on: 'Must be nice for you to be back.' She didn't respond. 'In France, I mean. Well, it'll be handy for us, won't it, you speaking the lingo? Course, I expect his lordship speaks it a bit, but if you and me wanted to go out in the evening or something, you could do the old Polly Voo—'

She interrupted him firmly. 'I don't speak French.'

'What? How come?'

And she said, in a completely different voice from the one she usually used, 'I'm not French. My name's not Marie. I come from Stepney, and my name's Mary Filmer, and if I'm going to be stuck in close quarters with you, you'd better stop all this nonsense and start behaving like a sensible boy. Polly Voo indeed!'

He stared at her in admiration. 'Why'd you do it? Pretend to be French.'

'Obvious, isn't it? The nobs all want French lady's maids. You want the best job, you've got to give them what they want. And, by the way, if you tell anyone, I'll kill you.' She gave him a level look. 'Don't think I couldn't.'

He was entranced. 'Oh, I believe you. I won't tell. I wouldn't anyway. I'm the same as you. My name's not James. I'm Sid – Sid Hook, from High Wycombe. My dad was a wood turner in a chair factory. He wanted me to go into it like him, but I didn't want to work in a factory. I wanted to be my own boss.'

'So you went into service?' she said witheringly.

'No – listen. You can save a lot of money as a footman. You've nothing to spend it on – everything's found. And I always meant to work my way up. A valet can make a good bit on the side, as well as his wages. By the time I'm thirty I'll have enough to set up my own business. That'll show my dad,' he added, in a bitter aside.

'What's his name, your dad?'

'Sidney, same as me.'

She nodded. 'Just as I thought. Bad blood between you – can't stand being called the same name as him, eh?'

James looked sulky. 'It's not that. All right, he did say some things when I wouldn't go into the factory like he wanted but, like I told you, I always meant to work my way up, and you can't be a high-class footman and be called Sid, let alone a valet. So I changed my name.'

She shrugged. 'You're not wrong.'

He took this as encouragement. 'We're alike, you and me, aren't we? We ought to join forces.'

She looked scornful. 'What on earth for?'

'Well, we both got secrets. We both want to get on. There's probably lots of ways we can help each other, make as much out of the situation as we can.' He rubbed thumb and fore-finger together. 'Me lord and me lady've got the butter, why shouldn't we have some of it? Two lots of brains are better than one.'

'Not when it's *your* brains,' she said.

'You don't have to be mean,' he said, hurt. 'We're going to be stuck with each other for weeks, we ought to try to get on.'

'I don't know,' she said, yawning. 'The whole idea of this trip bores me. I might not stick it out.'

'You what?'

'I only agreed to go for the free ticket. If I find myself in some place I like, I might skip.'

'Blimey,' he said in admiration. Even he hadn't thought of that. 'You are a one!'

'And if you tell anyone . . .' she said, with narrowed eyes.

'I know, you'll kill me.'

'And now,' she reverted to her French accent, 'I am going to read. So please to shut up!'

CHAPTER SIXTEEN

Rachel never received the letter from Victor Lattery. It arrived with the rest of the post, and Moss, sorting through, picked it out with a frown, then put it with her ladyship's letters. Lady Rachel was not of age, not even out, and for her to be receiving letters her mother did not know about was something Moss did not feel he could be responsible for. Added to which, the hand was plainly not a woman's.

Lady Stainton opened it at the breakfast table, and fixed Rachel with a basilisk glare. 'What is this?' she demanded, throwing the letter down on the table. 'Have you been corresponding with this *person*?'

Rachel's blush was automatic, but it made her look guilty. 'Who? What?'

Sebastian, in the seat next to Lady Stainton, looked at the signature and said, 'Victor Lattery? Wasn't there a daughter of that solicitor in Canons Ashmore married a Lattery? What was her name – Mildred? Tall, pretty girl.'

Rachel's mouth was dry, but she managed to say, 'I met him at the Brinklows' party, Mama. He said he was getting up a bicycle party—'

'So it seems,' she snapped. 'And has the impudence to invite you. Did you encourage him, after I told you not to?'

'No, Mama. But you didn't say – you only said – his aunt—' Rachel faltered.

'We do not know her,' Lady Stainton thundered. 'You

will have nothing to do with her or anyone connected to her, and certainly not this – this *youth!*' The word might as well have been *reprobate*.

Sebastian tried to intervene. He didn't like to see the girls so cowed. 'Now, Maudie, a bicycle party! It could hardly be more respectable. A group of young people, healthy exercise in the open air—'

She turned on him. 'Don't interfere!' she spat. 'You don't know what you're talking about. Rachel, go to your room. It's clear you meant to defy me. You are not to be trusted. You will not leave this house for any reason for a week.'

Rachel, in tears, ran.

Linda, who had been staying since the wedding and hoping for some reason not to go back to Dorset, said, 'You're quite right, Mama. Bicycles are so horribly middle-class. Knickerbockers and sketching parties. Not our sort of thing at all.'

Lady Stainton had a glare to spare for her, too, and breakfast was concluded in silence.

Afterwards, Alice went up to the nursery, where Rachel was just coming out of her sobs. She fetched a cold flannel and bathed her swollen face for her. 'It's so unfair!' Rachel cried. 'I didn't do *anything*! I didn't tell him to write to me.'

'You didn't tell him not to,' Alice pointed out. 'Oh, never mind, don't cry any more.'

'I would have asked permission, if I'd seen the letter.'

'Well, that's where you'd have gone wrong. You know Mama says no to everything. Much better not to ask – she never knows where we are, anyway. If anything like that comes up again, just go and don't tell.'

'Oh, Alice!' Rachel was torn between envy and disapproval.

'It's not as if you meant to do anything wrong,' Alice encouraged her. 'Why don't you write him a note, and slip it to him on Sunday?'

'He doesn't go to our church. They're Catholics.'

'Oh. Well, you could give a child a penny to put it through their letter-box.'

Rachel cheered up at the thought. 'I suppose I could.'

'Only be sure to tell him not to write to you here,' Alice went on, getting interested in the conspiracy. 'Now, who can we trust to receive a letter from him for you? Not Daisy – she'd tell straight away. Uncle Sebastian?'

'I don't think he'd go behind Mama's back.'

'No, you're right. Not Josh, that's for sure – he's hateful. Oh, but what about Axe? Victor could give a letter to him at the forge. And then Axe could give it to whichever of us he saw first.' They often stopped at the forge when they were in the village, for something to do. And Alice sometimes went over to his house on a Sunday afternoon.

'Do you think he would?' Rachel asked.

'I don't see why not,' said Alice. 'He's awfully nice.'

As the girls came out of church on Sunday, Alice was going to look out for Axe, when she saw Victor Lattery, leaning on the railings of the house opposite, hands in pockets. She nudged Rachel, who gasped. It was obvious he was waiting for her, because as soon as he saw her he pushed himself upright and started across. Rachel made a violent negative gesture.

Alice turned to her mother, who was just concluding a conversation with the rector. 'Mama, it's such a nice day, Rachel and I would like to walk back, instead of going in the carriage.'

Lady Stainton was indifferent. 'Very well. But don't dawdle. I'll take your prayer books.'

'What was all that about?' Lattery said genially, when they finally joined him. He was looking at Rachel. Again, Alice felt invisible – *just a child*. 'I stayed away from mass this morning on purpose to see you. Didn't you get my letter?'

'No, our butler took it to Mama, and she was angry because

I'm not out, you see,' Rachel said, blushing at the shameful admission, 'so I shouldn't get letters from men. So, please, you mustn't write to me at the Castle again.'

'Oh, Lord, I'm sorry. I never meant to make trouble.'

'We know,' Alice said. 'But the thing is, our mother absolutely *hates* your aunt.'

'Good God,' said Lattery blankly. 'Why on earth? Everyone loves Aunt Violet.'

'We don't know why. And Mama isn't the sort of person you can ask,' Alice said.

'I'll ask Aunty if she knows,' Lattery said. 'It's bound to be some silly misunderstanding. Honestly, you couldn't hate Aunt Violet, not if you tried ever so hard.'

'Oh, Mama's a good hater,' said Alice. 'I don't think she even likes us very much.'

'I'm sure that's not true,' Lattery said gallantly.

'Anyway, she's forbidden Rachel to have anything to do with you.'

'Ah,' said Lattery. 'Well, in that case, I suppose I had better say goodbye and make myself scarce.'

'Oh, please don't,' said Rachel.

'I don't want to get you into trouble.'

'It'll be all right if we're careful,' Rachel said.

'Clandestine meetings?' Lattery said. Alice couldn't tell from his tone whether he approved or disapproved. But then he grinned. 'How exciting!'

Alice said, 'Not very clandestine, standing here where anyone can see you! Ray and I are going to walk home now. We'll go the long way round, by Cherry Lane and up Mop End. There'll be nobody about. If you should happen to come across us on the walk . . .'

'That would be a very happy coincidence,' said Lattery, and walked away.

The girls turned in the other direction. 'Do you think it's wrong,' Rachel said, 'going against Mama's orders?'

'Not if they're unreasonable,' Alice said stoutly. 'If she really wants us to have nothing to do with him, she should tell us why. And even if she has a reason to hate Miss Eddowes, she shouldn't involve Victor and us.'

'I don't know . . .'

'Oh, Ray, you aren't going to do anything really bad, are you? Just walk along and talk to a person. There's nothing wrong with that.'

'I suppose not,' Rachel said. Then, more cheerfully, 'He's nice, isn't he?'

'He's all right,' Alice said. She thought he was a bit weedy, compared with – say – Axe Brandom. 'If you think he's worth it, that's all that matters.'

'I really like him. But you'll stay with me, if we do meet him?'

'Only as far as Shelloes, then I must go and see Empress's new litter. You know how one can't resist tiny piglets – so sweet! Like little fat ladies in tight shoes.'

'You'll get your dress dirty.'

'I won't. I'm only going to look.'

Crooks had managed to get away from the other servants, and lingered in sight of the north door until the choir came out. He strolled casually in the direction of the lych-gate, to reach it at the same time as the unmistakable figure of Axe Brandom. Brandom paused when he saw Crooks, and stepped out of the way, taking off his hat. The others streamed on past him with barely a glance. Service being over, there was the prospect of Sunday dinner for most and a pint or two for the rest. Either way, anticipation trumped curiosity.

'Good morning,' Crooks greeted him.

'Fine day, sir,' Axe said shyly.

'It is indeed. And the Te Deum was very lovely today. Thomas Tallis, wasn't it?'

Axe looked more comfortable, talking about music. 'Yes,

305

sir. Mr Arden, he likes all that early music. It's hard, till you learn it, but to my mind, it's finer than the more modern stuff.'

'You prefer polyphony to harmony? I think I do, too.'

Axe looked a little at a loss. 'You know bigger words than me, sir. I just know the way it sounds. Mr Evercreech, our lead bass, says it's too Roman, the Tallis, he don't approve of it. But my view is, if you're singing to God, it doesn't matter if you're Roman or C of E.'

'Well said,' Crooks exclaimed. 'We are too ready to make divisions where none is needed. It's a long time since I've seen you,' he went on. 'I've been in London with his lordship.'

'Yes, sir – got married, didn't he? Such a pity he couldn't have the wedding here. We'd have loved to do a choral service for him. But you didn't go away with him? Gone to France, I believe, him and his new lady.'

'Foreign travel doesn't agree with me,' Crooks said. 'His lordship kindly said I could stay at home. Which means I have some time on my hands. I wondered if you would like me to help you improve your reading.'

'It's most kind of you to offer, sir,' Axe said, blushing, 'but you don't have to worry about me. I couldn't take up your time like that.'

'Not at all, not at all. It would be my pleasure. Now, when would be convenient? Do you have a half-day?'

'Not a *half*-day as such, sir, but I finish early of a Tuesday, most in general. Mr Rowse lets me go about three o'clock, unless there's a big job come in.'

'Tuesday happens to suit me very well,' said Crooks. Actually, he was never wanted at that time of day. Mr Sebastian didn't need a great deal of valeting anyway, and until it was time to dress him for dinner, Crooks was pretty much at a loose end. 'There'll be too many prying eyes at the Castle – I don't want you to feel self-conscious. Suppose

306

I come over to your house, and we'll see how we get on. Where do you live?'

'I've a cottage over the other side of the Carr, sir. But it isn't much – not the sort of place for gentry-folk to visit,' Axe said anxiously.

Crooks smiled. 'I'm not gentry-folk, you mustn't think that. I'm just a working man, like you. I shall come on Tuesday – shall we say, half past three? I'll bring a few books and see what suits you best. We'll have you reading fluently in no time, I'm sure.'

He smiled, nodded, and walked past, under the lych-gate and away down the street before Axe could raise any difficulties. He felt immensely cheerful. Doing good was always a raiser of the spirits. He sang a little of the Te Deum under his breath as he walked.

There were so many museums and art galleries in Paris – and Giles did them all so thoroughly – that they were sure to last them for the two weeks. Kitty liked looking at paintings, in moderation, but Giles would stand for a long time before each, and after a few hours her feet and her back started to ache. Also, when she had said the few things she had to say about art, she was reduced to agreeing with him – not that she wouldn't have agreed with him anyway, but just saying, 'Yes,' to everything made her sound stupid. After a while, he stopped making comments, and they went round in silence.

One day they took a ride out to Versailles to see where the French kings had lived in such splendour. The journey was nice, and the park of Versailles was beautiful, but the fountains weren't running, and though the inside of the palace was very lavish with elaborate plasterwork and gold paint, it wasn't furnished, unlike palaces at home, so there wasn't much to see.

She'd have liked to look at the shops, but that was not

anything Giles suggested. Out of consideration to her feet, she'd have enjoyed sitting in one of the parks to watch people stroll by, or having a ride in one of the boats down the Seine, but that wasn't on offer either. He took her to the Sainte-Chapelle, which he said was finer than Notre Dame, and it might have been for all she knew, but she'd have preferred to stroll through the wonderful flower-market on the Île de la Cité, which she glimpsed as they were going in.

Still, she was in the wonderful city of Paris, and she was married to Giles, and she was plainly the luckiest girl in the world. Le Meurice, where they were staying, was simply gorgeous – more luxurious by half even than Dene Park – and all the staff were very attentive and called her 'milady' at every turn, which was awfully nice.

And the nights were wonderful.

Giles had no acquaintance in Paris, and it was the wrong time of year to encounter English visitors there. It was too hot in July: as with London, people started to go out of the city, and by August it would be deserted and most of the shops shut. It meant that he and his new wife were pretty much thrown on each other's company, which was perhaps not the best idea for two people who hardly knew each other and were not madly in love.

But he found ways to occupy their days. The Louvre alone, which contained a fine Etruscan and Roman collection, would have kept him happy. To begin with he tried to engage Kitty in conversation about the exhibits, but she tended to agree with everything he said, so after a while he desisted, and they walked about in silence. He was so used to being on his own that when he was fully absorbed with what he was looking at, he tended to forget she was there. He made sure she saw plenty of paintings, since he could not reasonably expect her to find a fragment of an Etruscan lamp as fascinating as he did, and even took her to Versailles and told her all about the Sun King and Le Nôtre and Le Brun. He thought, on the whole, he was keeping her amused.

The evenings were more difficult: sitting across a table from each other in silence seemed so awkward. The theatre was no use – neither of them spoke French well enough – but he took her once to the ballet and once to the opera. She seemed to like the former, but fell asleep during the opera, which he had to admit was very inferior.

All in all, he felt two weeks in Paris was probably too much. Italy, where he knew people, would be easier. What reconciled him to the whole business – apart from the knowledge that, even as they wandered about the glaring streets, his agent and banker were putting her dowry to work, paying off his debts – what reconciled him to his marriage was their nights together.

He could not have imagined that it would be so wonderful. From a nervous beginning he had grown in confidence, discovering with her and through her an experience so exquisite, so overwhelming, that he could hardly get enough of it. He felt gratitude towards Kitty, and great tenderness. He had dreaded it so much, but she had made it so easy! During the day, she was the shy, almost timid girl he had known in London, obedient as a child to an adult's commands, but at night, in bed, in the dark, she was the willing collaborator in this journey into a land of undiluted sensation. She seemed to like it as much as he did, to be ready, eager, as often as he wanted her. In the dark, he called her his 'little pagan', and she laughed delightedly. By day, she would hardly meet his eye. It was like being married to two different people. As he walked about galleries and examined exhibits, with his silent, obedient wife at his side, he often thought about the night to come, and it was as if he had a secret mistress – he felt almost guilty, as though he was being unfaithful.

Sometimes he asked her, 'Are you happy?'

And she always said, 'Yes.' By day she said it unemphatically, as if he had asked her nothing more than if she would like more coffee. By night she said, 'Oh, *yes!*' And his feelings would surge up and fill him with warmth.

It was very odd.

Nina suspected her aunt had manipulated her into friendship with Lepida Morris, but as she found that she liked her, it didn't matter. Lepida was tall and thin, with the sort of sensible face that people often described as 'horse-like', though why that should be derogatory Nina had never understood, horses being, to her, the most beautiful creatures on earth. Actually, she thought Lepida looked more like the hare she was named after, having very large eyes and a slight deficiency of chin. Either way, she was not unattractive, though no man would call her beautiful. She was very fair of skin, with mouse-brown hair, a long neck and long, expressive fingers. She was twenty-six, but Nina's education made the difference in age between them seem less.

Together they visited the drawing-rooms of wealthy ladies and asked for donations. This was the part Nina didn't like, though Lepida seemed unembarrassed by it. 'I've done it so often,' she said. 'You grow hardened in time.' It always involved explaining the scheme in detail, and in particular why it was needed and what good it would do. Many potential donors were instinctively averse to doing things for people who were not actually incapacitated; some others still divided the poor into the deserving and the undeserving, and suspected that most poor people fell into the latter category or they wouldn't be poor in the first place. The library, the girls explained again and again, would put people in the way of an education that would help them to help themselves, to lift themselves out of ignorance and thence out of poverty.

After one or two visits, they were always in need of tea.

In a tea-shop in Sloane Square, Lepida said, 'I have the schedule here of the evening lectures at the British Museum this autumn. I wondered if you'd like to have a look. I always go to one or two, and perhaps you'd be interested in coming with me. It's always more fun if one goes with a friend.'

Sipping her tea, Nina looked through the schedule, and one subject leaped out at her. 'Egyptology! Now, that would be interesting.'

Lepida looked. 'Oh, yes, Margaret Murray's lectures. I was quite interested in that myself.'

'A woman giving lectures?' Nina marvelled.

'She studied at University College London,' said Lepida. 'They're much more open-minded about women's education than the old Oxford and Cambridge colleges. The University of London started awarding degrees to women twenty years ago.'

'Did you never want to study at university?' Nina asked.

'I thought about it, and Papa wouldn't have been against it, but I decided it wouldn't really be for me. I don't have the right sort of mind. Mother says I'm curious, but lazy. And I couldn't see the point in doing all that hard work to gain a degree if I wasn't going to do anything with it.'

'You could teach.' Nina said.

'I should simply hate that,' said Lepida. 'Lazy, you see.'

'I don't think you're lazy. Look at all the work you're doing for the library.'

'Intellectually lazy, I mean. You've always got your nose in a book, but if I have an hour to myself, I'd sooner get out the water-colours, or go for a walk and gaze at nature. I don't mind learning, if someone else does the hard work – hence these lectures. One can sit still and be fed like a baby bird. So you're interested in Egyptology? Is that a new thing?'

Nina managed not to blush. 'Fairly new. Archaeology in general, but Egyptology in particular.'

'Well, Margaret Murray's awfully good. She studied under Flinders Petrie.'

'I've heard of him,' Nina said, sipping more tea to hide her face. Giles Stainton had told her how he had studied under Petrie, had been one of his favourite students, in fact. She wondered whether Margaret Murray would have known him. It would be a way to be connected with him, to be taught by her, even if it was only a public lecture.

Lepida was watching her covertly, wondering what she was thinking. 'You know,' she said at length, 'if you're *really* interested, you should think of going to university yourself.'

'Oh, I don't think I'd be good enough,' Nina said.

'I'm sure you would,' said Lepida. 'And there are so many more openings for women now – not just University College, but Bedford College too.'

'But I'm sure it would cost a lot of money,' Nina said. 'I don't think I could ask my aunt to keep me for all that time. That's why I'm going to be a teacher.' She sighed. 'I suppose I shall have to start after the summer, when the new term begins.'

'You don't sound very enthusiastic,' said Lepida.

'I expect I shall like it once I start,' said Nina. 'One must do something.'

Lepida left it at that, and poured more tea. 'What about the evening lectures, then? Do you care to join me?'

'Yes, please – if Aunt says I may.'

The leaves on the trees were July-thick and July-dark, the shadows deep and sharp under them. The tracks were dry, and the ruts had been beaten out into dust so Alice hardly needed to watch where Pharaoh was stepping any more: she could relax into his rocking canter and just enjoy the movement. She thought about Giles and her new sister-in-law, who would be in Italy by now. It seemed a waste to leave England just when England was at its best. She wondered how life would change when they came back. Rachel would be seventeen next month, so she supposed she would start going to parties, and be brought out next spring. Would Kitty chaperone her? Their mother had never shown any interest in them, or any desire for their company.

Pharaoh turned off onto the track of his own accord – he had been here several times now. She slowed him to a walk, and as they arrived in the yard, Dolly came bustling out with a single bark, announcing her. She freed her foot, unhooked her knee and slid off, stooping to caress Dolly's head.

Axe came to the door. 'Oh, it's you,' he said.

'You don't mind?'

'Welcome,' he said. 'Want me to tie him up?'

'I can do it.' The rope halter was hanging from the ring for her. Axe went to get an armful of hay while she loosened the girths. When she turned round, the three fat puppies had come wobbling out into the yard and were approaching her with large, inefficient enthusiasm. She knelt to do them justice. They pawed at her and licked her fingers, nudged and snuffled and overbalanced. Dolly went off to sniff in the bushes. 'She's not interested in them any more,' Alice said, as Axe came back.

'She's about sick of 'em,' he said. 'They're always at her, trying to suckle. Time they was weaned.'

She watched the puppies tumbling over each other, play-biting. 'And then you'll be getting rid of them, I suppose?'

He regarded her indulgently. 'They'll go to good homes. Dolly's famous hereabouts. Everyone'll want one of her pups.'

'Oh, good,' Alice said, standing up and brushing off her skirt. 'Only our head man Giddins got rid of some pups once, when Papa's spaniel was visited by the wrong dog.'

'Did you think I'd knock 'em on the head? My Dolly's pups?'

'No, of course you wouldn't.'

'Want to come in? I'll put the kettle on.'

'Thanks.' She followed him into the dark, cool interior. There was a book on the table. 'Oh, what are you reading?' she said, picking it up.

'It's not mine,' he said sharply. 'It's borrowed.'

She glanced at him, surprised. 'I won't hurt it. I know how to handle books.'

'Course you do,' he said, blushing slightly and looking away.

'*Gulliver's Travels*,' she discovered. 'It's good, isn't it? How far have you got? My favourite part is about the Houyhnhnms.'

'I don't know that bit. I'm only at the beginning, about the little people.'

'Oh, the Houyhnhnms are a race of intelligent horses. The horses are the masters, and the humans are the slaves – and they're horrible, primitive humans, too, nasty and violent. I've always thought Swift got that right – horses are so much more noble than us.'

He smiled faintly. 'I don't know about that. A horse'd never do you a favour, or look after you when you were sick.'

'Who did you borrow it from? It's a nice copy.' She turned it over in her hands – leather-bound, gilded, with marbled end-papers. 'We've got one at home just like this.'

'I'm practising reading,' he said, taking it from her and putting it on the dresser, out of the way. 'I learned in school, but I was never quick at it. I'd like to read better so I can enjoy stories and such.'

'Good for you,' said Alice, not noticing that he hadn't answered the question. 'I love reading, though most of the books in our library are pretty boring. But there's *The Seven Voyages of Sindbad the Sailor*. Have you read that? I'll get it for you when you've finished *Gulliver*. No-one will notice – I'm the only person who goes into the library now Giles is away.'

'Had any word from him?' Axe asked, pouring water into the teapot.

'No, but I wouldn't expect to. People don't write home from their honeymoons – or do they?'

'Your guess is as good as mine.'

'I expect they'd be too busy,' Alice said. He sat down opposite her, and put milk into the cups. She was facing towards the range and noticed the ornament on the mantelpiece. 'Will you tell me about your china shepherdess? I've been meaning to ask you.'

'What makes you think there's a story?'

'Well, it's the only ornament you've got, so it must be special.'

He poured the tea before he spoke again. He would never be hurried. It was one of the things Alice found so restful about him. What Axe did happened at Axe's speed. ''Twas when I was a nipper,' he said. 'Before I was prenticed to Mr Rowse. I went into service as boot boy to Mrs Eddowes, the solicitor's wife.'

'Is that the—'

'Miss Eddowes that lives there now, she's the daughter. Two girls there was, Miss Violet and Miss Mildred, and one boy, young Master Tom. Doted on him, the whole fambly, for all he was a rough boy, always in trouble. Teased them young ladies something cruel, spoiled their things. Always breaking stuff. Kicked a football in the drawing-room one time, smashed up a load o' things off of the mantelpiece. Only bit what survived was a china shepherdess, and that was cracked on the base.'

'That one?'

'The same. Had a shepherd to match, but he was in shards. Anyroad, Master Tom, like I said, he was always in trouble. One time, he bet he could swim across the mill-race – mill used to be down the end of the village.'

'Where Mill House is?'

315

He nodded. 'Mill wheel was taken away – what? – ten years since. But the river was in flood that day, race was running fast. In Master Tom goes, but he couldn't make any way, got swep' down and hit his head on something – tree root or summat. Well, I was just passing, and when I see him go by unconscious, I jumps in. I was big for my age,' he added reassuringly.

'You rescued him?'

'I got him to the bank, and others helped pull him out.'

'Alive?'

Axe nodded. 'Alive then. But he got pewmony and died a week later. They never got over it, the Eddoweses. Well, I left soon after, to be a prentice blacksmith, but Mrs Eddowes, she give me the china shepherdess to remember Master Tom by. Only I remember *her* by it. She was a real lady. Tom, he'd have come to a bad end, one way or the other.'

'What a lovely story,' Alice said. 'Well, sad, of course – but you were a hero.'

'Never thought about it,' he said indifferently. 'Just jumped.'

'And you still do things for Miss Eddowes.'

'Paying work, them gates. Where else'd she go for them?' he said, but added in a mutter, 'Keep an eye on her. She's the last of them. Got no-one else to count on.'

'What is it that she does – this philanthropy I've heard about?' Alice asked.

'Couldn't say,' said Axe. 'More tea?'

'Why does my mother hate her?'

Axe met her eyes. 'She don't. Not *her*.'

'What do you mean?' Alice begged, intrigued. But Axe wouldn't tell.

James was lonely and bored. There was not much to do in the middle of the day and, far from joining forces, Marie had taken to disappearing when they were not wanted. He couldn't talk to the hotel staff, who didn't speak English. It seemed no-one in the whole of Paris spoke English, and he was used to a whole household to chat to. He took to wandering the streets, feeling quite hard-done-by, though he could not exactly pinpoint whose fault it was.

He found himself one day in a rough, run-down sort of area, where there were a lot of small warehouses and artisan workshops. A canal came down to the river and there was a complex of cuts, wharfs and locks. He watched the boats working for a bit, then, wandering on, came to a sort of street market. It was not selling food, but pots and pans, household goods, things of that nature. One stall caught his eye – several pieces of battered furniture were stacked around it, and an old and very dirty man was seated there mending a chair. The chairback consisted of twelve narrow spindles, and he was fitting them into the holes in the top-rail. James watched for a while and then, driven by the desire for human contact, said, 'My dad was in the same trade as you. Making chairs. He was a wood turner.'

The man glanced up indifferently. '*Comment?*' he said.

'Mostly made legs,' James said. 'You know – legs.' He lifted his own and slapped the thigh.

The man shrugged, and went on with his work.

A woman who had been standing a pace or two off came close and said, 'You do not speak French?'

'No,' said James. 'You speak English?'

'Yes, I speak English good. My father, he does not.' She gestured to the chair mender.

James was eager for a chat. 'I was just saying, my dad was in the same business. Back in England.'

'You make chairs?'

'No, I never fancied it. I'm valet to an important English lord. He's here on his honeymoon.'

She looked puzzled for a moment, then said, 'Ah, *voyage*

de noces. You are valet, *hein?* Important job. Valet make very good money, I think.'

He swelled a little. 'Not bad,' he said. 'Plenty of perks, if you know what you're doing.'

The old man looked at her and reeled off a rapid sentence, and she replied in like vein, except that her voice was sharp and hectoring. He made a sound of disgust, and spat expertly onto the ground two inches from James's shoe.

The woman smiled at James. 'My father is not good temper since he be blind in one eye. He say we disturb him.' She stepped closer, fluttering her eyelashes. 'Would you like to buy me a glass of wine? Then we can talk.'

'Where?' James said, a little suspicious, but interested. She wasn't in the first flush of youth, but not bad-looking, and with a nice, generous figure – the way he liked them. And he hadn't had so much as a feel since they left England.

She pointed towards the water. 'There is a place over there. Not far. I would like to hear about you. Your *histoire.*'

'All right.'

'My name is Irène,' she said.

'James.'

'Shems. Oh, I like this name. Come, Shems, come, just over here.'

The place was small, dark and grimy, empty but for two men in working overalls and caps sitting up at the bar, and a few crude tables and chairs. She took him to a table by the open door, went to the bar, and came back with two glasses of wine. She sat down opposite him and lifted the glass. '*À votre santé.*'

He repeated the toast as best he could and she laughed and said, 'Oh, but that is ver' good. You will soon speak French *à merveille.*'

'Not me,' he said. Under her expert questioning, he told her about himself, and under the influence of three glasses of wine, he grew expansive. She leaned further forward,

318

giving him a better look down her front, gazed at him in fascination, toying with a curl of her hair. The Old Adam stirred. All *right*, he thought. If it's offered on a plate, I'm not going to say no.

A man came in, came up behind her and addressed her rapidly in French, in a rough and guttural voice. She replied in the same sharp, rebuking tone she had used on the old man. He went out, and she said, 'A friend of my father. He says I must go back and work.' She sighed. 'I must go soon. But not yet. Would you like to come out the back with me? You are so 'andsome man. I never had an English man before.'

There was a side alley. He looked round carefully, but no-one else was in sight. She stood with her back to the wall and drew him towards her. Then, with an enticing smile, she took both his hands and put them on her breasts, and slid hers around his waist, pulling him to her. He was enjoying himself, both hands and lips fully engaged, when he felt more hands – extra hands – coming from behind him, going into his pockets. He jerked in shock, then struggled furiously to release himself from her – she was holding his head now, kissing him smotheringly so he couldn't yell. Striking her hands away at last, he swung round, to meet a hard fist coming the other way. The expert blow to the point of his chin tipped him over backwards. The woman had jumped aside, and his head hit the wall. He slithered to the ground to the sound of running footsteps.

By the time he got to his feet, they were gone. He staggered out of the alley, angry, feeling a fool, and also obscurely hurt to have been taken advantage of. Fortunately, there had not been a great deal in his pocket-book, but to lose it in such a stupid way hurt his pride. Knowing it was useless, he made his way back to the chair mender's stall. 'Your daughter just robbed me!' he shouted at him. 'Her and her friend! I bet you knew all about it, didn't you?

I should have the law on you, you stupid old fool! Nice way to treat visitors, I don't think!'

The old man looked up and said something in French, then went back to his work. The back was all in one piece now and he was fitting the bottom of the spindles into the holes in the seat, completely absorbed in the task. James raised his fist threateningly – and suddenly there were a lot of other people around him. He began shouting. 'His daughter robbed me! Took me in a bar and robbed me! I bet she does it all the time! He knows – ask him!'

Everyone was talking now, jabbering at him in French, gesticulating. Some started arguing with each other. Others, he noticed unhappily, were grinning derisively at him. At the back of the group were several heavily built swarthy types, who looked as though they could do with some alleviation of boredom. It was time, he realised, to beat a retreat. He backed up, still expostulating, and turned and walked away, resisting the urge to run.

God damn it! So this was Paris. Huh! You could keep it! You could keep all of Abroad, for his money!

CHAPTER SEVENTEEN

It was hot in Italy. The train travelled through endless vistas of tan grass dotted with clusters of thin dark trees, clattered through small villages of achingly white cottages with red-tiled roofs. Kitty was exhausted by the time they arrived in Florence, too hot and tired to be charmed by the strange architecture as the cab, pulled by a thin horse that looked as though it might drop dead before journey's end, took them through the streets. But Giles sat up straighter, looked around him keenly, craning after every new sight with such rapid jerks she was afraid he'd rick his neck.

Her slightly sour thoughts were dispersed when they pulled up in front of a tall stone house with green shutters, and the door was opened onto a dark, cool interior by a handsome, motherly woman, who held out her arms to Kitty, and said, 'Oh, my poor dear, how tired you must be! Come in, come in and have some cold lemonade.'

She kissed Kitty on both cheeks, tenderly removed her hat, and said, over her shoulder, 'Dearest Giles, I shall kiss you too, but first I must take care of the little countess. Come and rest for a while before you go to your room.'

She led Kitty through the house – so dark after the vicious sunshine that she would have stumbled if she had not been so firmly led – and out into a courtyard garden where a table and chairs were shaded by a vine growing over a structure of poles and wires. Ferns and other greenery grew in dim corners, a fountain tinkled somewhere, and a pale pink rose scrambled over tall grey stone walls. The air was cool and fragrant. Kitty found herself seated almost without knowing how, before her a glass of lemonade so cold it was beaded with dew. The lovely woman beamed at her. 'Better?'

'Oh, much,' said Kitty, gratefully. 'Thank you.'

'And now, Giles, my dear!' Giles was engulfed in a hearty embrace. How delightfully demonstrative she was, Kitty thought, wondering if all Italians were like this.

After several exchanges in rapid Italian, Giles said to Kitty, 'You must let me introduce Signora Lombardi—'

'Lucia,' she broke in irrepressibly. 'You must call me Lucia – and I shall call you Kitty. Giles has told me about you in his letters. And here is my husband Flavio . . .'

A handsome nut-brown elderly man with swept-back silver hair.

'Professor Lombardi, head of the School of Etruscan Studies at the University of Florence,' Giles supplied.

'. . . and our daughter Giulia,' Lucia went on, bringing forward a tall, very dark girl of startling creamy-skinned beauty, who smiled faintly and bowed her head to Kitty. 'And that is all for now, so many names for you to remember, poor Kitty, when you are so tired and in a strange place! Have some more lemonade.'

'It's delicious,' Kitty said.

Lucia beamed as though she'd had the best compliment of her life. 'I make it myself, from our own lemons. Can you smell the blossom? There is a tree in the courtyard here.'

'Is that what I can smell?' Kitty said. 'It's lovely.'

'There is a small factory in the city that makes a perfume from the lemon blossom,' she said. 'You shall have a little vial to remember us by.' She sat next to Kitty and talked about the city while she drank her second glass. In the background, Kitty was aware of Giles, the professor and the lovely Giulia talking together volubly in Italian. It was probably only her tiredness, but it made her feel excluded and just a little resentful. *They shouldn't talk in Italian when they know I can't understand,* she thought.

When she had finished her drink, Lucia escorted her upstairs to a room with a high ceiling and white linen shades over the tall windows. The bed was large and high and covered with a white counterpane. The floor was stone, the furniture sparse and simple, and there was a large stone jar on the floor in one corner in which was a glorious arrangement of flowers, blue and white and scarlet. It all looked so inviting, she almost wanted to cry. 'Giles is next door, through here,' Lucia said, indicating a communicating door. 'And this is the bell.' A long sash hanging from the ceiling by the bed. 'I shall send your maid in to you, and you shall come down when you are ready – there is no hurry. Rest, dear Kitty, sleep a little if you wish. We are so glad to welcome you here.'

Kitty had never had a mother who exuded kindness like this. She would have liked to fall into Lucia's arms and rest her head on her shoulder. And possibly go to sleep there.

'I didn't realise you knew the Lombardis so well,' Kitty said, that night, as she and Giles climbed the steep stairs to bed.

'Didn't you?' he said, in vague surprise. 'I thought I told you we were staying with friends.'

'Acquaintances, you said,' she corrected.

'Professor Lombardi was my great mentor,' Giles said. 'The foremost expert on the Etruscans – he's led all the important digs. I've learned more from him than from anyone else. And Lucia made me so welcome when I was a lonely young man far from home.'

'She's very kind,' Kitty said.

'She's been more of a mother to me than my own mother,' he said.

'Giulia seems very clever,' Kitty said casually.

'Yes,' he said. 'She ought to have been a boy, really – minds like hers are rare enough in either sex – but it would have been a waste for her not to have been a woman.'

Kitty wasn't sure what to make of that. 'You talked a lot to her over dinner,' she said. He didn't respond, opening the door of her room for her. 'I didn't know you spoke Italian so well.'

'I had to learn it when I was studying,' he said. 'You can't really study Romans and Etruscans in the modern world and not speak Italian. And living here with the Lombardis helped, of course. It's the best way to learn a language, to immerse oneself in it.'

'You lived here for a long time?'

'Oh, many months,' he said. He was heading for the communicating door. 'And many visits since.'

'I must say, it does make one feel left out, not under-standing what's being said,' Kitty said cautiously.

'It was academic talk, mostly,' Giles said. 'You wouldn't have enjoyed it. I'll leave you to get undressed.'

Marie, who must have been listening outside, came straight in and undressed her as far as her shift, thankfully without speaking. She took down Kitty's hair, and then Kitty said, 'I can do the rest.'

'Thank you, my lady,' said Marie, and left.

Alone, Kitty removed the rest of her clothes, washed her face at the wash-stand, and slipped naked into bed. The sheets were gloriously cool against her skin. It had been a long day, and a long evening – a protracted meal out under the vine arbour, course after course brought by sturdy-looking servants who spoke with easy familiarity to their employers. So different from home. Her mind was a jumble of confused images – of cicadas, and red wine glowing in the candlelight, of huge stars glimpsed in the square of velvet sky above the courtyard, of night-scented flowers and blundering écru-coloured moths, of Italian voices tumbling

324

on and on like a stream, of the professor laughing, throwing back his head exuberantly and showing fine white teeth, of the dark red beaded gown contrasting so startlingly with Giulia's creamy skin. Of Giles smiling and talking, smiling and talking, as though he had finally reached the place on earth where he belonged . . .

She was almost asleep when he came in, shed his dressing-gown and slipped naked into bed with her. They had stopped wearing night-clothes – it was a waste of time. He drew her into his arms at once, without a word, and she felt his hot readiness pressing against her thigh. With a glad sigh she opened herself to him, and he entered her, more eager, more passionate than ever. They moved together in the familiar ecstatic dance. When it was over, he held her in his arms, and she felt him drifting into ready sleep. He had not spoken, and she felt, for the first time, not contented but oddly lonely. She had had his essence, but she wanted words too.

'Giulia is very beautiful, isn't she?' she said in a small voice. But he was asleep and didn't answer.

'I think his lordship's a bit smitten with Miss Giulia,' said James, polishing boots. The cool morning air came in through the open door to the small scullery beside the kitchen. Already, in the kitchen, there was a smell of coffee, pans were being clattered and voices were bantering back and forth. They did love their grub, these Eyetalians, he thought.

'She's all right,' said Marie, working on the countess's shoes. 'A bit full of herself, if you ask me. And her hair's coarse as a pony's – nothing to write home about. Nice skin, though.'

'Yeah,' said James. 'She can ring my bell any time she likes.'

Marie gave him a scornful look. 'You can dream about it.' She yawned. 'They keep late nights here.'

'Yeah, but at least some of 'em speak a bit of English. It makes a difference. That butler, Stefano—'

'Major domo,' Marie said. 'That's what they're called abroad.'

'Whatever he is. I had a good chat with him yesterday. He says English servants go down a treat over here. Everyone wants 'em – snob value, apparently.'

'You stick with his lordship,' Marie advised. 'You wouldn't last five minutes anywhere but England.'

'Huh!' James said, hurt. 'What about you, then?'

'Oh, I reckon I could make it here. I'm quick to learn. And I like the place.'

James was alarmed. He didn't want to be left on his own. Broken English wasn't enough for a gregarious man. 'You're not jumping ship?'

'Wouldn't you like to know?' she said.

Nina hadn't spoken to her aunt about university: it seemed too remote a dream. And the reality of taking a teaching job was looming ever closer. Aunt Schofield hadn't said anything, but Nina felt she ought to make some preparation. She visited Miss Thornton and talked it over with her, asked her what would be the best way of seeking a post. Miss Thornton told her her education was good enough for a girls' school, and said she would ask around and let her know if she heard of a place. She quizzed Nina about her new interest in archaeology, and suggested some books. 'I think you know everything,' Nina said admiringly.

Miss Thornton laughed. 'A little about most things,' she said. 'Just enough to appear to know a lot more – which is the teacher's great trick, Nina, my dear. Always keep one step ahead of your pupils . . . and their parents.'

Meanwhile, Nina was busy, and happy, enjoying the last of her freedom. Apart from working for the library, she was studying the basics of Egyptology, and spending a couple of mornings a week at the British Museum. Aunt Schofield had many charitable schemes, and she helped her every day with the correspondence. And her friendship with Lepida was flourishing. There were summer courses at the university, and they went to some lectures together, compared notes, shared reading lists. Nina found Lepida's orderly mind a great help – she was a good sounding-board. They went for walks together in the parks or along the river, and to one or two concerts.

Nina was becoming a regular visitor at the Morris home. She liked Mrs Morris, Isabel, who was a motherly soul, and enjoyed the relationship between the three of them, which seemed attractively egalitarian to one brought up to strict discipline. Henry 'Mawes' Morris was an extraordinary man: an artist, illustrator, and drawer of cartoons for *Harlequinade*, the satirical magazine. He had an original mind, a puckish sense of humour, and many talents: Aunt called him a polymath. He could draw and paint, play the piano, write songs, had collaborated on a comic play that had done very well in a London theatre, and had been in his youth a top-class cricketer and yachtsman. He liked to talk and to laugh, but had occasional ferocious bouts of temper when things went wrong, which scared Nina at first. But they never lasted long, and were not directed at anyone in particular, more at the perversity of a Fate that dropped objects in his way on which to stub his toes.

Nina was soon persuaded to model for him. 'I'm always looking for willing bodies,' he told her. 'Bel and Lepida are so bored by it, though they put up with me, bless them.' She never knew what she would have to do next: pose with a tennis racquet as though taking a shot, sit at a tiny table with a glass in her hand being in Paris, straddle a bicycle (scolding from the housekeeper about oil on the carpet), hold an inside-out umbrella and pretend to be struggling against the wind. Often it would involve dressing up in something hired from a theatrical costumier. It was all great fun. Aunt Schofield did not take *Harlequinade*, and she had to go to the library to see herself magically transposed into a cartoon. She loved the idea that people all over the country would be looking at her image without knowing in the least that it was her. She was immortalised – but anonymously.

As well as using her for his paid work, Mawes, as he insisted she call him (everyone did), was painting a serious portrait of her, sitting on a high stool by a window and gazing out pensively. 'That's it,' he would say sometimes. 'That expression of melancholy – that's what I want.' He never asked why she was sad. Sitting gave her time to think, and nothing to interrupt the thoughts. It was better, she thought, to keep busy – but she would always oblige him.

He thought it was going to turn out well. 'I might send it in to the Exhibition at the Royal Academy next year,' he said.

There were lively dinners at the Morrises', too – with as much talk but more laughter than at Aunt Schofield's gatherings. From his yachting days Mawes knew the King, who was a tremendous fan of his work. He had met many people of influence, while his journalism brought him together with people from all walks of life, politicians, courtiers, bankers, sportsmen, actors, writers. Mawes seemed to know everyone: you never knew who might be at the table.

One day while she was sitting for him he said, 'I met a fellow the other day who claims an acquaintance with you, Nina. He recognised you from that high-wind cartoon, you remember the one, and asked me about you. It was at a gentlemen's dinner in Manchester Square. Name of Cowling. Do you remember him at all?'

'Yes, of course,' Nina said.

'Really? I thought he must be mistaken,' said Mawes. 'Industrialist – frightfully big in boots and shoes, apparently. Couldn't think where you might have met him.'

'It was at a ball at Dene Park,' Nina said. 'He was in a party that came with the King. I danced with him.'

'Ah, yes, he is one of the King's coterie,' said Mawes. 'Well, that explains it. He sent his compliments and so on. You seem to have made quite an impression on him.'

Nina smiled. 'I don't remember saying very much. Mostly I listened while he told me about himself.'

Mawes smiled mischievously. 'That'll do it every time! If females knew how powerful being listened to is, none of us would have a chance. We'd fall like ninepins.'

Giles seemed in no hurry to leave Florence. He had disappeared into the world of academe – and, in particular, the archaeological section of it – and Kitty hardly saw him. It was left to Lucia to entertain her, and take her about the famous city to see the sights. More museums and art galleries. Lucia was very knowledgeable, and at least did not spend as much time on each exhibit as Giles tended to. Even so, Kitty's feet ached in concert with her head. There seemed to be an inordinate number of churches in Florence, but Kitty was glad of them: at least it was cool inside, and out of the glaring sun. She could even contrive to sit down for a while, and if Lucia wondered at the time she was willing to spend in rapt contemplation of a statue of the Blessed Virgin, she made no comment.

One morning Lucia said to her, 'What would you like to do today, my dear?'

Kitty smiled dutifully. 'Whatever you like. Had you something planned?'

'I think it's too hot for the Boboli Gardens. There's the Strozzi Palace – we haven't seen that yet.'

'I'm sure whatever you choose will be lovely,' said Kitty.

Lucia cocked her head. 'But Kitty, *cara*, what would you *like* to do?' Kitty couldn't answer. 'You are so polite, my dear, and I don't believe you have ever told anyone in your life what you really want. But you can tell me. I swear on all I hold dear that I shall not be offended, whatever it is. If you had the choice of anything today, what would you like to do?'

Kitty hesitated a long time. Obviously *go home* was not on the list. In the end, cautiously, she said, 'I would like to look at the shops. But I don't suppose—'

Lucia clapped her hands together. 'Perfect! But why didn't you say so?' She slid an arm through Kitty's. 'I have been thinking, my dear, that your clothes are not very suited to our Florentine summer. They are too heavy and too tight.'

'My mother chose them.' Kitty said. 'I don't suppose she has ever been to Italy.'

'Well, then, we should go at once to my favourite shops, and I shall have the greatest pleasure in seeing you dressed like a true Contessa di Firenze!'

Kitty almost pulled her arm away. 'But I don't have any money!' she blurted.

Lucia laughed. 'But that is of no account. The bills will all be sent here, and Giles will settle them. That is how it is done. Come – we shall have fun today.'

They did, and the new clothes were lighter and looser and much more pleasant to wear. But July turned to August and still Giles showed no sign of moving. And as well as missing him during the day, she was now missing him at night. His visits had stopped when her time of the month came, but that was over now, the Hygena rubber doily belt had been put away, and he had not come back to her. She was too shy to say anything to him, and even dropping a hint had seemed too embarrassing. But one evening when she went up before him, she went so far as to say, 'Will you be long?' She blushed at her own boldness, but he didn't notice. They had all been sitting round the table in the courtyard, as they so often did, and he was talking hard to the professor. When she spoke, he said, 'I'll be up soon,' dropping out of Italian into English for those four words, without even looking at her.

Still, she was hopeful, but she was also very tired – the heat did not suit her – and she fell asleep waiting for him. She woke with a start, not knowing how long she had been asleep. It had been close to midnight when she had come upstairs, but she had no clock in her room, and did not own a watch. She felt suddenly wide awake, and a charming idea came to her. She got up, put on her dressing-gown, and went quietly through into Giles's room.

His bed was empty. The clock on his mantelpiece showed a quarter to two. Where on earth could he be? She opened the door onto the corridor, and listened. The house seemed quiet and still. Worried now, she made her way downstairs – there was just enough moonlight coming in through the narrow windows to see her way. The rooms were empty, silent, the servants gone to bed, but then she heard a faint murmur of voices. Soundless on her bare feet, she went towards it, through the hall and the anteroom and, yes, towards the courtyard garden. Before she reached it, she could see through the door the shape of Giles, sitting at the table, leaning on his elbows, his profile picked out by the moonlight. He was talking to someone who was sitting back, in the shadows. His voice, which she had always loved, murmured on, and she knew by the shape of it that he was talking Italian. Then he stopped, as if waiting for a response, and the figure in the shade leaned forward into the silvery light and spoke. A woman's voice, light as a breeze. It was Giulia.

Kitty froze where she was, invisible to them if she did not move. Why it seemed important not to be seen she wasn't sure. She listened for a long time, to the soothing rhythm of people who know each other well, and are at ease. No other voices joined them. It was just Giles and Giulia. How hatefully well those names went together! Giles and Kitty – that was not a match. They were not a pair. They had never spoken to each other in that comfortable way. There was an ache low down in her stomach, as if her month-time was returning. She felt empty and without purpose. Delicately she backed across the cold stone floor until she reached the door, then turned and went quickly upstairs.

She lay in her bed, listening for him to come upstairs, but the walls were thick and she didn't usually hear him until he came through the communicating door. She hoped and hoped; but she feared. Then she fell asleep. So she never knew if perhaps he *had* come in, but finding her asleep had gone away again.

The Coronation finally took place on the 9th of August. Most of the foreign visitors who had come in June had gone home again, though the colonial representatives had stayed so, according to the newspapers, there was a pleasantly 'family' feeling to the celebration. The King looked well, and had apparently completely recovered; the Queen, slender and beautiful in a gown of gold tissue, looked ethereally young. Her serenity was unshaken by the fact that a special pew had been reserved in the Abbey for the King's favourites, including Mrs Keppel and Sarah Bernhardt. The King was hugely popular, and the crowds cheered him hoarse: it was a turn-out that rivalled the Jubilee celebrations of five years previously.

The grand families fled London in August, so their Coronation parties were held on their country estates, which left London to the real Londoners, who did not go away but rather relished the capital's quietness in the summer weeks. Aunt Schofield had been invited to a party at one of the Oxford colleges, but allowed Nina to accept instead an invitation to the Morrises'. In order to host as many people as possible, it was to be a buffet meal instead of a sit-down dinner, and Mawes had decreed everyone must come in fancy dress.

'Such a lot of nonsense,' Aunt Schofield said. 'It adds nothing to the occasion but embarrassment, and the costumes are uncomfortable and awkward. And no conversation of worth can be held with everyone standing up and talking at once.'

'I don't suppose conversation of worth is Mawes's idea,' said Nina. 'But it will be fun.'

'I do not share your idea of fun,' said Aunt Schofield. But she helped Nina to make a helmet and shield from gold-painted cardboard for her Britannia costume – a plain white dress with a red, white and blue shoulder sash that shouldn't be too hampering. 'Shouldn't I have a trident, too?' Nina asked.

'Nina, my dear, for the hope of any enjoyment at these costume parties you must keep everything as simple as possible. Helmet and shield are bad enough – you will not want to be carrying around an overgrown toasting fork as well. As soon as people have seen you, find somewhere to get rid of them.'

Nina saw the wisdom of this advice when she arrived at the Morris house and saw the lengths some people had gone to, and how uncomfortable they were as Elizabeth I or Mary Queen of Scots, Richard the Lion Heart or St George. Lepida was a very Millais Ophelia in a nice loose gown and flowers in her hair. Mawes was Mr Pickwick, which suited his growing *embonpoint*. Isabel Morris as Grace Darling was only incommoded by a plaid shawl. There were three other Britannias, which given the occasion, was not very surprising, and they all had tridents and large shields that got in everyone's way. But the atmosphere was tremendous, and everyone seemed bent on having an extremely good time.

When Nina was accosted by a rajah in gold tunic and trousers and a turban with a hackle, she wasn't surprised that she didn't recognise him – after all, hadn't Miss Thornton told them that the fancy-dress party was the modern incarnation of the *ballo in maschera*, whose purpose was to allow people to disport themselves incognito?

But as soon as he spoke, she recognised the accent, and the voice. 'Mr Cowling,' she said. 'Goodness, what a surprise! You don't look a bit like yourself.'

'I don't feel a bit like myself either,' he said, pulling out a handkerchief from under the tunic and mopping his face. 'I wasn't sure of the wisdom of it – dressing up – when I got the invitation, but now I'm thinking it's a damn silly idea at this time of year.'

'But you look very splendid.'

'Eh, do I? You're very kind. I didn't want to be looking foolish, at any rate. Some of the costumes – well there was one with knee-breeches and a great long wig. Louis the something – one of those French kings. Fine fool I'd have looked in that! And then the chap in the shop had a notion I'd look good in a turban. Why I listened to him I'll never know! It's damned hot.'

'But he was right,' Nina said. 'I'm not sure why, but it does suit you.'

'There's that silver tongue of yours again!' he said, smiling. 'I tell you what, though – the first thing he wanted was to get me up as Sindbad the Sailor. That had a turban all right, but then there were those silly baggy trousers and curly shoes! I told him what I thought of that.' He made a sound of disgust. 'They're an abomination, those shoes. What man in his right mind would ever have worn 'em?'

'I'm sure you'll see a lot of silly shoes here tonight,' Nina said.

'Aye, I've been looking,' he said.

'I expect historical people didn't have the same shoe-making equipment as nowadays. Perhaps we shouldn't judge them too harshly.'

334

'Well, maybe you're right – but curly shoes! No, I draw the line there.' He shook his head, then seemed to recollect himself. 'Dear me, where are my manners? You've done it again, Miss Sanderton, made me so comfortable I just jaw selfishly away without thinking. So, what are you supposed to be?'

'Britannia,' she said, pulling out a fold of the sash to demonstrate.

'Well, that's nice and patriotic,' he said. 'But isn't there a . . .' He twirled a finger over his head.

'Helmet? There is, and a shield, but I hid them in the cloakroom downstairs a while ago.'

He beamed. 'Very sensible. I think I might get rid of this turban the same way.'

'Oh, not yet! It does make you look rather splendid.'

He looked at her suspiciously. 'Now you're gammoning me.'

Nina, who had been, just a little, straightened her face and said, 'But tell me, were you at the Coronation? In the Abbey, I mean?'

He looked pleased again. 'I was. The King was so kind as to send me a ticket – one of the out-of-the-way seats, and I couldn't see everything because of the pillars, but it's something to say I was there.'

'But you weren't invited to the banquet afterwards?'

'No, no, I'm not that important. But when I told the King I'd got an invitation here, he said he wished he could come too, and that I'd have more fun than he would, for all the twenty courses. Of course, he knows our host very well, Mawes Morris. Makes him laugh every time, and His Majesty does love to laugh.'

At that moment, Mawes himself appeared, seized Nina's arm, and said, 'Nina, come with me. I must make a quick sketch of you as Britannia. I've had an idea for a cartoon for next week.' He frowned. 'Didn't you have a helmet?'

'And a shield, but no trident,' she said. 'I got rid of them downstairs.'

'All right, I'll send someone for them. Come along, while I'm on fire. Cowling, good to see you! You don't mind my stealing your companion.'

He didn't wait for an answer, but towed Nina away through the crowds. 'There are other Britannias, you know,' she said, 'with better costumes than mine.'

'But you have the face – particularly the profile,' he said. 'No, I must have you.'

'I see you invited Mr Cowling,' Nina said, as she followed him upstairs to his studio. 'I thought he seemed – well, a bit out of his usual place.'

Mawes swung round the turn of the stairs, so she saw his grin. 'Wasn't my idea. He invited himself, quite pointedly, so I couldn't refuse. I would never have imagined him enjoying a fancy-dress party of this sort, but you never know, do you? I half expected the King to slip in behind him – playing hooky from the official bun-struggle at the palace.'

Nina smiled at the thought. 'I wonder what he'd have come as.'

'Probably as the King of England,' said Mawes.

'It really is too hot in Florence,' Lucia said at dinner, in the scented, mothy half-darkness of the arbour. 'Look how your poor little wife is drooping, Giles, like a flower that wants water.'

'Yes, what are your plans, Giles?' asked the professor. His English was good, but not as perfect as Lucia's – she had been secretary to an English Egyptologist. 'You are welcome to stay here as long as you wish, but we do not remain in August, usually.'

'I'm sorry, am I disrupting your plans? I've been so happily occupied I haven't thought. Stupid of me! I had thought of going to Naples from here. I'd like to show Kitty the ruins of Pompeii.'

Both protested at once, and even Giulia looked surprised.

336

'Napoli? Impossible! Intolerable!'

'Giles, you cannot drag her round Pompeii in August. You cannot be such a brute.'

'Every man of sense goes to the sea at this time of year.'

'Is that where you're going?' he asked.

Husband and wife glanced at each other. 'We always take a villa in Capri for August,' said Lucia. 'We have lingered here for you – and glad to do it—'

'Then we must delay you no more,' Giles said. 'You've been too polite. I'm sure you're sick of us by now.'

Lucia reached over and slapped his hand. '*Cattivo!* We can never be sick of you. We want you come to Capri with us, of course. The villa is big enough for us all.'

Giulia said, 'Oh, do come, Giles! It is so beautiful there.'

'And there are ruins,' Lucia said wickedly, 'if you cannot bear too much pleasure. Lots of them. Tiberius built twelve villas there, remember.'

Giles turned to Kitty, who was pushing food about on her plate. 'What do you think, Kitty? Would you like to go to Capri?'

'I don't know what it is,' she said dully.

'It is an island,' Lucia said. 'In the Bay of Naples. Rugged cliffs, beautiful scenery, fresh air, shady trees, and the most beautiful, beautiful sea to bathe in.'

Kitty raised her head. 'I've never bathed in the sea.'

'Oh, then you *must* come! It is the best thing in the world. Tell her, Giles.'

'It is very nice,' he said. 'Would you like to go?'

He spoke so kindly, she looked up at him in hope. 'Would *you* like to go?'

'I believe all the ruins have been excavated to the limit,' he said, 'but I'd still like to see them. I never did get there before. And you can sit in a cool garden, go for boat rides, and swim in the sea. What do you think?'

'I would like that,' Kitty said. She would rather have gone

somewhere with him alone, somewhere that Giulia wouldn't be, but if the choices were staying here or going to the seaside, she chose the seaside.

When Giles's cable arrived, Lady Stainton said, 'Then we don't need to be here, if he's not coming back.'

'Good,' said Sebastian, looking up from the paper. 'We can be in Scotland for the twelfth.'

Rachel and Alice exchanged a glance. 'Oh, Mama, we don't have to go, do we?'

She raised an eyebrow. 'You most certainly do. We will all go to Kincraig. What are you thinking?'

'But there's nothing to do there,' Rachel cried. 'We don't like shooting or fishing and there's no riding and the midges are awful.'

'Couldn't Rachel and I stay here?' Alice asked hopefully.

'Of course not,' said Lady Stainton. Her eyes narrowed as she looked at Rachel. 'Stay here on your own? Nonsense!'

'I don't see why we couldn't stay,' Rachel grumbled, as the girls went upstairs after breakfast. 'Nobody wants us there. Mama never wants us around her anyway. And Mrs Webster could look after us.'

'I think she was suspicious,' Alice said. 'Did you see the way she looked at you? I think she knows why you want to stay.'

'Oh, well, she'll never agree, now she's said no,' said Rachel, gloomily. 'It's horrible Kincraig for us.'

'Your old Victor won't miss you for a few weeks.'

'That's what I'm afraid of,' said Rachel.

Richard decided not to go to Kincraig. 'I can't hold a gun with one arm, or make a cast,' he said. 'And I can hardly tramp over the heather like this. I suppose I'll just have to stay here.'

'Would you like to come with Grandmère and me to Biarritz?' Caroline asked kindly.

'Promenading up and down so that everyone can admire my clothes *would* be exciting,' he admitted, 'but I'm afraid I'd slow you down.'

'Don't be satirical. You know there's more to it than that.'

'Not a *great* deal more, surely.'

'There are the gardens, the galleries, the *plage*.'

'I'd forgotten the *plage*. I'd give a fortune to see you and Grandmère disporting yourselves in bathing costumes.'

She ignored that. 'There will be lots of parties. And Sir Thomas is conducting a series of concerts in the royal villa.'

'Ah, all is clear. You want me to increase the size of Sir Thomas's *claque*.'

Aunt Caroline gave him a severe look. 'If you don't want to come, don't. There's no need to be facetious. But I think you would benefit from the sea air.'

He leaned over to kiss her repentantly. 'You are the most gracious of aunts. I'll come.'

He went to say goodbye to the Sandses. It was a baking hot day, and although it was fairly cool inside the tall Georgian house, he felt uncomfortable about their confinement when he was going on holiday.

'I'm glad for you,' Mrs Sands said. 'It's been hard, I think, the inactivity since your accident.'

'Oh, I'm an idle fellow,' he said. 'Inactivity is my natural state. But I wish you and Miss Chloë could have a holiday. London in August is suffocating.'

'There are the parks and gardens,' she said lightly. 'And I expect we shall have a day-trip to the seaside. The steamer to Southend is always pleasant. If I can drag her away, that is.' She smiled. 'What do you think happened? We had a letter from your kind grandmama to say that Chloë could still go in and practise while she's away. She said she had told the caretaker to let her in. Isn't that good of her?'

Richard was surprised, but only that Grandmère had

thought of it. 'She thinks very highly of musicians,' he said. 'Music is a passion with her.'

'But I think you had something to do with it, didn't you?'

'Not at all. In fact, I'm ashamed it didn't occur to me. Is that really what you want to do?' he asked Chloë. 'Stay in London and practise? Where would you go, if you had your choice of anywhere in the world?'

Chloë looked faintly surprised. 'I have everything I need here,' she said. 'Why should I want to go anywhere else?'

For the life of him, Richard couldn't tell if she really meant it.

CHAPTER EIGHTEEN

The Villa Isabella was set in lavish vegetation on top of a cliff, with a view from the terrace over the Bay of Naples that literally took Kitty's breath away. She couldn't believe the sea could be so blue – it almost ached in the afternoon sunshine. The air was fragrant with pine and myrtle, and in the dense green there were splashes of colour from bougainvillaea and hibiscus, and the starry white flowers of jasmine. It was, she thought, as close to Paradise as one could probably get.

The villa was an old building, the rooms simply but pleasingly furnished. Life mostly took place on the verandah or the terrace: there they took their meals, and there they sat in the shade through the heat of the day, cooled by gentle breezes. There were winding walks along the clifftop, the Roman ruins to visit, boat trips around the island, and to see the Blue Grotto; and best of all, from Kitty's point of view, sea-bathing. The Isabella had its own small beach, sheltered at the foot of the cliff, with a zigzag path, intercut with steps, leading down from the terrace. She had been nervous on her first venture into the water, but once she had got used to it, she could hardly bear to get out. She bathed every day, going down in the cool of the morning through the scented trees, hurrying to the water as to a lover. Lowering herself into its supporting arms was the greatest bliss she had known, except for Giles.

The next house along, the Villa Caprini, was occupied by Lord and Lady Latham, their son David and daughter Louisa, who were twenty-five and twenty-three, and David's friend Matteo, with whom he had been at university in Oxford. They and the Lombardis knew each other from previous visits, and the two parties intermingled frequently. Now that most of the conversation was in English Kitty did not feel left out. That, plus being away from the stifling heat, lifted her spirits.

Matteo spoke very good English, as good as Lucia's, but he reverted to Italian for some conversations with Giulia – long tête-à-tête talks, which pleased Kitty. Matteo was darkly handsome in the Mediterranean way, and if his interest in Giulia did not entirely separate her from Giles, it broke them up a little. With her reviving spirits, she wanted Giles more than ever.

For the first few days he was attentive to her, took her to see the most interesting ruins, explained some of the island's history and told her the names of flora and fauna. When everyone gathered on the terrace for conversation, he chose the seat at her side. He did not seem particularly interested in the Lathams, whose conversation was light and general. Kitty liked it – it was easy and unchallenging, and reminded her of the five-o'-clocks she had enjoyed during her come-out, the unimportant chatter of the fashionable set. Giles usually sat silent at these times, joining in only when addressed.

Kitty and Giles did not have adjoining bedrooms – his was across the passage from hers. On the first few evenings they went up to bed at the same time, and she was able, through looks and a few hesitant words, to indicate that she would like him to visit her – and he did. She was happy: she felt that things had come right again, and Florence was fading into a bad dream.

But then Giles and Flavio went on an expedition together

to one of the ruins, and Giles, kissing Kitty lightly goodbye, said, 'You wouldn't enjoy it.'

Well, perhaps she wouldn't have. But she missed him. And that evening, when he and the professor talked about it, it seemed as much to Giulia as anyone that Giles spoke. They had all been talking English, for the benefit of the general company, but Matteo, changing his place to sit beside Giulia, began addressing her in a low voice in Italian. Giles frowned, and said sharply, 'In English, if you please. Remember, not all here are fluent in Italian.'

Lady Latham, who did not speak any Italian, said, 'Oh, yes, please, let us all hear.'

Giulia looked uncomfortable. 'We were talking of secret passages,' she said, in her soft, hesitant accent.

'Is it true,' Louisa asked, 'that there's a secret passage to the Blue Grotto, and the Emperor used it as his private swimming pool?'

'Quite true – is it not, Giles?'

Kitty listened absently. She was more interested in watching: Giulia's eyes were fixed on Giles, and Matteo's were fixed on Giulia. And Giles: where did his interest lie? He was talking about secret passages, and dividing his looks now between Lady Latham and Louisa, but where was his mind? Kitty knew every inflection of her husband's voice, and she didn't think he was giving his whole attention to the subject, even when it progressed to Etruscan catacombs. But whatever he was thinking about, she knew it wasn't her.

David, changing places to sit beside her, murmured, 'You seem to be miles away, Lady Stainton. Roman ruins not quite catching your attention tonight?'

She made an effort, and smiled. 'One can have enough of them.'

'True. And on a night like this – did you ever see such a moon? – one can't help thinking a nightingale would be more worth listening to than human voices.'

343

'I've never heard a nightingale,' Kitty said.

'Really? You should get Lord Stainton to take you to the San Michele gardens one evening. You can always hear them there.' They were silent for a moment, both staring at Giulia. Then David said, 'Don't you think Italians have an unfair advantage over us? All that lustrous black hair and such—' He broke off, and said awkwardly, 'I beg your pardon. I meant no comparison – so clumsy of me!'

'Don't apologise,' Kitty said, in a low voice. 'Every reasonable person must agree that Giulia Lombardi is beautiful.'

'I'm not sure,' David said, looking moodily at Matteo, 'that reason comes into it.'

That night, after the Latham party had left, and Kitty got up to go to bed, Giles did not rise with her, but smiled vaguely and said, 'I'll be up soon.'

And he didn't come.

Kitty hadn't slept well. When Marie came in, she asked, 'What time is it?'

'Half past nine, my lady. I didn't wake you when I came in the first time, you seemed so deep asleep.'

Kitty sat up, trying to shake the cobwebs out of her head. The intensity of the light on the blinds told her it was a hot day out there. Even in here it was warm enough to make her skin unpleasantly damp. 'Is his lordship up?' she asked.

'He's gone out, my lady.'

'Out?'

'To look at some ruin or other. It was thought it'd be too hot later so he wanted an early start. I believe he said they'd be back by midday.'

'I think I'll go for a bathe,' Kitty said.

She found her host and hostess sitting in the shade of the verandah reading, and looked at the professor with surprise. 'I thought you'd gone to look at a ruin.'

He glanced up and smiled. 'Good morning, my dear. Going for your swim? No, it was too hot for me this morning.'

'I think there might be thunder later,' Lucia said.

'Giulia went with Giles,' Flavio went on. 'She knows the way – and she knows as much about it as I do. Not much left above ground, but there are some interesting tesserae – nothing complete, of course, just fragments, but—'

'Flavio, *caro*, she doesn't need to hear all the details,' Lucia interrupted smilingly. 'I told them to be back by midday, so they'll be quite all right. The storm, if it comes, won't be until later, around sunset. Will you have some breakfast, my dear?'

They seemed so at ease about Giulia and Giles going off together that Kitty felt ashamed of her own inward reaction of anger and surprise. But she had seen, as perhaps they had not, the way Giulia looked at him.

The thought of food sickened her. 'No, thank you. I think I'll sea-bathe first. I don't feel hungry.'

'Shall I come with you?' Lucia asked.

'There's no need. The sea's calm and I only want to lie in the water. I shan't swim out.'

'Well, see that you don't,' Lucia said, too comfortable to get up. The thought of the walk down the path in the heat, and then up again . . .

Kitty was sitting on one of the sofas on the verandah when Giles and Giulia came back. David and Louisa had come over from the Villa Caprini, though without Matteo, who had gone to visit Italian friends elsewhere on the island. All five were having a desultory conversation about nothing in particular; the heat had become oppressive, and the sky in the distance looked congested, the blue faded to grey, then darkening to pewter on the horizon.

The returning explorers looked hot, but happy, as though they had spent a stimulating morning. 'You see, we're back before your storm, Lucia,' Giles called cheerfully, as they came up to the verandah. 'Is that lemonade? I'm terribly thirsty.'

'Did you see the horse's head mosaic?' Flavio asked. 'It is thought to be part of a mounted image of Tiberius. He was a fine soldier, you know,' he added to Kitty, 'before he went to the bad.'

'A noted general,' Lucia added. 'After the campaigns of his brother Drusus—'

'Oh, more history lessons,' David interrupted. 'Dear *madama*, it's too hot!'

Giulia ignored him. 'We didn't find any fossils,' she said to her father. 'Not even animal bones. I'm sure there were wild goats once.'

Giles had poured himself a glass of lemonade, and came and sat heavily by Kitty. He smelt hot and dusty. 'There's some dispute over whether the name of this island came from the Latin for "goat" or the Etruscan word for "rocky",' he said. Kitty supposed he was speaking for her education, but he had not so much as looked at her yet.

'You know there's no evidence for Etruscan connections with the island,' Giulia said, with mock sternness. It sounded like an argument they had had before.

'If I stayed here long enough, I guarantee I could find them,' Giles said. 'The style of that bird fragment we saw, even the horse's head, the way the bridle was reproduced—'

'Oh, Giles!' Giulia said with affectionate exasperation.

'Oh, everyone! No more antiquities!' David interrupted, laughing. 'We were having a nice time talking about normal things.'

'You must be hungry.' Lucia said to Giulia and Giles. 'I should stir myself and see about luncheon, but I'm so comfortable.'

'I'd like to swim first,' Giles said.

346

'Oh, yes,' said Giulia, at once. 'It's so hot! A bathe would cool us down.'

'We've brought our things,' said Louisa.

'Very well, swim first, and luncheon will be ready when you come up,' said Lucia. 'You can change in my room, Louisa – David, you can use the wood store.'

The young people jumped up, and the professor said, 'You make me feel old with your energy. If only the sea would come to me, rise up and collect me kindly, but that walk down the cliff, in this heat . . .'

Giles was almost in the house when he seemed to remember Kitty, and turned back to say, 'Are you coming?'

She looked up, but his eyes did not connect with hers. *I'm just an afterthought when she's around.* 'I bathed this morning,' she said.

He might have said, 'Come anyway, 'or 'You can bathe more than once, you know,' and she'd have jumped up. If he had even smiled at her . . . But he said indifferently, 'Very well,' and went inside to change.

By the time they came out, changed and ready, Lucia had hauled herself up to go inside and bespeak luncheon, while Flavio had sunk back into his book, and was verging on slumber. Kitty had picked up a book too. 'Ready?' she heard Giles say, and the four young people came past her, jumped gaily down the verandah step and trotted across the terrace to the dark place between the trees where the path began – twisting, winding, uneven, down the steep cliff to the rocky cove and the blue, rocking waves. Nobody looked at her or called to her before they disappeared into that dark mouth. She felt abandoned and bitter.

Luncheon was always light, cold meats, cheeses, salads and fruits, served at the big table on the verandah. There was easy talk, and laughter. The light outside was thick and strange, and the heat was so intense that even in the shade it was too warm. Conversation flagged after a while, except for Giles and Giulia, who continued to talk about the ruins they had visited, and the mosaics in particular – a conversation that wandered in and out of history and occasionally fell into Italian and out again, as though there were no difference between the languages. Kitty, her chair drawn back into the deepest shade, watched them, brooding, and felt the ache in her lower stomach again, an ache that made her clench all her muscles.

'The storm's coming,' Louisa said, into a pause. 'I think we ought to be walking back, Davy. Mama will be worried.'

'It may pass us by,' Lucia said. 'They sometimes go round to the south.'

'Still, we ought to go,' David said. 'Thank you so much for your hospitality.'

'Shall we see you this evening?' Lucia asked.

'Thanks, but Matteo's friends have asked us – the Morettis.'

When they had gone, Flavio yawned and roused himself to say, 'A *sonnellino*, I think, is the answer to this heavy air.'

Lucia agreed. 'We should all lie down on our beds until it makes up its mind whether to storm or not. My dears, won't you?'

'You're right,' said Giles. 'I can hardly keep my eyes open.'

They all went upstairs, Kitty trailing after Giles. The Lombardis turned one way at the top of the stairs, and Giles and Kitty the other. At the door to his room, Giles turned and frowned at Kitty. 'Are you all right? You're very quiet.'

Tears came to her eyes. Was this all she deserved? From the man who could chat to Giulia, it seemed, for hours at a time. Who seemed to be able to ignore her very existence when it suited him.

'What do you care?' she said, low and angry.

He seemed startled. 'What do you mean by that?' She had turned away. 'Kitty? What's wrong?'

She didn't answer, went into her room, threw the door shut behind her – but he was quick enough to catch it, followed her in and closed it quietly.

'Now, what is all this?' he asked, in the firm, reasonable tones of a man dealing with a fractious child.

'You should know!' she cried. 'You *would* know if you paid me the least attention. But I don't exist for you when *she's* around!'

'What are you talking about?' He sounded genuinely baffled, and it enraged her.

'You went off with Giulia this morning – just the two of you alone – and you expect me to put up with it. You talk to her as if there's no-one else in the world but the two of you, and I'm supposed to smile and bear it. I know she's beautiful – I could hardly help knowing when everyone talks about it, *everyone* – and I know she's much cleverer than me. But you married *me*! I'm your *wife*, whether you like it or not!'

He took a step closer. 'Keep your voice down, for Heaven's sake,' he urged. 'You don't want them to hear.'

She went on as though he hadn't spoken. 'You married *me*, and I know it was my money you wanted, I *know* that, I'm not a fool, but it doesn't mean you're entitled to pretend I don't exist! I deserve better, I deserve to be treated with respect!'

'I *do* respect—' he began.

'You don't even look at me. You don't address a word to me. Anyone who didn't know, seeing us at luncheon, would have thought I was one of the servants. You can't treat me like that, Giles! I won't have it! I expect – I expect—'

She was trembling with passion, and her rage had carried her, but now belatedly she had heard herself, and self-consciousness returned, weighting her tongue with dread.

How had she dared speak to him like that? It was against the habits of a lifetime. She was as shocked with herself as she had been angry with him. And as the rage deflated, she was left with the terrible fear that she had broken something. *What have I done? He'll never love me now. I've spoiled everything.* Tears, already close to the surface, welled up and spilled down her face in a terrible flood.

'Kitty, don't,' he pleaded. 'Don't cry. Tell me what you want. I don't understand.'

He didn't *understand?* Had he not listened to a word? It was the last straw. She was just an hysterical woman to him, a thing with unpredictable moods, like a wild animal there was no reasoning with. Soothe her, like a mad thing – but don't take her seriously!

'I'm your *wife*,' she sobbed again.

'Kitty—' He took a step forward, hand out, like someone approaching a snarling dog.

I'm not a dog! she cried in her mind. 'Leave me alone!' she sobbed aloud. 'Go away and leave me alone!'

And – God help her – he did.

Giles lay on his bed, bemused. What had happened to the shy little girl he had married? Where had this rage, this passion sprung from? He had been surprised – agreeably surprised – by the physical passion they had shared; but for him, it occupied a separate compartment in his head. He'd had very little to do with women in his life. He always treated them as he treated anyone else, and since there had never been an intimate relationship, that strategy had worked out all right. It had not really occurred him, not consciously, that having done what they did in bed together, at night, in the dark, there ought to be any change in how they behaved towards each other in daylight.

She was jealous of Giulia – he thought he had gathered that from her incoherent raving. He was genuinely surprised.

He had never had romantic feelings towards Giulia. She was like a sister to him – or, perhaps he should more accurately say, like a brother. He had known her for many years, had almost grown up with her, given that his important growing up had happened after he left home. He liked her mind, liked talking to her, but the idea of flirting with her, even if he had known how to flirt (Richard would have laughed at the idea) made him feel a bit nauseous. How could Kitty think it? It was a sign of her deranged mind. Him and Giulia? It was practically incest.

And yet – as he lay staring at the ceiling, where a thin line of light from the side of the blind tracked slowly from one side of the room to the other – and yet, deep down in his mind there was a seed of guilt, which he was unwilling to acknowledge. Women had not featured in his life as differentiated creatures – but there was one, wasn't there? He had deliberately put aside, deeply buried his feelings for Nina; but he'd had them, even while he had been courting Kitty. He took them out now and looked at them. He had loved talking to Nina, and it had not been at all like talking to Giulia. With Giulia it was purely intellectual, just the same as when he spoke to Lucia or Flavio. But with Nina, every encounter had been an exquisite pleasure, every word had seemed to have a deeper meaning. He had felt connected to her in a way he had never known before, as though a cord were attaching her to him, as essential and life-giving as an umbilicus. She had *mattered*, in a way that Giulia or any other woman did not.

He had married Kitty, but he had already given to another woman what the matrimonial state demanded should be for her and her alone. In that way, he had betrayed her, and a small part of him betrayed her still. He had been unfaithful to her, and she knew it – she just had mistaken the object.

He must make it up to her, he thought. And remembering how she had raged against him – like a tiny kitten suddenly turned to a tiger – he felt a stirring of desire. Did that mean he loved her, really? Could he feel that for one woman while loving another? Had he *really* been unkind to her? Had he got everything wrong? Was it really his fault? Thinking these woolly, confused but on the whole willing thoughts, he fell into an exhausted sleep.

The storm did pass by on the south. The clouds had come up in a purple-black bank, like a fist threatening the island, but had moved on, leaving a sky of pale, tender blue behind, and a fresher air, a light wind blowing away the thick, damp heat. The birds that had fallen silent struck up the afternoon chorus with restored vigour. The household awoke, rubbed its eyes, and wandered downstairs to regroup and think about evening pleasures.

Giles looked around. 'Where's Kitty?' he asked.

Lucia consulted the other faces. 'I haven't seen her. Isn't she in her room?'

'I've been here for half an hour,' said Giulia, 'and she hasn't come down.'

'Perhaps she's gone for a walk,' said Flavio.

'Yes, it's so pleasant now the heat has passed. I expect she'll be back in a little while,' said Lucia.

They waited, chatting in a desultory fashion, but Kitty did not appear. Giulia slipped away to ask the servants if they had seen her. It was James who came out from the house to hem softly at Giles's shoulder. 'I understand you were wondering where her ladyship is,' he said. 'I was taking a walk about an hour ago, my lord, once it'd got cooler, and I saw her going down the steps to the beach. I think she was going to bathe. She had a towel over her arm.'

'Thank you,' Giles said. Everyone was looking relieved. But an hour was a long time to stay in the water, when you were on your own. 'I think I'll go down and see how she is,' he said. 'She was a bit upset earlier – the heat, you know.'

'She bathed this morning,' Lucia said, 'but she does love it so, I'm not surprised she's gone again.'

'All the same,' Giles said, and went.

James watched him, and when everyone else had turned back to their conversation, he slipped away and followed, keeping a discreet distance. There'd been something about his master's expression – and Marie had said her ladyship had seemed upset earlier. If she was down there, there might be a row, and if there was a row, he wanted to hear it. You never knew how you might turn something like that to account. Knowledge was power, as the philosopher said.

The little cove was empty, though a towel, a robe and a pair of slippers lay neatly on the rocks.

Giles was scanning the water and calling when James emerged from the trees behind him, and registered the situation at once. The water was so clear, you could see there was no-one in it.

Giles turned, and stared at him as though he didn't recognise him. 'She never goes out far,' he said. 'She likes to lie in the water, but she doesn't swim much. Never beyond the rocks.' The rocks made a V-shaped inlet, with the cliffs rising up on either side. There was a small beach of pebbles, then the water dropped after a few feet into a deep pool. Perfect for bathing. Beyond the point, the sea was darker, and choppy from the breeze that had followed the storm clouds.

'Maybe she went up again,' James said.

'Without dressing?'

'She might have wanted to dry off in the sun,' said James. 'I'll go back up, look to either side of the path.'

'I'll come too.'

They climbed, checking every place a person might leave the path, every place where the tree cover broke and provided a sunning spot. Giles called, with increasing anguish. At the top of the path he turned and started down again, like a trapped animal running between two points. *What have I done? What have I done?* His thoughts tormented him.

James fathomed them. 'My lord, she won't have— I mean, I'm sure it's not what you think. She's wandered off somewhere. We'll find her, safe and sound, you'll see.'

Giles turned to him, seeing him now. 'We quarrelled,' he said starkly.

James looked away. He did not want to witness such feelings in his master's eyes. Knowing things like that made a relationship awkward later. But he felt a deep dread. There weren't many places a semi-naked lady might be found. She had gone down to the sea, it seemed, and not come back up.

They searched again, down the path, to either side. Giles called, and this time James called as well. He remembered seeing, on his walk, a sort of open headland that he thought might be reached from the path. A nice place to catch the sun or look at the view. There had been no-one on it when he was walking back. But she might not have reached it by that time.

Or, said his deep mind, she might have gone there and – not be there any more. He had stood at the top of a cliff once, looking down, and had felt a strange desire to jump off. And he hadn't even been unhappy at the time.

He left his lordship to carry on down and, in a moment, heard him calling from the beach, his voice echoing off the rocks. He found a side path he thought went in the right direction, but it petered out and he had to force his way through. After some time he finally came out on the headland, but he could tell no-one else had been that way, at least not today. He paused, looking around, hearing his lordship's distant shouts, and then a faint reply. A woman's voice.

He bellowed, 'Hey!'

Faintly, it came back. 'Help me!'

He thought it was from below. He stretched himself prone on the short turf, wriggled up to the cliff edge – it looked crumbly to him, and dangerous – and carefully inched forward until he could look down. 'Is somebody there?' he shouted.

'Help! Help me!' the cry came back.

Definitely down there. The cliff made an overhang: he could not see straight down. He eased forward a bit more. 'Is that you, my lady?'

'Yes, yes. Who's that?'

'It's me, James.'

'James. I'm so cold. I swam round, but I can't get back.'

'Are you all right?'

'I'm on a rock, but the waves . . . I'm afraid I'll slip off. Oh, help me!'

'I will,' he called, oddly moved. 'I'll get to you. Stay where you are! Don't try and swim. I'll come and find you.'

He wriggled backwards so hastily that he dislodged a lump of something and heard it tumble down. Hope to God it didn't hit her, he thought, as he scrambled to his feet and hurried back the way he had come, struggling through the vegetation, getting scratched and snagged in his haste. When he reached the path, he found his lordship coming back up yet again.

'She's there! I heard her!' James cried. 'Down the bottom of the cliff. She swam round. She's sitting on a rock, but she can't get back.'

'Oh, God!' said Giles, and his face paled with shock and relief. 'How can I get to her? We'll need a boat.'

'A boat'd take a long time,' James said. 'She must be getting cold. What if she slipped off? What if the wind gets up?'

'You're right,' Giles said. For once, common sense seemed to have abandoned him. He didn't know what to do.

'Can you swim, sir?'

'Yes, yes!'

'If *she* got round there, *you* must be able to. I'd—' James swallowed '—I'd go myself, but I can't swim worth a farthing. I could—'

Giles was already tearing off his clothes, his paralysis gone. 'Stay there. I might need your help,' he said, and plunged in.

James took off his clothes too, and got into the water, going as far as the end of the little cove, holding onto the rocks and treading water. He didn't dare go out beyond a hand-hold. It seemed a long time – an ice age – before he heard splashing sounds coming closer, and the two figures came round the bulk of the headland, both swimming. The countess looked all in, and was barely making progress, her weary head washed over by a wave every now and then. The earl was supporting her with one hand and swimming with the other, and seemed to be gasping for breath. James pushed himself off the rock and swam a stroke or two, reaching her as she sank under the water. When he grabbed her, she was limp, and her weight pulled him down. He fought off panic, got his head up out of the water, spluttering, trying to keep a grip on her slippery wetness.

'On her back,' Giles gasped. 'Turn her on her back.'

Between them, the two men turned her over, getting her face clear of the water, and then towed her together into the bay until they could find their feet. Giles was too exhausted for the moment to do anything more, so it was James who slid his arms under her shoulders and knees, lifted her up, and staggered with her to the dry beach, where he laid her down and then collapsed, panting.

Giles dragged himself out of the water, and hung over her. 'Kitty,' he said. 'Oh, Kitty.'

James had never heard such tenderness in a man's voice, and he turned his head away, feeling he was intruding.

* * *

Kitty opened her eyes and looked up into his beloved face. *I'm still alive*, she thought first. The swim back had been so exhausting, she had thought she wouldn't make it.

'Kitty,' he said. 'Oh, Kitty.'

'I'm sorry,' she said.

She had gone down to the beach in a state of anger, grief and frustration and, casting herself into the sea, had thought she did not care any more whether she lived or died. She had swum out beyond the headland, and the current had taken hold of her, pushing her away round the outcrop. When she realised she could not get back, fear had seized her, and she had known that she did *not* want to die, not yet. She had struggled and fought until the current had pushed her against the rocks, where she managed to get a hand-hold, and at last was able to pull herself out of the water. But she was stuck at the bottom of a cliff with no way to climb up, and to get back into the water was unthinkable.

At first it had not been too bad: she had assumed she would be missed. But then the sun went round and the shadow of the cliff was on her, and she grew cold, and the sea looked darker and more threatening, and no-one came. She longed and longed for Giles, and was more sure than ever that she had lost him. When she'd heard the voice calling she had been close to despair. And then the voice went away! She had waited so long she had thought herself forgotten – or perhaps she had only imagined someone had been there. But he had come for her, Giles had come for her, and now he was looking at her with an expression she had imagined (in the darkness when they made love) but had never seen.

'I'm sorry,' she said.

'No, I'm sorry,' he said. 'Oh, Kitty, you didn't – you didn't mean to . . . ?'

She couldn't answer the implied question – not truthfully. She sighed, a broken, pitiful sound.

'I don't care for Giulia, not in that way,' he said. 'I never did. Please believe me. She's no more than a sister to me.'

'It doesn't matter,' she said wearily.

'It does,' he insisted. 'You were right. You're my wife, and I've neglected you. You'll see a difference from now on, I promise you.'

She was slipping into unconsciousness. 'I'm cold,' she said. He wrapped her in all the clothes he could lay hands to and, with James's help, carried her up the cliff. She slept on and off in his arms. He had not said he loved her. But he had looked at her in that way, and had promised – had promised . . .

Giles wondered. He supposed he would always wonder. Had she simply made a mistake, or had unhappiness driven her near to suicide? Yet, oddly, it was not that which had moved him so much. It was the ferocity with which earlier she had faced him and told him she was his *wife* and deserved better. Where had that courage come from? Because he was sure it had taken courage to speak, when she had always been so meek and shy. He admired her for that; he felt a warmth towards her, and a curiosity, and wanted her to be well so that he could visit her bedroom again and engage with that passion in a greater knowledge and understanding than before.

There was a different woman inside the meek, child-like Kitty, a woman of spirit and fire. He had got a better bargain when he married her than he had compounded for.

CHAPTER NINETEEN

Aunt Schofield was invited to a dinner party by Lady Manningtree. It was not simply a card but a letter, citing their acquaintance at school, and speaking warmly of Nina; otherwise she might have made an excuse, *ton* parties not being to her taste. But to be invited so specifically and cordially . . . And when she mentioned it, she saw that Nina wanted to go, so she accepted for both.

Lady Manningtree engaged her at once in conversation, talking about school and their common acquaintances, and Richard made a bee-line for Nina.

'I haven't seen you in an age,' he said. 'Have you had a letter from the honeymooners?'

'Just one, from Kitty,' said Nina.

It had not said very much – had been little more than a list of sights she had seen – but it had ended with an emphatic sentence about longing to see her again. 'So much more to tell you than I can write down. You must come and stay with us at the Castle when we return.'

Nina did, of course, have a curiosity to see the Castle, and she missed the friend she had been so close to for three years; but she really did not want that invitation to arrive. To go in under the roof of a Kitty married to Giles Stainton, to see them together, to be forced to be in his company – no, that was not a good idea. Better for her, certainly, that the friendship should die, and that she should never see them again. She was not of their rank in life, anyway. Perhaps when – if – the invitation came she would be working somewhere as a teacher and unable to take the time off.

To Richard, she said, 'She sounded as though they were happy.'

'Really?' he said. 'Well, I'm glad, if surprised. I had a letter from Giles that was nothing but holocausts and mosaics and pillars and pediments. You'd think he had married the ruins of Pompeii, not a flesh-and-blood woman.'

'Was it very different from any other letter he's ever written to you?' Nina asked shrewdly.

'I'm not sure that he *has* ever written to me before,' Richard said, 'but I see your point. And, no, he is not the sort of man to gush about his feelings. Bits of broken columns alone have the power to move him. A dull stick, my brother. Well,' he dusted off his hands, 'that deals with the subject of our mutual friends. Now we can talk about something much more gripping – ourselves.'

'You really think that will be interesting?'

'Of course,' he said, feigning surprise. 'I'll go first. What have I been doing? I've been in Biarritz with my aunt and grandmother. Dull work, when the rest of the family was in Scotland for the grouse shooting. But I was still too knocked up to go.' He gestured to his injured arm. 'My uncle has a place on the Spey. Glorious scenery, if you like that sort of thing.'

'Don't you?'

'Well, I'm not completely insensitive to grand sweeping panoramas of purple hills and brooding forests – rather Biblical, I've always thought. And of an early morning, the reflections in the still waters of a loch would have me reaching for the water-colours, if I had ever learned to paint.'

'Goodness! How poetical.'

He narrowed his eyes. 'You mock me, Miss Sanderton?'

'I had put you down as a Town bird. I must humbly beg your pardon for misjudging you.'

'You *are* mocking me! Jolly good. Makes our relationship much easier. Of course, I'm a Town bird when I'm in Town, which is often, but I was brought up in the country, and it does have the power to move me, when it takes me unawares.'

'When you have small helpless animals to kill?'

'I am a hunter, Miss Sanderton, like my forefathers back to the dawn of time. I eat what I kill – little birds and great big fish. And don't give me that look! You eat birds and fish too, but leave the killing of them to someone else. How do you think that salmon gets onto the fishmonger's slab?'

'Salmon does not often come my way,' Nina said demurely. 'A little scrap of cod, perhaps, now and then.'

'Now you're being naughty. You look perfectly well fed to me. Now, your turn – what have *you* been up to?'

'Apart from having my likeness taken?'

'Good heavens, yes. I've seen your lovely features in the *Harlequinade*. Periodicals take a while to reach us in France, but I did see you impersonating Britannia with a very meek lion at your feet. Was it stuffed? Or did Mawes Morris import a real live animal to do you justice?'

She laughed. 'Neither. The lion was copied at the Natural History Museum.'

'I'm relieved to hear it. What else?'

'Not much. Reading and studying, mostly. And I've been looking for a teaching post.'

'With any success?'

'I did see one advertisement, but it was for a small school in rural Berkshire. My aunt said I would be teaching farm children their primers, and that it would be a waste of my education. And another was for a school in Scotland, but again it was only for little ones. I was hoping to teach older girls.'

361

'I do remember you said you were going to be a teacher,' said Richard. 'I hoped you weren't serious.'

'I was. I must earn my living. What about you?'

'I have no desire to be a teacher.'

'You know perfectly well what I mean. Don't you have to earn yours?'

'I suppose when my brother comes home the question will be raised. I'm enjoying the last of my freedom at this moment. It's like a beautiful dream – please don't wake me up.'

'Reality must be faced,' Nina said. 'What *can* you do? What are your skills?'

'All I've done so far is soldiering. Younger sons traditionally go into one of the professions, but the law requires years of training and I'm too old for that. And the Church requires something else that I'm not prepared to give.'

'No, I can't see you as a churchman. What's left?'

'I don't know. Dear me, how serious this conversation has got. Let's talk about something else.'

Nina didn't oblige. 'Perhaps you could marry an heiress, like your brother.'

'That bordered on the sharp, Miss Sanderton! The trouble is, he has a title to exchange, and I haven't. No, if anyone marries me, it will have to be for love. And I don't think I'm very lovable.'

'If you're fishing for compliments . . .'

He grinned. 'How refreshingly frank you are! I wish I could marry *you*. If only either of us had a fortune . . . I could marry you and save you from becoming a teacher.'

'If I had a fortune, I shouldn't need to marry you,' she pointed out.

He pouted. 'Now you've hurt my feelings. Don't you want to marry me?'

'You'd be very high on my list, I assure you . . .'

'. . . if you had a list,' he finished for her.

* * *

Giles had given James a present of money to thank him for his part in rescuing Kitty, and enjoined him not to talk about the incident. 'Of course not, sir,' said James, with his most loyal look.

Of course, everyone downstairs at the villa was talking about nothing else, in a mixture of English and Italian, and he enjoyed his moment in the spotlight as sole eye-witness and hero of the hour. Since no-one else had been there, he was able to adjust his part in the rescue until his lordship was little more than an onlooker. The Lombardi staff were impressed by James's courage and endurance in undertaking a long and dangerous swim to rescue the little contessa, and even more by his modesty in insisting it was nothing, really. That was so English! They couldn't hear the story often enough.

Marie gave him a cynical look as they were cleaning shoes together one day. 'You'll get caught out one day, telling all those lies.'

'What lies?' he said defensively.

'You told me you couldn't swim.'

'I can swim a bit. And when danger threatens like that – well, you find inner resources.'

'Inner resources? Where did you learn that piece of flannel?'

'Has her ladyship said anything to you?' he asked uneasily.

'Course not. Tight as an oyster that one, when it comes to anything to do with his lordship. I just know you, that's all. You're not the hero type.'

'Well, his lordship thought so. You saw the money he gave me.'

'For helping. Never mind, you can tell whatever story you like – I don't care. I'll just be glad to get away from this place. There was one of those lizards on the ceiling again this morning.' She shuddered.

'They don't hurt you. That gardener, Jacopo, says they're a good thing – they eat the scorpions.'

'I don't want scorpions in my room either, thank you very much.'

'You've changed your mind about getting a place out here, then?'

'I'm sick of being in service. From what I gather, my lord and lady mean to spend most of their time down in the country. That doesn't suit me at all.'

'Don't you like the country?' She shrugged. 'You could get another place.'

'That Miss Latham hinted she was looking for a French maid, but I'd still be a lady's maid, and she's not even a ladyship, so I'd be worse off. No, I want a real change.'

'Look here,' he said, 'why don't we make plans together? I'm sick of being in service, too. With that money his lordship give me, I've got enough now. I dare say you've got savings, too.'

'What if I have?' she said cagily.

'We should throw in our lot together, like we said at the beginning. Start up a little business.'

She gave him a distinctly unflattering look. 'Yes, and I know what other lot you'd expect me to throw in! No thank you.'

He was taken aback. 'Don't you fancy me, then?'

'Not half as much as you fancy yourself.'

'I bet you've never even done it,' he said, to hurt her.

But she just laughed. 'No, and I never will. I'm not that stupid! Men get all the fun, and all women get is toil and babies. I've got a plan, and it doesn't include you.'

'What plan? I bet you haven't.'

'I'm going to skip on the way back through Paris. Join one of those couture houses, learn a few tricks, then start up on my own. I know what ladies like – and they'll like it even more that I speak English. I can make a fortune in a few years.'

'I could help,' he said feebly. 'I could—'

364

'Be the chucker-out?'

Now he was offended. 'I'll tell,' he said. 'I'll tell them you're planning to run out.'

'If you do, you'll find a scorpion in your bed,' she said.

It was a good thing, James thought, as he returned moodily to rubbing a boot toe, that he had alternatives. It didn't look as though he was getting anywhere with Marie. But there was the plump Italian kitchen maid, Ignazia, he had been working on, and who had gone so far as to let him kiss her out behind the kitchen among the herb-pots – though he had to be careful as she was Catholic and he suspected Jacopo was her father.

In all, he was rather looking forward to getting home, now. He had irons in the fire there, too. He wondered if Dory was missing him.

At the Castle, with the family away, it was the chance to get the chimneys swept, a job that caused so much disruption it could not be fitted in around normal service. But it had to be done once a year. All along the Ash valley the story was still told of how a chimney fire had set Priestwood Hall alight twenty years before, and the entire Tudor house had burned to the ground, with the loss of two housemaids and old Lady Dunsmore, who had been overcome in their beds before the alarm could be raised. Since servants slept under the roof, with the longest way to go to safety, it was a cautionary tale useful in suppressing grumbles about the extra work.

Mrs Webster much preferred this sort of extraordinary effort to the day-to-day grind of routine. She threw herself into it, like a general planning a campaign. Mr Moss, Mr Crooks and Miss Taylor had gone to Scotland with the family, but everyone else had to help – even the grooms were brought in, after sternly supervised hand-washing and boot-wiping, to shift furniture and carry things. As the horses had been turned out for their holiday, they had no excuse.

In each room, the carpets had to be rolled up, the furniture moved to the sides and covered with Holland, every ornament taken down and separately wrapped. Small pictures and looking-glasses were removed for cleaning while those too large to move had also to be wrapped. Then the cloths were laid all over the floor, and the sweeps could be allowed in. When the job was done, the soot had to be carried away and everything had to be dusted and restored to its place.

The sweeps, of course, were black from head to toe, but everyone in the house became grimy, despite wearing housemaids' coarse aprons and covering their hair with mob caps. Mrs Webster was a great one for cleanliness, and mass bathing was arranged every evening before supper. The men washed in the yard in cold water, with a great deal of splashing and horseplay and ripe language; the maids had the privilege of warm water, and went in by twos to a tub set up in one of the pantries, and helped wash each other's hair and scrub each other's backs.

In normal times, dinner was taken at noon, but at chimney-sweeping time, the midday meal became a nuncheon of bread and cheese, and the proper meal took place at supper time, when the work was over for the day. Mrs Oxlea, like Mrs Webster, was at her best, stimulated by the challenge, shaken out of her usual melancholy. With the butler absent, protocol was abandoned and everyone ate together, indoor staff and outdoor, senior and junior. There were cauldrons of soup, vast joints, mountains of baked potatoes, lakes of rice pudding, treacle tarts and apple pies the size of tea-tables, and plenty of laughter and badinage.

The kitchen chimney was always the last to be done, as the fires had to be put out and the ranges would be out of use for two days. At the end of kitchen-chimney day, the outdoor men built a bonfire, cooked meat over the flames and roasted potatoes in the embers; trestles were taken out and everyone ate out of doors. The feast was washed down with a ration of beer. It was a happy evening, and a reward for all the extra work – as nice, they always said, as the old harvest festivals.

Boredom was the servant's greatest enemy, and though the work was hard, everyone enjoyed the change. Dory threw herself into it with energy, and if James had known how little she missed him, he would have been taken aback. The only time she actually thought of him at all was when she went into a prepared room to check that it was ready for the sweep and discovered the housemaid Mabel on a Holland-covered sofa with one of the grooms. His bare bottom was bouncing up and down so vigorously that Tiger, who had followed her in, pricked his ears and started ambling across to see what it was, bobbing away all white and gleaming. Probably thought it was some kind of animal, Dory thought, catching his collar just in time.

When his lordship was away, their young ladyships looked after the dogs, but since they had gone to Scotland the dogs had become a problem that no-one particularly wanted to solve. They haunted the place looking miserable, until Mrs Webster tripped over them one day and banished them to the stables. But they were even more miserable there, and Giddins had said one day that they were pining themselves to death, and did she want to tell his lordship when he came back that they'd let his dogs die.

They had all been at dinner at the time, around the long table in the servants' dining-room, girls one side and men the other, William at the foot and Mrs Webster at the head, so they had all heard. Dory had privately thought his lordship would not be much troubled, since the dogs had adopted him rather than vice versa, and he had gone away to London without a glance behind.

But when Mrs Webster had thrown open the question to the table, Dory had spoken up into the silence – she didn't really know why – and said she would have them with her

367

in the sewing-room, and take them out for walks morning and evening.

The housekeeper was just glad to have someone else bother about the wretched animals. Dory found no difficulty with them. They were not barkers, and once they'd had their morning run, they were content to doze on the floor beside her while she worked, or to pad along at her heels as she went from place to place about her business.

If she thought about anyone during the frenzy and toil of chimney-sweeping, it was certainly not James. Just before the family went to Scotland, she had gone along to Mr Sebastian's room with a basket of napkins to darn.

'Come in, come in!' he had cried when he saw her. 'I see you've brought some work. Good. Sit over there. I thought we'd have some Brahms today.'

He began to play, and she sewed automatically, fingers busy on their own, mind flowing with the music, like a loosed punt carried down a stream. The sunshine slanted in through the window, picking out the gently moving clouds of cigar smoke. Mr Sebastian held it in the corner of his mouth so that the smoke wouldn't get into his eyes, but his eyes were closed more often than not. Dory looked up at him sometimes, and wondered about him. His hair was a wild grey mop, like frosty vegetation sprouting from a rock; his features were carved in the granite; but he was still good to look at. She liked looking at him when he was not aware of it, for there was something in his face that went with his musical ability – a fine-ness and a good-ness beyond the mere casual kindness of one person for another. If she had not been kept so busy, she would have missed those occasions much more.

On Kitchen Chimney Day, after dinner outside at the trestle tables, one of the stable boys brought out a mouth-organ and old Frewing, the hall porter, fetched his precious fiddle. Between them they made enough noise for dancing country jigs. The dogs, who had been lying quietly under the table, came wriggling out in astonishment, and romped about among the dancers, thinking it was a game. The bonfire, falling in, threw golden fountains of sparks into the dark air, maids whirled with lads, clapping to the music and laughing, and Dory, setting to partner with the coachman Joe, had Brahms's Hungarian dances in her head, as Mr Sebastian had played them to her, instead of the shrill wailing of fiddle and mouth-organ.

The invitation was for Miss Sands to play for the dowager Lady Stainton and guests at her house in Bruton Street. The choice of music was left up to her, and a fee was mentioned that shocked Mrs Sands.

'You are behind this,' she said to Richard, showing him the letter. 'I know it is your kindness at work.'

'No,' he said. 'I promise I know nothing about it. Except that I've been invited, too. I had a card from Grandmère to a musical evening, with "you will come" written across the bottom in her own hand, and underlined twice. When Grandmère does that, you have to obey. I didn't know why she was so keen on my company, especially when I haven't a musical bone in my body.'

'That's not true, and you know it. You may have thought you didn't care for music, but you've discovered otherwise, haven't you?'

He grinned. 'Some music, and only in certain company. But you *are* making me a better person, there's no denying.'

Mrs Sands was off on another track. 'She'll have to have an evening dress to play in. That will deplete the fee. But it can't be helped. If there are influential people there, it may lead to other engagements. Do you know who else is invited?'

'Not a clue. For all I know, it could be just me,' he joked.

She was too tense to appreciate it. 'There wouldn't be a

card if it were just you,' she said. 'Chloë's so nervous. I wish I could be there with her, just to give her courage.'

'I don't see why you shouldn't be. Doesn't a pianist usually have a turner?'

'At a recital in a concert hall, yes, usually a student or someone of that nature. Although Alicia Ferrari's husband turns for her.'

'Well, then, Chloë Sands's mother should turn for her.'

'Do you think so? Would your grandmother think it a liberty, perhaps?'

'Grandmère never notices anything that doesn't discommode her, so as long as you are in the background, she will probably have no idea you are there. By the way,' he said, to distract her, 'if Miss Sands does become a famous international pianist, she'll have to change her name. Alicia Ferrari sounds so much more impressive than Chloë Sands. I think, actually, an Italian name is almost compulsory. How about Chiara Sabbia?'

Now she laughed. 'You really are an absurd boy!'

He liked the laughter, but didn't care for the 'boy' part.

He called on his grandmother. 'You didn't tell me Miss Sands was to play at your musical evening.'

She raised an eyebrow. 'When have I ever discussed the details of my entertainments with you? Do you wish to approve the menu of refreshments, too?'

'Now, *bellissima*, don't be facetious,' he said. 'You know I have a particular interest in Miss Sands.'

'Yes,' she said, 'I have noticed it.' She was more convinced than ever that he was in love with the girl. Why else had he rushed here as soon as he had had the invitation? 'And why are you speaking Italian to me?'

'Because I've just been talking about Alicia Ferrari, so the language was in my head.'

'Hmm. Not a bad pianist, but I don't care for her style. Sir Thomas had a little *histoire* with her, many years ago.'

'So it seems *he* liked her style, at any rate.'

'Don't be vulgar. Well, what else have you to say about my soirée? You will come. I will not accept any excuse.'

'Oh, I will come. I don't dare defy you when you resort to pen and ink. I suppose,' he said, trying to sound casual, 'you won't object if she brings someone to turn for her.'

Grandmère's eyes narrowed. 'I know that tone. What *tracasserie* are you plotting now? If you mean yourself – you are already invited. If you wish to turn for her, say so.'

'I don't read music well enough to turn. I think she would like her mother to do it.'

He braced himself for some violent objection, but his grandmother only looked thoughtful, and said, 'I see no reason to object. In fact, it would suit my purposes quite well.'

'What purposes?' he asked nervously. 'What are you plotting, Grandmère?'

'Not your business,' she snapped. 'She may come. That is all.'

'Will you come now, please, miss – and madam?' said the butler.

Mrs Sands and Chloë had been waiting in a small, book-lined room on the ground floor. They had heard the sound of music faintly from upstairs – someone playing the flute, accompanied by the piano. Then silence had fallen. And now this butler, with the manner so grand it would have served one of the more magnificent French kings, came to summon them. Chloë threw her mother a terrified look as they fell in behind him.

At the foot of the stairs they had to stop to allow someone to come down – a slender girl, even younger-looking than Chloë, carrying a flute case, and preceded by a dark young man in evening dress. The girl made a face at Chloë as she passed – a complex mixture of despair, relief and sympathy.

They mounted the stairs, towards a murmur of voices like the distant sea. The butler threw open the doors, and they stepped into the drawing-room. The two halves had been thrown together by the folding back of the dividing doors; the piano was pushed to the centre of one half, while in the other half little gilded rout-chairs had been arranged in rows, and an array of glittering people was sitting there expectantly.

Chloë had not known what to expect – something more casual, certainly: people grouped on sofas and in armchairs, chatting and drinking coffee or champagne while she played. This was arranged like a proper recital, and she faltered. There was no applause at her entrance, but the murmur of conversation died away, serious eyes examined her, and in some cases a lorgnon was raised for a better scrutiny. They all looked very rich and important and there were a great many diamonds in the room. Of the only two familiar faces one was Richard's – he was sitting in the centre of the front row next to an elderly lady, presumably his grandmother. Chloë had, of course, never met her, though she had played in her house for months. Richard was looking oddly nervous, which didn't reassure Chloë: he raised an eyebrow at her and gave a quirk of the mouth that could have meant anything from *All is well* to *Run like the devil*.

The other familiar face was even more unnerving, because – sitting on the other side of the old lady, handsome head thrown back in anticipation, a faint smile on his face, his evening dress gleaming and immaculate – it belonged to Sir Thomas Burton, pianist, conductor and impresario.

It was fortunate that at that point her mother administered a sharp pinch to the flesh of her waist – the nearest part to her – making her jerk into action, or she might have remained stranded halfway across the carpet. But as soon as she sat at the piano she felt better. For one thing, she could not now see the audience unless she made an effort to; and for another, the piano was familiar, an old friend. She knew its voice, she knew what it could do, and she had played all this music before.

Her mother had placed the music on the top and was about to lay the first piece on the rack, but Chloë put up a hand and stopped her, and exchanged the first piece for the second. They had discussed the order at home, and had assumed that people would be chatting while she played, certainly at first, so they had picked a quiet piece to begin with. But now, with Sir Thomas in the front row, she wanted to make an impression, have them all jump and pay attention. She pulled out the second piece, smiled and nodded at her mother, and as soon as it was opened in front of her, leaped into Dvořák's 'Capriccio'.

There was applause at the end. Chloë had almost forgotten about the audience by then, and it surprised her a little. Her mother put a hand under her elbow, urging her to rise, and she did, and bowed her head, smiling vaguely at the glittering people. Richard jumped up and came over to her as the applause died away and people began moving.

'You were wonderful,' he murmured. 'Everyone was listening, even Lord Strathmore, who usually falls asleep in these things. Grandmère was really impressed. She frowned all the way through, which is a good sign. When she smiles, it means she's hiding rage or disappointment.'

'Richard, stop, you're making her nervous,' said Mrs Sands. She was gathering the music together. 'We'd better go, so as not to be in the way.'

'No, Grandmère sent me over to ask you to stay where you are until everyone's gone. She wants to talk to you.' He gave them a reassuring smile, and went back to help his grandmother say goodbye to the guests. Chloë and her mother sat down together on the piano stool so as to be inconspicuous. Chloë began to shiver a little, and Mrs Sands felt a mother's crossness at keeping them waiting, when she really wanted to get her girl home and make her some cocoa. She supposed the old lady just wanted to thank her in person – at best, she might have another recital to offer.

Suddenly they were there, Richard, the very elegant old lady and, at her shoulder, the terrifying Sir Thomas Burton. Everyone else had gone, except for two servants quietly removing the chairs.

The old lady did not waste time. 'I am Lady Stainton, Miss Sands. You are Mrs Sands? How do you do? Thank you for playing for us. It was most enjoyable. In fact, of course, I have been listening to you playing for a long time, but I wanted to hear you properly, in the same room, and to see how you performed in front of an audience. I was not disappointed.'

'Thank you—' Chloë began, but a thin, ring-heavy hand was raised to stop her speaking.

'I have a proposition for you. Sir Thomas has a proposition, in fact. You know Sir Thomas Burton.'

'We know *of* him, of course,' Molly Sands said. 'I recognised you from your picture in the papers, sir.'

Sir Thomas smiled graciously at her and, after a tiny moment of thought, extended his hand. 'Delighted to make your acquaintance,' he said, then turned to Chloë with a look her mother afterwards classified as almost hungry. 'Miss Sands. I have been impressed by what I heard here tonight. Lady Stainton,' he turned his head to acknowledge her, 'has spoken to me about you, but of course one has to hear for oneself to be sure. You have a remarkable talent.'

'Thank you, sir,' Chloë said, in a very small voice. She was trembling like a vibrating leaf, though whether still with cold or something else now, her mother couldn't be sure.

'I like to take an interest in promising young musicians,'

he continued. 'Bring them on, help them to realise their potential. I would like to sponsor you for a place at the Royal Academy. I will cover all expenses,' this was addressed to Mrs Sands, 'so there is no need to worry about anything. You will study composition and music theory with the other students, but I will oversee your piano studies myself, with the expectation – if you develop satisfactorily, of course, it is not a guarantee – with the *prospect*, let us say, of a career as a soloist. I have connections and influence all over the world, and a protégée of mine can expect to go far, very far indeed.'

When they had all gone, even Sir Thomas, and only Richard was left, and he was preparing to take his leave, Grandmère said, 'Help me to my room, child. Simone will be asleep in a chair, and if I ring, it will take her so long to get down here, you may as well give me your arm instead.'

She moved slowly, and he shortened his steps to hers. Her hand was light on his arm. It struck him that she was more tired than he would expect after an evening of music.

'It was so good of you to arrange all this for Chloë,' he said.

'It was not for her, foolish. Or for you. It was for music itself. I have no time for personalities. The music is all that matters.'

'Well,' he said. 'As you say.' They climbed the stairs so slowly he felt the silence was awkward, and sought for something else to say. 'Sir Thomas really was impressed with her.'

'He will have her, of course,' Grandmère said indifferently. 'I know that look. But she has talent enough to survive. Not like that silly flautist. I hope, *petit*, that *you* won't mind too much?'

Her words had shocked him, but he rallied – he would

375

not seem unsophisticated in front of her. She could not really have meant it. 'Why should I mind?' he said lightly.

She gave him a sidelong look. '*Insouciance?* Do not you love her?'

'Good God, no,' he said. 'I just think she's jolly good. I like listening to her.'

'*Jolly* good,' she repeated, musing. Not the praise of a lover, she thought. So what was his game? Could it really be nothing but altruism? 'I think perhaps you are growing up, *chéri*,' she said.

'Gosh, not me, Granny,' Richard said. 'I intend to remain for ever twenty-five.'

He was happy for Chloë – he didn't take Grandmère's warning about Sir Thomas too seriously – but what he was mostly thinking was that, with Chloë away at the Academy all day, he would have Mrs Sands to himself.

CHAPTER TWENTY

Mary Caldecott had come to tea with Aunt Schofield, and brought with her a thin-faced, intense young woman, Octavia Liston. She was much exercised by the new Education Bill being brought by Mr Balfour, who had taken over as prime minister from his uncle Lord Salisbury when he retired owing to ill health. She spoke so rapidly it was hard for Nina to understand whether she was for or against it.

Mrs Caldecott's more measured tones sounded almost languid by contrast. 'Of course, the ratepayers won't like it. Some of them hardly accept that children should go to school at all, let alone after the age of twelve. If these new local education authorities start putting money into secondary education, they'll riot in the streets.'

'I hardly think so,' said Aunt Schofield. 'Rational people will see the need for more technical schools—'

'And for general education, too,' Miss Liston broke in eagerly. 'The LEAs will be charged with seeing that teachers are properly qualified, which surely *must* mean education beyond the elementary level . . .'

Nina felt herself sagging, and straightened her back hastily. She ought to be interested in this sort of thing if she was to be a teacher, but her mind kept wandering.

Mrs Caldecott turned to her as Miss Liston had to stop to draw breath. 'How is your search for a teaching post going, Miss Sanderton?'

'Oh, is Miss Sanderton going to be a teacher?' said Miss Liston, with new interest.

'I haven't found anything yet,' Nina said. 'But Miss Thornton says her sort of school usually starts a new year in January, so there's plenty of time. She's still looking out for something for me. May I offer you some more tea?'

Mrs Caldecott saw she didn't want to talk about it, and turned the conversation to the Free Library. 'How are things progressing? Have you any news?'

'I have indeed,' Aunt Schofield said. 'I think I told you we had located a building in the right place. Now we've received a most generous offer not only to buy the freehold for us, but to pay for all the necessary alterations.'

'How wonderful! Who is this philanthropical person?' Mrs Caldecott asked.

'I don't suppose you know him. He's what they call nowadays an industrialist, though he's one of the King's new circle. Nina met him during her Season, and he turns out to be a friend of Mawes Morris, too.'

'Oh, the very *useful* Mawes Morris!' Mrs Caldecott laughed. 'I wonder if there's anyone he doesn't know.'

'Apparently, he was at dinner there the other evening,' Aunt Schofield went on, 'and Lepida Morris was talking about the Free Library. He asked a great many questions, and presumably was seized with the idea, because his letter arrived yesterday.'

'Excellent man,' she said. 'Alexandra, my dear, you must positively have this paragon to dinner, and be sure to invite Quin and me. I should like to interest him in one of my schemes.'

Aunt Schofield smiled indulgently. 'Invite a person to dine and then pick his pockets? That would be shabby. But a dinner is an excellent idea. I should welcome the chance to thank him in person.'

'Tell me more about the building,' said Mrs Caldecott.

'We're going there tomorrow morning,' said Aunt Schofield. 'You'd be welcome to join us.'

'Oh, tomorrow I can't. Never mind – another time.'

The building was on the Commercial Road, a former warehouse. The agent was waiting for them in the rain when Aunt Schofield, Nina and Lepida arrived in a cab from the station. It was a poor area of mean streets and over-crowded tenements, and the Commercial Road itself was busy with traffic and full of small factories and workshops belching out yellow-grey smoke. But the building was solid, of red brick with a slate roof, the height of a two-storey house, with a row of windows set at second-storey level, the wall at ground level being blank.

'I like it,' Nina said, as they climbed out of the cab. A hansom was a tight squeeze for three, but they were all quite thin. 'The red brick is cheerful.'

'It would be if it were washed down,' said Lepida. The prevailing soot in the air had coated everything. 'But won't the lack of windows make it dark?'

'Could we put in another row lower down?' Nina wondered.

The agent said, 'I wouldn't recommend it, ladies. High windows make it more difficult for anyone to break in.'

Inside, the place smelt dusty, but not unpleasant. It was completely empty, a brick oblong with a concrete floor. 'It was used for storage,' the agent said. 'Dry goods in tea-chests waiting to go to the docks.'

'I don't see any puddles on the floor,' said Nina, 'so I suppose the roof is sound.'

'There may be the odd slipped slate, 'said the agent, 'but that's easily remedied. It's a good building. The only reason it's still empty is that, as a commercial property, it's rather small.'

A shadow darkened the door behind them, and a voice said, 'Do I intrude? May I come in?'

They all turned, and a male figure coming in out of the rain and doffing its hat resolved itself into Mr Cowling.

'Oh, good morning!' Nina said. 'How did you know we were here?'

'Mawes told me, when I happened to drop by, so I hurried out to see if I could catch you,' he said.

Nina realised that her aunt had never met him, though she could probably guess who he was. 'Aunt, may I present Mr Cowling? Mr Cowling, my aunt, Mrs Schofield.'

'Honoured to make your acquaintance, ma'am,' Cowling said, giving her hand a hearty shake.

She drew it back and discreetly massaged it. 'The pleasure is mine, Mr Cowling. This scheme has been dear to my heart for many years, and your generous offer has made it possible to realise.'

'A free library,' Cowling said. 'Not a bad idea, as long as there's good solid books of education, and not too many trashy novels.'

'Self-help is the main purpose,' she said. 'But knowledge of the classics can only enrich the mind. We need gardens, Mr Cowling, as well as factories. Mankind needs plants as well as plant.'

He seemed struck by that. 'Plant and plants – I hadn't thought of it that way. That's a good one! I shall remember that. Plants and plant.' He looked around with a sharply critical eye. 'It looks a solid place enough. What do you think, Miss Sanderton?' His voice underwent a modulation when he turned to Nina: he asked her opinion almost tenderly.

'I was wondering about the lack of windows,' she said. 'It needs to be inviting – people will be scared enough to come in without it looking dark and oppressive.'

'Aye, the thought of having to read a book would shake most of the folk round here to their boots,' Cowling said genially.

'You couldn't build bookshelves across windows,' said Aunt Schofield, 'so the more blank wall you have, the more bookshelves you can put in. The room is high enough to have two storeys, and my idea is to build a gallery upstairs, where the natural light is, to use as a reading-room.'

'But how will people down below be able to see the books?' Lepida said.

'If the gallery is made of pierced ironwork, it won't cut out all the light,' Aunt Schofield said. 'But there will have to be artificial light for the ground floor.' This was the point that had been worrying her most. There would have to be light anyway, because they wanted to open in the evenings, the only time most working people could get there. There had been no need of gaslight in a warehouse used only for storage, so there was no supply laid on. She didn't know how much their new benefactor was willing to spend.

Mr Cowling looked untroubled. 'Electric light's the thing. No sense messing around with gas, these days, specially when your stock's all paper. You don't want any risk of fire, now, do you?'

'That's a good point,' said Aunt Schofield. 'But wouldn't electric light be expensive?'

'No more than gas,' said Cowling. 'There's electricity all up and down the Commercial Road. Only a matter of tapping into it. Easier to lay electric cables than gas pipes, ma'am, I can tell you. But you leave all that to me. You don't need to worry about details. You just decide what you want, and I'll stand the nonsense, whatever it is.'

'That is very generous of you, Mr Cowling.'

'No, no, I said I'd do it and I will. I can't stand paltriness. I suppose you'll need an architect to draw your plans.'

'I can recommend a very good firm,' the agent began.

Cowling turned on him, like a cat pouncing. 'I don't doubt you can, young man – and a firm of builders as well, eh? All friends of yours, and greasing your palm to get the work.

Well, I wasn't born yesterday. You and me are going to have a serious talk about money very soon, but we won't do it in front of ladies, so bide there and hold your water till I'm ready.'

Having trounced the agent, Cowling clasped his hands behind his back, and stared around with apparent pleasure, rocking a little on his heels. 'Aye, not bad, not bad. I can see it all. That gallery – having the study part upstairs'll mean you can keep an eye on the books and not have 'em walking out the door. And pierced ironwork'll mean you can watch what folk are up to. You don't want the place getting a reputation for hanky-panky. You want decent folks to let their sons and daughters come here.'

'You seem to have thought of so many things that hadn't occurred to us,' said Aunt Schofield.

Mr Cowling beamed. 'Well, now, ma'am, I wouldn't expect ladies to recognise all the pitfalls the way I can, having been in business all my life. Ladies have the fine, grand ideas – they do the artistic bit of the thinking, which is right. Base folk like me can get down to the grubby details, being closer to the ground, as you might say.'

'I don't think you are in the least base,' Aunt Schofield said firmly. 'Your willingness to help with the Free Library shows you to be a superior person.'

He looked abashed. 'No, no,' he mumbled, in protest. 'You're too kind. I know what I am. But it doesn't mean I don't know superior when I see it.' Nina thought he was actually blushing. Then he pulled himself together. 'Now, this young man and I had better have a talk about the money, which is what you don't need to worry about. Are you done here, ladies? Can we get you a cab?'

'Yes, I think we've seen all we came for,' Aunt Schofield said. 'Mr Cowling, would you take dinner with us at my house tomorrow evening? I would like the other movers of our scheme to meet you.'

'At your house? I'd be honoured,' he said, seeming genuinely pleased.

'At seven, then? And we will dress.'

When the family went home from Scotland, Sebastian had gone to stay in his house in Henley, and had taken Crooks with him. The town was quiet with the regatta long gone and it had been pleasantly restful after the hurly-burly of Kincraig. But Crooks didn't really have enough to do, and he was glad to get back to the Castle.

The first thing he did was to walk out to the cottage at Ashmore Carr. He found Axe in his yard, sitting on a wooden stool carving a piece of wood. Dolly was lying under the stool, her forepaws crossed, the picture of ease now her pups were gone. One of the cats that had been sitting nearby unfurled itself and stalked delicately across to pat a curl of wood-shaving that had just fallen. Then Dolly gave her warning bark, and the cat scooted as though blown by a gust of wind.

Axe looked up, and smiled. Crooks thought his smile the most beautiful thing God had ever created.

'I heard you was back,' Axe said. 'Our Josh said they'd had orders to get the horses in because her ladyship and all would be back today. Didn't think I'd see you this soon, though. Thought there'd be some settling in to do.'

'I only had to unpack Mr Sebastian's things. But we'll be busy soon. His lordship and her new ladyship will be home the day after tomorrow, so I thought I'd come out and see you while I can. What are you making?'

'Oh, just whittling,' he said. 'I like to do a bit. Hands get stiff and stupid, blacksmithing.'

'May I see?'

'' Fyou like. I'll go and get you a chair – unless you want to go inside?'

'No, it's pleasant out here. I don't get out of doors often enough.'

Axe handed the piece of wood to Crooks and went inside. Crooks turned it over in his hands, fascinated. It was obviously going to be a doll, or a figure of that sort, about eight inches high, with arms and legs all of a piece with the body. But there was a neck, and the head had curly hair, and already the features of the face were emerging.

Axe came back, and Crooks sat down, still turning the figure round in his hands. Axe watched him for a moment, then said, "'Twas an old chair leg. Too broke to mend, so I took the legs for my carving – the rest'll burn. Probably burn that, too.' He nodded at the figure. "'Tis only practising.'

Crooks looked up. 'No, you mustn't burn it. It's amazingly fine work. The way you've done the hair! There are marble busts up at the Castle that don't have the hair as well done as this.'

'It's hard working that small,' Axe admitted. 'One little slip, and you've spoiled it. One I did previous, I'd just got the face all nice and I went and knocked the nose right off.'

Crooks handed it back, and watched the big hand take up the knife again, and go delicately to work. Axe tilted his face down, concentrating, thick golden lashes fanning his cheeks. Such a fair face. Someone ought to use *him* as a model, Crooks thought. That straight nose, the rounded chin and the sculpted lips would make him perfect for any Greek hero. He wished he could paint. Or even draw. Beauty was so evanescent that man was always driven to try to preserve it in some form – paint, charcoal, marble. Wood. Axe said he was exercising his hands, but wasn't he also trying to capture something, some fragment of beauty his soul perceived, though his education had no words for the concept?

Suddenly Axe lifted his head, the blue eyes looking frankly into his, faintly questioning. Crooks was scalded with embarrassment to be caught staring. 'I – er – I did bring something,'

384

he said, glad to have an excuse to advance. 'A new book for you to tackle.'

'That's nice of you, sir,' said Axe.

'You don't need to call me "sir",' Crooks said, not for the first time. He drew the book out of his pocket. 'It's by Mr Wells, H. G. Wells – have you heard of him?' A shake of the head. 'Well, he writes a lot of scientific books, but this one is a piece of fiction, something quite different. I thought you'd enjoy it.' He passed it over. Axe put down the wood and the knife and wiped his palms on his trouser legs. He always handled books reverently, as though they had been blessed by a priest. 'I think it's important, when helping an adult to read,' Crooks went on, 'that the book is interesting. You can't be expected at your age to read from a child's primer.'

'*The Time Machine*.' Axe read the title. 'Is it about a clock, then?'

'No, it's about a machine that lets people travel into the past, so that they can see what things were really like.'

'History?' He opened it and read a few words. 'It looks difficult.'

'We'll tackle it together. I think once you get interested, you'll fly through it. That's what I want for you – to be so involved with the story you don't notice you're reading.'

'That *would* be fine,' Axe said shyly. 'I think I know what you mean. There were times with old Gulliver when it was almost like I could see him, like I was there.'

'Yes, exactly! Would you like to get started now?'

'Have you got time?'

'We can do a little, just to get you off the mark, and you can go on on your own when you've time.'

'Better go inside,' Axe said. 'Don't want to get the book dirty. It looks like new.'

It was new. Crooks had bought it specially on one of his afternoons off in Henley. But he didn't tell Axe that.

'We s'd have a cup of tea,' Axe said. 'You must be dry after walking over. I'll put the kettle on.'

Inside, Crooks sat down at the table, and his eye jumped at once to another book lying there. 'What's this?' he said. 'Ah, good old *Sindbad*! Have you been reading it?'

Axe turned sharply. 'Doing a bit of practice, while you were away, sir.'

'Where did you get it from?' Crooks said, picking it up.

'Borrowed it,' Axe said, removing it firmly from his hands and taking it over to the dresser, out of reach.

'We have *Sindbad* in the library at the Castle,' Crooks said. 'The same edition, I think. How interesting. Who lent it to you?'

Axe was collecting cups rather noisily, and didn't hear. 'This time machine, sir,' he said, bringing them to the table, 'how would that work? I mean, if you was to go back into history, wouldn't people notice you weren't here? And what if you went to a place you'd already been – would you see yourself there?'

'Ah, said Crooks, 'you ask some very interesting questions. People have always been fascinated by the idea of travelling back in time, but there are reasons to believe it could never actually be possible.' Talking about the subject, he entirely forgot *Sindbad*.

'Nina, my dear, thank you for coming,' said Miss Thornton.

The parlour, where she had so often sat, studied and conversed looked just the same. Nina felt a pang of home-sickness for that time when everything had been so simple, when there had been nothing in her immediate future but the pleasures of learning and of friendship.

Miss Thornton was examining her. 'You've grown up,' she observed. 'You were an eager girl when you left me, now you're very much a young woman. And our Kitty is married! How quickly things change. Have you seen her?'

'Not yet,' Nina said. She tried to think of something to say about Kitty and her marriage, and failed. Her former teacher's eyes were so noticing, she was afraid she'd give herself away.

Miss Thornton observed the slight discomfort, and filed it away. 'Well, now,' she said, 'to business. I expect you've guessed that the reason I asked you to call is that I've heard of a place for you.'

The ginger cat, Rasselas, came stalking in, and selected Nina to receive his blessing. He jumped up and settled his soft bulk on her lap. Nina stroked him. His thick fur was cold from being outside, and he brought a smell of leaves in with him. 'I thought that might be it,' she said.

'You don't sound excited,' said Miss Thornton. 'Have you changed your mind about teaching?'

'Oh, no,' Nina said hastily. 'I have to earn my living. And I hope to do some good. If I can be to some other girl what you have been to me . . .'

'I don't want you to get your hopes up too high. With all due modesty I can say that not all schools are like mine. I wish I could take you on here, but I have no vacancy for a teacher.'

'Is the place you've heard of – not nice?' Nina asked falteringly.

'Don't be despondent. I think it is a very good place for you to start. Allely's Academy for Young Ladies has a vacancy for a junior mistress. The senior mistress is retiring because of ill health, and one of the present juniors will be promoted. It's in York, which is a very nice city, and has a lot of well-to-do families. Most of them will only want their daughters educated to drawing-room standard, but there is a section of York society, so Miss Allely tells me, that has quite a strong academic bent, and supports education for girls.'

'York!' said Nina. 'I've – I've never been to the north of England.'

387

'Dear Nina, you talk as though it's on the other side of the world! It's only about four hours away by train – and, as I said, it's a pleasant city. There are theatres and an assembly hall with regular concerts, several libraries, and some fine shops, I believe, though of course they can't compare with London. Now, you would share a bedroom with the other junior mistress, and all meals are provided, so although the salary is small, you would have no expenses but your clothes.'

Nina stroked the cat but said nothing. The loud purring was the only sound in the room.

'Well?' said Miss Thornton. She raised an eyebrow. 'Did you expect to step straight into the perfect position? In every profession you have to work your way up. You will learn a lot at Allely's, and those girls you *can* help, in the way that I hope I've helped you, will give you the satisfaction and sense of achievement I think you crave.'

Nina roused herself. 'Yes, I'm sure you're right. And thank you. I truly am grateful. When would I have to start?'

'When the new year begins, in January. In the normal way Miss Allely would want to interview you to see if you are suitable, but she knows something of my school and my girls, and she is happy to trust my judgement, so you need only say yes.'

Now that it was actually going to happen, Nina was realising with dismay that she *really* did not want to be a teacher. But what choice did she have? And Miss Thornton had gone to considerable trouble for her, and had recommended her. She could not let her down. 'Yes,' she said, trying to sound pleased. 'And thank you again.'

'Very well,' said Miss Thornton, still watching her. 'I'll write to Miss Allely – and, no doubt, she will write to you with further details. And now, my Nina, tell me what you've been doing. Have you been keeping up with your studies, or has it been all dancing?'

'Dancing?' Nina gave a short laugh. 'Not since Kitty's wedding. But I've been going to some interesting classes.'

She told her about the British Museum lectures and the summer courses she had been attending with Lepida, and her tone grew animated, and her face flushed with pleasure.

Canons Ashmore station again. Kitty noticed the details of it sharply, thinking that from now on it would be 'her' station, as Hampstead station had been for most of her life. The wooden roof with its decoratively carved canopy, the cherry tree, its leaves rusty now with the onset of autumn, the white-painted picket fence . . . Outside, the carriage awaited, with the lovely greys. This time the liveried groom bowed to her and murmured, 'My lady,' as he offered his white-gloved hand to help her in. *My lady*, she thought. *I'm the Countess of Stainton.* Somehow it hadn't been real when they were abroad – it hadn't counted. Now, here in the actual place, it came home to her.

She had felt different ever since that dreadful day when she had shouted at Giles, breaking through the barriers of a lifetime. She never would have thought she could talk to anyone like that, least of all to the man she loved with a consuming passion. But there had been an extraordinary release in it – terrifying and exhilarating at the same time. Then afterwards . . . Well, the details had become hazy now, and she didn't really remember why she had swum out into the sea. She only remembered how frightened she had been, how she had thought she was going to die, and how Giles had come fighting his way through the waves to save her.

The two things were mixed up in her memory. She did not think it in words, but there was a feeling in the back of her mind that he would not have tried to save her if there hadn't been the quarrel before. The Kitty he had saved was a different Kitty. She had *done* something – she to whom, before, things had always been done. She felt different inside, stronger, more *herself*. She had come once before to the Castle, trembling with apprehension, afraid of everyone and everything, hoping only to escape notice. Not to be seen, not to offend, not to be told off – that had been her highest ambition. Now she looked around with interest as the carriage bowled through the pretty village and then up the green hill. She remembered the shabbiness and the air of neglect and believed she could make a difference to the Castle. *I'll make it a home for him*, she thought. And there would be good works to do on the estate and in the village. People would come to love and respect her. They would bring their troubles to her and she would help them. She would matter.

Giles was looking out of the window on his side, his face turned away from her. What was he thinking? What *did* men think? To her he was as beautiful and exotic as a tiger – and as unpredictable. But she had made her stand, staked her claim. 'I am your wife,' she had said, and he had accepted it. Whatever happened in the future, that would not change. For the first time in her life, she looked forward to what was to come – still afraid, yes, but feeling she had something inside her that could face up to the difficulties and allow her to enjoy the good parts.

The servants were lined up on the steps as they arrived – in the same deer-trap formation as if, Giles thought again as he climbed out, he might try to make a run for it. The house looked so big, compared with the places they had been staying; it, and all the staff, and the estate made a burden he had to shoulder. The holiday was over: his work began. And now there was this small female beside him – his *wife* – whose happiness and welfare depended uniquely on him. He sighed, and looked up for a moment at the indifferent sky, before walking submissively in.

★ ★ ★

'Kitty's maid left us in Paris,' Giles told his mother.

Lady Stainton looked at Kitty as though wanting to ask, 'What did you do to drive her away?'

'My mother only took her on for the Season,' Kitty found the courage to say. Lady Stainton was undoubtedly the biggest of all hurdles to cross. 'I thought when she agreed to come away with us—'

'We thought she was permanent,' Giles took over for her. 'But evidently she thought differently.'

'Rose had better attend her for the moment,' said Lady Stainton. 'Rose is quite accustomed to attending female visitors who don't bring their own maid.'

Giles thought this sounded slightly disparaging, but it was not the moment to probe his mother's attitudes. He was glad there were others present to dilute the company – Linda and Cordwell, Uncle Sebastian, Aunt Caroline and Grandmère. And Richard, ready to defuse any situation with wit and jokes. The girls, hanging back as usual, seemed pleased to see him, and gazed at Kitty as if they longed to carry her away with them to the nursery.

And the dogs, who came to overwhelm him with passionate adoration: swinging tails, butting heads, yards of tongue. 'What have you been doing to them?' he asked facetiously. 'Beating and starving them?'

'We've tried to be nice to them,' Alice said, 'but they'd decided you were their new master and no-one else would do.'

Giles's things had been put into the Blue Bedroom. He had managed up until his wedding to resist being installed in the Queen's Bedroom, and had half suspected his mother would have ordered the change in his absence, but evidently she'd had other things on her mind.

Kitty had been put in the Tapestry Room. It was one of the grand rooms on the first floor, and Giles had never used it, or he might have made a protest on Kitty's behalf. Conducted to it by Rose, she looked around with misgiving. As its name suggested, it had walls lined with a series of ancient tapestries depicting the chase. All the colours but blue and green had been leached out of them over time, and the effect was consequently gloomy. There were heavy blue drapes at the window and over the massive bed; ancient black oak furniture, and dark oil paintings mostly featuring the results of hunting – limp birds, bloodied hares, dead salmon. The one opposite the foot of the bed depicted a stag, brought to its knees, rolling its eyes up in despair as the hounds tore out its throat.

Rose, standing behind her temporary mistress, wondered what sort of person would paint such a thing, let alone hang it in a bedroom to be the first thing you saw when you woke up. She also knew, from the servants of visitors who had slept there, that the mattress was the worst in the house. It was the largest room, after the Queen's Bedroom, which might be assumed to be the reason the dowager had assigned it to the new countess. Rose wondered, however.

'It's – rather sombre,' Kitty said.

'Yes, my lady,' said Rose. She was taller than her ladyship by several inches and felt suddenly rather protective towards her. 'There are other rooms.'

'You mean, I could change?' Kitty said doubtfully. Rose only gave her a sturdy look that said *You can do anything you like.* Kitty gulped. 'Perhaps I'll have a look tomorrow. I don't want to make a fuss now, when I've only just arrived.'

'No, my lady,' said Rose. If she was going to pitch her will against the dowager's either there would be a battle royal, or instant capitulation and tears. Not having any means to judge the new countess's mettle, Rose didn't know which. Personally, she wouldn't sleep in this room for a pension. 'The White Chinese Room is nice, though not as big as this.'

Kitty sensed friendship coming from this tall, rather gaunt maid. 'Could you choose something for me to wear tonight? I'm not sure how formal it will be.'

'Gladly, my lady,' Rose said, pleased. It was nice when new people didn't throw their weight around straight off. Boded well for a happy adjustment. 'I can do your hair for you as well, if you like. I'm accustomed to doing ladies' hair.'

First of all James sought out Crooks. Certain things had to be settled. 'Don't think you're going to walk back in as his lordship's valet,' he said brutally, cornering Crooks in the valets' room.

Crooks looked up from ironing Mr Sebastian's white tie – the valets' room had its own ironing board. 'I'll thank you not to speak to me in that tone of voice,' he said, temporising. He had been thinking for two days about the situation, unsure whether he wanted to go back to his old duties. He was comfortable with Mr Sebastian, who didn't need much looking after, which gave him more free time. And less responsibility. On the other hand, there was the question of status. He didn't want James lording it over him; and the other servants would think less of him if he meekly stepped aside.

'I'll use any tone I like,' said James. 'The fact of the matter is *I'm* his lordship's valet.'

'Temporary,' said Crooks. 'For the journey overseas, that's all.'

'Says you! You weren't up to it. You were making mistakes all over the place, remember? I stepped in and saved your bacon. Lord knows what'd've happened if you'd gone abroad with them. You'd never have coped.'

'I will always cope with whatever is required of me,' Crooks said, striving for dignity.

James put on his most scornful face. 'Oh, yes? And what

would have happened in Capri, if I hadn't been there? You couldn't have done what I did.'

'I don't know what you're talking about.'

'Of course you don't. But I'll tell you. I saved her lady-ship's life, that's all. She'd have drowned if it hadn't been for me – now then! D'you think you could've thrown your-self into the sea and swum to her rescue? I don't think so! His lordship'd've been a widower by now if I hadn't taken over from you. So don't think he's going to take you back after that. You just be grateful you've still got a job.'

'I don't – I didn't—' Crooks quavered. James had somehow made him feel that her ladyship almost drowning was *his* fault, when he hadn't even been there. 'How did it happen? How did she—?'

'Never mind. You'll hear. I'll tell it all tonight downstairs. You stay out of my way and you'll be all right. I'm in good with Mr Sebastian – I'll put in a good word for you.'

'Thank you,' Crooks said automatically, and James had whirled away before he could think straight. 'I don't need a good word from you,' he said, annoyed with himself. How was it that James always got him in a tizzy? An over-hot smell alerted him just in time to the fact that the iron he was holding was still resting on the white tie. *Damn that man!*

Dory was sorting out her work basket for the next day. 'I'm back,' James said, from the doorway.

'So I see,' Dory said, not looking up.

'Been in foreign parts. Got lots to tell,' he said enticingly.

'I expect I'll hear about it sooner or later,' she said indifferently.

He took a couple of steps closer. 'Did you miss me, then?'

Now she looked up. Luckily, the basket was between her and him. 'Of course not,' she said. 'Why on earth should I?'

'I thought you fancied me,' he said. He reached out to

stroke her forearm, but without her seeming to move, it wasn't where it had been and he missed.

'Of course I don't,' she said. And she didn't say it emphatically, or spitefully. She didn't seem to be trying to hurt his feelings, which made it all the more hurtful.

He pulled on his dignity. 'Your loss,' he said, and went away.

'I don't think so,' she said softly, taking out a shirt and turning it over to see where it was torn.

He hadn't noticed before, but Tilda had a bit of a moustache. Because it was gingery, like her hair, it only showed up in a certain light.

Still and all. 'Did you miss me, then?' he said insinuatingly.

She went scarlet, and her mouth opened, but no words emerged.

'I been in foreign parts. Want to hear all about it?'

She nodded.

'Say it, then. Say "please".'

'Please,' she managed, her eyes fixed on his face.

'Outside, then. By the dustbins. I've got something for you, if you're a good girl.'

She was about to ask what it was, then thought she knew. And it wasn't being a good girl that got it for you. But with James she was like a rabbit before a stoat. She had no will of her own.

The White Chinese Room had white panelling, picked out in gold, a green marble fireplace with a huge gilded mirror above it, a green and white Chinese carpet, and white damask bed hangings with gold tassels. On the mantelpiece was a collection of white jade Chinese figures, and the occasional tables and chairs were in Chinese bamboo from the Regency period. Giles thought them rather hideous, but it was certainly much pleasanter than the Tapestry Room.

'It's smaller, though,' he said.

395

'But much less dark,' Kitty said anxiously. 'And those pictures of dead animals . . .'

'We could have them moved,' he said.

'I'd sooner have this room,' she said. 'If you think it would be all right.'

'My dear, have whichever room you want,' he said.

'Um – but your mother . . . She chose the Tapestry Room for me.'

'Isn't that the one with the really bad mattress?' Giles dredged up a memory – hadn't Richard slept there once?

Kitty's lips tightened a moment. If he had visited her in bed, he would know. But his bedroom was down the corridor from hers, and he had not come to her, though they'd been at home five days. 'It is really bad,' was all she said. 'Like sleeping on rocks.'

'Well, ask Rose to tell Mrs Webster you want to move,' Giles said, and seeing doubt in Kitty's face, added impatiently, 'My mother won't care, Kitty. She just put you in Tapestry because it's the largest. How is Rose working out?'

'She's good,' Kitty said. 'I like her.'

'Well, if you want to look for a new lady's maid, I think you'll have to go to a London agency.'

'Oh, no, I'm happy with Rose, at least for now.'

'Very well,' Giles said, and turned away. Markham and Adeane were waiting for him in the library. A volume of work had built up for him during his absence.

'Wait – Giles! I have something else to ask you,' Kitty said.

He turned back with barely controlled impatience. 'What is it now?' he asked, managing at the last moment to modify his tone and not snap at her.

'This room,' she said. 'Well, I've noticed that it's next to your dressing-room.'

White Chinese didn't have a dressing-room. 'You want to swap with me? I don't really care, you can have Blue if you prefer.'

'I don't want to swap. What I thought was, if we moved that console we could make a door through into your dressing-room. And then you could come through into my room without having to go out into the corridor.'

She looked at him hopefully, and watched as the implication sank in.

Giles felt a quickening. He had been too busy since they'd got back to think about it – and being at the Castle had thrown him into a bachelor state of mind: it was something to do with his mother's presence and dominance, which made changing anything, including his own status, unthinkable. But now he did think about it, a warmth flooded his lower body. *His little pagan*, he thought. Since that outburst on Capri, he had realised how much of a pagan lived inside that quiet creature. Yes, it would be good to visit her again – and to do it without the danger of running into a staring servant.

'That's not a bad idea,' he said. 'I'm not sure how much work would be needed – these old houses were pretty solidly built. We could have the estate carpenter in to have a look. Yes, I think it's a good plan,' he concluded, turning away. 'Better run it past my mother first, though.'

Kitty watched him walk out, and felt that with those last words he had doomed it.

Miss Taylor met James on the stairs as he was taking them two at a time, going up with a clean shirt over his arm. He was surprised to find himself halted by a skinny but powerful claw.

'What?' he demanded crossly.

She stared at him like an inimical owl. 'Think a lot of yourself, don't you? Think you're very clever.'

'I *am* very clever,' he said.

'Last I heard, you were still James, not Mr Hook. His lordship's not confirmed you as valet, has he?'

James was going to argue that names don't matter, but of course they did. But the best form of defence was always attack. He painted a sneer over his lips. 'Still pining for old Crooky, are you? I reckon there was more going on between you two than met the eye.'

'Mr Crooks is a gentleman's gentleman. You're not any sort of gentleman. I've seen it before,' she went on, looking him over as if he were a rather inferior piece of meat. 'You can put a necktie on a pig and call it "sir", but it's still a pig.'

James bristled. 'You want to watch who you're calling names,' he growled. 'People that cross me always regret it.'

She was unmoved. 'I've seen upstarts like you come and go, but I'm still here. I know all the tricks your sort get up to. Just remember, Mr Still-a-Footman James, I'm watching you. I'll always be watching you.' And she went on down the stairs.

For an instant he felt a powerful urge to give her a shove and watch her tumble down. *Break her skinny, ugly neck!* he thought. How dare she threaten him? How dare she? Pig, eh? He'd show her who the pig was! She thought she knew all the tricks, but she didn't. There were a good few of his own he had up his sleeve. Pig! He'd get her back for that. He'd make her sorry. *Have to bide my time,* he thought. *Wait for the right opportunity.* But it would come – and when it did, she wouldn't be expecting it. He could wait. He was good at waiting. And he was good at hating. Pleased with the rhyme, he went on up the stairs.

CHAPTER TWENTY-ONE

'I'm going to a political meeting tonight in Kingsway,' Mawes Morris said at luncheon. 'I want to make some sketches. I wondered if you girls would like to come with me.'

'Am I included in the "girls"?' Isabel asked.

'Of course. What would I do without you?'

'You'd be bored.' Isabel laughed. 'Don't be deceived, girls – he doesn't think you'd enjoy it, he only thinks he won't enjoy it on his own.'

'Really, Daddy?' Lepida asked.

'There are two good speakers,' he said enticingly. 'You know the government is split on the subject of free trade? Chamberlain and his faction want to put punitive tariffs on countries that put tariffs on our goods, while Churchill and his gang want total free trade on everything, regardless. It'll be a ding-dong sparring match.'

'And which one do you want to draw?' Nina asked. She and Lepida had been working on the Free Library scheme, and she had stayed for luncheon.

'Churchill mostly. He has a distinctive face, better for caricatures than Chamberlain's, though I shall need both for next week.'

Nina was looking forward to seeing Winston Churchill, whom she had heard described as a 'rum cove'. She remembered Richard Tallant speaking about him once, telling how he had been a newspaper correspondent in the war and, having been captured by the Boers, had managed to escape out of a window, then had written the Boer leaders an impudent letter thanking them for their hospitality. He had recently been elected to Parliament, and was making a name for himself as a speaker.

The hall in Holborn was packed, and they could only get seats near the back, which was not ideal for Mawes. There weren't a great many women present, Nina noticed, looking around – just two near the front, and another two further along their own row. There were some rough-looking men standing at the back, presumably not having been able to secure a seat. 'Free trade is a popular subject, it seems,' Nina said to Mawes.

He stared round at the men. 'I don't think they're here for the debate. There's a certain sort of man who just enjoys heckling. Politics is a rough sport.'

'What's "heckling"?'

'You'll see,' he said, settling his pad comfortably on his knee, and rapidly sketching some of the faces around him.

The speeches were serious and impassioned, and Nina found herself swayed one way, then the other. Both sides seemed to have perfect, logical arguments, and she wondered how anyone could decide between them. Then the chairman opened the meeting to questions. A man stood up and asked a question, and those on the platform attempted to answer it, while the rough men behind shouted the occasional comment, and others in the seats turned and shouted back at them. It was certainly more lively, though perhaps less enlightening than the speeches. The questions seemed to have petered out when one of the women further along their row stood up, and a sudden hush fell on the hall.

The woman's voice rang out clearly, her accent pure, her tone the decided one of a person used to public speaking,

400

though she was plainly dressed with a very unemphatic hat. 'Will Mr Chamberlain tell us whether the government will give the vote to women?'

Someone near the front groaned, someone else said something Nina didn't catch, and several people around him laughed. The chairman scanned the room. 'Are there any more questions?' he said.

'I have asked a question,' the woman said.

Someone in the back row shouted, 'Sit down!' and the man in the seat immediately behind the woman grabbed her arm and pulled her roughly down.

'If there are no more questions, I propose we go to the closing speeches,' the chairman announced.

The woman rose again, and said, 'Why don't you answer my question? Will the government give the vote to women?'

Now there were shouts. 'Sit down!'

'Be quiet!'

'Rubbish!'

'Go home, woman!'

The men at the back were even more frank. 'Get off, you baggage!'

'Get back to the kitchen, you trollop!' And other suggestions less repeatable.

Mawes was sketching as though his life depended on it.

'Why won't they answer her question?' Nina asked him urgently.

'Women aren't allowed to speak at political meetings,' he told her, his eyes flashing up and then down, his fingers busy. Nina saw he was drawing Mr Churchill, whose chin was sunk in his hand, a grim, bulldog-ish look on his face.

The whole room was alive with shouts, harsh laughter and catcalls. A second woman tried to stand up but was pulled down. Someone at the back threw something at her – it looked like a balled-up pamphlet – and managed to knock her hat askew. The first woman rose again, but her voice was drowned out, though Nina, watching her lips, assumed she was asking the same question.

'It's so unfair!' Nina said. 'Why can't women speak?'

'Because we don't have the vote,' Isabel said.

'But they're *asking* for the vote,' Nina said. 'How can they get it if they're not allowed to ask?'

Isabel shrugged. 'Politics is men's business. You see how rough it is – too rough for women.'

Something was happening: a large man had advanced down the side aisle and was addressing the two women. Word came passing along the line. Mawes said, 'Apparently the chairman has said they must submit their question in written form.'

The hall was awash with loud conversation and the occasional burst of laughter. Nina watched as the steward accepted a piece of folded paper from the women and walked back down to the platform, where he delivered it to the chairman. The chairman unfolded it, read it, then screwed it up and threw it onto the floor behind him. The talk roared up in cheers and laughter.

'That'll teach 'em!'

'Go home where you belong!'

The two women stood up together, and in chorus began to shout, 'Votes for women!'

And now the back of the hall erupted. The women were grabbed. They struggled, and fighting broke out behind them, with oaths to turn the air blue. Stewards ran down the aisle again, someone fetched in the policeman from the door outside, and the women were dragged bodily away, still shouting, their words quite unheard in the din. One had her hat knocked off, and her hair half pulled down; the other's sleeve was torn almost from her coat, and Nina could see even from this distance that there was a bruise on the side of her face.

'What will happen to them?' she asked Mawes anxiously. 'Those men will hurt them! Can't we do something?'

'There'll be more policemen outside,' Mawes said, still drawing madly. 'They'll stop them being badly hurt. They'll be arrested and taken to the police station.'

'Arrested for what?' Nina asked. 'They weren't the ones causing the trouble.'

'Breach of the peace, probably. Or obstruction,' said Mawes. 'That's what they usually get charged with.'

'But it's not *fair*!' Nina cried again. 'They only wanted to ask a question.'

He looked at her with a faint smile. 'Very little in life is fair, Nina my dear.' He flipped his pad closed. 'Shall we try to leave, before the mob gets moving?'

'But *why* can't women have the vote?' Nina asked.

'Oh dear,' said Isabel, 'that's such a large question. Most women don't *want* to vote, you know. They don't understand politics and they're happy to leave it to their husbands.'

'You mean,' said Lepida, 'that it's a man's club and the men don't want to let women in. They want to keep all the fun for themselves.'

'It didn't look much like fun in there,' Nina said.

'Exactly,' said Mawes. 'It's a rough business, and any decent man would want to keep the women he loves out of it. And there's another reason, of course,' he added.

'What's that?' Nina asked.

'There are actually more women than men in the country,' said Mawes. 'So if they had the vote, they'd outvote us every time. What man could accept that?'

Lady Stainton's eyes flashed, her nostrils flared. 'Absolutely not!' she said.

Kitty wilted. It had taken her a long time to pluck up the courage to speak to her mother-in-law about making a communicating door, and the courage was too newly found to stand up to opposition, particularly when generated by centuries of privilege and a lifetime of being in the right. 'I – I'm sorry.' she stammered.

'Staintons have lived here for hundreds of years,' said Lady Stainton, icily. 'Yet what *they* have always found satisfactory, *you* have the temerity to object to. A girl barely out of the schoolroom! Not here five minutes and you want to tear the house down around our ears.'

'Oh, no, it's a lovely house,' Kitty faltered. 'I only thought—'

'You did not think at all, that's the trouble,' said Lady Stainton. 'I suggest you have the modesty to wait a few years before you begin dictating to your elders and betters.'

'But—'

'I will hear no more about it,' Lady Stainton said, and left the room, ending any possibility of argument.

There was a derelict barn over the crown of the hill, behind the woods, its roof too much fallen in to be useful for storage. As Rachel rode up to it, Victor came out, and stood waiting for her. He caught the rein, and Daystar threw up his head, knowing an inexperienced hand when he felt one. Rachel wished Victor wouldn't do it, but she knew he thought he was being helpful. She halted, untangled her leg, and let him jump her down.

'No-one about,' he said. 'I haven't seen anyone since I started up the hill.'

She led Daystar into the barn, where Victor's bicycle was leaning against the wall. There was an old ring and a bit of rope, and when she had tied Daystar and loosened his girths, she was free to turn her attention to Victor. The first thing was kissing. It was a new discovery for her – they had only done it for the first time at their previous meeting a week ago – and it was the most exciting thing that had ever happened to her. They stood for ages, mouths pressed together, while Daystar fidgeted about, scraped the ground with a hoof, sneezed, shook himself, making various bits of harness jingle. When they finally stopped for breath, Victor said, 'I brought a rug to sit on,' and took her out through the back of the barn to where someone had assembled a heap of stones at one time, perhaps meaning to effect repairs. He had rearranged them a little, and spread the rug over the pile, so that it was like a sort of sofa, with an unbroken bit of barn wall behind it for a back.

They sat, and Victor took possession of her hand. 'You got away all right, then?'

'Yes, all right,' she said. 'I had to hang around a bit. That horrid James was outside, lurking about. I had to wait until he went in.'

'James?'

'He was first footman, now he's my brother's valet.'

'Does he suspect?' Victor loved excitement. He half longed for conspiracy.

'I don't think so. He's not interested in Alice and me. I think he was having a smoke – or maybe waiting for someone. I don't like him, though.' She shivered. 'He has horrible eyes. He always looks at you as if – as if he knows what you're wearing underneath.'

'I'll knock his head off!' Victor said indignantly. 'I thought you said he wasn't interested in you.'

'I don't mean he looks like that at *me*, but I've seen him look at the maids. And Daisy – she's our maid – she says he tried to put his hand on . . . on her chest once.'

'If he ever tries to touch you, you tell me, and I'll see he suffers,' Victor said fiercely.

She loved Victor's protectiveness. 'What would you do to him?' she asked.

'I'd knock his block off. I'd kick him all the way to Aylesbury.'

'Oh Victor,' she breathed. 'Would you really?'

405

They talked in this vein for a while. Then Victor wanted to know every detail of how she had got away, and wanted to tell her every detail of his journey. And they kissed a little more. Eventually, as he always did, he got around to 'I wish we could meet openly. I'd love to come calling for you.'

She liked this game. 'What would you bring?'

'I'd bring flowers. Roses, as a pledge of my love.'

'There aren't many roses at this time of year,' Rachel said.

He sometimes thought she was too literal. 'I'd find them somehow – for *you*.'

'As long as it wasn't chrysanthemums. I hate the smell of them,' said Rachel. 'And what would you wear? Your blue necktie, because it brings out the colour of your eyes?'

'Whatever you want me to wear. I'd come up to the Castle, and you'd be waiting for me, and we'd declare our love for each other in front of everyone, without disguise.'

'I expect Giles would be all right about it,' Rachel said, 'now he's married himself. But Mama would be sure to say I'm too young.'

'You're *never* too young to be in love.'

'Mama's too old to remember what love is like. She'd never let me see you.'

'We should run away. We'd go to Scotland and get married there.'

'But I don't think I'd like that,' Rachel said uneasily. She wanted a proper wedding, with everyone there, a beautiful dress, and bridesmaids, and a carriage decorated with ribbons and flowers. 'Have you found out any more about why Mama doesn't like your aunt?'

'Nothing,' he said. 'I can't exactly ask her straight out. I've hinted about it, but she just closes her lips tight and changes the subject. But I think it's about something that happened a long time ago – that's all I can fathom.'

Rachel sighed. 'So there's nothing we can do.'

'Let's not talk about it any more,' he said. 'Let's just talk about Us.'

They talked about the first time they had seen each other, and what each thought about the other, and such lovery subjects that never failed to enthral. And in between there was more kissing. Time passed effortlessly, until Daystar began kicking the barn wall in impatience, and it was time to part.

As they went upstairs at the end of the evening, Giles said to Kitty, 'You looked very pretty tonight. Have I seen that dress before?'

'It was one I bought in Florence. Lucia helped me choose it.'

'She has a good eye. I like that colour on you. What do you call it? Blue?'

'Lavender,' Kitty said. His words and his look gave her a warm feeling inside. The dinner party that evening had been tedious. It was one of a series Lady Stainton was giving to introduce Kitty to the neighbourhood, but her part in any of them had been minimal. Her mother-in-law had made all the arrangements, chosen the guests, and conducted the evening, like a general directing a battle. Giles was all right, because he knew nearly all of these people – or, at least, knew who they were, having had them in his background since birth. And it was always easier for men to talk to each other – they had politics and sport to resort to. There had been talk of shooting parties to come, and the beginning of hunting. 'Will you hunt this year, Stainton?' they had all wanted to know. And then it was horses and dogs and guns, description and comparison of, the recounting of hunts and shoots past, and beloved horses and dogs fondly remembered. Even though – and she had watched him so she knew – Giles tended not to talk very much, even on these subjects, he had listened with apparent interest and passed a tolerable evening.

For Kitty, there was always the catechism – who was she,

where did she come from, who were her people – and when the answers were found unsatisfactory, as they always were, the conversation turned to people she didn't know, and children, and ailments. She was not confident enough to start or to lead a conversation: if she was asked a question, she could answer, but that was the end of it.

It was no better when the divided company rejoined in the drawing-room. The two sides went on talking about their own subjects, and there was little cross-fertilisation. Richard had gone back to London, so his help and support were not available, and the Cordwells had gone back to Dorset – though Kitty had been almost as afraid of Linda as of her mother, she would at least have distracted attention from her. Uncle Sebastian was kind, and sometimes tried to draw her in, but he tended to fall asleep after dinner.

And the dinners – oh, the dinners! The food, which she had noticed on her first visit to the Castle was poor, did not get any better. She could eat little of it, and noticed that the guests divided into those who would put almost anything into their mouths, and those who skirted round it with an air of resignation. Evidently no-one expected tasty food at the Castle. She remembered the meals in Italy, the simple but luscious tastes. She didn't understand why a large estate should not be able to produce good-quality meat, and fruit and vegetables in season. Even in Hampstead they had had a succession house, though it was small. At Ashmore, surely they had room for acres of glass.

It was one of the many things she meant to bring up with Giles, when there was time – at the moment, he was occupied with urgent estate business that kept him locked in the library day after day. But had not the money she had brought to the marriage solved his problems? And could there not now be some of the improvements she had dreamed of?

As soon as she could get him to herself, she would raise

408

the subject. Just now, however, they had arrived at the door of her bedroom. 'Goodnight, my dear,' he said, and gave her a peck on the cheek.

She looked at him longingly. Dared she ask if he would visit her? She put all her yearning into her look, and it seemed to get through to him. Meeting her eyes, he laid a hand on her arm. The feeling of his hot palm against her bare skin made her shiver with desire, and she saw that it had communicated itself to him. His breath was warm and sweet on her cheek as he whispered, 'May I come to you? In fifteen minutes, then.'

In her room, Rose got up sleepily from the chair, and came to help her with buttons and hooks. Kitty was in a frenzy to be ready in time – if he came in while Rose was still there, he might go away again! She wanted to cry, *Hurry up, hurry up!* but restrained herself. Perhaps Rose felt it anyway, because she quickened her fingers, and did not waste time with conversation. She left Kitty sitting up in bed with a 'Goodnight, my lady,' and as soon as she had gone, Kitty struggled out of the nightdress and lay down, pulling the sheet up to her chin.

There was a soft sound at the door, and Giles came in, in his dressing-gown. He hurried across the room, threw it off, and she had one glorious glimpse of his naked body before he jumped into bed beside her. Her arms went up around his neck, and she felt him shudder with passion. They sank into each other with a sigh of relief. There was no time for conversation. If only, she thought, before thought was obliterated, we could always be in bed . . .

In the morning, he kissed her goodbye, and as he climbed out of bed he said, 'What happened to the idea of the communicating door?'

'Your mother said no,' she told him sleepily.

* * *

409

'Giles, may I speak to you for a moment?'

Giles looked up, and curbed his immediate reaction of irritation at being interrupted, remembering the sweetness of the night before. But Kitty saw that he looked at her with a stranger's eyes, and her heart misgave.

'Give me a moment, Markham,' Giles said, and the agent bowed and went out. Kitty clasped her hands before her, like a child summoned to a stern father's study. 'Well?' Giles said. He didn't say, 'Be quick,' but it was in his tone.

She summoned her courage. 'Dinner last night,' she said. 'In fact, dinner every night. I see that you don't eat much—'

'I'm not a great eater,' he said.

'You ate in Italy,' she said. 'I saw you enjoy your meals. And you put on weight. Now you're getting thin again. I see our guests pushing the food to the side of the plate. We invite people to dinner, and they can't eat anything. It's – humiliating.'

'The food at the Castle has never been much different in my lifetime,' Giles said, turning a pen round and round in his fingers. 'My father—'

'But now *you* are the earl,' Kitty said. 'You ought to have meals you can eat and our guests can enjoy. We need a new cook. The one we have is useless.'

'Then do something about it,' he said. 'Running the household isn't my business.'

'But it isn't mine, either. Your mother orders everything.'

'I can't be drawn into an argument between you and my mother,' he said impatiently. 'You must sort things out for yourself without involving me every time.'

Kitty felt tears start, and tried to suppress them, knowing it would annoy him if she cried. 'I don't want to involve you,' she said, 'but she won't listen to me. I asked about having the communicating door made between our rooms, and she said no.'

'Well, don't ask her. Tell her. You're mistress of the house.'

'But you told me to ask her. And you know very well I'm not mistress,' Kitty said. 'She won't allow me to "interfere", as she calls it.'

'I'm sure she's just trying to help.'

'You *know* she's not. She runs the household, and nothing will change that unless you say something to her!'

His nostrils flared. 'Have you the slightest idea of what's involved in running a house this size? You're very young, and you've never done anything like it before.'

Kitty pressed her nails into her palms to keep the tears back. 'How can I learn if no-one will teach me? I don't want to take everything over all at once, but I want to start. Some things need changing, you know they do, and she won't change *anything* unless you tell her to let me have a say.'

Giles put his head in his hands for a moment and inwardly cried, *Oh, God! Why do I have to put up with this?* He wanted to shout at Kitty, tell her to go away and sort things out for herself, and above all *stop bothering him*! But then he thought of his mother, and her cold haughtiness, and he knew he could not in fairness expect young, unarmed Kitty to fight the dragon with bare hands and no help.

He sighed and said, 'I'll speak to her about a new cook. Now, I really must get on. Will you ask Markham to come back in?'

Dismissed, Kitty went.

'Out of the question,' said Lady Stainton.

Giles leaned against the mantelpiece and fiddled with a china figurine. 'I don't think it is. The one we have – what's her name? Oxhey?'

'Oxlea.'

'I think you must admit, Mama, that she is not very good. If we are to entertain, as I assume you must want us to, we must have a better one. Good heavens, this is an earl's house

411

– we ought to be serving the finest food. What if the King were to come?'

'The King thinks altogether too much about food. It is vulgar.'

'I'm not talking about twenty courses, larks' tongues and fillets of unicorn,' Giles said impatiently. 'Just well-cooked English food that I can eat.'

'You have learned finicking ways with all the time you've spent abroad,' Lady Stainton said. 'No-one else but you complains.'

'Well, I'm the earl, so who else matters?'

'Yes, I thought that would come!' she said angrily. 'Arrogance, Giles! Disrespecting your father's memory! Dismantling everything he stood for! Trampling on my feelings as a widow!'

'I'm not doing any of those things,' Giles said, exasperated. 'I just want a new cook.'

'The food at the Castle was always good enough for your father.'

'For heaven's sake, Mama!'

'There is no question of dismissing Mrs Oxlea,' Lady Stainton said, with absolute determination. 'No *question*, do you hear?'

She was trembling with rage. Suddenly he felt an unwilling sympathy for her. She had been in charge of a household since her own mother had died when Uncle Stuffy was only an infant and she was just a girl. She was an autocrat who had run first Cawburn Castle, and then Ashmore, and to be usurped by a much younger woman must be difficult for her to contemplate.

He tried to speak reasonably, gently. 'I just want to make my life more comfortable, that's all. It is my home, after all.'

'*Your* home!' she cried furiously, and then quite suddenly grew icily calm. 'I suppose you'd like to pack me off to the Dower House?'

412

It gave him pause. He knew what she was saying. If she went to the Dower House, he would have to pay her jointure, and it would be most inconvenient just now to find the money. She could hold that over his head whenever a dispute arose. It was blackmail. He had a flare of anger. 'I will be master in my own house,' he said.

She glared at him with white fury. 'Burn the whole place down, if that's what you want! As you so elegantly remind me, *you* are master. I have no rights here any more.'

She swept out, and he sighed wearily and rubbed his temples. How much more of this would he have to endure?

Everyone had been at the Commercial Road property in the morning, with the architect's drawings, and now, after luncheon, they were settled in at Aunt Schofield's house discussing the plans. Tea was brought in, and Nina did her duty with the teapot, and helped Haydock and Minny hand the cups round. In the general changing of places, she found herself on a sofa beside Mr Cowling. He was looking different lately, she thought. He seemed to have had his hair cut in a different way, and his suit was new and his necktie had a certain jauntiness. Becoming involved in the Free Library project seemed to be invigorating him.

The first thing he said to her, however, was 'That's a pretty dress you have on, Miss Sanderton, if you don't mind my saying so. Is it impertinent to comment on it?'

'Not at all,' she said, rather touched – he seemed so anxious not to offend. 'As you must know, sir, a female takes to compliments as a duck takes to water.'

He smiled. 'You have such an original way of talking! You always amuse me. I wish all ladies were as conversable as you.'

'Not all gentlemen like ladies who talk,' she said. 'I was at a political meeting a while back—'

'Aye, I know. Morris told me about it. Not that I'd have taken a lady there myself. It's no place for a woman – though

413

I wouldn't criticise him, for he's as good a fellow as ever lived. But politics is not the business for females.'

'Politics controls every aspect of our lives. Should we not have a say in it?' Nina said.

He thought about it. 'I can see why you'd say that, you being a very clever young lady, and a thinker, but someone has to be in charge. I wouldn't like it if my workers wanted a say in how my factory was run. I treat them well – you don't get good work out of unhappy folk – but what I say goes. It has to be that way.'

Nina saw many obvious flaws in the argument, but she didn't want to upset him, so she said instead, 'I'm sure you are right. Have you any new shoe styles coming out for the Little Season?'

'Now that was an obvious change of subject,' he said genially. 'You think I'm an old fellow not worth arguing with, don't you?'

'Oh dear, not at all,' she said. 'I just didn't want to be disputatious. And I would never think of you as an old fellow! Whatever put that into your mind?'

'Well, I'm a widower, and most folk think that once you've buried a wife, you can't have any more love in your life. I'm sure your good aunt has the same thing thought about her.'

Could he be interested in marrying Aunt Schofield? she wondered. It hadn't occurred to her before. It was an odd thought – no two people could be more unsuited, in her view, and in any case she didn't think her aunt would ever consider marrying again, having no need to. 'I think,' she said, to let him down gently, 'that she's still dedicated to my uncle, in her heart. I expect you miss your wife, don't you?'

'I used to,' he said, 'very much. My Emma was a good creature, and I shall always honour her. But I don't think about her often, as I used to. Which is not to say I'm not lonely sometimes. Work keeps a man busy, but when he stops at the end of the day, why, there's an empty space by the hearth that needs filling.' He shook his head. 'I'm not explaining myself very well.'

'Oh, but you are,' she said. 'I understand perfectly. Work is important, and life would be empty without it, but a life with nothing *but* work . . .' She thought, briefly and unwillingly, of Giles Stainton. 'The heart has its own priorities,' she said quietly. 'And it won't be argued out of them.'

He was silent a moment. Then he said diffidently, 'I heard tell that you had an offer of a teaching place. Somewhere up north, I believe.'

'In York. Apparently it's a nice city.'

'Aye, it's very nice, and quite grand. A lot of fancy folk live there. I expect it'd be an expensive sort of school for young ladies?'

'Yes, where young ladies are sent to learn how to catch expensive husbands,' she said; and then was sorry. She should not make public her doubts about Allely's School. And Mr Cowling was not the person to entrust with her secrets.

But he looked at her with unexpected sympathy. 'I think you don't much want to go there – am I right?' She didn't answer. 'Is it going up north that bothers you?'

'Oh, I've nothing against the north, in particular,' she said.

'Then it's teaching in general, is it? Don't you want to be a teacher?'

She resisted for a moment, but it broke out of her. 'I thought I did, but the closer it comes, the less I like it. Yet I have to do something.'

'Can't you stay with your aunt?'

'She isn't trying to get rid of me – you mustn't think that – but she can't keep me for ever. I have to earn a living.' She shrugged. 'There aren't many things a genteel girl can do.'

'What would you *like* to do?' he asked. 'In the whole world – say you could choose, and money didn't matter?

She smiled. 'Make-believe, is it? Would you have chosen to make shoes, if you had the choice of the whole world?'

415

'Why, yes,' he said, as if surprised. 'It's what I've always liked. Though I wouldn't choose to be living all alone, and having no son to follow me. But though shoes chose me in the beginning, I chose 'em right back. I'm happy with that part. But we're talking about you, Miss Sanderton. What would *you* choose?'

She thought. 'I'm not entirely sure just yet. But I would like to go to university.'

'Would you, by heck! I beg your pardon, I mean, would you really?'

'Yes, I think so. I love to study, to learn.'

'Aye, you're about like my secretary, young Decius. Decius Blake – you've not met him yet. He never misses a chance to learn something new. Makes him right valuable to me. But that's not something to spend all your life on. University's only a few years, isn't it?'

'Yes, and that's why I say I'm not sure what I'd like to do. Eventually, I'd like to do something good for other people, to make their lives better.'

'Poor folk, like?'

'Yes, and girls in particular.' She smiled. 'Being one myself, I know the disadvantages.'

'Well, you may say so. But I must say I like the fact that girls are different from boys. It wouldn't be half as nice a world if they weren't.'

Yes, you would say that, she thought. But she didn't say it. She smiled, and said, 'I expect you're right. And may this girl have the pleasure of getting you another cup of tea?'

CHAPTER TWENTY-TWO

Nina was in the morning-room, struggling to write a letter. She'd had one at last from Kitty, to confirm she was now at the Castle, hinting of difficulties of adjustment, talking again of longing to see her friend. There was no direct invitation, but Nina felt it was in the offing. How could she write a suitably encouraging letter back, while being discouraging about a visit? And yet – and yet . . . She would like to see the Castle. And Kitty talked about horses, showing her round the estate on horseback. She hadn't ridden in such a long time. And to see Giles again . . .

No. There must be no seeing Giles. That was poison. Double poison – to her, and to Kitty. She must find a way of avoiding going to Ashmore Castle.

The maid, Minny, came in. 'There's a visitor, Miss Nina,' she said. Nina realised she had heard the doorbell without really taking it in. 'Mr Cowling has called.'

'Did you tell him Mrs Schofield is out?'

'Yes, miss. But he said it's you he wants to see. Wants to talk to you particular.'

'Oh, very well, then,' Nina said. 'You'd better show him in.'

Mr Cowling had on what appeared to be another new suit; he had shaved very closely that morning and there was a faint smell of eau de Cologne about him. But he seemed nervous, even agitated.

'Won't you sit down? My aunt is out, I'm afraid,' she said. He neither answered nor sat, but walked to the fireplace, and then away again. 'Is something wrong?' she asked.

Her words seemed to release him. 'No, nothing wrong.' He sat down on the chair catty-corner to her. 'I must talk to you, Miss Sanderton. Will you listen?'

'Of course I will. Has something happened?'

'Aye, but not in the way you mean. I'm not in trouble – don't think it. But I've something to ask you.' She gave him an attentive look while he assembled his thoughts. He was usually such a calm man: to see him winding his hands together was disturbing. She was about to prompt him when he resumed. 'When we talked yesterday, I mentioned to you that I often felt lonely. I missed my wife at first, but she's long enough now in her grave, God rest her, that I can put her out of my thoughts without feeling guilty. And clearing the way in my mind, as you might say, I've come to the conclusion that I would like to get married again.'

Good heavens, she thought. *So he is thinking of marrying Aunt Schofield.* She liked him too much to want to see him crushed by rejection. She must discourage him as gently as possible. 'Mr Cowling, I must say—'

He held up a hand. 'Please. You are a very kind young lady, so you'll understand that I have to say what I want to say, now I've wound myself up to it, without stopping, or I'll lose my nerve. If you'd just let me say it right out, then you can say what you like in reply.'

'Please go ahead,' she said, with an inward sigh, and folded her hands in her lap to indicate that she wouldn't interrupt again.

That seemed to unnerve him, and he was silent, staring at his hands. Finally he began: 'Miss Sanderton, when I first met you at Dene Park, I was struck by what a nice person you were, so easy to talk to, and not too proud to listen to a man of my class. Nor, being a very young lady as you are,

418

too proud to listen to a man of my age. We did talk a lot, didn't we, Miss Sanderton?'

'We did,' she agreed, baffled.

'And you seemed not to be too bored – though that might just be your politeness.'

It was clear he wanted an answer, so she said, 'I wasn't bored. I enjoyed talking to you.'

'I'm glad to hear you say that. Because I know right enough – no-one could know it better, I promise you – that I'm a lot older than you, and though I was a decent-looking chap in my youth, I've nothing to boast about now by way of looks or person. But I'm an honest man, Miss Sanderton, and a hard worker, and I have a warm heart. And I'm very well to do, if you'll pardon me mentioning it. I have as much money as any sensible man could want – though I've nothing much to spend it on. I have two houses, one in Northampton and one in Market Harborough, but cold hearths they are to me with no wife to come home to. And I've no son to pass on my fortune to. My dear wife never fell for a child, and it was a great sadness to both of us.'

'I'm sorry,' said Nina. Surely he could not hope to have a child with Aunt Schofield. Even if she were not too old – and Nina wasn't sure about that – she would certainly not want one. She had spoken on many occasions of her dislike of small babies, had often said she had never wanted children, any more than the professor had.

'So there it is,' he said, sitting back slightly. 'I've laid all out as fair as I could. I took a great fancy to you that evening at Dene, Miss Sanderton, and every time I've met you since, my feelings have grown stronger. If you could see your way clear to marrying an older man, I promise you I would love you as well as any younger man, or even more. And with all my money, I can make your life easy and your path smooth. And as to good works, well, they're nothing without money, are they? But you shall spend mine as you please,

419

for I know that you are as kind and honest a lady as I'll ever meet, so I can trust you with my fortune. And if you could be so obliging as to present me with a son, well, nothing in the world would be too much for you, or for him.'

There was no mistaking him now. 'You want to marry *me*?' she said.

He nodded, looking at her with unbearable hope. 'If it's not too much to ask. But you've listened to me so kindly – aye, you guessed what was coming, didn't you? And you didn't laugh at me, or tell me to push off, so I'm thinking, maybe you don't find me repulsive.'

'No, no, of course I don't,' she said, trying to hide her distress. *Not Aunt Schofield, idiot – you!*

'Well, I don't need to say how lovely I think you are. Far too lovely for me. But I love you, Miss Sanderton, with all my heart. I think about you all the time and – and you shouldn't think I'm going about asking any girl who might take me. It's you or no-one, I promise you that. My hand and my heart and my fortune, that's what I'm offering, fair and open, to you and you only.' He stared at her urgently. 'What do you say?'

What indeed?

'I – I can't answer all at once,' she said. 'It's come as a surprise to me. I wasn't expecting it.'

'That's your modesty, then, for I thought I'd made it plain enough how I felt. Mawes Morris gave me the hint the other day that he'd noticed. But he's a gentleman so a hint was all it was.'

Didn't see fit to hint to me, Nina thought bitterly. She liked Mr Cowling so much, and the last thing she wanted to do was to hurt him. She couldn't say 'no' right out, as she wanted to. 'Will you give me time to think about it?' she said. 'And – and I ought to ask my aunt.'

'Aye, of course,' he nodded. 'I know you're under age, and I ought to have gone to her first. But I wanted you to

420

know this is not a business proposition, which if I'd gone to her without speaking to you, you might have thought it was. But you talk to her, and tell her it wasn't disrespect for her, and I'll come and ask her formally in the proper way, just as soon as you've made up your mind.'

He stood up.

'And I'll leave you now in peace to have a think. But don't keep me waiting too long, will you?' He gave a nervous smile. 'I suppose a lover always feels like this but, like I told you, I never had much courting to do of my first wife, us growing up together in the same village. And I never felt about her the way I do about you, either. No need to ring, I'll see myself out.'

He was gone. Nina sat down again rather suddenly, found her hands shaking, didn't know whether to laugh or cry. No, not laugh – there was nothing ludicrous about him or his offer.

And as she thought about what he'd told her, she began to move away from her first instant idea of rejection. Because it was a way out for her, wasn't it? It was an answer to more than one question.

Richard had never been to a hospital before. The Middlesex, with its strange smell, hushed atmosphere, and the disagreeably large number of sick people everywhere, daunted him, and he found it difficult to maintain his usual devil-may-care attitude, even before the relaxed Dr Dangerfield. But Dangerfield had persuaded him to undergo an examination of his bones by the Röntgen method. The Middlesex Hospital had been the first to obtain one of the machines, which was installed in a small room above the out-patient department.

Dangerfield was at his most chirpy. 'Did you ever as a child hold your hand up against the sun? Remember how your fingers glowed red? That's because the flesh is partially translucent – that is, light passes through it.'

421

'I suppose so,' Richard said sulkily. He was out of his place and out of his element – both sensations he resented.

'Very good. Well, a German physicist called Röntgen discovered a special sort of extra-strong light that can be passed right through the human body – flesh, organs and all – and is only stopped by the bones.'

'Very clever. What's the point of that?'

'It means that we can see inside you, Mr Tallant, and take a photograph of your bones,' Dangerfield said happily. 'We can see if they're broken and, conversely, if they've healed. The rays are also stopped by foreign objects,' he added, as though Richard were interested, 'so, for instance, if someone is shot, we can see where the bullet is. Makes it an awful lot easier to get the thing out. I tell you, this machine is going to change medicine! We're only just beginning to work out all the applications.'

'All I care about is that you want to apply it to me,' Richard said.

'Your fractures were severe,' Dangerfield said, 'and you are an impatient patient. I want to be sure they've healed before I let you loose. The alternative,' he added casually, 'is to lock you up for a few more months to stop you using your arm and foot.'

'You don't deceive me for an instant,' Richard said. 'You're just hell-bent on using this new thing-a-ma-jig.'

Dangerfield grinned. 'I am. It's a beauty. Well – don't you want to make medical history?'

'You mean I'd be the first person to use it?' Richard asked, half excited, half appalled.

'Well, no – they've had it since 'ninety-six,' Dangerfield admitted. 'But you'd be the first of *my* patients,' he added temptingly.

The result of this disagreeable experience was that Dangerfield dismissed him as 'healed, as near as dammit'. His arm and his foot were usable now, 'though the muscles will need to be built up again'. The shoulder fracture had healed, but Richard found it stiff, and if he lifted his arm too high, or rotated it too far, it hurt. Dangerfield told him he might never have a full range of movement with it. 'However, gentle exercise will improve it to an extent. The more you use it, the better, but don't strain it. And,' he added wisely, 'I advise you not to break it again. Try to keep out of accidents, especially those involving the high impact of your body with immovable objects.'

'Such sage advice,' Richard said. 'How much am I paying you for it?'

Giles rarely came in to breakfast, eating earlier than the females of the house and getting straight to work. So Kitty had to seek him out in the library, much as she disliked disturbing him. But she found him looking more cheerful than usual, and before she could speak he said, 'Come in! Adeane has suggested it's time I went about the estate and looked at some of the things he's proposing. He was for going in the dog-cart, but I haven't been astride a horse for so long, I decided to ride. Would you like to come too?'

Her heart lifted – he wanted her company! 'Oh, yes – yes, please,' she said. 'Is there a horse for me to ride?'

'You can have Queen Bee – my mother's mare. I checked and she isn't riding today. Can you be ready in half an hour?'

'Oh, yes – but, Giles, there is something I wanted to ask you.'

'Fire away, then.'

'I ought to pay a visit to my parents. I haven't called on them since we got back. And I thought, if you agree to it, I could take the girls too. Not so much to see my parents – I shan't stay long there – but for a day in London, to give them a change of scene. We could look at the shops, and have luncheon somewhere – now I'm a married woman,' she parenthesised shyly, 'I can chaperone them, so it would be quite respectable.' He smiled at the thought of her, a chaperone. In her eagerness she looked no older than Alice. 'And they're so much confined here, I think it would do them good. What do you think?'

'You should ask—' he began.

The shine went out of her eyes. 'You're going to say I must ask your mother. And she's sure to say no.'

'I don't think so. She doesn't mind much what the girls do, as long as they're kept away from young men. But, if you like, I'll mention it to her myself today. You may go ahead and make your plans. It will be all right.'

'Oh, *thank* you!'

He gave her a quizzical look. 'Is their company such a treat for you?'

'I like them very much,' she said, not understanding his point.

He waved it away. 'I was going to suggest that while you're in London, you should call on Aunt Caroline. The girls will like to see her, and she was very helpful in bringing us together. We both owe her a debt.'

'I'll do that, gladly,' Kitty said. 'I'll go and tell the girls. And Rose – she'll have to help Daisy find them something to wear.' She paused, looking at him doubtfully. 'They ought to have a new dress each. While we were looking at the shops, do you think . . . ?'

He anticipated. 'Yes, of course, buy them whatever you want. Set up accounts at the shops and they'll send the bills here.' He didn't add, 'It's your money, after all,' but he puzzled to himself as to how she could still be so humble about spending it. And then, remembering Lady Bayfield, puzzled no more.

Nina was silent at luncheon, and after one or two attempts to start a conversation, Aunt Schofield gave it up and retreated into her own thoughts, where she was always comfortable. But when they rose from the table she said, 'You seem out of sorts, Nina. Do you feel well?'

Nina wasn't ready to talk yet. She said, 'Quite well, thank you. I've been indoors too long, that's all. If you don't need me this afternoon, I think I'll go for a walk.'

She walked down to the Embankment, and then along the river under the turning trees, watching the laden boats coming up with the tide on the grey-brown river. She walked until her feet were sore and the streetlamps started to be lit, then took an omnibus home, choosing one with strong, fresh-looking horses, a habit of hers – silly, as if adding her weight to the load could make any difference! The shops were beginning to be lit up in the dusk, which always made her think of Christmas. Christmas, in a home of her own – she had always wanted a Christmas tree, but Aunt Schofield would never have one. And she could decorate the house too, in any way she liked. It was a small, unimportant thing, but it made her realise that she had actually made up her mind. The walk had done its job.

They were dining out that evening, with academic friends of Aunt Schofield's at a house in Bedford Square, so she would have to speak to her as soon as she got home, before they went up to dress. And suddenly her mouth was dry.

'There's something I must talk to you about, Auntie.'

Aunt Schofield looked up from her letters. 'Yes, I thought there was. Is anything wrong?'

'No, not wrong.' Nina frowned. There was nothing for it but to come straight out with it. 'Mr Cowling was here this morning.'

'Yes, Haydock mentioned it. What did he want?'

'He asked me to marry him.'

Aunt Schofield was silent, absorbing the news. She would never be precipitate in her reactions. 'And what did you say?' she asked at last – though she knew it could not have been a refusal, or Nina would have said so. And so, what then?

'I said I would think about it. And that I must speak to you, of course. He said – he said that asking me before speaking to you wasn't disrespect, but to prove to me that it wasn't . . . a business transaction, I think he said. That he loves me.' She was watching her aunt's face, and there was no trace of a smile at that point, of which she was glad. She found herself more anxious all the time that he should not be ridiculed.

'Very well,' said Aunt Schofield. 'I have no need to ask if you have been thinking, because you have been out walking the soles from your shoes. So what have you concluded?'

Nina swallowed. 'I want to accept.'

Aunt Schofield put aside the letters, sat up straight and folded her hands in her lap. 'You have my full attention. Let me understand your reasoning.'

Nina met her gaze, but she said, 'Do I have to have reasoning? When a girl is asked by a man to marry him—'

'An older man, of a different class, whom I have no reason to believe she loves.'

Nina gave a shaky smile. 'You have always poured scorn on love,' she reminded her aunt.

'Not on love, on "falling in love". You are thinking that I married an older man, and that I was not "in love" with him. But I loved the professor's mind, Nina. Do you love Mr Cowling's mind?'

'He loves *my* mind – he tells me so,' she answered. Her aunt waited implacably. 'He is a kind, generous, honest man, and I believe he cares for me. He will give me a good home, an establishment. I shall never want.'

'You are marrying him for his money, then?'

Nina was stung, as Aunt Schofield had meant her to be. 'Isn't that always what marriage is about – any marriage you would approve of, at any rate? I know you wouldn't approve of two young people without means marrying just because they were "in love". A man offers a girl a home and a fortune. Except,' she remembered Kitty, 'when it's the other way round.'

Aunt Schofield nodded calmly. 'And you believe that this is your best chance of happiness? You are very young, and you have met very few people. This is an irrevocable step to take so soon.'

Nina's eyes narrowed. 'If I said I was in love with him, would you think differently?' Aunt Schofield didn't answer. 'Is it just his age you object to?'

'I haven't said I objected. I wish to understand your train of reasoning, to be sure you have thought fully about the implications. Mr Cowling is not so very old. You may have twenty or thirty years of marriage with him. Have you considered what that means?'

'I have considered that I must do something, and that I really don't want to be a teacher.' There, the secret was out. She felt shaky, and gripped her hands tightly together. 'I'm sorry, but I've realised I have no vocation for it. And teaching or marriage, those are my choices, aren't they? Because I know I'm putting a strain on your household. I've seen you worrying over your accounts. My Season cost you a great deal. And however frugal I might be in the future, you can't afford to keep me here.'

Aunt Schofield looked uncomfortable. 'You were not supposed to worry about my financial position. At all events, you must not think that I would ever begrudge you a home with me. Better we both live frugally than that you rush into an unwise marriage.'

'But better that we both live comfortably than that I hang round your neck and force you into miserable penny-pinching,' Nina said. She felt quite calm now. Her aunt's words had made up what little was left of her mind to convince. 'I don't think it's an unwise marriage. I think he would be very good to me, and I would be very comfortable. And just think of the good I could do! He is *very* rich, Auntie, and he says I can spend whatever I like on charitable works.'

Aunt Schofield nodded. 'These are all good points. And I find it encouraging that you are defending him so stoutly. That means you do care for him. But there is no need to decide in a hurry. Take a few weeks, or months. If he really wants you, he will wait.'

'There *is* need,' said Nina. 'If I'm not to take up the post at Allely's, I must tell them soon.'

Her aunt was silent a moment. 'Is that what's behind it? Do you hate the idea of teaching so very much?'

'It's not that. If I had to, I would teach. But don't you see? I *don't* have to. I can be a rich man's wife, and a great patroness. In a fashionable girls' school, my mind would dwindle – *I* would dwindle. I don't want a small life, Auntie,' she concluded passionately. 'I don't want that.'

Aunt Schofield was silent, thinking. Finally she said, 'Very well, Nina. You are an intelligent girl, and have the right to choose your own path in life. Will you wait one more day? Sleep on it, and speak to me again tomorrow. And please believe, you will never be homeless. I am not casting you out, and never will.'

Nina smiled affectionately. 'I know. You've always been so good to me.'

Rachel and Alice had a superb day. Going up to Town with Kitty was so different from going with Mama. Everything was fun, even the train journey. Kitty did not require them to sit still and be silent – they could jump up and down and stare out of the windows and cry, 'Oh, look!' as much as they liked.

There was the visit to Kitty's parents in Hampstead, but that was interesting. They always liked seeing inside other people's houses, even if, like the Bayfields', it was dark and gloomy and smelt a bit mushroomy. Lady Bayfield was obviously a Tartar, but they were inured to the breed after their mother, and Sir John seemed very nice, smiled at them and called them pretty, asked in a pleasant way what they would be doing in London, and then – what they always liked best in grown-ups – excused himself and left them alone. And while they were there, coffee was brought in, and the most delicious little cakes and biscuits – they had nothing like them at home. The visit did not last long: Kitty, they noticed, did not seem to be enjoying it very much, and seemed to perk up as soon as they left.

They had luncheon not in some dull, terribly proper place, but in Gunter's, where Kitty let them have poached eggs on toast followed by wonderful ices. When they stepped out again, Alice groaned and said, 'I'm having such a lovely time! I'm not sure if I can bear any more wonderfulness.'

And Kitty laughed and said, 'But we're going shopping!'

'Oh dear,' Rachel said. 'I'm like Alice. I think I shall burst.'

They survived it, even though looking at shops was their favourite activity – they even liked looking at the ones in Canons Ashmore, where they knew everything in the windows by heart. London shops were bliss, on such a different scale it was like a banquet compared to nursery tea. Kitty took them to Kensington, which was a place they had heard Mama speak about with scorn, but there were two enormous stores right next door to each other – Barker's and Derry & Tom's – with ladies' clothing departments offering a range of dresses such as they had never dreamed of. Usually when they had something new to wear, Mama chose it from a pattern and it was made by her dressmaker. Kitty let them choose for themselves, and they could actually try things on and, best of all, buy them at once instead of having to wait for them to be made and sent home. They begged her to let them carry the things away right there and then, and she saw the point at once. The only drawback was that, with all the parcels, they had to take a cab rather than go on the omnibus, which they'd been longing to do.

And so, then, to Berkeley Square and Aunt Caroline's. Aunt Caroline was always nice to be with, and Richard was there, and Grandmère, so it was like a delightful party. Sir Thomas called in, and he spoke to them rather pompously and asked whether they practised every day, which was bad, and demanded Rachel play the piano for them, which was worse, but he very quickly stopped her and said that was enough, and soon afterwards took his departure. He gave them each half a crown as he left, which mortified Rachel because it meant he thought she was only a child, but Alice pinched her hard and thanked him gushingly for them both. Half a crown was half a crown, after all, and a fortune to someone who didn't often have money to spend.

And then tea. Aunt Caroline always did excellent teas, and their light luncheon was nothing but a distant memory. There were muffins and strawberry jam, and cress sandwiches, and Gentleman's Relish sandwiches because they were Richard's favourite and which the girls adored but never had at home, and macaroons, and not just Madeira cake, which one would expect, but actual chocolate cake. What a day!

'How did your first visit home as Lady Stainton go?' Richard asked, patting the seat beside him, as Kitty brought him his tea.

Kitty frowned. 'It was rather odd,' she said. 'Papa seemed almost shy with me. He talked in a sort of hearty way as though I was a stranger, and dashed away as soon as he could.'

'Well, you're not his timid little girl any more. You're a grown woman,' Richard said. 'I expect you did seem like a stranger. But your mama was pleased to see you, I expect.'

'It's hard to tell. She talked a lot about the wedding. She asked me about the places we visited on the honeymoon, but she didn't listen to the answers. She seemed more interested in telling me about all the parties *they*'d been to. They seem to have been having a gay time since I got married,' she added, a little wistfully.

'I expect your mama enjoys telling all her friends about her daughter, the countess,' said Richard, who had a fair idea of what made Lady Bayfield tick. 'So you've given her great pleasure.'

'I suppose you're right,' Kitty said, but with a sigh. She was silent a moment, then said, 'I mentioned something about Christmas, hoping they'd come to the Castle, but she didn't seem happy about that. She said they'd have to see – that they already had lots of invitations for the Christmas season.'

'Now look here,' Richard said, 'do you miss your parents dreadfully?'

'Well – no,' Kitty admitted, ashamed. 'Am I horrible? I've hardly thought about them. When I lived at home, I didn't see much of them. It was only during my come-out that we spent much time together. I'm an unnatural daughter, aren't I?'

'Not at all,' Richard said easily. 'Believe me, not caring much for your parents is more the rule than the exception. Aunt Caroline is much more of a mother to me than Mama – and Grandmère even more so. And all I really remember of Papa is him thrashing me and telling me it would make me a better man.'

'Oh *dear!*' Kitty cried in sympathy.

Richard leaned close, as if basking in her warmth. 'I must say, if I ever have a son, I shan't ever beat him. I shall let him turn out as bad as he wants. I wouldn't beat a dog the way Papa beat me – and I was his favourite. God knows how Giles survived. It's no wonder he's a bit strange.'

Kitty began to protest, then looked at him cannily. 'I think you're roasting me, aren't you?'

431

'Just a bit. But when you have a son, do remember my words and persuade Giles to spare the rod. I can imagine him turning into a stern disciplinarian.'

Kitty blushed at the thought of having a son with Giles, then smiled at the remembrance of their night together. Richard observed both reactions, and said, 'You've grown up. You're not the frightened little mouse I used to see around Town in the Season.'

'But that's better, isn't it?' Kitty asked.

'Oh, certainly. Speaking of your Season, have you seen much of Miss Sanderton?'

'I haven't since we got back. But I do miss her. I'd have liked to see her today, but there wasn't time with everything else, and I wanted to take the girls shopping – they really did need new clothes. I must make a separate trip for Nina – we'll have so much to talk about.'

'I think you'll find her changed, too,' said Richard, wondering if the friendship would survive such upheavals.

'I suppose it has to happen. People do change,' said Kitty wistfully.

'Except me. I stay resolutely the same in all circumstances.'

Grandmère, as Richard called her, beckoned Kitty over, and required her to sit beside her. Kitty had been admiring her *toilette* across the room: she was so elegant, the colours so suited to her complexion, the jewels fine without being overpowering. Kitty wished she could ask her to teach her how to dress. She had always thought she was part of one homogenous social class – wealthy people who brought their daughters out in style – but she was learning that there were strata within that class, and not only did Lady Stainton think Lady Bayfield was from a different stratum, she actually *was*. It made Kitty feel she had married Giles on false pretences, and that she would never really be a countess.

Grandmère smelt of face powder and verbena scent, which

432

was nice. 'How are you settling in at the Castle?' she asked. Kitty hesitated just long enough for Grandmère to give her a shrewd look and say, 'It was always bound to be difficult. Such adjustments take time. And your mother-in-law is a difficult woman.'

Kitty demurred. 'Oh, no, I'm sure . . .'

Grandmère laid a wrinkled but elegant hand over hers. 'You wish to be nice to everyone. *Bien*, that is a virtue that cannot be taught. But there comes a time when it ceases to serve. There cannot be two mistresses in one house.'

'But I never thought—'

'That you would be mistress? But you should, and you must. Attend: the great houses always build a dower house, for the exile of the dowager when the new countess comes. Otherwise life would become *un cafouillage*. Intolerable. But Maud, your mother-in-law, does not like the dower house. I did not like it either, and preferred to live in Town. Maud does not like Town. So she lingers.'

Kitty shrank. 'I couldn't ask her to go.'

'Of course not.'

'And I don't know how to run the house, anyway.'

'*Entendu.*'

'Then what must I do?' Kitty asked helplessly.

'Invite me to stay,' said Grandmère. 'I make the offer at great cost to myself because I do not like to live in the country. But I will come for a few weeks, teach you what to do. How to dress,' she added, with a comprehensive glance at Kitty's appearance. 'And make sure that Maud does not trample you, like a great rampaging elephant.'

'But she's not *fat*,' Kitty protested, slightly shocked.

'Elephants are not fat. Merely one cannot ignore them. Maud will not acknowledge the fact that she is now the dowager until someone makes her, and that cannot be you, *ça se voit.*'

'May I ask a question? If she is the dowager, what are you?'

'I am dowager too. You may think of me as the double-dowager.' Kitty laughed. 'Usually there are not two, because countesses have many children and are so worn out with child-bearing they die young. I had only the one, so I shall live to a ripe old age. You must do better than me, but do not have as many as Maud.' She sighed. 'Poor thing, one must pity her. She has not had an easy life.' She gave Kitty a frank look. 'I shall tell you her story one day, and you shall pity her, too, but not yet. For now, you must have no pity, or she will crush you. So?' She raised her eyebrows at Kitty.

'Yes, ma'am – your ladyship?' Kitty was confused.

'Invite me to stay,' she said impatiently. 'And you may call me Grandmère.'

'Would you please come and stay at the Castle – Grandmère?' Kitty said dutifully.

'I shall think about it,' said Grandmère. 'I do not like the country very much, and I have a great many engagements.'

At that moment Richard joined them. 'I can see you are looking thoroughly bewildered, Kitty. Is my wicked grand-mother winding you in her toils?'

'I asked her if she would come and stay at the Castle,' Kitty said doubtfully. 'I'm not sure if she said yes.'

Richard saw his grandmother's teasing smile, and leaned down to kiss her cheek. 'Cruel creature! Tormenting little kittens. Remember our Pusscat doesn't understand your ways yet.'

Grandmère was intrigued by 'Pusscat'. '*Tu sens quelque chose,*' she said, looking from Richard to Kitty.

'*Bien sûr,*' Richard shrugged. '*Pourquoi non? Elle est vertueuse et agréable.*'

'Hmm,' said Grandmère.

'Her ladyship enjoyed herself so much this morning,' Giles said. 'She ought to have the opportunity of riding whenever she likes. What is there that will carry sidesaddle?'

434

Archer and Giddins looked at each other. 'Did Bee not go well for her, my lord?' Archer asked.

'Yes, her ladyship managed her nicely, but my mother likes to ride most days. What else is there?'

'Well, my lord, nothing really,' said Giddins. 'Kestrel *has* carried sidesaddle in the past, but his paces are poor. And he's got a hard mouth. I wouldn't like to trust her ladyship to him – she might not be able to hold him.'

'Then we must buy something for her,' Giles said. 'You must look around for me. I'm too busy to do it myself right now. Try to find something as soon as possible.' He was turning away, and turned back to say, 'Why are we keeping Kestrel, if he's hard-mouthed and poor-paced?'

'His late lordship liked him for hacking, my lord,' said Archer. 'They got on together, as you might say.'

'You'd better sell him, then. I shan't ride him.'

'Very good, my lord. Er – will you be hunting this winter, my lord?' Archer asked. 'Because we did ought to look into getting a couple of hunters for you, if you are, you having sold his late lordship's youngsters.'

'I suppose time is getting on,' Giles sighed. 'Put the word out for me, will you?'

Both men brightened. 'Nothing easier, my lord,' said Giddins. 'In fact, I heard that Lord Shacklock had some nice hunters he was selling. I could drive over first and try them out, and if they seem suitable, you could have a look at them after, when it was convenient.'

'If they're nice, why is he selling them?' Giles asked suspiciously.

The men exchanged a glance, and Giddins answered reluctantly. 'His younger son's mounts, my lord. Mr Crispian had a bad fall, racing across country in the summer. Killed hisself.'

'Ah,' said Giles. They obviously thought it was a sore point.

* * *

435

Nina went in to breakfast, to find her aunt absent. 'She went out early, miss,' said Haydock. 'She said she wouldn't be long, but for you not to wait.'

Nina took her lone breakfast in silence. She had had a restless night, but her thoughts were tranquil now. She had gone over and over the arguments in her head, and was satisfied that she had come to the right decision. She was lingering over her second cup when Aunt Schofield came back. She heard her in the hall, talking to Haydock as he took her coat and hat; and then she came in, with a parcel under her arm. Unusually, she closed the morning-room door behind her.

'I have something to show you, Nina,' she said, and there was tension in her face, as though she had had to come to a difficult decision. 'Clear a space at the end of the table.'

Nina obeyed, and Aunt Schofield put down the parcel, unwrapped it, and removed a large book. 'I have gone to some trouble to borrow this,' she said, 'because women are forbidden to look at it. I had to ask Mr Carnoustie, who obliged his friend Professor McLaren at the Royal Free to do him a favour. He lectures in anatomy.'

'Anatomy?' Nina said, surprised.

'Yes, child. There are things that I'm afraid most girls go into marriage in ignorance of, but I will not have that happen to you. Whether you marry Mr Cowling or someone else, you shall understand what is involved. Come and stand beside me.'

Nina went, feeling very awkward. She saw there were bookmarks at various points in the large, cloth-bound tome. *Anatomy. That means bodies. Am I going to be embarrassed?*

'To begin,' said Aunt Schofield, and opened the book at a drawing of a naked woman, but with the inside parts drawn in. 'You have a tube in your body, which allows excess liquid to pass out – here.'

'Yes,' said Nina. It *was* embarrassing – but interesting.

436

'You may or may not know, that in the male of the species, this tube is extended beyond the body, in a sort of pipe.'

Ah, thought Nina. 'In India, when I was a child, I sometimes saw the gardeners – um – relieving themselves in the bushes. They had—'

'Very well. This male pipe is properly called the penis. And it contains not only the tube for excess water, but another tube that connects with the part of their body that makes the seeds of life. Just as you have, inside your body, another tube, or passage *here*—' She showed Nina on the drawing '—connecting with the womb, which is the place that new life grows.'

'I've heard of the womb,' Nina said. 'And I know babies grow in there. But I didn't know – I wasn't sure . . .'

'Of course not. Girls are not *meant* to know. The very idea of discussing it out loud as we are now doing is shocking, and the main reason men have always resisted the idea of women becoming doctors. Fortunately, I married a most enlightened man, who borrowed a book very similar to this one in order that I should understand that most important process for the continuation of life. So I, in my turn, am enlightening you.'

'Thank you,' Nina said hesitantly. She didn't feel very grateful.

'Very well,' said Aunt Schofield. 'To continue. When a man and woman are married, at time of passion, the male pipe, or penis, becomes rigid, enabling it to be introduced into the female passage, to pass the seed into her. The seed thus travels up into the womb and implants itself.'

'Oh,' said Nina. Her cheeks felt very hot but her stomach felt cold.

Aunt Schofield went on relentlessly. 'In good time, when the baby is ready to be born, it passes out of the female body through the same passage, which is extremely flexible and can expand sufficiently to allow the infant to pass. Do you understand?'

437

'Yes,' said Nina. 'I think so.' She supposed it was better to know than not to know, but it was a lot suddenly to digest.

'I mean, do you understand why I am telling you this?' Aunt Schofield insisted.

Nina looked at her, then quickly away. 'Oh,' she said. *Now* she understood.

'If you marry Mr Cowling, you will go through this process with him. He will expect it, and it will be your duty to co-operate. Men differ from each other, but in general they get great pleasure from the process, which makes them eager to do it often, sometimes every night.'

'I see,' said Nina.

Aunt Schofield closed the book. 'It is something for you to think about, before you make your decision.' She began to turn away, then turned back. 'Is there anything you want to ask me?' she said, in a kinder voice.

'Yes,' said Nina, but she didn't know how to phrase it. She rehearsed it in her head, but it was still hard to say. 'Did you—?' No, that was not the way. She cleared her throat. 'What I mean is – you say it is pleasant for the man. But is it not for the woman? When you were married, was it hard for you to – to bear it?'

Aunt Schofield paused for so long, Nina thought she wasn't going to answer. 'It was not *un*pleasant. Not hard to bear. I'd say it was a tiresome necessity, on the whole. But sometimes . . .' Another pause. 'Sometimes there was a feeling of – of warmth and comfort. And one likes to please one's husband, if one cares about him.' She turned firmly away. 'That is all I have to say. Think about what I've told you.' And she left the room, taking the book with her. Nina realised now why she had shut the morning-room door – so that Minny should not come in and see it by accident.

CHAPTER TWENTY-THREE

Richard was let in by the housekeeper, and ran up the stairs two at a time, hearing the thumping sounds of a piano lesson from above. He tapped on the door to be polite, but opened it at once. A small boy was sitting at the piano, feet dangling above the pedals, watching his hands with intense concentration as if they might come loose from his wrists and prance away without him. Mrs Sands, who was beating time with a baton on her palm, looked up. The boy glanced up too, his hands fell over themselves, and the music stopped.

'Do I intrude?' Richard said gaily. He held up a paper bag. 'I've brought sacrifices to appease the gods.'

'I'm teaching,' Mrs Sands said. 'I'm always pleased to see you, but I can't have you interrupting my lessons. I have a living to earn.'

'I'm sorry,' Richard said meekly. 'I'll sit quietly in the corner until you're finished.'

'You'll do no such thing. I wouldn't be able to concentrate with your eyes boring into my back. You must go away and come back later.'

At least she'd said he should come back. He pressed his advantage. 'At what time?'

'Twelve,' she said.

'And then I'll take you to lunch.'

'I have another lesson at a quarter to one.'

'Then lunch shall come to you. I'll leave these, for now,'

he said, and put down the bag on the table. 'In case you have time between pupils.' He winked at the rather startled boy, and withdrew before she could say something severe.

At twelve, he passed a different pupil on the stairs, a twig of a boy with a long neck, whose sleeves and trouser legs were too short, as if he had grown rapidly in the past hour.

The first bag he had brought was still on the table, he noticed. He put down a second one. Mrs Sands paused from sorting out music. 'Hot pies. Fetch plates,' he commanded her. 'And glasses. I brought a bottle.'

'I can't drink wine, foolish boy,' she said. 'What would my pupils think?'

'How would they know what wine smelt like on the breath?'

'My next pupil is a girl and her mother brings her,' said Mrs Sands.

'Well, the bottle isn't wine, anyway. It's ginger beer. Do you think I don't know how you work by now? Ginger beer, so we can pretend it's champagne.'

'You are a most *in*sistent, *per*sistent person,' said Mrs Sands. 'You bother me like a fly at a picnic.'

'Since I brought the picnic, that's most ungenerous,' he said. She had fetched the plates from the chimney cupboard, and he was laying things out. 'But I forgive you. What would you have been eating if I hadn't?'

'I think there's some bread and cheese,' she said vaguely. 'I don't bother much with luncheon when Chloë isn't here.'

'Just as I thought! You neglect yourself. It won't do, you know.'

'Hm, those pies smell good.'

'From the stall on the corner of Green Park.' He saw how hungrily she ate. Things were a struggle, he guessed. Chloë was getting her tuition free, but there would still be incidental expenses – clothes and music, and food for Chloë while she was out during the day. And there was nothing he could do about it. He had nothing himself.

He amused her with light chatter while she ate the pie, and then he produced the earlier bag. 'Custard tarts,' he said. 'I know you like them.'

'Pastry and pastry,' she said. 'What a shocking diet.'

'You should have let me take you out.' He could charge at most restaurants.

She cocked her head. 'Why do you bother with me?' she asked. 'I thought—'

'You thought? Yes, I tried that once. Didn't take to it at all.'

She laughed. 'You like to pretend you are careless and frivolous, but I know you are a good, kind person.'

'You don't know the half of it! I'm not at all good, and rarely kind. It's just that you bring out the best in me.'

'I thought,' she went on, with a sort of determination, 'that you came here for Chloë's sake. In the beginning, you seemed struck with her. And she *is* very beautiful – though I'm her mother, I can say that, because her beauty is of a special order.'

'She is one of the most beautiful girls I've ever seen.'

'And she has extraordinary talent.'

'She has. I admire her extremely. And I'm so glad she is at the Royal College every day, so that I can have you to myself.'

Her cheeks reddened, and she looked away. 'You mustn't say things like that, Richard,' she said quietly.

'*Mustn't* I – Molly?' he replied.

'Don't joke,' she said. 'I've thought sometimes – you've been so kind – it's ridiculous, I know – but I've thought—'

'That it's you I come here for, not your pretty daughter? Yes, that's pretty ridiculous, isn't it? But it does happen to be true.'

She put her hands to her face. 'Don't!' she cried.

'Why not?' he said. 'Chloë is sweet, but she's a child, and I'm long past childhood. Naïve innocent girls don't appeal to me, haven't appealed to me since before I went away to Africa. I'm long past sops and cocoa, Molly Sands. I want a woman of intellect and character, a woman who can talk to me on my own level, a woman,' he slipped from his chair to his knees before her, capturing her hands, 'who shakes all my senses to their foundation.' She tried to pull her hands away. 'No, no, you invited me into your parlour, remember? I'm tangled in your web. You are the spider in this case, and I am the helpless fly.' He lifted her hands and kissed them.

With a determined jerk, she pulled them free. In a harsh voice, she said, 'Richard, get up! At once!'

It was the sort of voice that was obeyed. He resumed his seat, looking at her with a raised eyebrow, not yet upset, not yet accepting rejection. Her cheeks were hot. 'That colour suits you,' he said conversationally. 'You should wear it more often.'

'Richard,' she said desperately, 'you must stop this.'

'Don't you like it?'

'Don't you understand? I was your father's mistress. I slept with your father. Your *father!*'

He hadn't thought of it quite like that, and for a moment he was taken aback. She saw the thought permeating his mind as clearly as if it had been water trickling down a glass. And then, shockingly, he grinned. 'Oh well,' he said. 'what's that jolly song Vesta Tilley sings? "Following In Father's Footsteps"?'

'*Richard!*'

'Dear, darling Molly, don't fret. What does it matter? It isn't a case of incest. We aren't related by blood. You slept with my father, but you're not my mother, for God's sake! If I don't care, why should you? Don't you fancy me? I thought you did. Did I get it completely wrong? I'm not usually so insensitive, but if I've mistaken your feelings, I'll apologise and clear out.'

'I—' she began, and stopped. Her eyes moved away.

'Ha! Thought so,' he said triumphantly.

'I think you should go now,' she said quietly.

He looked at her for a moment, and then got up. 'All right,' he said, quietly too. 'But you haven't got rid of me. I came to tell you that I'm going down to Ashmore for a few weeks. My brother has summoned me – I suppose he wants to find out what I'm going to do to pay for my keep. I came to take my leave, and to tell you that I shall miss you. But I shall be back. And in the mean time, if there's anything you need, anything at all, send me word, and I'll come hurrying to your side as fast as the train will carry me.'

'You're very good,' she said, in a subdued voice. 'But we'll be all right.' She got to her feet, and went to the door to show him out.

When he reached it, he put his hand over hers on the doorknob to stop her opening it. She looked up at him. Their faces were very close. Their eyes met, and a message passed without volition between them. He closed his eyes – his eyelashes were very thick and very dark, she noticed – and he laid his lips softly against hers. They were warm and firm, like the touch of a sun-ripened fruit. It was a feather of a kiss, and lasted only an instant, and then he tipped his hat and was gone.

She put her fingers to her lips in dismay, and thought, *My God, what next?*

Footsteps up the stairs, that's what – her next pupil and her mother.

Alice rode into the yard, and saw Axe's cottage door open, though he was not in sight. Dolly barked and came running out but, seeing her, sat down in the middle of the yard, waiting for her, eyes bright and stubby tail beating the dust. Alice halted Pharaoh and jumped down, expecting Axe to come out. But perhaps he was at the back, or even out in

443

the woods. He wouldn't mind leaving his door open out here – there was no-one to bother him.

She and Rachel had started out for a ride together, but once they were away from the house, Rachel had told her she was going to meet Victor Lattery. 'You can come too,' she said. But it was plain she didn't mean it – and Alice had no wish to sit and listen to their silly talk. 'I'll come back for you,' she said. If they arrived at home separately, questions might be asked.

So, naturally, she thought of riding over to see if Axe was about. She half thought he wouldn't be, so the open door was a pleasant surprise.

'It's me,' she called, leading Pharaoh over to the ring. He knew the pattern by now, and was nosing about on the ground for spare wisps of hay as she tied the rope round his neck.

As she reached the cottage door, Axe appeared at last, but he seemed put out. His cheeks were very red, and his hair was ruffled, as though he had run his hands through it backwards.

'I was just passing, so I thought I'd stop by and see you,' she said, and heard a sound from inside the cottage, a suppressed cough. 'Oh, have you got visitors?' she said.

'Just one,' he admitted. He wasn't moving to let her in, and she was a bit puzzled.

'Oh,' she said. 'Well, that's nice for you. Is it one of your family?' He had a large selection of brothers and sisters. 'I'd love to meet them.'

'No, it's not—' he began.

Someone inside moved, hurried across the cottage behind Axe's back in what was almost a furtive scuttle. She only caught a glimpse, but she couldn't mistake him. 'Is that Mr Crooks?' she said in surprise. 'I didn't know you knew him.'

Axe looked away, and then back, his gaze direct, though

444

his cheeks were flushed. 'He's helping me to read,' he said. 'He gives me lessons.'

'But I'd have done that,' Alice said, disappointed. 'I brought you books, didn't I?'

Axe shuffled his feet. 'He offered first,' he muttered. 'You're both very kind.'

Alice realised he was embarrassed by the situation, and that it was up to her to end it. 'Never mind,' she said. 'I've got to go. Can't leave Pharaoh standing – he'll get chilled.'

She turned away. Axe started forward. 'I'll help you up,' he said awkwardly.

'No need,' she said stiffly. She felt a little hurt.

But she couldn't get up on her own, and the alternative was leading Pharaoh away until she found a gate or tree stump. So she let him throw her up, and he stood holding the rein lightly, looking up at her with a frown of thought. When she gathered the rein, he let go, but said, 'I like your visits. Mr Crooks – well, he's kind. He's helping me. But . . . I like your visits,' he finished helplessly.

She couldn't think of anything to say. She turned Pharaoh and rode away.

A message sent to Brown's Hotel, where Mr Cowling liked to stay when he was in London, brought him to Draycott Place, looking very nervous and subdued. Haydock admitted him, with a face as carefully wiped of expression as was possible in a butler, giving him no inkling of what his reception would be. He was shown into the drawing-room, but had to wait only a few minutes – not even long enough to open the thoughtfully placed newspaper – before the door opened and Nina came in. She was in a grey-blue dress that he thought suited her colouring perfectly and made her eyes look darker, and he wondered, not for the first time, at her beauty, and why the young men of London were so blind to it they let her get away. He looked automatically at her shoes, and saw with approval they were Cowling & Kempson heeled kid lace-up ankle shoes, smart and practical.

He got his word in first. 'I know you are a kind person, Miss Sanderton, so don't keep me on tenterhooks. Tell me right away if it's "no".'

'It isn't "no",' she said.

He had been so expecting a rejection that he didn't take it in for a second, and then an incredulous smile spread across his face. 'Are you saying – you will marry me?'

She couldn't help smiling too. 'Yes, I will marry you. And thank you for asking me.'

'Oh, no, no! Thank *you*! You've made me the happiest man in the world.' He stepped forward and took both her hands, and she had to let him. His were hard, the hands of a working man, but dry and smooth. She was glad they were not damp and clammy, like those of some young men she had danced with during the Season. Hard, dry hands that she would be living with for the rest of her life. For a moment she misgave, and swallowed – but she had made her decision carefully, and, no, she didn't repent of it. It was still the rational thing to do, and the course that promised her the best chance of happiness.

'I will do everything in my power to make you happy, I promise you,' he said. 'Anything you want, you just say the word. I mean it. Oh, I don't know what I've done to deserve you!' He was beaming at her, holding her at arms' length. Then he said, 'Can I – may I – kiss you?'

She nodded. He drew her to him by the hands, dipped his face, and kissed her on the lips – a dry, firm kiss, brief, unfrightening. His breath smelt of peppermints. When it was done, he stepped back and beamed at her again, and said, 'I had better go and talk to your aunt, hadn't I? Do it all fair and square.'

'She's coming here to speak to you,' Nina said.

'Oh, right, then. And when do you want to tie the knot?'

he asked. 'I should warn you,' he added, with a smile, 'I'm not in favour of long engagements.'

'Nor I,' she said. Now she had committed herself, she wanted to get it done. 'I think we should get married quite soon – before Christmas.'

'Aye, I should like to have Christmas with you. Mind you,' a thought seemed to occur to him, 'I don't know what you'll think about the house. I have a housekeeper, Mrs Mitchell, she keeps it clean and aired, and it's comfortable enough in a simple way, but I wouldn't call it smart or fashionable. But once we're there, you can say what you want – new wallpaper, new furniture, anything you like. Decius shall put it all in hand. He'll get good people on the job. An invaluable young man, Decius Blake. You should meet him as soon as possible. You'll like him.'

Mawes greeted Nina was a smacking kiss on the cheek. 'Congratulations!'

'You know already?' said Nina.

'Cowling was here this morning – couldn't wait to tell his good news. He was as happy as a sandboy. Speaking of which, I'd like you in the studio when you've had your chat with the girls – just half an hour, to be a lady sculptor, if you wouldn't mind.' He grinned. 'These female suffragists are going to be jam for me, I can tell you – top-class strawberry! So many glorious situations!'

'Probably not glorious to them,' Nina said, 'being bundled away by policemen.'

'No, but there's something irresistibly comic about a beefy, red-faced policeman having his helmet knocked askew by a little old lady in a bonnet. You must admit!'

'You're incorrigible,' Nina said, and went on into the parlour.

Isabel was grave. 'I suppose I must congratulate you.'

'You don't approve? I thought you liked him.'

'I like him very much. But you're so young, Nina dear. I

447

can't help fearing it's too hasty, and that you'll regret it in a year or two.'

'Lots of girls get married at seventeen.'

'Yes, they fall in love—'

'And love never lasts. I've heard *that* so often from my aunt. Well, my head isn't turned, my senses aren't aflame, and my eyes aren't dazzled, so surely I've a better chance of being happy than most.'

Isabel pressed her hand. 'I shan't say another word. I do wish you every happiness, and if there's anything friendship can do to advance it, it shall be done.'

'There is – come to my wedding, and dance with a light heart,' said Nina. 'Oh, and do you think Mawes would give me away? Because I'm awfully short of male relatives.'

Nina and Lepida walked off together to get the omnibus, on their way to University College where they hoped to receive a donation of books from the librarian. The Free Library had already secured the services of a book-binder, who would repair for a nominal fee damaged books that had been donated.

They walked in silence, but at the omnibus-stop, Nina turned to her companion and said, 'Isn't there anything you want to say to me? Not even "why"?'

Lepida scanned her face. 'No. I understand why. I think Mama doesn't realise that your aunt is – well, not able to keep supporting you. You don't want to be a burden on her.'

'But you think I should have been a teacher?'

'No,' Lepida said. 'I never really believed in that. You're the marrying sort, whether you ever thought it or not. You wouldn't be happy with the spinsterish life of a school. And, truthfully, if someone like Mr Cowling came along for me, I'd do what you're doing.'

'I thought you were happy at home.'

'Oh, I am. Mother and Daddy are hardly like parents, most of the time. We're more like friends. All the same, there are times when I would love my own house, my own establishment. And the freedom. Married women can do things single women can't. You'll find out. No, I don't blame you at all. And you're sensible enough to make things work in your favour. I'm sure you'll be happy. Just—'

'Just?'

'Don't forget your old friends,' Lepida said.

Nina smiled. 'You'll be the first to be invited to stay when I'm Mrs Cowling.'

'Everything in the house will be covered with dust,' Mrs Webster complained.

'Well, you won't have to clean it up,' said Rose.

'I'm *responsible* for the cleaning,' Mrs Webster said shortly. 'And the noise of hammering!'

News had reached them that her young ladyship wanted a connecting door between White Chinese and the dressing-room, and old Lady Stainton had managed somehow to get her ladyship to agree to it.

'Then it'll be sawing. And the smell of paint,' Mrs Webster went on bitterly.

'I'm sure it will all be worth while when it's finished,' said Moss emolliently. 'Wouldn't you say so, Mr Crooks? You were always a great advocate of the dressing-room.'

'Why are you asking him?' said James. '*He*'s not his lordship's valet.'

Crooks ignored him. 'A dressing-room is essential for fashionable living, but her ladyship ought to have one of her own. In a truly elegant suite, her ladyship's dressing-room and closet would be on the other side of her room from his lordship's.'

'I think it's a shame, all this knocking about of good rooms,' Rose said. 'Pulling the house to pieces. Then, as

449

like as not, a few years down the line they'll be wanting to put it all back the way it was.'

Moss turned graciously to the newcomer at the table, the lady's maid who had been brought in to take care of the young countess. 'What do you think, Miss Hatto? Is a dressing-room essential for an elegant lady?'

Miss Hatto was a youngish woman, neat as a pin, pleasant in face and manner, although she hardly ever spoke. But where Miss Taylor's silences were taciturn in origin, Miss Hatto's seemed to stem from a curious kind of completeness. Mrs Webster found her intriguing. You couldn't imagine her ever making a noise, or gossiping, or laughing at a joke, but she did not come across as prudish. It was as if Miss Hatto said the last word there was to say about Hatto-ness, and that was that. William, whose fixation on Milly had been waning, had already transferred his mute, doglike devotion to her.

'It is a great convenience,' she said now. 'Though historic houses should be respected.'

Rose rolled her eyes at Mrs Webster, who returned a minute shrug. In her view, the fewer people who were contentious, the easier it made her job.

Moss had picked up the word 'historic'. Are you interested in history, Miss Hatto? I have a wonderful book called *The A to Z of Universal Knowledge*, a great instrument for expanding the mind. I learn something new every day. It has many entries on history. I'm reading about the history of India at the moment.'

'You've been reading about India since last Christmas,' Mrs Webster muttered.

Moss didn't hear. 'The Indian Mutiny, for instance, most interesting. The Indian soldiers, who were called Sepias in their own language—'

'Sepoys,' Mrs Webster corrected irritably.

'—objected to biting their rifle cartridges because they were greased with pork fat—'

450

'Cow fat! Have you never heard the expression "sacred cow", Mr Moss? Where do you think it came from?'

Grandmère's maid Simone, who had been moved a place down the table by Miss Hatto, whose mistress outranked her own, lifted her hands in a very French gesture of exasperation. 'This is a madhouse! It is true, all English are mad. Thank God my lady is going back to Town tomorrow.'

'I'd be happy to let you look at my book some time, Miss Hatto,' Moss rumbled on, undeflectable. 'There is an interesting piece on architecture, as you seem interested in that subject. Of course, I have progressed far beyond the As myself.'

'You are learning alphabetically?' Miss Hatto asked. Mrs Webster's interest quickened. Was there a hint of satire in the question?

'The information is arranged alphabetically,' Moss explained kindly. 'That is why it is called *The A to Z of Universal Knowledge*.'

Giles was surprised to see his grandmother in the stable-yard. He hurried towards her, fearing for her shoes, pale grey glacé kid. 'What are you doing here? You'll get yourself dirty!'

She waved him back, concentrating on the ground. 'Do not fuss. Do you think I have never seen a stable before?' One of the grooms rushed forward with an empty sack to spread, Raleigh-like, before her feet. She gave him a smile that he remembered for the rest of his life and stepped upon it. 'I have come to see the new horse, Giles. You may bring it closer. A gelding, I see. Good. I do not agree with that nonsense that women must always ride mares. Geldings are more reliable, less temperamental. I always had geldings.'

'I don't think I ever knew you to ride, Grandmère,' Giles said.

'You have only known me in London, where one cannot ride,' she said, as if it was obvious. 'But I was the lady of Ashmore Castle once. Was I not, Giddins? He was a very young stable boy when my poor Compass Rose broke his leg and had to be shot. How you cried!'

'Yes, my lady. I remember it well,' said Giddins, thrilled that she remembered him. Giles observed his expression and thought *That is how she makes the servants her slaves. It's all done with love.*

'Walk him up and down,' she commanded, and Giddins obeyed. It was a fifteen-two chestnut with one white sock and a small white star.

'He belonged to Lady Bexley at the Grange,' Giles said, 'but she's giving up riding, so Giddins thought he might do for Kitty.'

'*Why* is she giving up riding?' Grandmère demanded.

Giddins and Archer exchanged an embarrassed look. Lady Bexley had got so fat recently that she found it impossible to mount, and the gelding wasn't up to her weight, but they could hardly say that to the gentry-folk. 'Couldn't say, my lady,' Giddins said, and then, to distract her. 'What would your ladyship's opinion be of the colour? Archer and me thought it a bit flashy, like.'

'A good horse is never a bad colour,' said her ladyship, sternly. 'How does he go? That is the point.'

'Young Miss Eveline showed him for us at the Grange, my lady, and he went very nicely indeed, carries his head well and doesn't pull.'

Archer said, 'I had a quick little go of him bareback, my lady, after Miss Eveline had done, and he seemed quite light in hand, but of course you can't tell what a horse is like sidesaddle when you ride him across.'

'I wish I could try him for you,' her ladyship said wistfully. 'Seeing him makes me wish my riding days were not done.'

'I'm sure if—' Giddins began eagerly.

'Thank you, Giddins,' Giles interrupted, before he could offer to take her out. At her age!

Grandmère gave him a level look, divining his thoughts.

But she said, 'Bring him to me again, Giddins.' She stripped off her glove and caressed the horse about the head and neck, seeing that he was comfortable with hands, and friendly. Obviously he had never been roughly treated. Giddins sidled up to her and shyly offered her some horse-nuts from his pocket, which she accepted to give to the animal. He snaffled them up gently, and she was satisfied. 'I think he will do very well,' she said. 'What does Kitty think?'

'She hasn't seen him yet. He was to be a surprise for her.'

'Then I hope she likes him.'

'It's her wedding gift from me,' Giles said. Grandmère raised an eyebrow. 'I didn't know what to get for her,' he excused himself. 'People seemed mostly to think it should be jewellery, but Mama told me she would have liked a dog, only Papa bought her paintings.'

'Ah, those Corots!' Grandmère sighed. 'Not his best work. Very well, a horse is a more thoughtful gift, if that's what she will like.'

'I think she will. She loves horses. They're . . .' He hesitated, then went on. 'She's never been afraid of them, the way she is of people.'

Grandmère nodded. She stroked the chestnut's muzzle, and he half closed his eyes. 'What is his name?' she asked Giddins.

'Apollo, my lady.'

'Well, that is very nice. *Eh bien*, Giles, give me your arm as far as the house. Thank you, Giddins.'

When they were away from any ears, he said, 'Did you really come to the stable-yard to see the horse?'

'Why should you doubt? I like horses. When Simone said Moss had told her it had come, I said, "I must see for myself, because I go home tomorrow, so I shall not have another chance."'

'Hmm,' said Giles. 'So there wasn't anything you wanted to say to me in private?'

'I think I should like a turn on the terrace,' she said. 'Oblige me by walking with me.'

She would never be hurried. He fitted his steps to hers, and waited. Her hand was feather-light on his arm. She walked him up to the stone balustrade, below which the ground fell away towards the valley bottom, with the view over the Ash. Ashmore Carr was along to the left, and the village of Canons Ashmore nestling in its fold was straight ahead, the spire of St Peter's poking up through the golden trees.

She sighed. 'Sometimes I miss it – the Castle. The place. The long view. In Town, there are no horizons.'

'You could come back,' he said.

'And live here?' She gave him an amused look. 'You wish to compound your problems even more? Besides, Maud and I could never live under one roof. But you are a good boy for suggesting it. I wish I had got to know you better, Giles, but you were never here. Always running away.'

'I didn't—'

'You did. But you cannot run away from yourself, because yourself is always waiting at the other end. And there is one thing that will bring you back, however far you run – reel you in like a fish on a line.'

'The place?' he suggested, amused by her philosophising.

'Duty,' she said. 'Ah, you laugh inside. Foolish old woman, you think. I see it in your eyes. But there is always one in every family on whom duty alights, like the wicked fairy with the unwanted gift. Don't fight against it, Giles, *mon cher*, or you will be miserable. And now you had better go and find Kitty and show her her horse, before someone else tells her about it and she wonders why she is the last to know. Poor Giles,' she said, as they turned and walked towards the house, 'you really don't know much about women, do you?'

'I've never had to,' he said, a little stung.

'*Ça se voit*. But it is never too late to learn,' she said blithely.

CHAPTER TWENTY-FOUR

Rain and wind were stripping the leaves from the trees, changing the look from autumn to winter. Riding was impossible for several days, and when a still, dry day finally arrived, Rachel hoped that, having been kept apart by the weather for so long, Victor would know without being told that she would be at the old barn, and would go up there without a definite agreement.

The path was slippery in places, and she had to go carefully, which was not Daystar's plan. Having been shut in for days, he wanted to gallop. Holding him back fretted him, and made Rachel's back ache. So when they got up onto the top, she decided – or he decided and she went along with it – to let him go. He took the bit, stretched his neck, laid himself out, snorting eagerly, and she was half exhilarated, half afraid. She was like that about everything – the secret meetings with Victor were not entirely a joy to her, because the conspiracy and danger alarmed her as much as they thrilled.

Ironically, it was not the gallop that brought her to grief. She pulled him up after a long stretch, then turned and walked him back towards the barn. There were a lot of rooks whirling around above the woods and making a racket, and he was paying attention to them and not his surroundings, so that when Victor stepped out of the barn and waved, he gave an enormous start. His hoofs skidded on the slippery turf, a section of it peeled back like skin, and he went crashing down on his side.

Rachel had the breath knocked out of her. She heard Victor's cry of alarm. For a moment the weight of the horse was on her legs, but then he had scrambled and heaved himself up, and for a fortunate instant was too surprised to bolt, giving Victor the chance to grab the rein. Luckily her foot had come free of the stirrup, or when the horse got up it might have broken her ankle.

'Are you all right?' Victor was crying, wanting to get to her but having enough wit to realise he must not let go of the horse. 'Rachel, are you hurt?'

She could feel wet mud soaking through the shoulder and back of her jacket, her hat had fallen off and her hair was coming down. She sat up, wishing she could curse like the grooms when a horse trod on their foot. 'I'm all right,' she called shakily. 'Tie him up.'

He dithered for a moment, then saw the point and led Daystar into the barn. By the time he returned, she had managed to get to her feet, and was surveying the ruin of her appearance. 'Are you hurt?' he asked again. 'When I saw him come down on top of you—'

'Some bruises,' she said. 'That's all. Ow!' She put her weight on her right foot and took it off again. 'Twisted my ankle, I think.' It would have been caught between the saddle and the ground.

'It's not broken, is it? Let me see.'

'It's not broken.' She took a step or two and found she could walk, limpingly. 'I must look dreadful,' she said.

'You've got mud on your face,' he said, which she thought a little less than gallant. *You always look lovely to me* would have been better.

'Have you got a handkerchief?' she asked, a little impatiently. He produced one, and wiped gently and rather inexpertly at her face, while she felt around behind and managed to get her hair back up into its net. 'My hat?' she said. It was lying nearby, with the semi-circular dent of a hoof print in it. She pushed it back out and put it on.

'You look fine,' he said belatedly. 'A bit muddy, but fine.'

Holding his arm, she limped into the barn, where Daystar was standing, looking smug – as well he might, being plastered with mud all across one side. This was far more serious than her own appearance. 'Josh will kill me!' she cried.

'Isn't it his day off? Someone else will have to clean it up.'

'Oh, that's true,' she said, with relief. 'But they're bound to tell him. And he'll grumble that he wasn't washed properly and make a big fuss about blue-bag and everything. That's the trouble with a grey – everything shows.'

Victor's interest in horses had reached its limit. 'Come and sit down,' he said. 'I've got something to tell you.'

'What is it?'

'No, come and sit down. It's really exciting.' They sat on the rug on the pile of rocks, and she turned to him, eager for kisses. He kissed her, but gingerly, she thought. 'There's still a lot of mud on your face,' he said, pulling back. 'I can't get it off without water.'

'Oh, never mind. Mud won't kill us,' she said. 'Is your news really exciting?' she asked, after a while, when they stopped for breath.

He faced her with an eager expression, took both her hands, and as she waited breathlessly for something concerning her, something about love and potential marriage, he said, 'I'm going away!'

It was as though he'd struck her. 'Away? What do you mean, away? Where?'

'To America!' He was waiting for her reaction.

She looked bewildered. 'But why?'

'A cousin of my aunt's has a shipping business in New York, and he's going to take me on as a clerk. Once I've learned the business, I can work my way up. It could lead to really big things for me. There's a tremendous amount of money in shipping, and you can go anywhere in the world. Aunt's cousin has offices in Hong Kong and Singapore and Alexandria and – oh, everywhere!' He surveyed her face again. 'Isn't it exciting? Aren't you pleased for me?'

'I thought you were settled here for good,' she said. 'I thought this was your home now.'

'Well, I have to have a job. I've been looking around for something to do, and I thought I'd get something near here, or even in London, and travel back and forth. But this is so much better! She had an idea this cousin might help, so she wrote to him, and we got the letter back from him just on Friday. I'm to leave on Wednesday – no sense in delaying, especially as the crossing gets worse the later in the year you leave it.'

'Wednesday?' she said in dismay.

'I'm so glad I saw you today. I was afraid I'd have to leave without saying goodbye. I was wondering how I could get a letter to you without making trouble for you. I say,' he said with concern, 'you're shivering.'

'The mud's soaked right through,' she said miserably. 'I think I should go home.'

'Well, I should hate you to catch cold.' He stood up, helped her to her feet and gazed at her affectionately. 'Oh, Rachel, it's been wonderful, these last few weeks. You really are a tremendous girl. I shall always feel lucky to have known you.' She looked at him in dumb misery. 'I'd give you a hug, but the mud would come off on me, and my aunt would ask questions.' He leaned in carefully and kissed her. Her lips clung to his, but he broke away before she was ready. 'I'll help you mount.'

Daystar seemed irritable after his fall, and fidgeted about, making it difficult for Rachel to mount – Victor wasn't very good, in any case, at throwing her up. At last she was in the saddle. He placed a hand on her knee and said, 'Go carefully, won't you? Ride slowly. Don't have another fall.'

'So – this is goodbye, is it?' she asked, feeling her throat close.

'I won't be able to get away again before Wednesday,' he said. 'There's so much to do, and Aunty will want me to be with her. But, Rachel, I'll never forget you.'

She couldn't speak. She rode away without looking back, tears streaming down her face and washing clean tracks in the mud smears.

'I always said them horses were dirty, dangerous beasts,' said Daisy, helping Rachel to sit down in the bath.

'It wasn't his fault,' Rachel managed to say. But tears were very close, and Alice stepped in.

'Could you take her clothes away and do something about them?' she asked. 'I'll help her bathe.'

'She needs arnica on the bruises as well,' said Daisy.

'I'll do the arnica. And, please, it'd be better if everyone didn't know.'

'Oh, they'll know all right,' said Daisy. 'That Pobbo in the stables, he'll tell Aggie, and it'll be all over everywhere. Galloping about like a mad thing, I suppose you were. Not ladylike at all.' But she gathered up the clothes and left, and Rachel was able to dissolve into the tears she had been holding back for so long.

'I wasn't galloping,' she sobbed first. 'We were walking when he slipped.'

'Daisy doesn't know anything about horses,' Alice said. 'What happened?'

So she told her. 'I th-thought he loved me,' she sobbed at the end. 'I thought we'd be together for always. I thought we would get m-*married*!'

'Oh, Ray,' Alice said helplessly. 'I bet he wasn't worth it. If he'd really loved you he'd have taken you with him.'

'But I love him!'

'I don't suppose Mama would have let you marry him anyway. You know what she's like.'

'She'll never let us marry anyone. We'll have to stay here for ever and be *old m-maids!*'

Alice didn't answer that, thinking it only too likely. She worked the sponge over Rachel's narrow back with nice, round, comforting movements, while her sister cried the stormy tears of thwarted first love.

James and Speen came out of the church together into a foggy November midday. Crooks was a few steps ahead of them in the crowd. The sight of him reminded Speen, who said, 'How come you're still James, anyway? Hasn't his lordship confirmed your place? Are you his valet or aren't you?'

'Course I'm his valet. Who's been saying contrary?'

'No-one in particular. Just general speculation.' Speen shrugged and pushed his hands into his pockets. 'If I was you, I'd have a word with his lordship. Make him announce it, then you'll know you're safe.'

'Look, I'm safe all right,' James said firmly. 'They got a new maid for her ladyship, didn't they?'

'Hatto? She's a queer one,' Speen retorted. 'Can't make her out. But she's not got the style for a lady's maid, not a countess's, anyway. You got to put it on a bit. My opinion, she was never no *titled* lady's maid before. Got a middle-class sort of look about her. I bet—'

'The point *is,*' said James irritably, 'that they got her in to take over from Rose, because Rose was only temporary. All right? Well, then, if I was only temporary, they'd have done the same with me. Done it at the same time. No, his lordship knows he's got a good 'un. And I saved her ladyship's life, didn't I? So I'm safe as houses. He'll never get rid of me after that.'

The crowd was shuffling forward as they talked, and they saw the white head of Crooks up ahead of them disappear under his hat, then bob away to the right. 'Where's he going?' Speen asked. 'The brake's the other way.'

'Oh, he doesn't go in the brake. He likes to walk back from church, often as not.'

'Does he? That's a bit queer, isn't it? He don't look like a walker to me. I'd have said he was soft as soap.'

'Well, he is in general,' said James.

'I never told you what happened in London, did I?'

'What, then?'

'Let's see where he's going,' said Speen. They followed round the side of the church, and were in time to see Crooks standing at the lych-gate, in conversation with Axe Brandom. Axe had removed his hat, and his fair hair was a flag of brightness in the dull air. 'Who's the pretty boy?' Speen asked.

'Blacksmith's assistant. Pretty boy? He could break you in half with his bare hands.'

'Yeah, but he wouldn't. That sort, the stronger they are, the softer inside. Come on.' He turned back the way they had come.

'Thought you wanted to know where he was going,' said James.

'Know now, don't we? Come on, we'll have to hurry or we'll miss the brake, and *I* don't want to walk up that hill.'

'So, what was you going to tell me about Crooky in London?'

'Tell you later. Not in front of the ladies. But it explains a lot, does this,' said Speen. 'Secret assignations with pretty boys? Explains a lot.'

'I don't know what you're talking about.'

'Course you don't. Dead innocent all you country folk.'

'I'm as smart as any Town valet,' James said angrily. 'You'd never survive in the country.'

'I wouldn't want to,' said Speen. 'If Mr Richard stays here, he'll have to look for a new man.'

* * *

461

'May I speak with you, my lord?' James said, holding out the waistcoat for Giles to slip into.

'Yes. What is it?' Giles asked, not really listening. He was pondering a list of barn and cottage repairs Markham had given him. So many roofs! So much rain!

'Am I giving satisfaction, my lord?'

Giles jerked back to the present. 'What are you talking about?'

'Well, my lord, you asked me to go on the trip abroad in place of Mr Crooks, him being too old and p'r'aps a bit frail for so much foreign travel. And I was wondering whether you were satisfied with how I looked after you.'

'I'd have damn soon told you if I wasn't,' Giles said, scowling. 'What is it you want? Speak out. I haven't time for all this Uriah Heep nonsense.'

James didn't know what a uriah heap might be – did he mean the dung heap in the stable-yard that the grooms wee'd on? What had that got to do with him? But he knew better than to provoke a wasp. 'I'd like to know if the position is now permanent, my lord.'

'Of course it is. Why are you asking me now?'

'It's just that a gentleman's gentleman is called by his surname, and I'm still known as James, which is a footman's name.'

Giles was about to snap, but reflected in time that these little points of status were important downstairs. 'I wasn't even aware you had a surname,' he said, to lighten things.

James's stony look said it was no joking matter. 'I have, my lord, and it's Hook. If it's not too much trouble, would you be so good as to tell Mr Moss that I'm to be referred to as Mr Hook from now on?'

'Very well, James – Hook, I mean. I'll speak to Moss. Anything else?'

'No, my lord. And thank you.'

As he left the Blue Bedroom with a soiled shirt over his

arm, he looked to his left and saw Miss Taylor just starting down the stairs. 'That'll teach you, you old bitch,' he said softly. He'd get his revenge on her. Call him a pig? He wouldn't forget that. He never forgot a slight, and he was patient. He'd wait for his moment, and his revenge would be a good one.

And that Speen would have to show him a bit of respect now.

Giles and Richard walked their horses side by side down the hill. 'What do you think of him?' Giles asked.

Richard patted Lucifer's black neck. 'He's fine. He'll carry you all day, if I'm any judge. What's yours like?'

Giles was riding dark bay Zelos. They were the two hunters they had taken on approval from Lord Shacklock's stable. 'He's fast. I like him.'

'So does that mean you will be hunting this season?'

'I would like to go out now and then. I haven't time to be hunting the way our father did, three times a week. What about you?'

'I'm not sure the shoulder will take it. Even the best horse will pull if it's excited. And if I should have a fall . . .'

Giles looked at him with concern. 'I didn't realise it was so bad. Does that mean you'll never be able to hunt again?'

'I hope not. The sawbones said it ought to get stronger in time. I'm just a bit tender of it at the moment.' He tried a smile. 'Wounded twice, you know.'

'Oh, you mean the bullet in South Africa? Yes, it was unlucky it was the same arm.'

'Anyway,' Richard went on, 'I don't yet know where I'll be this winter.'

'I thought you'd be here,' said Giles, with the beginning of an annoyed frown.

'Brother dear, you haven't told me what you've decided about my fate,' said Richard. 'That's the trouble with you thinkers – there's so much going on inside the skull, you forget the rest of us don't know about it unless you say it out loud.'

'I thought we'd discussed your helping Markham,' said Giles.

'Discussed it – but you didn't actually ask me. Am I to assume this is a formal offer – come live with me and be my agent?'

'Assistant agent to begin with. But I'd really like Markham to become more like a secretary to me – especially if I take up my seat in the Lords next session – so you would eventually step into his shoes. And you'd have to work with Vogel on the financial side.' Giles frowned. 'It's a big job, and a lot of work. If you take it on, you'll have to be serious about it.'

'And you think I'm the right man? I'm flattered. Surprised, but flattered.'

'I don't know if you are or not,' Giles said frankly. 'You seem to make a joke about everything.'

'Doesn't mean I'm not serious inside.'

'Well, I know I'd sooner have you than a stranger. And, besides, there's the problem of what to do with you if you *don't* take it on.'

'Ah, the younger son!' said Richard. 'What *do* you do with the blighter if he's not needed to inherit? I'm not cut out for the Church.' Giles laughed at the idea. 'Thank you. And it would be pressing our luck to hope for another heiress to come along for me to marry. What does that leave? Politics?'

'You need money to go into Parliament. And if I have to pay for you, I'd sooner you did the job *I* want doing.'

'So unless I can find a billet in commerce, it's the estate for me.'

'You might sound a little more enthusiastic. And grateful.'

'Oh, I'm grateful all right.' He was, but only up to a point. He would sooner not have a job of any sort. But

Giles, for such a dreamer, was hard as flint underneath. He had refused to pay Linda the allowance the old man had been giving her, so there was little chance he'd go on supporting Richard *ad infinitum*. If only he had a private income . . . He thought fleetingly of Mrs Sands. If he had some kind of income, he could make her comfortable, get her into a proper house, and maybe then she'd look kindly on his suit. An image of marriage flashed briefly across his mind like a comet.

'Perhaps I could get a position in a bank,' he said. He didn't realise he'd said it aloud until Giles laughed explosively.

Kitty was sitting in the lobby as Nina came in, and stood, her face breaking into such a smile that Nina hurried to her thinking, *I didn't know how much I'd missed you.*

'I feel as if I haven't seen you for a hundred years,' Kitty cried. 'Oh, this is so good!'

'You're looking well,' Nina said. Kitty had changed, she thought. That frightened-kitten look was gone. She held her head up now. Her face had filled out into adulthood. Her hair was rolled all round and the topknot was hidden by a small jaunty hat with a cocked brim and curled feathers held by a brooch – had she chosen that for herself? It seemed bold. Automatically she noticed her shoes (black kid with a decoration of jet beads all across the toe) and smiled at herself for doing so. Kitty looked every inch a prosperous young matron. Marriage must be suiting her. 'I think you've put on weight.'

'I can't think how,' Kitty said. 'The food at home is worse than ever – it's even made me sick a few times.'

'You called it "home",' Nina noticed.

'I suppose I did,' said Kitty. 'I almost think of it as home. After all, I didn't much like Mama's house in Hampstead, so I've no other. But, Nina, why are we talking about me? *You're* the one with the wonderful news! Tell me all about it!'

'When we've sat down,' Nina said, as the hovering attendant waited to conduct them to the dining-room.

Kitty gazed around as they were settled at a table. 'I do love this restaurant. And isn't it fun to be eating out without a chaperone?'

'You're my chaperone,' Nina pointed out. 'Married woman of great respectability.'

'I suppose I am. It's hard to believe it's real, sometimes. Being with you, I feel like a schoolgirl again.'

'We're neither of us that any more,' Nina said, with a touch of sadness. 'Are you getting on better with your mother-in-law?'

'Not sure. I know she doesn't like me, but I think she's learning to ignore me – as long as I don't try to change things too much. But Grandmère intervened about making the door through into Giles's dressing-room. Oh, and Giles has bought me a horse!'

She described Apollo, and the rides she had taken with her young sisters-in-law, the repairs Giles had ordered to various roads and tracks on the estate and how much the work was needed. Nina listened, injected a word here and there to keep her going. She reflected that, for all the wonderful things that were happening, Kitty's loquacity suggested she didn't have anyone to talk to. She imagined Giles always busy, Lady Stainton cold and distant, the girls always with their heads together, sufficient unto each other. She felt sorry for her, for all her new wealth. And yet Kitty had married the man she loved – and from the way she spoke about Giles, she still idolised him. So what was there to pity?

Following her thoughts for a moment, she forgot to prompt Kitty, who wound down, and looked at her with concern. 'I'm still talking about me – and you're encouraging me,' she said, with unusual percipience. 'Is something wrong? Don't tell me your engagement is off – is that why you don't want to talk about it? Is your heart broken?'

466

'No, no,' Nina said hastily. 'I'm still getting married. I wanted to hear all your news, that's all.'

'But yours is so much more important,' Kitty said, not quite reassured. 'You haven't even told me his name. Is it anyone I know? Where did you meet him? How did he propose? Tell me everything! When is the wedding to be?'

So there was nothing for it but to tell. 'You met him once, at the same time as me,' she said. 'At Dene Park. I danced with him. He came with the King's party.'

Kitty frowned in recollection. 'But they were all quite old, weren't they, the King's friends? I don't remember anyone you danced with. Oh – except wasn't there a funny old man who talked to you about shoes?'

'He's not old, and he's not funny. He does make me laugh sometimes, but on purpose. He likes to see me laugh.'

'*Nina!*'

'Don't look like that, Kitty, or I shall be sorry I told you at all. His name is Joseph Cowling and he loves me dearly. He will be a good husband to me, and make me comfortable.'

'But you can't love him,' Kitty said falteringly. And then, 'Can you?'

'Don't you remember when we were at school, and you talked about falling in love? And I always said I never would?'

'I didn't really believe you.'

'It's not important to me the way it always was to you,' Nina said, which was not true, of course, not now. But she couldn't speak about love to Kitty, who had married the one man . . . 'And, remember, I have no fortune. My best chance of happiness is to marry a rich man – and Mr Cowling is very rich.'

'I thought you were going to be a teacher.'

'I was, but I've discovered I really dislike that idea. Mr Cowling is a nice man and will give me anything I like.'

Kitty pondered that. It would be good to think of Nina being able to have all the new clothes she wanted: she remembered the sartorial difficulties of her come-out. And – and books, she supposed. Lots of books. But Kitty thought of her passionate nights with Giles, and how dreadful it would be to be in bed with a man you didn't love. To do *those things* with an old man and without the fire in the belly that made it all so easy and exciting . . .

But the tabu against married women talking about those things to unmarried women had shut down her tongue. It was awful. Nina probably thought being married was just sitting across the breakfast table from each other. She would be quite unprepared for what would happen. But Kitty couldn't tell her. She just – *couldn't.*

Nina smiled. 'Don't worry, Kitty. I've thought about it very carefully, and I'm sure it's the best thing for me.'

Kitty sought for something positive to say. 'If he's really rich, you could have a horse. You've always wanted a horse.'

Nina laughed. 'Yes, and he has a house in Market Harborough, right in the Fernie country, so perhaps I shall be able to hunt. Will you be hunting this year?'

'I may do. But I need time to get used to Apollo and learn the country. I might just go to a meet or two. But, Nina,' Kitty refused this time to be distracted, 'you're really, really sure?'

'Really, really. Be happy for me, Kitty dear.'

'Well, then, I am. When will the wedding be?'

'The sixth of December.'

'And are we invited?'

Nina had known the question would have to be faced. She didn't want Giles to come to her wedding. She didn't want so much pain, on that day of all days. But there was no help for it.

'Of course,' she said.

* * *

468

She had gone to see Miss Thornton to tell her in person, feeling she owed her nothing less, after the trouble she had taken to get her the post at Allely's. She had expected another inquisition about her choice, but Miss Thornton had been very pleasant about it.

'I'm not entirely surprised,' she said. 'You would have made a good teacher, but there are other paths you can take. With money, you can do a great deal of good.'

'That's what I was hoping,' Nina said.

'You might found a school of your own,' said Miss Thornton. 'It's much more satisfying than merely teaching in someone else's. If you ever do, come and see me. I can give you lots of good advice.'

'Thank you. I might do that. And thank you for being so understanding.'

'You were always a favourite pupil of mine,' Miss Thornton said. 'I think you have remarkable abilities. But more than that,' she smiled suddenly, 'I always just *liked* you. You'd be surprised how rare that is.'

After parting from Nina, Kitty took a cab. But she didn't want to go straight home. She felt restless, her mind full of swirling thoughts, her stomach full of swirling acids. The food at the Castle was poisoning her, she thought. Now she couldn't even eat the lovely luncheon at the Savoy without suffering! She wondered if she might be actually ill. Nina had said she looked well, but she felt as though something was going on inside her that she couldn't quite put her finger on. It was making her nervous.

Halfway to the station she rapped on the roof, and when the cabbie opened the hatch she said, 'I've changed my mind. Bruton Street, please.'

'Yes, miss,' he said. It ought to be 'ma'am', Kitty thought. Do I still look like a miss? But what would a miss be doing in a cab on her own?

Luckily, Grandmère was alone – or, at least, she had only Sir Thomas with her, taking tea and chatting. She waved Kitty to a chair, rang for another cup and continued talking to Sir Thomas about music, a conversation Kitty couldn't have joined in if she'd wanted to. Sir Thomas balanced his cup and saucer on his plump knee, and made expansive gestures with his other hand, his little beard jerking up and down as he talked. Kitty began to feel quite sleepy. And then suddenly he was on his feet, bowed over Kitty's hand and said, 'Two Lady Staintons in one room: what a lucky chap I am!' and was gone.

Grandmère got up, took the untouched tea from Kitty's hand and put it on the table, saying, '*Eh bien*, what is the matter? And do not,' she added, as Kitty opened her mouth, 'waste my time by saying "nothing". You came here.'

'I didn't know who else I could talk to,' Kitty began, but didn't go on.

Grandmère saw she needed to be led up to the fence. 'What are you doing in Town? Did you come up to shop?'

'No, to see Nina – my friend, who was my bridesmaid. She's getting married.'

'Yes, I have heard. Richard told me. Sensible girl, a good choice.'

'Do you think so?'

'*Bien sûr*, she is doing just as she ought, securing an establishment for herself. Do you tell me you have become upset because of this?'

'No, it's not that. Of course not. She says she's happy so I believe her. It did shake me up rather, but I've been feeling – well – rather odd lately anyway. I think I might be ill.'

Grandmère raised an eyebrow. 'So you come to ask me about it, though I am not a doctor? But I understand. Doctors are fools and brutes. What is wrong with you?'

'I feel – funny.'

470

Grandmère clicked her tongue. 'You must give me more than that.'

'Well, I've been sick a few times at the Castle, but it can't only be the Castle food because I've just eaten at the Savoy and that's making me feel ill too. And when I get up from a chair I get dizzy sometimes. And—' She stopped, and a slow, rich blush spread up from her neck.

'Speak out,' Grandmère said impatiently. 'I am very old. Nothing shocks me.'

'Well, I haven't – I mean, you know how one, from time to time . . .' She pulled herself together. 'I haven't needed my doily belt for ages,' she blurted out, and then had to look away. How could she have mentioned such a thing to a dowager countess? The humiliation!

Grandmère suppressed a smile. 'How long ago did you last need it?' she asked briskly.

Kitty, still hiding her face, said, 'In Italy. On our honeymoon. In August. Not since then. I heard one of the maids talk about someone dying of a blockage inside. Is that it? Am I – going to die?'

'*Alors*, you are not ill. It is as I thought when you came into the room – one gets an instinct for it. You are *enceinte*, child. You are going to have a baby.'

Kitty looked up, the colour draining away. 'A baby?' she said, in a whisper of a voice.

'Why not? That is what honeymoons are for. Did not Giles visit your bed? That is how it happens, foolish. Let me see . . . August.' She counted on her fingers. 'Three months. A May baby. You have timed it very well. Best to get it over before the hot months. You would not wish to be carrying through July and August.'

'I'm going to have a baby?' Kitty said in wonder.

'You are being very slow. Yes, a baby. And what should you do, then? Nothing! Go home, tell Giles, be happy. Do not let them treat you like an invalid. Walk every day, eat

471

enough but not too much. And hope it is a boy. It is always best to have a boy first.'

'Thank you,' Kitty said, her face transformed. 'Oh, *thank* you!'

'You are thanking entirely the wrong person.' But she smiled. 'Do not be afraid. The world is full of women who have given birth. I shall come and stay from time to time to make sure they aren't ruining you with neglect – or indulgence. Be at peace, dear child. You are doing your duty, and that is a good thing.'

CHAPTER TWENTY-FIVE

It was hard to tell Giles. He was busy, as always, and it wasn't something she wanted to say in front of other people, at the dinner table or in the drawing-room. It was something, she felt, that belonged to him especially. He must be told first and privately.

In the bedroom, then. But he didn't always come to her room, and after that day in London, not for several nights. The secret grew inside her as she imagined the baby growing. She was not tempted to tell Hatto, but once when she went into her room and found Rose there, replacing the jade figures she had just washed, she almost told her.

'My lady?' Rose said, turning and seeing the eager face and parted lips. 'Was there something?' she pressed, when nothing was forthcoming.

But no: Giles must know first. 'Oh, nothing,' Kitty said.

'You're looking a bit flushed, my lady,' Rose said. 'Are you quite well?'

'Oh, *quite* well,' Kitty said.

Rose went downstairs thoughtfully, and cast her mind back over the weeks she had been lady's maid, and realised what had not happened. And then she smiled to herself. Obviously it was a secret for now, but it could not remain a secret for ever, because Hatto would start to wonder for herself sooner or later. A lady's personal maid was always the first to know.

★   ★   ★

Kitty lay wakeful, too racked with indigestion to sleep. She thought about Giles, wondered how he would take the news, what it would be like to have a baby, whether it would hurt, how Nina would fare marrying that funny old man (she had only the vaguest memory of him – perhaps he was much nicer than she remembered). She sat up and drank a little water, and the heartburn eased a little. And then she felt lonely. It had been so nice seeing Nina again. She wished she had someone like that to talk to. She loved Giles wildly, consumingly, with utter devotion, but he was not *company* in the same way Nina had been.

But perhaps when she had his baby, things would change. It must make them closer, mustn't it? Suddenly, she couldn't wait to tell him. That was what the communicating door was for, wasn't it? She went and put her ear to it, but there was no sound, so either he had not come up yet or he was already in bed. Cautiously she opened it, and saw across its darkness a hair-fine filament of light below the further door. She crossed, listened, heard no murmur of voices or rustle of movement. James (she always thought of him as 'that horrid James') must have gone.

She went in. Giles was sitting up in bed reading, and looked up, frowning. 'Kitty? What are you doing here?'

It was rather a silly question, and it dispelled her nervousness and made her want to giggle. She scudded across the room and climbed in beside him. It was not etiquette for the countess to visit the earl rather than vice versa. His room smelt different from hers, his mattress was harder and a bit lumpy. She felt instant concern for him – he should have a new mattress, she would order it for him if he was too careless of his own comfort to do it. Hadn't he married her so that her money could make Ashmore what it ought to be? He was looking at her with such a puzzled expression that she did actually laugh.

'I missed you,' she said. 'You didn't come and see me last night, or the night before, or—'

'I was tired,' he interrupted, and heard as the words hit the air how churlish it sounded. But she shouldn't be here. Suppose James – Hook, rather – came back in for some reason. Still, he must be gentle with Kitty. 'I'm sorry,' he said. 'I have so much work to do.'

'I know,' she said, 'but you needn't do it all at once. You shouldn't make yourself so tired every night.'

This was a different Kitty, he thought – not the shy daytime girl, or the little night-time pagan, but an oddly *wifely* Kitty he hadn't seen before.

'What's got into you?' he asked. 'I've never seen you like this before.'

'Put those silly old papers away,' she said. 'I've got something to tell you.'

He put them aside, on his bedside table, and said, 'What, then?'

She was looking at him as though she had never seen him before, tracing his features with her eyes. And then she traced them with a finger, running it over his eyebrows, down his nose, then over his lips. He bore it patiently.

I hope it's a boy, and he looks like you, she was thinking. The focus of her eyes changed, her breath grew heavier. She whispered. 'Oh, Giles!'

It lit him like a match to a bonfire, and entirely forgetting that he had not locked the door, he rolled her over and engulfed her, kissing her, excited by her readiness, entering her with relief and desire, the tensions of the last few days spending themselves – as had become the satisfying pattern – and leaving him breathless, warm, relaxed, content.

Kitty lay in his arms, her face against his neck, breathing in that special scent of him that was behind his ear and nowhere else, that made her feel she knew something about him no-one else knew. That he belonged to her, almost as much as she belonged to him.

'What was it you came to tell me?' he murmured.

He would be asleep in a moment – she knew that voice. She moved her head a little so that her lips were against the shell of his ear, the beautiful curves of which she had gazed at so often, and loved. 'I came to tell you that I'm going to have a baby.'

She felt his arms stiffen around her in shock, and then he pulled his face back from her, fully awake, to look at her, eyes wide and questioning. She smiled with complete happiness. 'It's true,' she said. 'I'm going to have a baby. We're going to have a baby. Oh, I hope it's a boy!'

He said nothing, but he drew her close again. He held her tightly and kissed her brow and her hair and her eyes, then her hair again. She would have liked him to say more, but the kissing was very nice.

Giles held her almost in fear. *What had he done?* Now there was no going back. It was absurd, because of course the die had been cast long before: from the day his father had died his path had been laid out. But, still, he felt as though this was a defining moment. He felt the jaws of the trap close round him.

Mr Cowling invited Nina to inspect his house in Northampton. 'I don't know what you'll think of it,' he said. 'It seems all right to me, but I don't pay much heed to such things.'

'But it's your home, isn't it?' Nina said.

'Well, as far as I have a home, I suppose that's it. I've not been there much since my Emma died. I've always moved around a lot, for my business. When I'm in Leicester, I stay in lodgings, and when I'm in London, Brown's makes me comfortable. But Beechcroft House is where I keep my things. I thought you might prefer it because it's close to London. It's not a bad journey by train from Northampton.'

476

'Prefer it to what?' Nina asked.

'I have a house in Market Harborough, as I think I mentioned. It's bigger, but it's an old place and very plain. I bought it because it was a bargain. Chap who was selling it had got into trouble and needed the money quick. I won't go into details. I thought I might have parties of people to stay for the hunting. You can do a lot of business that way. But that never came off. Emma – well, she wasn't a great one for parties. And she never liked it much. Thought it gloomy. She was happy enough in Northampton.'

'Then I'm sure I shall be,' Nina said, not wanting to cause him anxiety.

'Aye, you say that, but you've not seen it. It mightn't be to your taste. I don't want you thinking you're stepping into someone else's shoes. Anything you want to change, you go right ahead and do it. You don't need to think I hold anything sacred because it was Emma's choice. Or if you find you really don't like it, I can buy you a different house. Or we can pull it down and build a new one. I want you to be happy.'

Mr Cowling was very correct. He invited Lepida Morris to accompany her, in case anyone thought it wasn't respectable for her to come alone.

They went by train to Northampton. Mr Cowling had gone down the day before, 'to see to things', as he told them. 'Decius will meet you at the station and bring you to the house,' he said.

Northampton, as they ran into it, seemed to have quite a lot of factories, surrounded by the usual sort of Victorian red-brick terraced streets. They crossed a river, which Lepida said was the Nene. 'I looked it up,' she said. 'And the factories make boots and shoes, and also hosiery. And bicycles. And furniture.'

As soon as they stepped through the barrier, they were approached by a man in a neat, plain suit, who swept off

477

his hat and bowed to them. 'Miss Sanderton, I believe? And Miss Morris? I'm Decius Blake, Mr Cowling's secretary.'

Nina said, 'How do you do?' and shook his hand, and was amused to see Lepida looking slightly confused, for Mr Blake was almost ridiculously handsome, with thick, wavy dark hair and eyes so blue they seemed shocking by contrast.

'I have a cab waiting,' he said. 'Did you have a comfortable journey?'

'Very, thank you,' said Nina, as Lepida was obviously not going to help. 'I hope you don't mind my asking – Decius? Such an unusual name. Were you . . . ?'

'The tenth?' he said. He had a charming smile. 'I'm afraid so. I come from a numerous family.'

'And are all your brothers and sisters named numerically?' Lepida asked, recovering at last.

'Fortunately for them, no,' he said. 'I have a brother Sextus, and a brother Octavius, but the rest are girls, and my parents spared them.' There was a four-wheeled cab waiting, and he let down the step and helped them in.

'It isn't far,' he said, as he settled himself opposite them. They were driving through streets of the same red terraces they had seen from the train, but soon they passed into a broader thoroughfare, with plane trees planted at either side.

'How did you first meet Mr Cowling?' Nina asked.

'My father was the parish priest in the same village where Mr Cowling was born,' he said. She nodded encouragingly, so he went on, 'When he had made his fortune – or, I should say, the first part of it – he went back to the village to see what good he could do. The church, All Saints, was a little dilapidated, so he made a generous donation for repairs and improvements.'

'That was an admirable thing to do,' Lepida said, finding her voice at last.

He looked at her. Did Nina imagine it, or did Lepida

478

shudder at the impact of those eyes? 'He is a very fine man, generous and good.'

'So after that, I suppose, he became friendly with your father,' Nina prompted.

'Indeed. And finding that, as usual, a large clerical family is not a rich family, he undertook to send us boys to school at his expense, and when school was finished, he offered me a position as his secretary. You can imagine,' he concluded, 'how grateful all the Blakes are to Mr Cowling. We pray every day for his continued health and happiness.' He gave Nina an almost urchin-like grin. 'It seems our prayers have been answered.'

He pointed out various landmarks. 'The river is over that way. The green space over there is the racecourse. And here we are, Beechcroft House.'

It was a red-brick building in the Victorian with narrow 'church' windows, gables, decorative pinnacles and so on. There was a sweep in front, skirting a thick, old-fashioned shrubbery, and a very large tree grew to one side, though Nina noticed it was not a beech but a yew.

Blake noticed the direction of her gaze, and said, 'It's thought there was a church on this site a long time ago.'

'Oh, yes,' said Lepida. 'Churchyards nearly always have a yew tree in them, don't they?'

'Yes, for the magic, to ward off evil spirits, I believe,' said Blake. 'There's no trace left of the church. Beechcroft House itself isn't old – it was built in about 1870. The yew is probably six or seven hundred years old.'

'Let's hope the magic still works,' Lepida said.

And now the door of the house had opened, and Mr Cowling had emerged, hurrying to open the cab door and let down the step. Blake hopped out of the other side and made himself useful paying the driver, while Cowling dispensed handshakes and a modest kiss on the cheek for Nina.

'Come in, come in, and welcome. Luncheon will be ready directly – you'll be hungry after your journey. Oh – your coats! Decius, take the coats. And your hats – aye, I want you to be comfortable. You're at home now – you too, Miss Morris. I hope you'll visit whenever you feel like it. You'll always be welcome here. This is Mrs Mitchell, my house-keeper, who's looked after me for years. Miss Sanderton and her friend Miss Morris.'

The housekeeper dropped a dutiful bob, but her eyes flicked over Lepida indifferently, and lighted on Nina with what Nina felt, before it was veiled, was quite definitely hostility.

'Well, are you satisfied with your new house?' Lepida asked, as the train trundled towards London.

'It wasn't what I expected,' Nina said.

The Gothic style needed some getting used to. The house was not large, only six bedrooms, but it was pretending to be a medieval mansion. The heavy oak doors, stained glass, coloured tiles, baronial fireplaces, elaborately carved panel-ling and grim black-iron gasoliers all made an emphatic statement in what was, after all, a suburban villa. Mr Cowling was obviously indifferent to architectural style, and appar-ently had not spent much time there anyway, but to modern eyes, Gothic was a joke, and could one be happy living in a joke? Still, she would have an establishment, and for a girl without dowry that was everything. She should be grateful. She *would* be grateful.

Along with the house, of course, she would inherit the servants. The elderly manservant, Moxton, was Mr Cowling's valet and also acted as butler. He was tall, with skinny legs and a shock of white hair, and when he bent over Nina serving the soup he had smelt strongly of mothballs. The house-parlourmaid, Nellie, plump and shiny of face, helped at table, and there was a cook, though she lived out and

480

only came in when required, Mr Cowling being away so much. When he was not at home, Mrs Mitchell and Nellie did the cooking between them.

'What did you think about Mrs Mitchell?' Nina asked Lepida. 'Did you think there was anything, well, odd about her?'

Lepida knew immediately what she meant. 'I don't think she liked you.'

'So it wasn't my imagination! But why?'

'Probably because she's looked after Mr Cowling for years and years, and now you've arrived to put her nose out of joint.'

'But I haven't—'

'She's jealous,' said Lepida. 'You often see it with these old servants. They become possessive. Don't worry about it, she'll get used to the situation.' She didn't add, because she didn't want to make Nina any more apprehensive, that it was possible Mrs Mitchell was a bit in love with her master. Cowling was a decent-looking man and had obviously been handsome in earlier years. And his wife had been dead for five years. That, too, would sort itself out, she thought. There was no need to stir up trouble. 'It will be better when you get more servants in. She'll have other people to think about then.'

'I don't know if we'll need them.'

'Mr Cowling talked about entertaining, in which case you certainly will,' Lepida said. 'By the way,' she went on, as Nina was about to protest, 'are you always going to call him "Mr Cowling"?'

'Until after the wedding, anyway,' Nina said; and felt a bit peculiar at the thought of being married to him.

When Giles made the announcement, Richard jumped up from the table and ran around it to kiss Kitty in congratulation, the girls clapped their hands in excitement, and Uncle

Sebastian rumbled his approval and pleasure. But the dowager looked at Kitty through narrowed eyes, as though she had done something underhand, and then said coldly, 'You will not ride any more, of course.'

'Not – ride?' Kitty faltered.

'Until after the baby is born.'

'Oh, yes, that's right,' Giles said. 'I hadn't thought about it, but ladies in a delicate condition mustn't ride. It's too dangerous.'

'But you've just bought me Apollo.'

Richard intervened. 'I'll keep him exercised for you.'

'Will your shoulder stand the strain?' Giles asked.

'You wouldn't have bought him if he was a puller,' Richard pointed out. 'I can amble about gently with him. It will be a good way to get back into action.'

'If he'll carry a cross-saddle.'

'Oh, Giddins and I between us will persuade him.'

All right for you, Kitty thought. A little sulkily, she asked, 'Is there anything else I mustn't do?'

Nobody said anything, but she met Giles's eyes and the same question occurred to both of them. Of course, it was not something either of them could ask his mother. They both looked away, embarrassed.

The anniversary of the old earl's death came, and there was a memorial service at St Peter's, with the whole neighbourhood attending, and a very beautiful choral work performed by the choir. The following day, the dowager went up to London for a week, to buy new clothes and meet old friends. The anniversary marked the end of her mourning period. 'Couldn't wait to get away,' Sebastian remarked to Giles. 'Unseemly haste?'

But Giles said, 'I can't blame her. I don't suppose, from what little I can gather, my father was an easy man to live with.'

482

'Mourning's not about feelings,' Sebastian said. 'it's about perceptions. Still, I don't suppose there's any harm in it. You broke the mould by getting married. And,' he went on, before Giles could comment, 'that was a very good thing you did for Ashmore.'

Giles thought he was referring to Kitty's money. Sebastian smiled, knowing exactly what was on his mind, and went up to play the piano, hoping that the sewing-maid would appear. He played better with an audience. No, little Kitty would be good for Ashmore in many other ways – as soon as Maud could be persuaded to loosen her grip.

Next, the traditional farmers' dinner was held at the Crown in Canons Ashmore. The fine old coaching inn was finding a new role for itself, since the railways had killed coaching. There was a new fashion for Londoners to take pleasure trips out into the nearby countryside. Visitors sought the historic, the picturesque, the quaint, but they still wanted London-class food and accommodation.

The farmers' dinner was a male-only event, at which Giles, assisted in this case by Richard, beguiled the local farmers with a slap-up meal, and plenty of port and cigars, to talk about local matters, to moot improvements, to air problems, and to renew their devotion to the hunt. Giles had attended it once with his father, and had woken the next morning with a head like a pumpkin from the port and a throat like a cheese-grater from the cigar smoke. He did not relish having to do it every year and, in the coach on the way home, said to Richard, 'You seem remarkably chipper. How do you cope with this sort of thing?'

'Practice,' Richard said unhelpfully.

For a few days it was mild for December, and actually sunny after the early fog had cleared. Kitty begged Giles for his company in a walk around the gardens. He was surprised by the novelty of the request, but the glimpse through the window of the hazy sunshine persuaded him. Besides, the dogs needed a walk.

It was almost warm outside. Around the horizon, the trees were bare, a black mesh of branches against the faded blue of the sky, and the air smelt of woodsmoke and leaf mould. The dogs greeted the outing with rapture, coursing about nose to the ground, running back every few moments to laugh up at the humans and urge them to hurry. *So much to smell! So little time!* Giles had brought a cane with him, and slashed occasionally at a weed, or used the point to turn over a clot of leaves, looking about him keenly, his mind on the estate. Only when Kitty stumbled did he notice her and offer his arm.

'How are you feeling?' he asked dutifully.

'Very well,' Kitty said. 'I'm not being sick any more. How are your improvements going?'

'Slowly. There's so much to do. And everything involves expenditure,' he added awkwardly. 'Markham and Adeane sometimes get carried away, but I do question everything to make sure it's really necessary.'

'You don't need to worry about spending my money,' she said earnestly. 'It's yours now. I would never question anything you did.'

He looked down at her. The low sunlight, illuminating her face, only showed how young she was. *She was having a baby – his baby!* The thought gave him a cold feeling at the pit of his stomach – not distaste, but fear of not being good enough. 'You'll turn me into a tyrant if you agree to everything I say and do.'

'You would never be a tyrant,' she said contentedly. They turned into the walled garden. 'This was what I wanted to talk to you about,' she said. 'I've been thinking about it since I first came here. We ought to grow a lot more vegetables and fruit for the house. Mrs Oxlea really only understands potatoes and cabbage, but there's room here for much more variety.'

484

He smiled. 'Is this what a well-bred young lady thinks about all day? Cabbages and potatoes?'

'We need those too,' Kitty assured him, 'and carrots and turnips and all that sort of thing. And that's what the kitchen garden is mostly full of. But if we build a second walled garden next to it, we could have spinach and chard and peas and – oh, everything!'

'How exotic! Fruit too?'

'We grow apples and pears enough, but in the second garden you could have peaches and apricots. Gooseberries and currants. And strawberry beds. Think of fresh strawberries in the summer!'

'I like raspberries better.'

'Raspberries, then. And, Giles, if we built greenhouses all along one wall, we could have fruit out of season. And a vine-house.'

'What brought all this on?' he asked.

'I remember how you ate in Italy, and I see you pick at your food here. I know Mrs Oxlea isn't very . . . adventurous—'

'A masterly understatement, my dear.'

'—but if she had better ingredients, perhaps she could learn. There must be recipes somewhere, and she'd only have to follow them. That is,' she added, in a low voice, 'if she can't be replaced.'

There was a brief, awkward silence. He did not want to tackle his mother again on the subject. He did not want to participate in a civil war in his own house. Perhaps Kitty was right, and an influx of new ingredients would do the trick. They were worth having, anyway, for their own sake.

'Very well,' he said, 'you shall have your walled garden and your greenhouses. It shall be just as you want it. We must speak to the head gardener,' Giles said. 'I'm sure he won't object.'

'I did actually speak to him,' Kitty admitted shyly. 'He seemed very pleased. But he'll need more boys if there's more to do.'

485

They walked about, discussing the plan, pointing out suitable spots for this or that delicacy, and for a little time were in perfect harmony, Giles dreaming of warm ripe figs and peaches, Kitty of Giles putting on flesh and looking less haunted. The dogs ran about, jackdaws chacked from the bare trees, a robin flew down onto the top of a wall and twittered at them, and as they turned a corner of the walk, Giles pressed her hand against his side in an unstudied gesture of affection.

'Are you sure it's me he wants to see, and not Miss Nina?' Aunt Schofield asked.

'Quite sure, madam,' Haydock said.

She sighed, and went into the morning-room. Cowling was there, warming himself before the fire.

'Mr Cowling, how can I help you?' she asked briskly.

She had so much to do with the upcoming wedding. For Nina's sake, she wanted it to be fine. It would not be luxurious, like Kitty Bayfield's, of course, but there must be no hint of shabbiness. And that posed a problem. She lived on a fixed income, and she had spent her savings dressing Nina for her Season. She didn't begrudge Nina her wedding, but she would have to sell gilts to pay for it, and her future income would be correspondingly reduced.

Nina was at that moment at a fitting for her wedding-dress – a simple ivory silk fitted underdress, and an overdress of embroidered cotton gauze with loose sleeves, flowing into a short train behind. Isa Morris, who was very good at dressmaking, had undertaken it with the help of her personal maid Sarah. She had always made clothes for Lepida, and would probably have loved to be making a wedding-gown for her own daughter, so Nina was the next best thing. They had pored together over magazines and pattern books, and chosen in the end something with simple, graceful lines.

Back in Mrs Schofield's morning-room, Joseph Cowling

was looking ill-at-ease – almost, she thought, hangdog. A brief worry flashed across her mind that he had come to call the whole thing off, but she dismissed the idea. She might deplore Nina's marrying a man of limited intellect, though probably that was more often the case than was generally realised, but she had no doubts of his sincerity.

'Was there something you wanted to ask me?' she prompted him, when he seemed to have difficulty in coming to the point.

'Yes, ma'am,' he said at last. 'I've come to ask you a favour.'

'A favour?' she said in surprise.

'A very *great* favour,' he said, 'and I'd not ask it, I promise you, except that – well, it seems a matter of plain justice to me, and I know you are a fair-minded woman – person – beg pardon, lady.'

Mrs Schofield waved away the distinction. 'Please speak freely, Mr Cowling. What is it you want?'

'Well, ma'am, I know right well that it's the bride's family who pays for the wedding, and I know you'll do everything tasteful and nice. But, you see, I want to invite a lot of people to see me off – a very large number of guests – and it doesn't seem fair to do that and land you with the bill. So what I wanted to ask was whether, as a great favour to me, you'd let me pay for the wedding-breakfast. I know it's not the done thing, but no-one ever need know except you and me, and that way, I could ask anyone I liked, and not be racked with guilt about making you feed 'em all. So, what do you say, ma'am? Could you go along with me on this one? I'd take it very kindly.'

Mrs Schofield was silent for a long moment, and Cowling's brow furrowed more and more, thinking he was going to be slapped down. 'I've offended you,' he mourned. 'I never meant to do that. I only wanted—'

In fact, she had been trying to control her laughter. Now

she got hold of herself and said, 'I'm not offended. Indeed, it's a very generous offer, and I accept it gladly.'

He was almost too surprised to be pleased. 'Really? You mean it?'

'Mr Cowling, please arrange the wedding-breakfast exactly as you like, and invite everyone you want. I am more than happy to pass the entire responsibility to you.'

'That's right good of you, ma'am,' he said, beaming. 'I'll undertake all the arrangements. You needn't lift a finger. My fellow Decius will handle everything, and he's a great man for detail. It'll go like clockwork. All you have to do is give me a list of people *you* want to invite. And don't go easy on me – have as many as you fancy! It'll be a slap-up do, I promise you. No half-measures. It'll be, well, not good enough for her, because what could be? But as near as money can make it.'

'I'm sure it will,' said Mrs Schofield.

'And you can hand off any other arrangements you like onto Decius – he can do everything. All you'll need to do is turn up at the church on the day with Miss Nina. Oh, my,' he concluded, rubbing his hands, 'it'll be something like! I'll send Decius to talk to you, if I may, and you can load him up like a pack-mule with all your worries.'

Mrs Schofield smiled and thanked him again. It was a weight off her mind, and she was truly grateful. Nina had spoken highly of Decius Blake, so perhaps he would control the quality as well as the quantity – and, after all, Cowling had dined with the King, so he must know something of how things were done.

In any case, she thought, when she had seen him out, even if it should turn out to be a vulgar display of wealth, well, it was his wedding, too, wasn't it?

CHAPTER TWENTY-SIX

The time had all run out, and here was Isabel Morris's maid Sarah – who had a proprietorial attitude to the gown she had largely made – helping Aunt Schofield's Minny to dress her for her wedding. Nina stood in front of the large cheval glass, imported from Aunt Schofield's room for the occasion, and watched the transformation with an almost academic interest. It didn't look like her – it didn't feel like her. The whole thing was oddly dreamlike. *Someone* was being decked out for a wedding, but it couldn't be the Nina Sanderton whose mind she lived in.

The gown was beautiful. It felt soft and delicate against her skin, and fell in graceful folds, the train moving when she moved. It had been a surprise when Aunt Schofield brought out her mother's wedding lace for her to wear. 'Your mother asked me to keep it for you, for your wedding.' It was rather yellowed, and careful repeated washing had only partly remedied the problem. Luckily, the gown was ivory rather than white, so the discrepancy was not as obvious as it might have been. And Nina would rather have worn her mother's yellowed lace than anything new and perfect.

Along with her pearls, it was the only thing of her mother's that she had. She had assumed she would wear the pearls on the day – she had nothing else by way of ornament – but then, a week ago, Mr Cowling had called and, with a touching air of shyness, had given her a flat leather box that turned out to contain a diamond necklace. She had been overwhelmed, and her first instinct was to refuse it. She couldn't imagine how much it had cost, but it was altogether too much.

Luckily Aunt Schofield had been present, and had read Nina's expression correctly. Before she could say more than 'I can't—' she had intervened. 'The groom's gift to the bride,' she had said firmly to her niece. 'It's traditional. Diamonds are very suitable. You'll wear them with your wedding-gown, Nina.'

Mr Cowling had also been watching her face. 'Not if she doesn't like it,' he said anxiously. 'I can change it in a snap for something else.'

Nina looked up almost tearfully. 'It's beautiful. The most beautiful thing I've ever owned.' It was like a string of raindrops. 'Thank you.'

So now on her wedding day Sarah was fastening the diamonds round her neck, and she looked more than ever a stranger, glittering as well as white. 'Are you going to swoon, miss?' Sarah asked sharply.

'Pinch her earlobe,' said Minny. 'That'll fetch her back.'

'I shan't faint,' Nina said hastily.

They brought Lepida – Lepida was to be her sole attendant – looking unusually pretty in a gown of harebell silk, which suited her colouring, and wearing round her neck the groom's gift to the bridesmaid, a sapphire drop on a fine gold chain. Lepida had been equally impressed, though not quite as overcome: she had not for an instant considered refusing.

And now it was time to go. Nina caught Lepida's hand with her cold ones. 'You'll come and visit – afterwards?'

'Of course,' said Lepida. 'Smile, Nina. It's your wedding day. You're not being burned at the stake.'

'I am smiling,' Nina said.

'Well, smile more.'

490

Downstairs, Mawes was waiting to escort her, looking distinguished and unusually tidy in morning dress. He made a soundless whistle as Nina appeared, and said, 'Wish to God I had my sketch-pad with me. You look a picture, Nina. An absolute picture.' He crooked his arm for her. 'Your carriage awaits, Cinderella.'

It all passed in a blur – the ride to the church, the slow walk down the aisle between ranks of people she didn't know (Aunt Schofield had invited shoals of her friends so that the bride's side shouldn't be too empty), the familiar words of the service which sounded odd and jarring being applied to her. Mr Cowling was the most blurred of all – she couldn't see his face, and was only aware that he had a white rosebud in his buttonhole because she puzzled all through the ceremony where he could have got it in December. He briefly became real when he took her hand, and she felt the hardness of it, dry, and nearly as cold as her own, and was shocked into realising that she was marrying him – *marrying!* – *him!* – right that moment. But immediately it became unreal again.

His supporter was Decius Blake, looking even more outrageously handsome in morning dress. They had been seeing a lot of him while the wedding preparations were going on. Aunt Schofield had approved of his quiet efficiency: he would ask one or two sensible questions and then the thing would be done. And since Lepida had been exposed to him a good deal, Nina thought she had become a little more hardened to the impact of him. When he handed the ring to Mr Cowling, he met Nina's eyes for an instant and smiled encouragingly, and his beauty seemed only reassuring.

There was the short drive to the Palace Hotel on the Park where the wedding-breakfast was to be held – a grand place, with a multitude of liveried servants. Nina had to stand with Mr Cowling to receive the guests, and though he, and Aunt

491

Schofield on her other side, did their best to tell her whom she was greeting, it went in at one ear and out of the other. Familiar faces emerged from the fog and retreated again – Miss Thornton, some of the girls she had come out with, academic friends of Aunt Schofield, gay bohemian friends of the Morrises. She began to feel very tired.

And then Kitty was before her – Kitty in old rose silk damask, with a cut velvet coat in grey and pink, and a grey velvet hat – Kitty smiling widely but with tears on her cheeks.

'Oh, Nina! Dearest Nina!' She laid her wet cheek against Nina's for an instant. 'I hope you'll be very, very happy.' Then she gave her hand to Mr Cowling and said, 'Take care of our Nina for us.'

Suddenly Nina was out of the fog, into the real world, saw where she was, because there was Giles, tall, burning like fierce sunlight against the contrasting dullness of everyone else, his eyes boring into hers as though he was about to dive inside her through them. Giles. He was going to touch her. He took her hand. He leaned down and touched his lips to her cheek. He didn't speak. She knew he could not. Because she couldn't either. Her throat closed. The pain was terrible. And it was worse when his hand parted from hers – she wanted to snatch it back and cry, 'No!' He had to go on and shake hands with Mr Cowling. And she hated them both in that instant for being so different from each other, and for occupying the wrong places.

Mr Cowling – her *husband* – shook hands with Giles and said, 'We're honoured you came, my lord. I hope we'll see you at Beechcroft House, our wives being the best of friends. Or maybe in Market Harborough – I've a nice house there for the hunting. You hunt, of course?'

Giles murmured something. Cowling let go of his hand. It was time to move on and let someone else take his place. But he looked once more at Nina, and she held the after-image of that look for a long time. She imagined someone drowning might look up through the water like that, as they sank for the last time.

Hearts don't really break. If only they did, she thought, then it would all be over.

They weren't going abroad. Indeed, there wasn't to be a honeymoon of the sort Kitty had had because Mr Cowling had too much work on hand with only a few days to Christmas, and he couldn't spare the time. But he promised her a trip in the spring, if she cared for it. 'Once I've got the new styles jigged, I can take two or three weeks. We can go to France, or Italy, or whatever you want.'

He said these things to Nina in the train going down to Northampton. It was late and she was very tired, but he'd wanted to go. 'I'd as soon not spend our first night in an hotel,' he said. 'Your own bed's always the best, I say. They're expecting us. There'll be a bit of supper laid out, if you're hungry, and fires lit and hot bottles between the sheets. We may not be grand, but we're comfortable.' He looked at her when she didn't answer, and said, 'You're tired. I can see that. Why don't you have a little nap till we get home? Here, rest your head on my shoulder, that's right. Just close your eyes and let go.'

His kindness pierced her. He was nicer to her than she was to him. She didn't sleep, but she dozed a little, caught in a strange place that was half real, half dream, where the sounds of the train became other things – a waterfall, a roaring animal – and the ticket collector sliding back the compartment door and saying, *Tickets, please* became a knight riding a horse too small for him, dragging the point of his lance along the ground and crying, *Dragons! There be dragons!*

'I've got a little present for you,' Cowling said, when she had been divested of her coat and hat. 'Come into the drawing-room.'

493

A fire was lit in there, but it was a big room and none too warm for a girl in flimsy wedding clothes. Cowling in his suit and waistcoat was better equipped. 'There,' he said. 'What do you think?'

Above the fireplace, in pride of place, was the portrait Mawes Morris had been painting of her. It had come out very well, in Mawes's opinion. Nina, on a high stool, hands folded quietly in her lap, looked out of the window with a pensive expression, a diffused light brushing her face with soft shadows.

'He didn't want to part with it,' Cowling said, watching her for reaction, 'but once I saw it, I had to have it. I gave him a pretty price for it, I can tell you! He looks soft, does Mawes Morris, but when it comes to business he knows his own worth.'

'I thought he wanted to exhibit it next year,' was all Nina could think to say.

'Aye, well, I've told him he can have it back for the Academy exhibition. I'm proud of my wife and want the world to admire her. It's a good likeness – though nowhere near as beautiful as the original.'

She had to look at him. He smiled hopefully, and she could no more disappoint him than smack a child's face. 'It was a lovely thought, to buy it. I'm touched that you want me hanging over your fireplace.'

'I've already hung you in my heart,' he said, and then seemed so surprised at his own lapse into poetry, she felt a surge of affection for him. 'Could you fancy a bite of supper?' he asked. And she could. If talking was difficult, there was always eating.

And so to bed. Nina was wide awake now, lying in the big bed (the sheets had been warmed, she was glad to discover, because she was very cold) waiting for the man to come through from the dressing-room for the final act. She remembered the book Aunt Schofield had shown her, remembered what was to come, and couldn't decide whether she was glad or sorry that she knew. Perhaps, unless you were madly in love, it was better to come at it in ignorance because there was something awfully – well – *unecstatic* about it.

There was one light still on, turned down low, at the other side of the bed but that was still too much. She'd have preferred complete darkness. When the door opened and he came through, she closed her eyes, not wanting to see him in his night clothes. He put out the light and got into bed, and she heard his breathing, too loud in the absence of any other sound.

He inched up close to her, his hands stroked her face, he kissed her brow, then her cheek, then her lips. A change came over him. His kissing became harder, his breathing harsher. He pushed up her nightdress and she felt his touch on her bare skin. *Well*, she thought, *he was married before. He knows what to do*. She tried to relax. The man finds it intensely pleasurable, her aunt had told her. She must not spoil his pleasure. He touched her breast, and she gasped at the feeling. Aunt hadn't said anything about this. She tried to remember what she'd said about 'the pipe' – but it was rather horrid to think of the pipe in relation to Mr Cowling, so she concentrated on making her mind a blank. He was breathing like a man running, and there was fumbling and touching down below, which she forced herself not to resist . . .

And then his weight was gone from her, he rolled off and lay beside her in the darkness, and his breathing gradually slowed. Was that it? she wondered. It didn't seem to accord with what Aunt Schofield had told her. Of course, she didn't know how it would feel so perhaps she was mistaken. She didn't know what to do, whether she was expected to speak, or touch him in any way. She wondered if he was falling asleep.

Then he turned on his side facing her, and laid an arm across her, and said quietly, 'I'm sorry.'

She hadn't expected that. She was going to ask, 'What for?' but at the last moment swallowed the words. She was so ignorant, despite Aunt's efforts, that the whole subject seemed too fraught with potential embarrassment. She waited in silence for some cue.

Then he said, 'Come here, you're cold.'

She was. He drew her against him, arranging her with her back to his front, and folded his arms round her, and she was warmer at once. It was rather nice. Very soon she became drowsy with the warmth, and then she fell asleep.

Kitty wanted to go to a meet, so Giles drove her in the dog-cart, and let Archer and one of the stable boys, Timmy, hack the horses down. 'Then Timmy can drive you as far as the first draw,' Giles said. 'And drive you home afterwards.'

'I can drive myself,' Kitty said. She'd been having lessons with Alice. 'And Biscuit knows the way.'

But Giles said, 'I don't want you driving on your own in case anything happens.'

He was glad now he'd had the tracks repaired. He knew vaguely that going over bumps was not good for expectant ladies. When they came to a pothole, he drove through it carefully, saying, 'We're not on my land now. This is Shacklock's responsibility. I must have a word with him.' The road took a bend, and he checked Biscuit. 'Look back, over that way, Kitty. You see where that clump of three trees is?'

'On a sort of hill?' said Kitty.

'That's right. That hill is the old motte, where the original motte-and-bailey castle was.'

'I read about it in the guidebook,' Kitty said, pleased.

'You get the best view of it from here.'

'It said in the book there were no stoneworks left.'

'That's right, nothing of the castle at all. Though I suppose there might be something under the ground.'

'You should excavate it one day,' Kitty said. 'Just to keep your hand in.'

He felt a sharp pang at her words, of loss for the old life. For an instant he saw the diggings in Thebes, the hard-edged sunlight, the acid sky, the dazzling sand, the tents, the camels and mules . . . He came back with a shocking bump to the grey-green, damp reality of England.

And yet, as he looked around like a man waking from a dream, he discovered he didn't hate it any more. It was his burden, his responsibility, the thing that tied him to this place so that he could never escape. For the rest of his life, he would carry it. But he couldn't resent it, any more than he would a child's hand slipped trustingly into his. He must look after the land, which was his child; and the family; and Kitty; and the heir she was carrying. He felt a thrill of excitement at the thought. He had understood with his mind before; now he understood with his guts and his blood and his inner core why the estate must be cared for and passed on.

There were clattering hoofs up ahead. 'Oh, there are the girls. And Richard,' Kitty said. 'How nice Apollo looks,' she added wistfully. Richard was taking her horse to the meet, just to show him hounds.

Giles gave her a sympathetic look. 'It's a pity you can't ride, just when the hunting season's starting.'

'Best to get it over with before the hot weather comes,' Kitty said. 'One wouldn't want to be carrying in July and August.'

There it was again, he thought, that unexpected wifely Kitty. He didn't know, of course, that she was quoting. He thought that pregnancy had made her wise.

* * *

497

The first week of marriage passed more easily for Nina than she had expected. Mr Cowling was out all day, seeing to his business. And she had enough to do. She had to learn the house and the routines. Mr Cowling had said she should change anything she pleased, but she knew Mrs Mitchell would resist, albeit silently. Shopping was always fun when you had plenty of money. She had the town and the area to explore. And lots of neighbours were making their formal visits, which she had to return in the few days available.

She saw Decius Blake every morning, when he called to take Mr Cowling to his business. And in the evening, when he brought him back, and the following day's plans had been discussed, Cowling would as likely as not say, 'Stay and eat, my boy. Don't go back to those lodgings of yours. There's enough for three.' His company and conversation were very welcome to Nina, and he created a bridge between her and the unknown quantity of her husband.

So, all in all, married life was less difficult to adjust to than Nina had expected. It was only in the bedroom that she had misgivings. Kitty, she knew, had a separate bedroom from Giles, but Cowling slept in the same bed with her, and most nights witnessed that silent struggle under the bedcovers. She was fairly sure now that it was not going the way it should, though of course she could not possibly ask him anything about it.

One evening at dinner they were talking about Christmas. He was as excited as a child at the thought of decorating the house. 'Mrs Mitchell never approved of it,' he said, 'and it seemed a bit daft anyway, with only me here. But this year we'll go all out, won't we?'

There would be a grand party on Christmas Eve, with thirty expected for a buffet supper. 'I saw it done in Russia once. You can pack a lot more in that way, and nobody minds at Christmas-time. But we'll have proper dinners next year.'

Decius told Nina about Cowling's Christmas good works, saying his employer was too modest to mention them. Cowling scowled at him, but seemed pleased all the same to talk about them. Every year he paid for a special party and presents for the nearby elementary school; and at the local hospital he provided a turkey to every ward for the patients who couldn't go home. 'They cook 'em in the hospital kitchens, and the doctors go up to the wards to carve them, like it was the operating theatre. Lot of jokes made on *that* subject, let me tell you.'

Then Decius talked about Christmas back in Wigston, with his family. 'Everybody manages to get back, wherever they are, so there's a grand houseful,' he said. 'Nobody but a Blake could stand that many Blakes in one small space. But we like it.'

'It must be nice to have so many brothers and sisters,' Nina said, with a touch of wistfulness. She thought it must be like her childhood in India – the sort of warm, happy-go-lucky, loving atmosphere – but with more individuals to share it.

When Decius had taken his departure, and Moxton had finally left them alone in the drawing-room to finish a last drink before bed, Cowling sat down on the sofa beside her, captured her hand, then stared at her intently and, she thought, rather mournfully.

Eventually, feeling uncomfortable under such scrutiny, she said, 'What is it? Have I done something wrong?'

He looked startled. 'No! On the contrary, it's me.'

'I don't know what you mean,' she said.

'You're so wonderful, and I don't deserve you.'

'I'm not. You do,' she protested.

'No, I know what I am,' he said certainly, preventing further argument. 'But I want you to have everything. What you said about having brothers and sisters, I heard from your voice how much it meant to you. Well, it's too late for that, but you should have lots of children. And you *shall*.'

He was staring past her with an introspective frown, and she wasn't sure the last words were actually directed at her rather than to himself. But something seemed to be called for, so she said mildly, 'That would be nice.'

'I'll not be beat,' he muttered, and then, with a visible effort, roused himself to smile and speak lightly. 'You like Decius, don't you?'

'Very much,' she said.

'Aye, he's a grand fellow. And a great one for the amateur dramatics. They always play charades when they get together, those Blakes, and you never saw the like! Young Decius, well, he hardly needs a scrap of cloth or a bit of paint to his face, and there, he's a sultan or a pirate or I don't know what, to the life, so you entirely forget it's not real. He could have gone on the stage, that one! But me, well, one time when I only had to made a speech at the Free Trade Hall, I got stage fright so bad I couldn't say a word. Decius had to prompt me word by word till I got going. Then I was all right.' He nodded, and again she felt he was no longer talking to her when he concluded, 'Aye, I've got a bit of stage fright. That's all it is.'

They played charades at the Castle, where everyone had gathered for Christmas: Linda and Cordwell and the children, Aunt Caroline, Grandmère. Uncle Stuffy was expected on Christmas Day – he had been staying with friends at Asham Bois for the last few days and would drive over on Christmas morning. Aunt Schofield and Sir John and Lady Bayfield were to come after Christmas to stay for a few days.

Mrs Oxlea was at her best at Christmas, with vast turkeys, geese and ribs of beef to roast – cooking she understood. The puddings were made to an old family recipe that could not go wrong, and Mrs Webster had persuaded Mrs Oxlea to hand over all mince-pie responsibilities to the head kitchen-maid, Ida, who could make pastry that didn't break teeth. It was just as well, because the traditional Boxing Day hunt was to meet at the Castle, and a vast number of patties had to be made for the field, while Moss was busy looking up stirrup-cup recipes and trying them out to choose the best one. 'It's three years since we had the meet here,' he said, to anyone who asked. 'We must get it absolutely perfect for his new lordship.'

Then, of course, there would be shooting, and lots of comings and goings from other house parties in the area, and the whole season would culminate with the servants' ball on Twelfth Night. Kitty was glad her parents wouldn't be staying for Twelfth Night. She could just about see her father dancing with a housemaid, but trying to imagine Mama dancing with a footman gave her a headache.

The best moment for her came on Christmas Eve, when the carollers came up to the Castle, and were brought into the great hall to sing. Everyone gathered to hear them, mulled wine and mince pies were served, and there was much chatter and laughter. A big Christmas tree had been brought in that morning and set up, and the young people had dressed it, and now it stood in its glittering glory, scenting the air with pine. Kitty remembered how Nina had said her aunt would never have a Christmas tree, and wished she could be there to see it. She wondered what Nina was doing, and how she was enjoying married life. They had sworn always to be friends, but she was wondering whether she would ever see her again. Their lives were so far apart now.

Then Giles was at her shoulder, and said, 'Come outside. I've got something to show you.'

'Outside?'

'Yes. I've got a coat to put round you. Don't tell anyone – I only want you.'

The words warmed her. She slipped away with him, out of the great hall, through a side lobby where he picked up a thick coat – she had no idea whose it was – and led her outside onto the terrace.

'It's snowing!' she said in delight.

'That's what I wanted to show you.' He guided her to the balustrade at the front of the terrace, beyond which the ground fell away down to the valley and the river. Already the snow was settling, turning a familiar scene unfamiliar, known shapes ghostly in the failing light. The river ran black between whitening banks; beyond, the village was showing the first warm yellow lights.

'It's so pretty,' Kitty said, entranced. 'Like—'

'A scene from a Christmas card,' he anticipated. 'All it needs is a stagecoach-and-six going over the bridge.'

'Well, it does! Make fun of me if you like.'

'I wasn't making fun,' he said, and put his arm round her. She loved the weight of it, and the warmth of his big body close to hers. She closed her eyes a moment in bliss, thinking how lucky she was to be married to him. 'This time next year,' he said, 'our son will be here. It's hard to believe, isn't it?'

She assented. So much had happened in such a short time. This time last year she had been a child in school. This time next year she would be a mother.

'I'm so grateful to you, Kitty,' he said.

She would have preferred him to say, 'I love you, Kitty,' but she had to settle for what she could get. His arm was round her, and he had chosen *her* to see the snow with him.

'We must go in,' he said, brushing flakes from her hair. 'It's getting heavier.'

At breakfast on Christmas morning, Mr Cowling and Nina exchanged presents. Hers to him was a pair of amber and gold cufflinks. She was a bit ashamed that she'd had to buy his present with his own money. She'd had to ask Decius for his advice, since she actually didn't have any money at all. He had been upset on his employer's behalf, because he knew Cowling had meant to arrange an allowance for her. 'He doesn't want you to have to ask. But for now, you can always charge anything, you know. Just sign the bill and it will be sent to me.'

Cowling seemed delighted with the present, and insisted on putting them on immediately. And then he gave Nina her present – a large box in which something shifted alarmingly as she tried to move it. 'Just open it where it is,' he said. So she knelt on the floor and opened it. Inside was a small white dog.

'It's a Jack Russell,' he told her, searching her face for pleasure. 'They're very loyal, they are. And intelligent.'

She picked it up, and it squirmed and licked her face. She looked at her husband, and her heart melted at his anxious expression. 'I've always wanted a dog,' she said.

His expression relaxed. 'I thought, as you're on your own so much, with me being out at work, he'd be company for you. I thought of a cat at first, but you like going on those long walks, and a dog could go with you where a cat couldn't.'

'You're absolutely right. It's the perfect present. I love him already.'

'His name's Trump. That was the name of the very first Jack Russell, Parson Russell's terrier, only his was a bitch. But I reckon Trump works for dog or bitch, don't you? But you can change his name if you want,' he added.

'I don't want to change it. Trump's a good name.'

She put the dog down and it ran about, sniffing at things, while Cowling watched it proudly. Nina found she wanted to cry, and she didn't altogether know why.

'I like your present,' Cowling said, pushing a sleeve back to display a link, 'but there is one thing more you could give me, if you would.'

He said it so diffidently that her mind jumped for a moment to the bedroom – but he couldn't mean that. There was nothing she could do about that – or was there? 'Anything,' she said, embarrassed.

'I'd like you to call me Joseph. You never have.'

It was true. She had never called him anything when they were together. In her mind she always called him Mr Cowling.

The dog came back to her on its circuit, and she scooped it up. Having licked her ear, it settled happily enough against her shoulder. She went over to where he was sitting, bent down and kissed him softly on the lips. 'Thank you for my present, Joseph. I love it.' It was the first time she had kissed him, too – that is, without him kissing her first.

It was, he thought, shaping up to be a grand Christmas.